WOLF
IN NIGHT

By Tara K. Harper
Published by The Random House Publishing Group

LIGHTWING
CAT SCRATCH FEVER
CATARACT

Tales of the Wolves
WOLFWALKER
SHADOW LEADER
STORM RUNNER
WOLF'S BANE
SILVER MOONS, BLACK STEEL
GRAYHEART
WOLF IN NIGHT

WOLF
in NIGHT

TARA K. HARPER

BALLANTINE BOOKS • NEW YORK

Wolf in Night is a work of fiction. Names, places, and incidents either are products of the author's imagination or are used fictitiously.

A Del Rey® Book
Published by The Random House Publishing Group
Copyright © 2005 by Tara K. Harper

All rights reserved under International and Pan-American Copyright Conventions. Published in the United States by Del Rey Books, an imprint of The Random House Publishing Group, a division of Random House, Inc., New York, and simultaneously in Canada by Random House of Canada Limited, Toronto.

Del Rey is a registered trademark and the Del Rey colophon is a trademark of Random House, Inc.

www.delreybooks.com

ISBN 0-345-40636-2

Manufactured in the United States of America

First Edition: February 2005

OPM 10 9 8 7 6 5 4 3 2 1

For my beloved niece, Anne, who was brave enough
to go canoeing with me at midnight and
who loved forging through the big waves at dawn.

SPECIAL THANKS TO

My neighbor Karen Castro, who graciously let me pace irritably in her living room while ranting and writing out loud;

Ed Godshalk for our annual midnight-to-dawn discussions of bayonets and kings (our spouses are saints);

Tamara Hanna, for letting me paint whatever I wanted on her living room walls (talk about a big canvas), and then for saying she loved it;

Detective Amber Lewis, of the Portland Police Department, for excellent advice and suggestions, and for correcting my misconceptions;

My brother, Detective Kevin L. Harper, of the Clark County Sheriff's Office, for pointing out all those pesky flaws, and for helping define the intrigue;

My father, Dan Harper, for the new computer, without which this story would not have been completed;

Peter Honigstock, of Powell's Bookstore at Loehman's Plaza (formerly the store at Progress, later known as something else, and now known by a completely different name that I've never figured out), for finding me marvelous, exactly-what-I-wanted books, although our wood floors are starting to sag because of the excessive weight of my library;

Artist Paul Missal, who lent me his cabin to write in during a fine coastal storm, and who helped me understand the first writer's block I've ever experienced;

Dr. Karen Gunson, Medical Examiner, Portland, Oregon, for helping me refine the plague; Chief Engineer Mike Roset, of the SS *Independence,* for unexpected information about steam engines; and Dr. Ernest V. Curto, for the moons;

My readers Doug Hartzell (who gets killed off at the end, to his own great satisfaction); Rich Wilson, who pinch-hitted in a most excellent manner; Mike Fitzgerald, whose insight was invaluable; and Stephanie Castro, who never lets me down;

Cindy Bertelman for a completely unexpected and amazing book of old formulas for metal oxides, tints, and what have you;

My editor, Shelly Shapiro, who was more than gracious in not overpressuring me;

Sandy Keen, for friendship far above and beyond;

And my husband, Richard Jarvis, who rebuilt, rewired, reconfigured and restored everything I broke, fried, crashed and destroyed during the course of writing this story.

Wolf in darkness
Wolf in night
Wolf in shadow
Wolf in light

—from *Resist the Mist*

Prologue

South, on the coast, in a city called Sidisport . . .

The dark-clothed man watched the black, glistening bay with the patience of an oldEarth Job. His gaze flicked toward each movement in the dark, and his body was poised against the cold seawall with deliberate negligence. His well-trained ears were tuned to the slapping of water on the rocks and wall below, to the couples who strolled behind him. To the soft laughter and murmured words as lovers pried at shuttered hearts beneath six of the glowing moons. He noted and discarded each couple automatically as they passed the wall where he waited. Not them, and not those two. Not that couple, either . . . It was a constant mantra, a steadying of his heartbeat in the dank spring air. It wouldn't be long now. An hour at most. The Tamrani woman liked dancing enough to stay late, even if she was with the dandy, but she was almost always home by two. He glanced at another couple who stepped up onto the waterfront. Too tall and thin, the hair too light . . .

His small boat waited in the slick water below. He had no worries that it would be seen. It was just another smudge against the seawall, a thicker edge in inky shadow cast harshly by the hovering moons. The only thing to draw the eye to his boat was the sea ladder that stretched down the stone wall. The ladder rungs glinted faintly, but since there were ladders all along the wall, no one paid attention. This one was even darker than the others. He'd sanded it himself to make sure his slide would be smooth, then had darkened it again with blackwash. No metal splinters there, though he'd have to watch his footing on the rocks near the boat. He could still get scraped up, and one didn't go into the water with wounds. Not near the shore, anyway, not after the spring currents shifted. The parasites that bred in the bay would eat a wounded man alive, leave him screaming, begging for the death that could be days, even ninans away. He'd seen it before. It was a classic lesson-killing, to dip a slashed man in the bay.

A closed carriage pulled up to the left, waited a moment, then took two couples away while the Haruman stared out at the water as if lost in thought. No one spared him more than a glance. It was understandable. His coat was well cut but of chancloth, not of silk. His boots were shined but neither rich nor new. His gloves were white and spotless, but cut in last year's style. Everything about him said acceptable but unimportant, not someone to notice. Even the city guard had done no more than nod as they passed him twenty minutes ago. They wouldn't be back for an hour. It was a good time for the Tamrani to show. There were few people left on the waterfront to watch or interfere, and those he saw were drunks, not paladins. That was another luck of the moons. The first thing his father had taught him was how to avoid the eager heroes and blend in with the drunks and darkness.

Soon, soon. Footsteps faded off to the right: a gentleman walked quickly, nervous in the night, his thick cloak flapping in the chill marine air. The Haruman dismissed him with a glance. The Tamrani lady, she was out with someone like that: slender, aesthetic, concerned with his clothes. Fentris the Fop, they called her dancing partner. Rumor said he'd killed his older brother in an alley, stabbed the man in the back with his own knife. The word was that the fop had backed away from every challenge he'd received since then. Gossip also had it that the fop was lucky the Tamrani's brother hadn't caught the two of them together, but that if the brother had, the fop would have run like a hare before worlags. A coward like that would be no trouble.

The Tamrani lady, now, she was a different piece of work.

He'd have considered negotiating other terms for her, but the Tamrani were powerful, they protected their own, and her House wasn't one in decline. He had no wish to bring that down on his head. Quick kill, quick silver, that's what his father had said, and his father had managed more than four dozen targets before he was taken down. Whatever the lady knew that had bought this kill tonight, it would die with her in the dark.

In the distance, a carriage let another couple off on the elegant waterfront and drove away. In the night, the Haruman glanced their way and felt himself tense. Ah, there were the two he sought. He turned back to the bay and made himself breathe slowly, softly as he heard them strolling toward him. He timed the steps and the soft murmur of her voice. His heart rate was up, but it made him poised, not skittish. Fast heart, fast reflex; fast hands, fast catch. His father had known all the old sayings.

They were almost on him when he sighed as if bored, straightened, and turned. "Excuse me," he murmured, and made as if to step past them. The knife in his left hand came out of its sheath like a silent snake. His arm moved smoothly, swinging up as he turned, and the razor steel slid into her heavy clothes, unopposed and unseen, like a needle through layers of lint. And in, in, cutting the bodice, the tip on her ribs, starting to sink in, slick as sweat, so easy, so fast, and the woman made no sound. She stiffened like a doe caught in light. He didn't look, but he knew her eyes had shocked wide as the tip slid into flesh. He started to press the thrust in and out to cut through her lungs as he slipped past—

Something clamped around his wrist and jerked before the steel could sink in halfway. There was a sting on his arm, and his body reacted before thought was formed. He tried to twist the blade out to rip flesh as much as possible, but he couldn't hold on to the hilt. Sloppy. Too much blood; his fingers were nerveless. He went for his other knife. Then he choked out a scream. His left hand was half severed at the wrist. It was the Haruman's blood that spurted out, not that of the Lady Jianan.

Lamplight bleached the motion like a black-and-white drawing. The fop slashed the Haruman's upper arm like a flash of light, then back-cut across his neck in the other fraction of a second. The carotid vein split like an overripe plum. Rich, red blood arced out. Kerien staggered back, clutching the hand that dangled by a strip of tendon and flesh. Gods—the fop? The fop was cutting him again, shoulder, arm, chest. He kicked out desperately, twisted and flailed back in defense, slashed hard and fast, but it was already too late.

With one steel hand on Jianan's arm, Fentris jerked her out of the way and side-kicked the other man's knees. He back-slashed at the blader's arm even before the man started to fall. Then he spun Jianan back and hilt-punched the Haruman's face as the blader began to drop. Bones splintered; the assassin screamed again.

Jianan's green eyes were wide and frozen, and she was sagging onto his arm. "Jianan," he snapped. He dragged her back farther. The assassin was on his knees, crawling, his good hand pressed over his carotid. Blood washed out in pulses from between the man's fingers, but he could still be a danger. It would be seconds before he was fully unconscious, minutes before he was dead.

Fentris cradled Jianan, his hands over hers to keep her from jerking the knife free. "Leave it," he said urgently. "It has to stay. Let the healers take it out."

"It . . . hurts," she whispered.

"I know. I'm going to set you down now and try to stop the bleeding." The knife hadn't gone all the way in, but she was a slender woman. It could have pierced her heart.

"Assass . . . sin."

"A robber," he soothed. "A second-rate blader. Don't talk." He yanked his handkerchief from his pocket and wadded it over the wound. He looked quickly around. "Help us," he shouted. "Guards, anyone!" The two couples in the distance didn't even glance back.

Jianan cried out as he shifted her, clutched his black jacket weakly. "Not . . . robber."

"We're on the boardwalk, late on a Pendian night, strolling around like anyone's prey." His handkerchief was soaking through. Her dress was silk and useless as tissue for stopping the blood. He said sharply, "And if he isn't just a robber, what could you possibly have been doing to make yourself a target?"

"Don't be . . . angry," she whispered. She was having trouble seeing. And cold. She was icy cold. She forced her lips to make the words, but they came out at a great distance. "Did you . . . hurt him? Is . . . he dead?"

He glanced at the other man's body. The assassin was weak enough now that his left arm lay limply across the sidewalk, and his other hand barely covered his neck. "Yes." There was a cold note in his cultured voice. "I'd say he's well on his way to the moons." He shrugged quickly out of his jacket and rolled the tailored garment into a pillow for her head.

"Oh, gods," she gasped as he shifted her. "Hurts."

"Lie still, love. Don't worry. You'll be fine."

"You'll ruin . . . jacket."

"It's for a good cause." He tore the sleeve off his shirt and folded it into a thick pad over the handkerchief. "Dik-spawned street scum," he cursed, not quite under his breath. "I'll see him rot in the seventh hell."

Jianan almost fainted as he pressed the pad down on the wound. She barely had breath to speak. "Fentris, he was an assassin. Not . . . robber. Have to know . . . who hired him. Find out. It's important. Promise."

He packed the cloth tightly around the blade. "If he was an assassin, I'll find out." His usually calm face hardened. "You can trust me on that."

There had been no bubbling in the blood on her chest, and she wasn't bleeding from her mouth, but it could be free-flowing inside. He looked desperately around. There was a carriage in the distance, but it had turned away down the street, following the path his own carriage had taken to the lot where it would wait. The waterfront businesses were closed, and the few apartments over them were dark. Four blocks away, the city guard had just stepped around the corner as they circled the blocks farther and farther away. "Guard!" Fentris shouted. "Help us! Guard, she's been stabbed—"

The two men looked his way, seemed to peer through the dim light, then finally broke into a run as he waved urgently with one

arm. One stopped for a moment at the lamppost to release a
warning bell, and the peals clapped out across the stone streets
like the pulse of the gods of the dead.

Jianan's fingers clutched his wrist weakly. "Fentris. Listen.
Papers, notes," she breathed. "Secret place."

He felt a chill. "The lockbox in the courtyard?" If she was
hiding something important enough to kill for, that was the
worst place to put it. He himself could count six people who
knew which bricks to move.

But she surprised him. "Bedroom," she whispered. She
breathed raggedly for a second. "Closet . . . door."

He stared down at her. They had talked once of hiding places.
He'd been twenty-five, he remembered, two years ago. The
month before his brother had died, the month before he'd become an outcast in his own family. He recalled every detail of
that time with the clarity of glass. It was only in the two years
since that he'd ceased to care about remembering anything.

Two years ago, they'd been in the courtyard, and Jianan had
showed him the lockbox hidden in the bricks beneath her window. He'd scoffed and said that if he had something to hide—
papers, letters, deeds—he'd put them someplace obvious. Inside
something that everyone looks at but no one sees. The closet
door, perhaps. Or inside a handle. People look into the spaces
beyond such things, not at such things themselves. He said
lightly, "You have six closets, Jianan."

She couldn't smile. "Fourth closet, fourth door. Lift it . . . off
the tracks. Hollowed out from the bottom. Papers there. Take
them to . . ." But each breath she drew in was a blast of crushing
pain. "Oh, it hurts. Fentris, it really hurts."

By the moons, how long did it take two men to run two hundred meters? The lights had gone on in an apartment over a
milliner, and in the distance another pair of city guards appeared. "Get a healer," he shouted at the first two. "For moons'
sake, get a healer." He didn't ease off the pressure on her ribs.
"The pain is a good sign," he told her firmly. "It means you're
going to be fine."

"How . . . would you know?" She smiled weakly. "You've . . .
never been . . . stabbed."

He had—twice—but it wasn't something he spoke of. "I'll find the papers," he said instead. "Stop talking now."

"Feels like . . . being crushed."

He hid his unease. That could be a sign of heart damage. "Help is coming. You'll be with the healers soon, and everything will be fine."

"Listen," she whispered. "Get the papers to my brother. No one . . . else. Promise me."

"To Ero? He's at sea. It would take me months."

She started to shake her head, went bone white even in the pale lamplight, and barely managed, "Con."

Crap on a stickbeast, Fentris cursed silently. Condari Brithanas had been one of his brother's best friends. Brithanas had been out in the western counties for the past two years, but he would have heard every story and rumor before he left Sidisport again. The man's one day in town had been short enough that Fentris had easily avoided him. Fentris had already sent his secretary ahead to listen in on the Ariyen councils, just so he wouldn't have to face the other man. After all, according to everyone down to the tailors and the cooks in the poorest homes in town, he'd murdered Condari's best friend. To seek him out deliberately, after Jianan had been stabbed in his care?

"I don't think—" he started.

"Yes." Her nails dug in. "Promise. Catch him . . . Deepening Road. Stay with him till he . . . gets to Shockton. Fentris." She clutched him weakly now. "Keep him safe."

It was Fentris, not Condari Brithanas, who would need safety. Fentris looked down at his bloody gloves. He said flatly, "You don't know what you're asking."

"I'll . . . do it myself, then."

She struggled to sit up, gasped, and he barely had to press her down before she collapsed back onto his jacket. "Don't be an idiot," he snapped.

"Promise."

"I swear, by the rust on a silk hat, you'll be the death of me." He looked skyward for a moment. "Alright, I'll do it, though after your brother finds out how I've left you, I'll come back as a ghost, not a man."

"You'll . . . go tonight."

His lips tightened as he felt the heat of her blood.

"Sw-swear," she whispered.

"I swear on the seventh moon I'll ride out as soon as you're safe in the hospital. Now shut up, love."

A ghost of a smile crossed her lips. "Not your love."

"Might as well be after the way we were dancing tonight. We shocked Lady Seigan like two mudsuckers in her sink. We'll have to do that again."

Jianan choked out a laugh, gasped at the pain, and fainted.

Fentris was left pressing his white-gloved hands into her bright red blood while the city guard came running.

I

A wolf doesn't choose his wolfwalker,
He can't help being drawn to your side;
There's a tiny place in his brain and yours
Which seeks the other's mind.

It's a need, a desire, a hunger in both,
An addiction that pulls like a chain,
It resonates between you, like the sun
Blinding and swamping your thoughts,

Like the wind rising and falling, falling,
Like the packsong calling, calling.
It binds you like two halves of a knot
That cannot come undone.

—excerpt from *Who Hunts the Wolves*

Afternoon, just west of Willow Road . . .

The wolf watched from the shadows with a predatory sense, an animal tang of hunger. Evening was approaching fast, when color would shift into shades of grey and the air would grow cool with danger. The young wolf knew what would come with the darkness. He was a year old, experienced enough that the hunt was no longer fearsome, but still young enough that it was something he eagerly sought. This time, he hunted alone.

He hunched beside the roots with a waxleaf tickling his fur. He flicked his ears absently. The yearling liked the weak warmth of spring. Deep winter was hard hunting, especially since it would be two more years before he came into his full strength. Spring meant creatures weak with hunger or heavy with their young. It meant easy running in soft earth, not deep drifts of snow. He inhaled quickly, trying to catch the scent of his prey. From the shadows, his golden eyes stared unblinking,

9

seeking even a blurred glimpse of movement, but the thick hedge remained impenetrable to his gaze.

Overhead, dark vines climbed along the spiny barrier bushes. The vines here were old enough that they stretched up into the arch of trees that hung over the man-made trails. They were two wide streams of white, those man-trails, made of wood so firm it was hard as stone. He'd run on such trails in winter when their wood-warmth kept them from freezing. At night, they glowed like the moons, and the humans used them like highways, clattering this way and that. They didn't seem to care that any hunter could hear them. They didn't care about scents, either, for dozens of strange, nose-clogging odors clung to that long line of movement.

It was hard to separate out the things from which the odors came. Some were forest smells carried along with the man-things, like the smell of the danger-fang, the tano, and that of the tiny, venomous weibers. Others were strictly man-scent: sharp smells, unpleasant ones, metal grease and oils. Then there was the smell of the spiny barrier that the yearling crouched behind. It was a man-thing, too, planted deliberately, according to the pack elders. It stank to keep the beasts away and wouldn't harm the wolves. Unpleasant, yes, but the other side meant safety.

The yearling's ears flicked again at an impression of motion much closer to his position. He was not mistaken. At the base of the bushes, slow blue flowers closed their soft, hungry mouths on the gnats that fluttered nearby. Everything was thickening and strengthening, not just with spring, but with the coming dusk.

On the other side of the hedge, the behemoths rumbled, unaware, unflinching, unstoppable. Rishte could hear little over their noise, but he knew his prey had moved beyond him. He scanned the roadside fruitlessly. He could feel the creature like the prickling of fur when one steps up to a trap. It was waiting, faintly wanting him as much as he wanted it. Calling for him to approach. Like an itch just under the skin, it clawed at his consciousness.

It had been there all day. At dawn it had begun to tug like a packmate on the rough edge of play. In the grey light of morning, it had crept through the forest. It had grown stronger as the pack moved out warily to hunt the thin eerin that grazed eagerly on fresh spring grass. It wasn't like the danger sense of the beetle-beasts that was making First Father so worried. It was more subtle, like a fern touching an ear or the sweep of wind-grass across the back, and it was stronger to Rishte than the others. Then the midmorning warmth had begun to saturate the air, and the sense of it had become sharper and harder to ignore. Since then, it hadn't stopped pulling, digging at his mind.

The young wolf flexed his paws as if ready to run. He stayed low, where it could not see him. He feared its eyes, the binding eyes. Pack Mother said that human eyes could trap a wolf like a dog. They could fill a mind with nightmares, split him off from his pack, and starve him for the grey. He believed her. There were images in the older songs of things the Grey Ones feared. He could feel that in his prey. But still he watched its passing. He couldn't help it. Nor could he help reaching out toward its mind. It pulled like a tether, and he howled back, scratching at its mind.

He rose and slunk along the road, slipping through the brush like a ghost to follow the deafening monsters. For a quarter day's run, he had followed his curiosity, till he'd been all but run over with sound. He'd had to force himself to approach the hedge that stank like rotting stingers. The noises didn't hurt his ears, but they masked other sounds so that he felt uneasy and vulnerable. Another monster banged by, and he cringed at the rumbling that his human ignored. He wondered how it could hear anything, even its own thoughts under that torrent. A lepa flock could descend on them all like a rockfall without them knowing.

The line of monsters curved again, and he knew they were starting to circle the den-hill. He was actually closer to his pack home now than before. The thought gave him some comfort, although he wished the human would leave the monsters and follow him to a quieter place. Its eyes would not be so terrifying if he met it within the pack. He was beginning to feel a need, not just a desire, to explore this odd and itching packsong.

The dying breeze ruffed the grey-and-white fur unevenly across his back. He had disturbed a monkeybush that morning, and two spurs were now caught back by his shoulder. He twisted and bit at them irritably, but they were hard-tangled and sharp as the human's mind. He snarled quietly, then turned back to the road. His paws itched to run, to flee from the monsters and scent of men. But that mental needle stuck in his thoughts, changing the tone of his voice in the packsong to one of longing and distance. The sense of muted smells, oddly sharp tastes, and smoothness instead of fur—they confused him. They had blinded his mind all day so that he'd actually slipped off a boulder at dawn when crossing a stream with the pack. Grey Helt and Second Mother had laughed, but Pack Mother had been grim as if facing a full-grown worlag. After that, Helt—First Father—had turned the pack back to the den, cutting off their hunt. Rishte had lagged behind, first slowing, then turning east, away from the pack, as he heard the strange voice in his mind.

Now he was close, close enough to smell what he sought. He saw them now, the humans. He could see their eyes. Flat, wary, they looked his way often, and there was no trap, no binding. He barely even felt them, just the one human he sought. Even amidst the musk of the riding beasts, even above the man-scent, he could smell that one in his mind. The feel of legs moving, tottering, never quite falling forward—it made his ropy thighs tense. He crept closer to a break in the brush. The grey shades shifted. He could see the monsters now. Huge—they were bigger than badgerbears, bigger than the boulders at the base of the cliffs. They made a line as long as a glacier worm.

Fear knotted his belly as if he were still a cub. Humans. Danger. The mind that seemed so close to his seemed to turn and look out to the forest. Instantly Rishte backed deep into green-black shadow. He tasted the edge of those thoughts. It could feel him, yes. It was seeking the predator who watched it, the wolf who gnawed at its mind. Rishte flattened down like a poolah against the soil, but the sunlight glinted in the human's eyes, and it was blind as it looked toward the shadows. Then it was moving on, moving away, leaving him behind.

He didn't realize how far he'd slunk back until his hind leg slipped on a slick pile of leaves. His black-rimmed eyes stared toward the road. It was looking back again, he could feel it. He scrambled to his feet, but did not run. He had to see its eyes, but fear held him fast. The human was more focused now, as if it knew where he was. Poised on the wide trail, he wanted to race back to First Mother and the strength of the pack. He was too far out of the hunting grounds, where even the poolah were wary. A wolf alone, without his pack? His thoughts stretched out like grey spiderwebs to test the air for hunters. He should go. It was dangerous to stay, but he wanted that human.

He growled low in his throat. It was moving away—he was sure of it. It was growing more distant already. His nostrils flared with disappointment. Then he smelled . . . water. He licked his lips and tasted the flat sense of it on his own tongue, felt the tepidness of it slide down his own dry throat as the human-creature swallowed. It pulled him, that sensation. The visceral sense of it clung to his mind like a leech. He howled his frustration in his mind.

And froze.

Something cut back at him through the grey. It was the human. Yes. It was listening for him again. He howled again, and its mind shifted, turned, touched his so faintly that the wolf almost whined out loud. He was on his feet before he realized it. He loped after the moving monsters. He brushed through catear shrubs with their fuzzy cones. He worked his way warily around the tangled start of a greendup patch, then hurried through wispy ferns. Then he halted again abruptly. The human was no longer riding away along the line of behemoths. It was on the ground in splintered sunlight, moving toward the forest. There was a steady drum, heavy, like that of a bollusk, unnervingly even as only two feet hit the white road, over and over, left, right, left, right.

Rishte's lips curled back in eagerness. The human slowed and crossed the second wide man-road. Closer now, it came through the brush. A surge of joy flowed into the young wolf's mind like the hot moment of biting into a hare. He stretched out his mind. *Come,* he sent eagerly. *Come.*

Now the human was ahead on the trail. Sweet-musk. It

14 Tara K. Harper

smelled like sweet-musk and leaf dust, not the bitter-musk of Grey Helt after a run. Rishte's nostrils flared as he sucked in the odor and set it in his mind. Leather, oil, water, metal, smoke and meat, bitter roots, and that sweet-musk scent that was all its own: human—and female, he realized.

He filtered the scents and moved toward the creature carefully, listening for her movements. Loud she was, like a clumsy eerin. Beneath her voice, her mind was sharp, like a claw barely sheathed, or a broken stone. There was a cold spot there, as if part of her thoughts were frozen. The sensation triggered a deep memory, and Rishte growled low in his throat. There was a deadly threat centered in the female's mind, a danger the wolves avoided. It was something that had become stronger in the forest in the last few years. It was even in the minds of men, as if they could sense it and now directed their violence around it. And it was in the mind of that human.

The human female—the woman, pack memory supplied—didn't seem to notice the hard spot in her mind. Instead, her thoughts flowed around that spot like blind water over a branch. Rishte's ears flicked as he reached carefully toward the rest of that mind. The woman didn't have the hard focus of some of the humans the Grey Ones sensed. The wolves had always avoided those kinds of men. There were memories passed down, as recently as two father-mothers ago, of such hunters. Such men had tried to chain wolves to them through fear and death instead of the bond. Rishte knew that wolfwalkers had saved the Grey Ones then, but this female wasn't a wolfwalker. Still, she knew the pack. She had the tone of wolves in her thoughts. And that death-spot in her mind might be as yellow and harsh as a thin winter sun, but the rest of her mind was as grey as any packmate.

Rishte lifted his head and howled softly.

To the east, the woman halted. Then she raised her head and howled back. The sound rose and then fell, fell, fading into shadow, exactly as she should answer. Rishte's hackles raised at the unfamiliar rightness of it. Finally, he howled his answer. Then he loped away on the trail. She followed as if she had understood.

The woman's coverings brushed against ferns—he could hear that behind him like the rasp of a tongue. He could hear her every step, but the sounds were sharp in his mind, not his ears. He paused, and she came closer, but the noise of the monsters was still too loud behind them, and he turned onto a different trail to take her back to the pack. She would stay with him now, he was certain. She had glimpsed him in the shadows, and even though there was a chill in her mind, her eagerness mirrored his own. *Come,* he sent again. *This way.*

He didn't stay to meet her eyes, but broke into an easy jog. The woman picked up the pace. Rishte hesitated at a bend in the trail, but she saw him turn in the late sunlight, and now ducked beneath the branches. He sent a shaft of approval through his mind, and she seemed to laugh. I'm coming, she seemed to sing.

Rishte's lips curled back as another scent lifted on the evening breeze. He sniffed the air quickly. They were still near the grouse hills and were working their way up the ridges toward the den, but other hunters were beginning to stir. They would have to be quick to avoid the poolah he could smell on the failing breeze. He slipped onto another trail, and the woman didn't argue. Good, good. Her voice was already changing, smoothing out on the edge of his packsong. Now that he could hear her, her eyes were no longer frightening. That sharp iciness deep in her mind, that was worrying, but he'd take her to meet Pack Mother. Grey Vesh would know what to do to fix her if Rishte brought her home.

II

Sometimes the touch is subtle

—Ariyen proverb

East of the ridge, on Willow Road . . .

It was late on the long, empty stretch of road. Dusk had fled into night, and the line of colorful wagons was now only a writhing black shadow, a massive serpent of motion. Two moons were visible, and two more floated beside the pewter-edged clouds, lighting the way. There was no need for anything else. The rootroad gave off a ghostly luminescence, and Kettre's night sight had always been good.

She reined in at the back of Payne's old wagon and rapped sharply on the side panels. They were fully expanded, like a rolling home, so people could sleep and work as they traveled, but these, more dented than most, flexed beneath her knuckles. "Aye, Payne. Get up," she called. "Twenty minutes to duty."

Inside the wagon, in the near-pitch dark, the young man woke abruptly—and froze at the sounds of rustling. Something feathery was touching his face with the swaying of the sling bed. He jerked upright and grabbed for his knife. Weightless things popped as his bare legs plunged down through the fragile balls. Brittle fragments burst out like feathery shrapnel against the hairs on his legs. The faint scent of fresh green leaves puffed back. "Chak take it—"

His brain finally kicked into gear, and he jammed the knife back in its sheath. In the dark, as he stopped moving, the inflated leaves settled lightly back into place. He batted another wash of tissue-thin things and cursed, "Dammit, Nori-girl." He was chest-deep in dried leaf balloons.

He held his breath as the leaves popped and burst. He knew how she'd done it, damn his sister anyway. She'd simply waited till he was asleep, then hummed while she worked. She'd been a caller since she was a child. At twenty-two, she could soothe almost any beast. Keeping him asleep while she packed in the leaves would have been child's play.

He shoved through to the wagon door, stubbed his toe on a heavy sword bag, then tripped on the pack he'd discarded earlier. He flung the wagon door open with an oath that would have shocked his mother.

Kettre burst into laughter.

A wash of leaf balloons flowed out and piffled away in wounded waves as if from a broken dam. Some bounced off onto the grassy verge; others drifted under the hooves of the next team of six-legged dnu. The tired team didn't even blink. They just plodded on like bloated centipedes, barely noting the noise as their flexible hooves popped and crushed the balloons. Tied to the back of the wagon, Payne's own mount merely chittered at the smell of the dusty leaves, and shifted out of the way.

Payne's violet eyes narrowed as Kettre stifled her giggles. He was covered in leaf dust, missing his tunic, and his toe throbbed like a drum. He jerked a dried stem out of his mussed black hair and smiled tightly.

The brown-haired woman grinned. Kettre and Nori had been friends since Kettre was fifteen. Kettre wasn't sure if it had been their opposite natures that had drawn them together or just the need for friendship. With Nori twenty-two and Kettre twenty-four, that was as close as any of their traits had ever been. Nori was lean from running and riding, had long, black silky hair, and the violet eyes of legend. Kettre was brown-haired, hazel-eyed, and muscular enough that she'd heard more than once that she looked like an amazon next to Nori. Kettre had been the rebellious one, while Nori had been the quiet guide who got them back to the wagons in one piece—mostly. When Kettre went into the cities, Nori had gone to the eastern counties where the forests were even thicker. They hadn't seen each other for years, but three days ago, when Kettre joined the caravan as it passed through Sidisport, they were like schoolgirls again with nothing changed between them.

"Don't look at me," Kettre told Payne innocently at his dark look. "I've been doing my *chovas* duty for the last four hours, riding guard for one of the elders."

"Sure, and you didn't see a thing." He kicked the last of the leaves off the gate. "Moonworms on a poolah's back, but she must have spent the whole afternoon inflating the stupid things."

"Oh, it took barely forty minutes."

Which meant she'd had help, then. "Where is she?" he asked ominously.

"Back with Mian, I think. Working with the weibers."

He snorted. The venomous creatures could use some work. Weibers were small and fast and could be deadly when they escaped. He doubted that this batch would ever be truly tame, but the cozar girl Mian was determined to keep the tiny beasts along with some of the other nasties: tano, pripri, fileleg bugs. The toxins were good for trade with healers and apothecaries, but so far, Mian hadn't managed to keep any of them well secured. Last ninan, three days after Payne and Nori had joined the caravan, the weibers had gotten loose while Nori was waterproofing her gloves. The tiny creatures lived only six months from birth to death, but they were born with noses like magnets. They had zeroed in on the glove oils like arrows to a target. If Nori hadn't been so fast on her feet and so good with animals, they would have swarmed her before she could get the gloves off and away from the rest of the circle. As it was, she was bitten twice on her left arm—a record for her, since she wasn't usually bitten at all. She had spent the next two days in the healer's wagon while her forearm swelled and bulged with purple veins. She'd had some interesting words for Mian when she was on her feet again. Payne didn't blame her for tearing into the girl. Her arm had been disgusting.

He finger-combed his hair and shook out the last of the leaf stems. "How close are we to the river?"

"Twenty minutes," the woman answered. "The last ring-runner

said the line was almost gone. We should be able to cross pretty quickly."

He nodded. A temporary bridge had been laid across for wagon traffic, but it would be a slower crossing, one-direction traffic only, and only a few wagons at a time. Slow enough, he thought slyly, that he might have time to climb down and try to collect some algae. If the growth on the broken bridge was thick enough, he could tear off a piece and press it right there to get a few drops of catalyst. A bit of that mixed with a few other things to make a pretty dye, then spread it on Nori's toothbrush and, he grinned to himself, let her see how widely she smiled.

He ducked back into the wagon and lit the lantern. "Tell Nori-girl I'm up, will you?" He threw the words over his shoulder. "She's supposed to be on lead-rider duty with me and Wakje."

He dressed quickly, kicked one last leaf out of the wagon, and stuffed a small bag of jerky and dried fruit in a belt pouch. Automatically, he surveyed their gear before leaving. Sword boxes, bow carriers, arrow-tip molds, knives—everything seemed in its place. He frowned at the three quivers that hung neatly over his sister's sling bed. She was carrying only one quiver on duty again, and he muttered a mild oath. Her arrogance at handling wild beasts was going to get her killed.

The rest of her gear was stowed as usual. Her guitar was in its case, her sword in its holder, her books in their bin. Carving tools were in their box, tanning tools and oils were racked above the sling bed, dyes and scents in their vials. The only things not secured were the strings of rough stone beads she'd been filing down that morning. He snorted to himself. She didn't travel light, his sister, but at least she traveled neatly. Between her and Payne, their uncle Wakje, and their uncle's tough-faced driver, the place looked like a cross between a mobile weapons shop and a crafter's transport. Payne had been offered a place in a dozen homier and roomier rides, but had always said no. This one, dinged up like an old hunting dog and cluttered with stray shafts and sharpening gear, was as sturdy as his uncle.

He made a quick stop at a peetree, refilled his bota at the water wagon, and headed for the front of the line. Past the chittering rookery with its white-haired message master muttering beside her driver. Past the healer's wagon, dark inside now that the Ell's broken ankle was set. Past the trade wagons, the family wagons, the well-lit meeting transport. One of the dnu teams bit irritably at his mount, and he jerked his own beast away. With the number of mishaps this train had sustained, he couldn't blame the teams for being nervous. Three fractured axles, five cracked wheels, two broken bones, and a bridge out? The Ell would be lucky if he brought this train into Shockton in anything close to one piece.

Payne picked up his uncle Wakje on the way and rode past the Ell, who led the caravan. The old man's broken leg was propped up on the footboard of the lead wagon, where the cast was a white splotch in the dark. The white-haired Ell nodded shortly as Payne and Wakje passed, then went back to arguing with the three elders who rode nearby.

Payne and his uncle joined the other lead riders and cantered ahead to a short rise where they could see the river. In the dark, it was a slick black line pocked with streaks of dirty grey and spattered with lantern light. The rains had stopped two days ago, and the water level had dropped, but the river was still swollen like an old woman's legs.

The temporary bridge was set up just downstream from the regular bridge. Three folded sections floated out from each side, and cables and winches secured and controlled the V-spans so that debris that built up at the broken bridge could pass through the gap. As Payne reined in with the other lead riders, the bridge crew began harnessing fresh teams of dnu to the massive capstan that squatted up on the bank.

Payne studied what was left of the permanent bridge. The tops of its stone arches were barely visible on the two remaining spans. Grey-black water rushed through the gaps, slick and thick looking, turning with the swells, and fouled with the smell of winter rot and mud. Masses of debris were caught on the remains of the pillars. One support was almost completely engulfed by branches, wood planks, and what looked like clumps of root-balls and shrubs. The other three pillars looked like logjams. Even as Payne and Wakje watched, one of the outside logs broke free and began to turn downriver.

"Log free," called the bridge watch.

"Log free, aye," came the return hail.

The men along the temporary span had their boat hooks out and ready. The long, telescoping poles were a favorite tool for sparring among the bridge crews. They'd stand on the floating logs and hook at each other till one of them went into the drink to the tune of boisterous laughter. Payne had earned a few dunks that way himself, though never in heavy current.

There was no sign of levity now, not with a log breaking free. Like some of the other logs before it, this trunk was thick and heavy with mass. The limp wash of evergreen boughs still attached dragged in the water like sea anchors, but as the log hit the current, it managed to gather speed.

The bridge crew rushed to meet it. "Left, left," one man shouted.

"Got it," and, "Shift a bit," and, "She's coming in—"

"Watch it, watch it—"

The snag hit the temporary span a few meters in from the gap. Two men staggered with the impact. One went to his knees, but they managed to keep their boat hooks against the mass. They jabbed in concert, working to sharp directions and curses, keeping it near the surface. Until it passed, the trunk could submerge then punch up through the bridge, or catch and hold so much debris against a span that the entire section sank.

Seconds passed, long seconds before they could work it away into the main current. It started to swing before it was fully free, then it caught in a slick, grey suck spot. They hooked at it futilely as it ripped free and submerged.

"It's under," one man yelled. "It's passing."

"Brace up," another shouted. "It's under."

It rolled once at the edge of the span, just beyond the bridge. A moment later, it was gone in the dirty, grey-black water.

The crew casually respaced themselves along the span as if the moment had been nothing more than a break from tedium.

Payne rested his forearms on the saddle horn and studied the setup. "Looks alright now," he murmured.

His uncle watched the water with narrowed eyes. "Too much debris in the river."

"We've got enough outriders to help with the poles."

"Won't matter much if they can't see what's coming." The older man pointed with his chin at a flat spot in the river. It was moving like an oil slick, and it wasn't till the spot approached the gap in the original bridge that the thing that made the flattened spot surfaced. It was a wide sheet of wood, probably torn off some villager's boat dock far upstream. It swung into the debris mats and was slowly pushed under. It didn't come back up.

Kettre cantered up with another group of *chovas,* and Payne glanced back. The caravan was winding into sight at the rise, the lead wagon like the nose of a serpent. "Did you find her?" he asked the woman.

Kettre shook her head. "She wasn't with Mian. Someone said they'd seen her back in the line, so I passed word to send her forward."

Payne hid a frown. Nori wasn't usually late to duty, especially after she'd pulled a prank. But outriders—or *chovas*—were beginning to gather as the caravan rumbled up, and his dnu was nudged aside to make room for another group.

There were plenty of the *chovas* to crowd the riverbanks. The biennial Tests and Journey assignments were a draw for all three central counties. Every caravan was mixed with both travelers and traders. The former went to watch their sons and daughters test for rank and compete for the Journey assignments. The latter went to make their fortune plying the former with wares. This caravan had grown by a dozen wagons in Sidisport, plus eight family transports taking their youth to Test. There were six flat engineer wagons, each carrying two precious flywheels. There was only one metalsmith, but his wagon was always surrounded by six guild guards, and sometimes other outriders. Even Nori and Payne had done a turn yesterday, helping guard the ores. Raiders weren't the only threat. This close to Sidisport, even other traders could be a danger to something as precious as metals. Hells, there were at least four merchants in this train whom Payne wouldn't trust with a blunt knife at ten paces. At least they were easy to identify. Each one's wagon flew its pennant proclaiming its House or guild. It was harder to tell the allegiance of the two dozen *chovas* who rode guard, handled the dnu, and did other mundane tasks. Some of them seemed too much like raiders for Payne's comfort. He wasn't alone in his thinking, either—not judging by the way Wakje had weaponed up after the *chovas* had joined the train.

Payne glanced at the youths in his own group. Aside from him and Nori, there were twenty-two other young men and women riding to Test. Half were in small groups with chaperones, while others rode alone. There were at least a dozen more Test youths traveling among the cozar. Then there were the tag-along riders who were neither cozar nor *chovas* nor Journey youths, but men and women taking a break from their own monotonous travel by stopping overnight in this or that caravan as they outpaced each set of wagons.

One of the outriders who reined in caught sight of Payne and nudged a partner. "Hey, neBentar," he called. "Heard your wake-up call from Black Wolf sort of ballooned out of control."

Payne grinned. "Aye," he called back. "But I'll have to tell you about it later. Right now we have to pop over to the other side of the river."

The *chovas* chuckled and shook his head. Beside Payne, his uncle snorted, then went back to watching the crew ready the bridge as the V-spans came down slowly, cranking inexorably into place as the harness dnu worked the massive cable wheel.

Payne half stood in the saddle to look back along the wagon line, but he didn't see his sister. He started to rein around, but Wakje stopped him with a grunted command. The bridge crew was almost finished dropping the temporary bridge in place, and it was starting to be secured.

Brean, the caravan's half leader, or Hafell, didn't waste any time. The lean, greying man rode up swiftly, looked over the washed-out bridge in the dark, and cursed silently. It figured, thought the Hafell. This wasn't even one of the better V-spans. There were no stanchions, so there were no safety lines, and it had already cost several someones dearly. He could see wagon debris and muddy gear in a growing salvage pile.

Two hours late to the circle, a flood crossing at night, and half the harness teams as nervous as four girls on their first date. Behind him, the old Ell perched on his wagon box like a damaged general, peeved as a half-plucked chicken, while the caravan rattled apart. It was Brean's job to bring up the rear, but with Ell Tai's ankle snapped like a twig at noon, Brean was riding both front and rear, overseeing his own second, a cousin, who had already made three mistakes and cost them another hour. It was closing in on midnight, and if Brean wasn't careful, he'd lose more than another hour here.

The Hafell pointed to Payne's group and ordered curtly, "Take your dnu across. Then come back and man the poles. You—" Brean motioned to the next group. "—start sorting the wagons for crossing."

Payne hesitated, but obeyed. With the dnu this anxious, Nori had probably been roped into helping to soothe them. Ever since she'd passed her third bar and transferred into the trade ranks, she'd been swamped with vet duty. One would think that half the dnu in this train were getting sick every day. Add being a natural caller on top of being an animal healer, and she was working even more than he was. Payne cast one more frown back, but pushed down his worry and moved into place.

Like Wakje, he studied the river carefully. The embankment was steep enough that the wagon ruts had cut deeply into the gravel. The drivers had to brake hard to keep from overrunning the bridge. The spans themselves were barely two wagons wide, just enough for a man to stand on either side and not be knocked over by the dnu. There were no real rails, just a guide beam, barely a hand's length tall, running along the edge of the spans. "It's a widdermaker, alright," Payne heard one man mutter. "Just enough to trip over."

The first four riders went across carefully in slightly staggered pairs to balance their weight. Then Payne's group rode across. They had a bad moment when a wash of debris caught on the ramped underside of the bridge. The spans trembled; the bridge crew rushed to the jab at the mass with their poles. The debris finally submerged. Payne's group urged their dnu onto the last span. Half of them balked, and Payne had to spur his beast hard to get it started again. Like all dnu, it loved to bathe in the shallows, but didn't like deep water. A swollen river like this could spook any beast; it would suck a man down like thread.

His dnu picked its way nervously onto the last span, then plunged with relief up the graveled bank. Payne hadn't realized how tense he himself had been until he reached the top of the bank. He whispered a quick thanks to the moons for the safe passage and flushed when Wakje glanced back. He didn't apologize. That *chovas* had been right. Fall in that river, and Payne would never have to worry about impressing a girl again, not unless she was on the path to the moons herself.

He handed his dnu off, picked up a boat hook from the bridge crew, and made his way back onto the span.

Payne and Wakje weren't stationed quite in the middle, for which Payne was grateful. The crack where the center spans met wasn't wide—he couldn't see the water through it, but the bridge shivered there like a Tumuwen winter. On the upstream side, the river roiled toward the floating bridge like an inexorable storm. On the downriver side, it slid slickly away into blackness.

One of the *chovas* looked at the water, over at Payne, and made the sign of moonsblessing. She was a husky woman, one of the few strong enough to do debris watch, but this wasn't her choice of duty. "Too deep, too fast," she muttered when he caught her nervous expression.

He nodded silently.

The Ell's was the first wagon forward. The old man's driver braked cautiously down the steep embankment, but the harness team was tired. The two dnu tossed their heads but didn't fight the slope or the men who strode beside them. They pranced a bit as they hit the first section. Their flexible hooves tested the shivering bridge like birds dipping into dark water. But the Ell clicked to them, and the irritable team obeyed and moved onto the floating bridge.

A trade wagon was next, then a family wagon with its side panels folded down to lower its profile. *Chovas* and single riders passed, with the few caravan dogs trotting ahead. Another trade wagon, fully expanded, two guild wagons, and a string of family wagons plodded along. One by one, the nervous teams rolled down the slope and onto the bridge while Payne and the others jabbed at debris. The heavy gear wagons were near the end of the train, and the cozar seemed to hold their breath while the first of the flywheels crossed. The third had a team that was spooky, and two more *chovas* moved in to pat and soothe the dnu.

They were just past the halfway point near Payne when one of the dnu jerked as if stung. It tossed its hammer head and struck its guide, Murton, right in the chin. The wagon veered, the bridge tilted at the uncentered weight. All six dnu spooked forward, and the outrider staggered into Payne.

"Look out—"

"Haw, haw," the driver shouted. "Easy there—"

Payne's heel hit the stub of the bridge rail. Instinctively he grabbed for the *chovas* with one hand and slapped out with the hook with the other. He missed with both. Murton still had one hand on the harness, and the startled team dragged the man forward. Payne's boat hook caught on the edge of the rail—and was knocked free by another man running to help. "Man in the water," the *chovas* shouted. "Man over—"

Payne twisted, felt the cold rush of water like a wind at his back—

A thick hand clamped over his wrist. He corkscrewed; his legs slapped the river's surface. His boots filled instantly. Frigid waves shocked his skin. For a moment, the river sucked with millions of liters rushing, pulling like a giant maw. Rocks, pebbles, grit hit and ground through his pants. Something struck his knee, something else tangled on his left boot. He dug his fingers into his uncle's hand. He was being swallowed whole—

Wakje heaved. Another man snagged Payne's wrist. A third man fisted his jerkin. His shins hit the rail, then his boots scrambled for footing. The other men steadied him. "Moons," he gasped.

"Alright?" one man demanded. "Alright?"

"Aye, gods, I'm okay." He caught his breath and straightened. "My thanks, to you—and the moons."

One of the men glanced at the river's maw. "Damn lucky, neBentar."

He glanced at the grey, greasy flood and hid his own shudder. "Lucky enough," he agreed.

"Best get changed," Wakje said curtly. "You'll slip more easily now."

Payne nodded. His heart was still pounding, and his breath was quick. That outrider had almost slammed him off the bridge. If Wakje hadn't been so close, so ready for anything . . . He shook his head at the moons. Nori would give him hell about his clumsiness when she heard. She would never have slipped like that.

He made his sodden way across the span, then slogged up the bank. Ahead of him, the caravan stretched out with long, black gaps. The last of the wagons would fill those holes as they were put back into order. In the meantime, the cozar were taking the chance to check tack and pick river gravel out of hooves. Test youths and inexperienced *chovas* milled around, while older outriders talked in low voices and cantered back and forth with messages. With the lanterns sharpening the dark, it was a demonic dance of shadows.

Payne caught a hint of movement to the side and instinctively stepped back behind a footbox. It was just a young woman sneaking out of a wagon, her long braid swinging slightly as she dropped softly off the gate. Payne grinned to himself as the slim shadow listened furtively, straightened her tunic, then disappeared into the night. Passion, he thought, was hard for even the *chovas* to deny. He glanced ahead to Vina's wagon, then sniffed his sleeve and made a face. He wouldn't be that lucky tonight, not before a shower.

He took an outrider's offer of a ride gratefully as he trudged along. By the time he was dropped off at his wagon, he smelled like wet dnu, not just river rot. He waved his thanks, ignored the cozar and *chovas* who wandered through the wagon line, and clambered up on the gate. There he stripped off most of his wet clothes. There was a faint scent already inside the wagon when he opened the door, and he drew his breath in deeply, but all he smelled was himself. "Hells," he muttered as he held the dripping clothes over the gate. He was getting more than paranoid. Nori always had some odd-smelling craft in the works or some dusty herb drying.

He tossed his own clothes over the drying rope. The threads were packed with silt, and he fingered them with sober realization. Few men lived who went into floodwaters. There was too much soil in the flood. The waters tumbled a man, packed the silt into his throat and lungs, till he couldn't even choke out the silt plugs to breathe. Payne let out his breath carefully and savored the taste of the air. Luck of the moons, he thought.

He had changed and was heading back to the bridge when he realized that there were only ten wagons left to cross the river, and he still hadn't seen his sister.

III

Night Hunt
Dry, your mouth where breath rasps out;
Numb, your thighs which strain;
Bruised, your feet that pound the earth;
Black, your blood—night stains.

Trapped, your heart which climbs your throat;
Clenched, your fists on steel;
Wild, your eyes that pierce the dark;
Fear, which claws your heels.

Harsh, the hungering sounds that chase;
Chill, the fog that hides;
Grey, the granite earth and graves;
Grey, the wolven cries.

   —from *Night Mares and Wolfwalkers, Tales to Tell Children*

Just shy of midnight, west of Willow Road . . .

   She wasn't fully panicked, not yet, but she was tiring hard, and her breath now choked her like flour. She bit at the growing fear as though she could spit it out. They were close behind her. They had to be. They would not have abandoned her trail at dusk. Not with her blood to mark it.

   Shadows leered before and behind her, shapeless monsters that breathed themselves bigger and blacker in the deepening night and reached down to whip her arms. Nori ducked, shoved through a menacing spring growth. Tripped on a half-buried boulder and skidded a meter in slick spring clay before she regained her balance. Another thin bough snapped at her, split her skin in a short, shallow slash. In the gloom, the smell of the blood on her arm was hard and hot and sweet.

   Wolves growled around her, and she snapped back. She had

nothing to protect her shoulders. Her trail pack had been clawed off her back by the beetle-beasts when they attacked the Grey Ones' den. Her shirt was now a crude sling for the two tiny wolf pups she'd saved. Gods, what she'd give for another bow. Hers had cracked in half when she'd drawn the third bolt. Her quiver, her jerkin, her belt and its pouches, she'd lost them all to the worlags—the beetle-beasts. With them, she'd lost her scout book. She'd actually stopped as she'd scrambled to safety and had reached back down to snatch it. A worlag claw had raked up, slashed the back of her arm, another had snagged on her belt—

She couldn't go back, not now. She could only clutch what was left of her shirt and run through the deepening night.

She splashed through a glinting puddle and fought the urge to look back. For a devolved species with only ratlike intelligence, the worlags were clever hunters. She'd managed to climb to safety on the short cliff behind the wolf den, but the worlags had found her trail again barely an hour later. She'd been herded away from the lake path almost as soon as she'd left the ridge. Now she was racing for Cotillion Cliffs and praying the rocks were close.

Never run under worlag moons . . .

She ducked under a forked bough too quickly, and her black braid caught in the brittle branch. She jerked free and snapped the wood like teeth. She didn't bother to curse. She'd already left so much sign on her trail that a blind man could have tracked her at a dead run. The beasts behind her were much more competent.

Fear sharpened her thoughts, and a slitted gaze flickered in the back of her mind, watching from a distance. Nori tried to ignore it. It wasn't the golden, predator-hot gaze of a wolf. It was cold and sharply yellow, alien and eerie as a moonghost. She felt a flash of hysterical laughter as the gaze touched the edge of her consciousness while the forest scratched at her body.

Centuries ago, the yellow-eyed birdmen called Aiueven had allowed humans to stay on this world only because of the worlags. In exchange, humans had engineered the barrier bushes to protect the Aiueven breeding grounds. The telepathic birdmen couldn't sense worlags as they could humans and other life-forms; the minds of the beetle-beasts were simply too different. The Aiueven had barely managed to strip the worlags of their technology before they could fully decimate the Aiueven population. Slow to breed and centuries old themselves, the birdmen were now only a fraction of their former number, while the worlags continued to spread. The worlags' hatred of the birdmen seemed bred into their very ichor. Now that hatred was aimed at Nori as if they could sense the taint within her.

Nori had been linked to the birdmen since she'd been in the womb. That was the taint that chilled her thoughts and made the Grey Ones growl. That cold spot could watch her thoughts, shift her perceptions, even punish her if it wanted. It had saved her more than once. But the worlags weren't of this world, and Nori couldn't feel them any better than could the birdmen. Now she ran a kay, just one kilometer, ahead of the worlags. And the beetle-beasts behind her were gaining.

She pressed the ragged sling to her chest and ducked blindly under branches. Slashed through a wide puddle that the wolves leapt like deer. Dodged a half-cracked rock and vaulted a fallen tree one-handed. The trail straightened, and three wolves flashed past her. In the patchy moonlight, she threw herself after the ghosts. She didn't bother to watch for forest cats or poolah traps. The noise she was making would scare almost everything away, and the wolves would sense a poolah trap or badgerbear like a hound dog does old cheese long before she ran over them.

Gods, she was an idiot. She had thought to leave the wagons for just a few minutes. She hadn't questioned the sudden, self-ish need to keep that haunting wolf Call to herself instead of sharing it with her brother. And when she'd reached the trail-head, the yearling had been waiting. He had loped away, just ahead of her, always just in sight, but slipping away through the forest like a grey will-o'-wisp. Her twenty-minute run had turned into a five-hour hike. Two more hours at the den, watching Rishte and First Mother until the rest of the pack returned. By the time she'd finally been accepted, the worlags had already set their trap. They had rushed the den like a flood. It had been all the wolves could do to slow them down while Nori tore the pups from the earthen den and ran for the rocks.

Now her fists clenched futilely. She had no weapons to protect the pups or herself, just her hands, scraped by rocks and branches, and her mind, with fear strangling her thoughts.

Grey Ones growled and she snarled instinctively back. She had no energy for words as she thrust through a tangle of ferns. The mix of weeds and hotflowers burned, and she hissed at the silk slime that slapped her forearm, blistered and raised her skin. The blisters would go down on their own in forty, fifty minutes—if she lived that long.

She staggered out of the thicket on the heels of the small pack. Dashed through another grass clearing. Back under the trees, a rise in the trail, a sharp dip, a switchback that almost defeated her as its edge crumbled away. She felt it give and grabbed at branches, dirt, roots that dangled like twisted fingers as the earth collapsed beneath her. Her knees hit the edge of the trail, but the dank soil broke away. A tiny stream had cut the trail back under the clay, and what was left of the ground scrabbled away beneath her kicking feet. She grabbed at muddy roots and tried to jam her knee up onto the soft edge. Instead, the slick clump gave way. She cried out as her hands stripped the roots. Acidic sap burned her fingers. Mud skidded past, and the roots stretched out like coarse wires as her weight dragged them down. They would snap and drop her on the boulders below. She knew they wouldn't hold. They couldn't hold. Instinctively she started to cry out toward slitted eyes—

The wolves howled in through her skull like a storm.

Like a stiletto, her mind sharpened. Energy surged in her strained muscles. Her left toes caught on a knob of rock exposed by the fresh slide. She thrust up, dug her free hand into the raw edge, and clawed into the soil. The other grabbed a fist-sized root just as the knob of rock let go. A wash of earth dragged at her boots, but she kicked and scrabbled up, hunched like a cripple over the sling as she elbow-crawled onto the trail.

The Grey Ones circled, dashing in and out, blinding her with movement. She didn't have to be linked to their minds to hear them: Get up, hurry. Hurry, run. She shoved herself back to her feet. She was sucking air like a chest wound. Her legs were shaky and her hands were raw with root sap. Half bent, she glared at the yearling who got too close. He shied away like a slal bird. They were wild creatures, these wolves, not raised with men. They would never trust a scout like her, not with the taint in her thoughts, but they'd bargain with the seventh devil to save their precious pups. She looked toward the yearling again and caught a glimpse of golden eyes. For a moment, they were tight in her mind like a noose. Then the Pack Mother growled from up ahead.

"I hear you," Nori snarled back. She kicked the mud off her moccasin-boots, then clutched the wolf cubs close to her chest and threw herself back to a run.

How far had she come? Three, four kays in the last thirty minutes? At night, with the worlags, with a pace too fast to maintain, her stamina had fled like fire.

One of the wolves dropped back until its smell was harsh in her nose. Golden eyes gleamed as it turned its head to meet her gaze. There was a harsh shock of intimacy. Engineered nerves triggered like sparks, and wolf thoughts hit like a fist: *Hurry. Danger. Closing.*

The creature broke the visual contact and stretched back into darkness. Nori stumbled with the loss of the link. The voice had been like a blast of air that rushes past one's mouth. Too much, too fast to bring into the lungs. It taunted her with the power of the pack. She cursed them for keeping it from her.

How far now? Her thoughts worried the distance like a rat on rawhide. She heard something hard behind her and whirled. The stitch in her side stabbed like a knife, but she forgot it as her own breath choked her with the clicking sound of the hunters in the shadows.

The worlags were closing.

She trembled in place, tried to catch her breath as she stared. She saw nothing, nothing. Just the swaying branches she herself had slapped aside while a flash of grey frayed the edge of her mind. It was them, the wolves, she realized, not she who had heard the beasts. The pack knew where the worlags were: Each slick and callused carapace that scraped along those boughs, each hardened, brown-black leather arm with its eager claw, impatient to slit her skin. Each black and lidless, bulbous eye that sought her now bloody trail.

She turned and ran. Around her, grey wolves snarled like a winter storm and crawled inside her skull to probe what was left of her strength. Without eye contact, they were only impressions that blued and yellowed the edge of her vision, so that she saw contrast more sharply, branches like streaks of black in a lighter blue-black sky. When they knew she could keep going, they left her as subtly as they had entered. It took seconds to realize that the night had not become deeper. Instead, it was simply the wolves giving her back her own dimmer, duller human sight.

Protect. Hurry. Water. Hurry. Without eye contact, the mental images weren't even words, just growls in the back of her head. She'd heard it all her life, that howling. It had grown stronger last year with each term at the university. She'd been more than impatient to finish her third bar so she could return to the trails at home. Wolves in the wilderness, just out of reach. Wolves on the edge of her mind. Gods, she had almost tasted it. Then the pack itself had Called. She had Answered like a shot, but was only now starting to understand them.

Hurry, water—the stream? The faint grey din snarled approval as she interpreted the image correctly. Ironjaw Creek? It was still four kays away.

The lead wolves disappeared over a small rise. A moment later, a faint eagerness came back through the packsong. Her ability to read the wolves was growing, in spite of the taint inside her. It lurked like a poolah, that taint, just waiting to tear at the grey. It frightened the pack as much as it frightened her. But the taint was from a distant source, and the wolves were with her now. She focused on the image they sent and let her mind go grey. Eagerness . . . The hunted turning, biting? The hunted becoming the hunter? An odor sent to her from the wolves tickled a mental nose.

"Ahh," she breathed. There was something on the trail ahead, something that loomed and waited. Something that didn't want the hot flesh of wolves or the iron-red blood of a human, but the dark, cool ichor of a leathered beast. She felt a feral grin stretch her lips. Blackthorn. It had to be a thicket of blackthorn.

When the trail split again, she followed the wolves without hesitation. Through a stand of silverheart, past a wash of thistles, and then she could smell the thorny shrubs as clearly as licorice. She sprinted toward the thicket, ducked under the first thin vines, and found herself in a nightmare weave of growth. A long thorn tore at a boot lace, and her hair caught in a vine. Blackthorn odor, acrid-sweet, now clogged her mouth like blood. She ripped free without slowing her pace. It was a mistake. Black vines clutched at her shoulders and feet. She stumbled in the dark, caught herself on a branch, and had to stifle her cry as two soft, bright green thorns pierced the palm of her hand. Silent—she must be silent.

She shoved through, and three more barbs raked her neck by her ear. They were spongy from the early rains and eager to feed after winter, but she tore away and ignored the shallow wounds. The thorns were not deadly, not, at least, to her. Three months, and they would harden into finger-long spikes. By fall, this track would be closed to all but the smallest creatures. Right now, the thicket would trap the beetle-beasts, if only for a few moments. The barbs that had torn her softer skin would catch in the worlags' leathered joints, and the venom that had no effect on her would slow the predators.

The wolves caught the triumph in her thoughts and howled in her head. She lifted her head and laughed wildly. It was powerful, seductive, the animal strength they projected. It was like growing fangs and biting at a meaty fist that tried to grab one's pelt.

Taste that, she snarled silently at the worlags. Behind her, the vines that had pierced her human blood writhed and shrank and shriveled up, and turned a pallid black.

Night leached light and vision as much as it did her breath. Shadows hid uneven ground; roots were ropes at her ankles. The pups were mostly silent now, enduring the jolting run. She went toe-heel with her knees loose to take up the shock when, in the dark, the ground wasn't where she expected it. Twigs snapped beneath her weight, and wolves snarled at each crack.

Danger, worlags. Faster.

She bit back in her mind. To them, she ran like a one-ton bollusk, but it was her hands, not her silence they needed.

She burst out onto a more open stretch. It was unexpectedly wide, and in her confidence she went to a heel-toe stride for speed—for two paces. Then she half tripped on the slick edge of an old wagon rut and nearly went face-flat across the ridges. She caught a branch on the way down, stripped the bark and more skin with it, and hit the rutted ground on one hand and knees.

"Dammit to the seventh moon," she burst out. What the hells was a wagon track doing out here? The cliffs, she realized with a spike of hope. She had to be close to the cliffs.

The wolves growled uneasily as she shoved herself back to her feet. They didn't like the turn of her thoughts. One of them—the mother wolf—snarled as she met Nori's eyes. The punch of lupine dread of the cliffs made Nori almost bolt from the ruts. She had to fight her gaze away. Pack memories could be years old, but the beetle-beasts were behind her right now. Whatever had bothered the wolves at the cliff wouldn't be worse than the worlags.

The mother wolf snarled again. Grey Vesh, Nori realized. She was beginning to distinguish the names of other wolves, too. Grey Helt was the pack leader, and the wolf who ran there to her left, the one who had Called her, was Rishte.

The yearling's thin voice sharpened as she caught his gaze. It triggered a flash like lightning in the grey. Time stuttered. Nori sucked in a breath as lupine paws seemed to clench around her heartbeat. Then the sense of wild, grating voices smoothed into the rhythm of her pulse. She felt herself reach toward him. *Rishte?*

Golden eyes dug into her mind. The deafness caused by a thousand faint sounds flooded into her ears. Tastes and dirt and odors and fur filled her mouth, sank down into her throat. *Wolfwalker.*

It was the sense of a name, a faint Calling, a hint of recognition. *Rishte?* she sent more sharply.

Do not! the mother wolf snapped across human and lupine minds.

Nori choked on the grey.

The young wolf veered off like a frightened deer. The pack-song bristled, and Nori dragged in air that was flat and wrong. The voice of the yearling hung for a moment on the edge of the din, howling as he snarled at Vesh. Then he slipped back into the grey. Nori bit her lip till it bled. The loss . . . hurt.

Hold the cubs, the mother wolf snapped. Grey Vesh was old enough to have strength in her voice and force in her Call. Once Vesh had touched the human mind, she didn't need to meet the human's eyes to force the human to listen. But the human was reaching toward Rishte again, and Vesh could see how their voices matched. The mother wolf snarled. There was a cold spot in the human, a death-spot like the fire that went with the wagon tracks. It made the mother wolf's hackles raise. To bond a pack-mate to this one? Even if it was meant to be, the grey beast snarled even more sharply and warned her yearling back.

But Nori could taste wolf in her lungs.

Fear. Hurry. Worlags. Run. Water ahead, water on the legs. The impressions cluttered her mind.

Water on her legs? They wanted to ford the creek, but that would only delay the beetle-beasts. Vesh didn't understand her answer, and she tried to focus her thoughts. The ridges were close, right there, to the east. All she had to do was climb to safety.

Water, swift water. The grey insisted.

Nori snarled back. She couldn't outrun them that far.

The Grey Ones tasted her sense of helplessness, of being weaponless and weak. It angered them. They gathered their minds and threw energy at her like a war bolt. She knew what to do with that mental power. She'd been taught almost from birth how to use it when it would finally be offered to her. But her contact with the pack was too new, too fragile. She barely touched the edge of that strength before it ripped past. She could grasp none of it on her own, hold nothing for more than an instant.

The wolves snarled at her ignorance, at the roughness be-tween them, at her insistence to head for the cliffs. Gathered themselves more tightly, turned their minds, and speared her with urgency. It was a blinding sliver through her brain, twisting, turning, diving down. The needle cut deep. She cried out, unable to be quiet.

Instantly the wolves drew back. She twisted with them, seeking the mesh and easing of pain. They shrugged with her, pulling her mind left and in, left and down. For a moment, her mind struggled against them. Then she felt the other. Deep in her thoughts, that older, more ancient, yellowed pattern fought to assert itself against the lupine weave.

The greysong stiffened in shock. Then Rishte howled in over the harshness. It was a wash of grey that smothered the alien patterns, like a rough-nubbin cotton after scraping against bark. It wasn't just strength she received. It was the confidence, the assurance of the pack, no longer through Grey Vesh and Helt and the others, but solely through the younger point that was Rishte. Nori's feet were suddenly lighter. The pups in her arms weighed nothing. The wolves were ghosts in the twilight, and she was a specter of fire on their heels. They fed her energy through their yearling, and she paced them now almost easily. Pounding, drumming the earth with her feet.

Finally the pack leader pulled them all back, forced Rishte to let go, to withdraw their strength. The point of power that was Rishte faded with the grey. Nori shuddered and stumbled. Without the packsong, she seemed more of a shadow, less than a wolf, less than human, and less somehow than herself. Where urgency had swamped her aches before, her calves now burned, and her arms were seared from the thorns. And she was tiring. She staggered as the ground suddenly collapsed beneath one foot. Dik-dik tunnel, rast hole—it didn't matter. She didn't stop; she merely caught herself on one hand like a sprinter at the mark, and hurled herself back to her feet.

Grey Helt snarled, but Rishte's voice was stronger. *Worlags, worry, fear. Run. Hurry. Hurry.*

She nodded. She was beginning to understand him. Chittering, clacking feet on leaves—that was the sense of the worlags. Urgency: *hurry.* Fear: *run.* The impressions themselves formed a language.

Behind Rishte, the grey din wasn't just some sort of fog, but the sounds of a hundred distant wolves. Each was distinct, like a point of light, but together they blended until there was only one song. It was the individual notes she was starting to hear. Each physical blow of her feet on the earth expanded her senses so she could hear them better. Each brush of a branch on her arms burned in a thousand more nerves on every point of skin. She had never felt the wolves like this, not this deeply, not on her own. Always before they had been a shadow, no more than the sense of a dream.

Since they'd left the den an hour ago, she had heard Rishte more and more clearly. Now she knew his name, his young strength, his open eagerness. She knew, too, that he was a year old, wild as spring eerin, and already set in the wolf pack ways. For kays he had led her away from the wagons, out along the game tracks before he'd allowed her close. With the taint in her mind, Nori hadn't been surprised when the pack mother had not been pleased. She could soothe a dnu or dog in seconds, but Grey Vesh saw through her soft voice easily. It was the danger of worlags that had finally forced them to accept her. The beetle-beasts had staked out the wolf trails and moved in while the rest of the wolves were hunting. Rishte's pack had barely come back in time to help Nori save the cubs.

It should not have been so difficult for her to offer help. The wolves had been engineered to work directly with humans. But Nori was tainted, and the Grey Ones could smell that like sulfur. Only because they could also sense the grey in her, not just the taint, and because their need to defend the pups was stronger than their fear, had they gone after the worlags and let Nori climb out with the pups.

Now their senses meshed with hers like a tapestry, thick with hundreds of years of fear. The oldEarthers had given them racial memories, not just mental communication, and the packsong tied them together from wolf to wolf, from birth to death. Deadly encounters with worlags had been burned into their minds like a brand. They poured it all into Nori.

Fear, fear. Feet, faster. Heart, strong. Hurry. Hurry.

Wolfwalker—The yearling's voice was urgent and sharp. *Close. Closing like badgerbears.*

She didn't waste thought to answer. She could almost hear through his ears that the worlags had hit the blackthorn stand just over a kay behind her. Now they were thrashing through. A kilometer. One kay. It was all the lead she had. She tried to pick up the pace, but she could not chance her final run. Not till she saw the cliffs for herself and a place to start her climb.

Boulders seemed to throw themselves at her feet, while branches clutched her shoulders. Stickbeasts scrabbled away in the trees, and sprits flew into her face. The snap of broken dills and the crackle of winter's littered leaves—they were careless sounds, the sounds of prey being run down. The forest held its collective breath to listen. A hunt like this could end only one way, and creatures watched with unblinking eyes, waiting with hungry, hard-earned patience for the tens of small meals that would follow.

And then, suddenly sharp, Vesh's voice, *Not there. This way, through here.*

Nori caught a glimpse of white rock and almost ran over a wolf who dodged close to herd her away. Rishte's sense of danger flared, and slitted eyes flickered open in the back of Nori's mind. She tasted metal, mold, dust, death. The wolves felt the tainted gaze deep within her and recoiled like a snake. *Death,* they howled. *Power. Old death. Burning, new fire, new death.*

The slitted eyes seemed to glow.

"Don't—" she cried out.

The packsong blasted back through her, cascading over the slitted gaze. Her mind seemed to right itself, twisted up and out, back to the clarity of chill night. Yellow eyes faded. Wolves nipped at her thigh and turned her away from the fork. Blindly she obeyed.

"Old death?" she tried to ask. "New death?"

Grey Vesh ignored her question. *Not that way,* First Mother snapped instead as she tried to look back. *Hurry. Clumsy human.*

That last was an afterthought, almost a goad, and Nori forced herself after the wolves. The Grey Ones feared the fork toward the cliff even more than they feared the worlags. What shocked Nori enough to follow was the sharpness of their fear. Old death, fevers, and burning pain—she recognized the taste of disease. But it should be faded, faint in their minds. Moons, but it should be years, even centuries old. There was only one thing could make such a memory:

Plague.

She'd seen it. She'd felt it. Her mother had made sure she could recognize it through the memories of the wolves: The slight tremors and rising fever. The convulsions that could snap a man's arms and back as his muscles contracted like vises around his bones. The blinding fire that burned in the veins and twisted a man's mind into coma and death. Full half of the colonists had perished in the first wave of alien plague. A third of those left had died in the second epidemic. And then there had been the martyrs. Even after eight hundred years, it was still viable, the plague.

Nori had been to the Ancients' domes twice, where the colonists had lived at Landfall. There had been bones there, hundreds of human skeletons, strangely lit rooms where the walls glowed without sign of a single lantern. There had been papers that had fractured or powdered when she touched them, odd equipment she didn't understand. Plague lived there, in the ruins of the first county halls. No one knew what caused the disease, only that the Aiueven, the alien birdmen, had sent the plague, and man could still contract it.

Plague here, in the forest? Nori must have misunderstood. With the bond so new, the fear of worlags was simply confused with other images. It was impossible to catch the death-disease away from the Ancients' domes.

But Grey Vesh nipped at Nori's knee, and another wolf bit at her heels when she tried to turn again to the cliff. She jerked back onto the forest trail. They snarled and pushed her into a wide arc around the ridge where they shied from death.

"Dammit," she cried out. "It's safety. I can climb out at the cliffs."

Death, death. Grey Vesh slammed into her thigh and snapped at her elbow.

She staggered left and missed another game trail that led toward the stone ridges. "Damn you, it could save your pups."

Burning death, Grey Vesh snarled back in her mind. *Dead wolves, dead pups. Dead humans,* the wolf finally snapped.

She had no more breath to argue. The best she could do was glimpse the rocks, pale and steep. In the moonlight, the cliff bit at the earth like a stone jaw half sunk into flesh. There was a darker scar on its face, as if the rocks had broken in recent years. It gave the ridge the look of a snarling poolah. She noted the location in the back of her mind, then raced on in the midst of the wolves. Now there was only Ironjaw Creek three kays away and shallow as a bigot.

Behind her, the thick trees swallowed the rancid scent of a drying seep and its rotting richness of reeds. She never saw the turquoise sheen of the shallow puddles that the rain had been diluting. Never saw the faint, yellow-green glow from the dying lilies that wept into the swamp.

IV

An ally makes a good friend,
Except when he's at your back.

—Nadugur saying

East, on Willow Road . . .

Payne's sister didn't turn up at Wakje's wagon, nor among the crafters, nor with the last of the cozar wagons. Payne was about to check with yet another merchant when he caught sight of the wagon's *chovas*. The man riding guard was Murton, the Sidisport chak who had dumped him in the river.

The *chovas* glanced back and caught sight of him. "Hey, neBentar," the man called out. "Sorry about that dunking."

Inside one of the wagons, three men went still. Then there was a flurry of quiet action. The blond man snatched the lists and papers on the table and stuffed them into his jerkin. The second man grabbed a map they'd had handy and laid it out over the now bare wood. The third reached back and picked up a packet of trade agreements to spread out over the map. As Payne's dnu reined in beside Murton, the three inside began a quiet murmuring about trade routes in the east.

Payne hid his disgust at the greeting. Murton's voice had been, of course, loud enough to catch the attention of every outrider nearby. The man got on Payne's nerves like a splinter in his shorts. But Payne smoothed his expression. With a ninan left to reach the Test town, he figured he'd better get used to splinters. "I'm asking along the line," he said shortly. "Have you seen my sister in the past few hours?"

"Black Wolf?" The outrider gave him a speculative look.

43

"Moons, neBentar, you worry more about her than a rabbit in a lepa's den."

He shrugged.

The older man said dryly, "If you can't find her, it's probably because she doesn't want to be found, especially after that leaf trick. How she knows where to find those things . . ." The *chovas* shook his head. "She's probably waiting near the front of the line."

Payne kept his voice steady. "No one's seen her ride forward."

But the man caught the undertone anyway. "Dik spit, neBentar, you're not thinking of calling a search? That's a hell of an overreaction."

Payne dropped his pretense of a smile. "Not if she's actually missing."

"Don't get your shorts in a twist, boy. Black Wolf will laugh her head off when she turns up at Chileiwa Circle after you've started a panic. Your parents will have a field day when they hear about that."

Payne stifled his instinctive response. There might be ten folk left in the county who didn't know he was the youngest son of Aranur of Ramaj Ariye and the famous Wolfwalker Dione. Attention from the girls he didn't mind. Taking flak from a chak like Murton was a different story. It was one of the reasons he preferred traveling with the cozar when he wasn't in a hurry. The cozar didn't care if he was Aranur's son, only that he worked his share of the line. In fact, with few exceptions, the only real ranks or titles used among the cozar were those of location, not lineage. A message master was the wagon with the birds and ring-runner supplies, not the person most skilled at writing, carving, or hawking. Duties rotated, depending on who was in the train, and people were judged by what they did, not by how they were born. Only the *-van* at the end of a task indicated someone whose skills were high enough to hold a permanent title, and the *-van* was used only for strangers who required the formality. Among themselves, the cozar were known simply by their rep-names, like Repa Ripping White or Tatsvin Ten-Bones, or in Nori's case, Black Wolf.

Murton cast him a sideways look. "She's probably out planning tonight's antic in spades," the man prodded again. "The painted faces on the dnu? The wheezing saddle? You should watch your backside more. She'd pick on a lepa if she thought it would bite The Brother."

There it was. Payne shrugged grimly. He should have expected Murton to get his name in sooner or later. The cozar had called him The Brother ever since he was twelve, but every time Murton said the rep-name, it turned into an insult. Payne prayed the rep-name didn't stick past his Test. It was depressingly accurate. His life in a nutshell: always watching out for Nori, always responsible for her. Sometimes, hearing "The Brother" made him want to pound some bones in, as if he would never be a man himself, just one more appendage of Nori.

Murton shook his head at Payne's shrug. "Even if she's out on the trail, she's four times as skilled there as you. You might as well worry that a poolah can't find its own den." The man's dnu danced nervously at a crackling sound, but the *chovas* controlled the beast easily. "She's playing a joke, nothing more. She'll be back by fireside."

"She's already played her prank for the day, and she would never make me worry on purpose." Not when it could rouse the cozar. The caravan folk would descend on the forest like a flock of pelan. They'd pick apart every bush in case she'd fallen or been set upon. They'd scour the creek banks, check every ravine. She'd never intentionally cause the kind of search she herself had led so often.

"She's made no bones about not wanting to Test."

"Doesn't matter. This is my Test, not hers. Besides—" He shrugged and hid a wince at a deep bruise. When it came to the fighting rings, his sister was no gentle teacher. She had fists like small steel hammers, elbows even harder, and a stubborn determination to train him up right for rank. Compensation, most likely, for not being able to Test herself. With the specialized training she had received, he might never achieve her skill in the rings, but at least he could best almost any student anywhere near his own age. He tried to force another smile, as if it was indeed a joke. "She'd never miss watching me get thrown around by a dozen ranking fighters."

The older guard chuckled. "That's not something I'd miss, either. I hear you're finally taking your firsts in Abis and Cansi. Been a bit of speculation as to why you haven't done so before. I would have thought the son of a weapons master would be encouraged to Test early, not late."

Payne's smile thinned. "Rank isn't everything."

Murton nodded. "I hear that a lot from the unranked. I mean no offense, of course."

"Of course," Payne bit off.

Inside the wagon, the men grinned slyly at each other. They had two bets riding on The Brother. The first was when Murton would get him to challenge. The second was how badly the outrider would crack the boy open once he had him down. They had argued briefly over the near-accident on the bridge, but had finally decided it didn't count toward the bet. They were hoping for blood on the boy, not just for a missing body.

Outside, Murton added, "I don't see why you're so upset, neBentar. They say she's been looking out for you for years every time you two hit the trails. She's old enough now to not to want The Brother tagging along every time she leaves the train. In fact—" He gave Payne a sly look as he picked a burr off his dnu. "—she was walking out with B'Kosan last night. She's probably riding the frontage trail with him and not wanting to be disturbed."

"I'll look into it, thanks." He spurred his dnu away at a canter.

Murton called after him, "Give my regards to B'Kosan."

"Moonwormed pissant," Payne muttered to his dnu. Nori might be more at home on the trails, but she hadn't walked out with B'Kosan. She'd had to rebuff that *chovas* ever since the man had joined them. It had been B'Kosan who followed Nori around, not she who encouraged the guard. Hells, for Nori to walk out with B'Kosan was like a wolf stepping out with a dog: it was bound to end in violence. Not just from Nori, either. Last night, when Nori had gone to gather night herbs from the verge, Payne had barely had time to sling on his swordbelt when B'Kosan had come back to fireside. Payne had smothered a dark satisfaction. The *chovas* had been limping.

Payne looked along the wagon line, then out again at the forest. No moonbeams penetrated the thick, textured folds of black-greens. The only lights now were the glowing road, the lanterns inside a few of the wagons, and the four moons overhead. On the ghostly road, the spoked wheels made illusive, hypnotic patterns. Payne listened as much with his mind as his ears, but the moons glowed silently above the rumbling wagons. He breathed, "Nori-girl, where are you?"

No wolf howls answered him. No badgerbear roars or bihwadi cries broke the quiet on the other side of the verge. If there were Grey Ones nearby, he could not hear them. Just the stuttered trot of the wagon teams, and the tiny cries of the tree sprits. He muttered another silent curse and rode forward along the line.

V

Nori was two kays south of Ironjaw Creek, running hard for the water. She had husbanded her strength, but her breath came now in urgent rhythm. Her hands were slick with sweat.

She turned onto a wide game track that, even in the dark, felt familiar. The wolves snarled, but she refused to change direction. They were adding distance to her path, distance the worlags didn't have to run. She built a picture of human scouts and projected it desperately into the packsong. *Men. Where are the nearest men?*

Rishte caught the sense of the question and passed it on to the grey. From him, it swept out from wolf to wolf, pack to pack in the night. The images snarled back. Men at the rock circle, men at the fork, men on the wide river trail . . .

Without the eye contact, Rishte's voice was too thin to understand. A river trail? Perhaps Deepening Road? It was the major route along the steep, rugged canyon that contained the River Phye. She knew dozens of scouts along that route and half the council ring-runners. But Deepening Road was seven or eight kays away, at least four oldEarth miles, too far with worlags behind her.

Men at the fork—she didn't get that. Pira Forks, perhaps, but that was clear on the other side of the cliffs. It might as well be on a moon. The men at a circle of rocks felt closer, north and west on a hill. Bell Rocks was in that direction. It was a scout camp, only four kays away, off the main trails on a side loop.

48

This time of year, with the worlags hunting, someone else might have been forced there to wait out the night. She felt a spur of hope. Ariyen scouts were well armed.

She projected a memory of the place, and Rishte growled. One of his packmates nipped at her heels as the wolves again tried to turn her off the track. *Death, death. Danger.* Rishte seemed to beat the words into her mind.

"Armed men," she managed. "Bell Rocks is safety."

But Rishte growled again, and his teeth seemed to bite at her thoughts.

Danger like the cliff? She didn't realize she had projected the question so strongly, but Rishte answered.

No. New death, cold death and marrow.

She gagged. She could almost taste the marrow. Cold death—cold bones? The wolves feared the cliff because it reminded them of plague. There was no sense of plague up ahead. So they avoided Bell Rocks for some other reason. Carcasses would draw worlags and bihwadi, so this was probably just an instinctive reaction to avoid the predators. Men would never butcher an animal where others might later ride. She tried to form an image of the slinking, doglike bihwadi, then of poolah with their tooth-ringed maws.

All she got back was a wary sense of danger. It was scavengers, then. The idea was actually a relief. She couldn't chance running into more worlags, but she could easily outclimb bihwadi. Rishte sensed her determination to go on and snarled into the pack. Another wolf snapped back, then slammed into Nori's thigh to try to turn her away from the loop path. She was almost thrown from the trail. Rishte snapped at the other wolf, but Nori shoved through them both. The other wolf didn't hit her again.

Ahead, Rishte whipped under a heavy log. Nori dove after him and rolled, following through a scurry of leaves and rotting twigs. She was spitting out debris when she realized that she could as easily have vaulted that log as rolled through underneath. She was too close to the wolves, too caught up in their urgency. It was now affecting her judgment. She pushed back the wolves, hit her stride, and went into the clearing in a full-legged run.

And tripped on the half-fleshed corpse.

She tucked up and jumped awkwardly, but her toes caught the bloody rib cage. Tangled bones tumbled thickly into a wash of moonlight. She landed in a crouch and whipped around, her breath ragged and tight.

Human. Dead.

New death. Near death. Cold.

Now she understood. "Gods—" She couldn't help the word. And not one body, but two. The wolves had known. That's why they had tried to herd her away.

She took in the scene as fast as she could. Scavengers had already eaten most of the flesh and guts. The doglike bihwadi had had their meals first. The dung and musk marks were a dead giveaway for the sly, pink-eyed creatures. The antlike largons had started in after the bihwadi, their insect jaws tearing out perfect half-circle bites. Now thin lines of writhing black led away through the crumpled grasses. The tiny nightants were still working where the largons had had their fill.

She squatted and quickly lifted leaves away from the bones. The edge of a metal button gleamed under a fern like a forgotten note of fear, and she identified the guild pattern as she turned it over in the moonlight. Messengers, then, or what was left of them. But all the way out here? She was in Gambrel Meadow, at least a full kay off the main trail. The only claim this clearing had to usefulness was as a hunter's meadow, and that was in early fall. In spring, with the worlag packs scouring the woods, it was as dangerous as an off-trail swamp. There were thick logs jammed up against the trees where flooding along the creek had wedged them in—good for shelter or for defensive fire, or for forest cats or poolah. Nearby she caught sight of the bolts permanently sunk into the trees from which to suspend the gambrels. Now a long, stained rope dangled from one set and twisted in the cold wind. Nori felt suddenly sick. There were older bones in a rough pile to the left, cracked and missing their marrow.

She stumbled across the clearing and yanked at the weeds already growing through the barely cleaned bones. There were rotting clothes and skulls for at least four skeletons. Her hands trembled as she pushed aside a scapula and caught a dull gleam of light too clean and regular to be natural. It was wire, and it circled two wrist joints still held together by taut-dried ligaments. She stared back at the fresh bodies, as if the moonlight lied. Then she groped for her scout book. She needed to mark this down, get this information to her father. But her hand scraped only air. "Oh, heckfire and damnation."

She had no scout book and only a few minutes to spare. She looked around to set what she could in her memory, but she was missing something. The boots, she realized, and the socks were gone. There weren't any packs or belt pouches, either. She lifted the trampled grasses near the fresh corpse and found five small message tubes opened out and empty. Heavy brush, trussed limbs . . . The ring-runners hadn't been caught on the loop trail. They had been marched here barefoot, through hotflowers, blackthorn, and brambles. Which meant the raiders who had caught them were staking out the main trails.

Death. Fresh death. The wolves had known. They hadn't wanted her to take this trail, nor to risk their cubs at Bell Rocks. They had known: the kill trail led like a road map from here to the creek to the camp. She'd find no scouts at Bell Rocks now. It was raiders up ahead.

"Dammit, godsdammit." She didn't even notice she cursed as she sucked in air to catch her breath. She could go on, could try to get around the camp, but if the raiders noticed her in the dark, she would look like another ring-runner. Raiders were always eager for news of a rich shipment or merchant train. Men like that would not lift a hand to help her. They would laugh while the worlags tore her apart outside their circle of fire. Then they would search her for any message tubes, and burn her limbs for their panbread.

Moonlight shafted through the trees, lighting the bloody bones. Black shadows darkened further with the brightening light, and the grisly skeletons stretched into distortions of human beings. The night breeze lifted and fell, and her sweat grew cold and clammy. Then, behind her, the worlags' chittering burst out excitedly. They had caught the smell of the decomp bodies—and her fresh blood smell on top of that. Nori's spine turned to ice.

A blood-rush surged in the wolves' mental voice. *Wolfwalker, the worlags,* Grey Vesh snapped.

Nori took off across the clearing. Rishte snarled and raced after her. On the edge of the wolves, she snarled back. For an instant, the two tones meshed. Her legs pounded faster. Her hands stretched out. Voices blended, emotions caught. Fear met and fed fear. The fragile communication twisted, clung. Her mind and Rishte's began to turn in the same direction till the link became a stronger cord, wound with lupine fury. It was the strength of hunting and feeding, of fighting for food against a stronger beast. It was the strength of survival, and it blinded her.

She slammed shoulder-first into a tree. "Dik spit!" She staggered back out of the roots.

Rishte snapped at her, as shocked by the abrupt, broad pain as she was. Even the pack stiffened with their link. The bond, the link, the change—

Her mind shifted through pain, and the wolves poured in more smoothly. Speed, they urged. Run, run.

Half deafened, half paralyzed by the pack, by Rishte's voice, Nori stumbled back onto the trail.

Hurry. Fight-protect. Pups. *Run.* The wolves passed each sense along through the faint mental voice of Rishte. Mud, darker, wetter—that way. And, footworm there. Jump over—

She could hear the rush of water now. The fear that ate at her throat would choke her soon, and the wolves were feeding that terror. Everything her mother had told her was clear as claws on glass. The wolves, the bond, the creeping grey in her mind that turned into a torrent. The need to run, to turn and slash at the worlags that hounded her. The desire to bristle and bite at the danger up ahead. She tried to wrench back from the mental snarls as she'd been told to do when the bond got too intense, too uncontrolled. Her mind twisted to the right, up, out of the fog. Away from the grey, just as the Ancients had been taught to do, just as the alien birdmen had taught the Ancients themselves. It cleared her vision abruptly. The silence cut like a knife, both ways.

Rishte howled.

Nori cried out.

The worlags raised their voices.

With dull human sight, Nori plunged toward the stream. She glimpsed the tiny whitecaps that topped its slick black expanse. The light of the fourth and seventh moons glistened dully on the waters. She risked a glance back.

Forty meters.

Moons help her, but the worlags had seen her even as she saw the stream. They were spreading out to trap her, to catch her against the bank. Their chittering grew as they closed.

"Rishte," she cried out. "Upstream, quickly. Two-Log Crossing."

Rishte howled back into her mind. There was an instant's struggle, as if they pulled at each other with their teeth. Nori snapped the command. Abruptly, the younger wolf obeyed. He disappeared into shadow. Four of his packmates went with him, but Helt and Vesh hovered by Nori, lunged away, and came back to their pups again. Vesh snarled with the desperate need of a mother who will do anything, use anything to save her cubs. Grey Helt felt his mate's need, but like the others he hated the nearness of the human. Even as he had been engineered to trust that wolfwalker bond, he feared the taint in Nori's mind. But the human had his cubs. It was an intolerable tension to the male, and Nori's own fear made it worse.

He leapt in front of her, planting his feet. Nori stumbled to a halt.

Wolfwalker, he snarled, glaring into her eyes.

"I can cross," she snapped back. "Get to safety."

Our pups—

"I have them," she snarled. "Now go, if you want us to live!"

She ducked past him, slipped in the clay, and dodged through the rocks toward the stream. It was fast and thick with spring runoff, but the worlag's chittering was almost loud enough to hear over the rush of the water. She grabbed up a thick, muddy branch that was jammed among the rocks and splashed in without looking back. Her shoulders were tight as if the worlags' claws would catch in her skin before she abandoned the bank.

The icy water was a shock to her heat-tightened skin. Her calves cramped like hammers. She gasped, staggered over the rocky bottom, knee-deep in the black surge. Quickly she jammed the stick in the rocks to catch her balance. She risked a glance over her shoulder. "Dear gods." She backed almost blindly.

Ten meters separated them, the woman and the worlags.

Ten bare meters between her and those claws, between her and the beetle fangs. In the moonlight, it could have been inches.

But the worlags halted on the bank, pacing, chittering, watching her in the water. One tested the creek, but jerked its claw back from the white-tipped water. Another eyed her and scuttled upstream, seeking a shallow crossing. Its six legs carried it over the rocks like an exaggerated skeleton.

Two worlags dropped to their fours as they watched her wade farther out. Their smaller, middle arms wrapped around the notches between their bellies and upper bodies. The semi-vestigal limbs would stay out of the way until they were needed to climb over boulders or rocks, or to start carving up her flesh with their more articulate claws.

A fifth beast chittered sharply and tested the few rocks that stood above the water near the bank. Nori's hand clenched on the branch as if her fingers would somehow find a knife, a sword, any kind of blade instead of brittle wood. The wolf cubs were very still in the sling. She hugged them closer, then steeled herself and turned her back on the worlags.

The frigid water in her boots burned grittily on her hot feet even as it chilled them. She refused to look back at the beetlebeasts. Instead, using the branch for balance, she worked her way into the stream.

The worlags chittered, scuttled, watched with unblinking eyes while swift water wrapped her trousers tightly around her legs. A broad, flat boulder squatted in the middle of the stream, tall enough that its upper half was dry. It tempted her as a place to rest, but she moved away from it, angling upstream toward a broader curve. There were deep pockets at the base of such rocks, places where the stream had eaten away its bed. A raft or kayak could be pulled in and under. Nori would be sucked down like a twig.

She forced her breathing to slow. In the gloom, it took her a moment to realize that the worlags were gone from the bank. If they weren't scuttling after the wolves, then they were seeking some other ford. They couldn't swim, but they went into the water often enough. They simply let the current sweep them along till they fetched up on the other bank.

In the distance, Grey Rishte felt her thrill of fear at the thought. Even without eye contact, his faint voice was still with her. She reached, focused, strove toward the grey. Before, there had been nothing to grasp into but a wispy sense of fog. Now she felt something more concrete. Now she felt an Answer.

The voice disappeared, wisped back in, then began to solidify. It wasn't just the young wolf, she realized. The other wolves had recognized the link that was forming between Nori and Grey Rishte. They put their own strength behind the yearling and pushed that force at Nori. *On. Move on.*

The wolves felt urgency, not fear now. The worlags must not have followed them upstream, but found some other ford, or she would have sensed the wolves' need to flee from an immediate danger, not just to return to the cubs.

Meet, need, agreed Rishte.

"To meet up?"

Rishte seemed to acknowledge that, and Nori's calves almost cramped again with the force of the grey wolf's sprint.

"Hurry," she tried to send in return. Her boots slid on slick rock, and she stumbled in the stream. "I need you to see for me." She didn't know how much he understood, but at least she knew he was coming.

She staggered out of the water and collapsed on a log. She took precious minutes to empty her moccasins, wring out her soggy trousers. Then she worked the limp clothes back on, adjusted the sling with its tiny balls of warmth, and scrambled up toward the trail.

VI

Who rides closer on the road:
The friends at your side,
The ghosts in your mind,
Or the dangers to which
You are blind?

   —from *Journey East to Far Away,* by Dici Criana

On Willow Road . . .

Payne's jaw was tense as he yanked open Nori's duffel to see what was missing. If she had gone out to run trail, she would be wearing her lightest jerkin, not the one she used for doing lead-rider duty. He pulled out a shirt—his, he noticed, and tossed it toward his own bag, but her lighter jerkin wasn't in the bag, nor were her scouting mocboots.

He pursed his lips, thinking, then stuffed the mess back in the bag and turned to his own gear. Quickly, he stuffed in a fresh set of clothes, then transferred his long knives from weapons rack to pack. He hesitated at the newer quivers, then finally took another one, this one for badgerbears and worlags, not raiders. He had grabbed a second emergency kit when he halted with a frown. Then he twisted and picked up his old hunting quiver again.

One by one, he pulled the arrows and examined the points. He ran his fingernail around the base of the fletching, but the glue was set on each quill and the binding was firm. Still, he frowned as he put the bolts back in the quiver.

He had his saddlebags in hand as Kettre reined in. "Aren't you packing a bit heavy for lead-rider duty?" she teased. "I mean, it looks like you've got something old, something dnu, something borrowed, and something blue all in one place."

He snorted as he tossed one of his sister's blue-edged bags over the rump of his dnu. "No one's seen Nori in hours."

Kettre abruptly lost her smile. "She's missing?"

"She sure as hell isn't in the caravan."

"Well, hells, Payne. Have you checked with the healer? Nori does have her first bar in human medicine. Your mother insisted. She might be helping with the—"

He cut her off. "I've checked with the healer and the message master, and with every wagon between. She's not here." He lashed a bag behind his saddle. "After pulling that leaf prank, she should at least have come by to gloat." He slapped the second bag behind the first.

Kettre eyed the doubled gear. "Maybe she went to check trail conditions, or the water levels for crossings."

"I thought of that, and it would make sense, if we were back at Four Forks. The creeks run close to the road there." He untied his dnu from the wagon, then swung smoothly into the saddle. "But that's a twenty- or thirty-minute run, and it's on the frontage trail. She wouldn't be gone eight hours for that. It's midnight, Kettre. She wouldn't have left the train so long, not at night, not without me, and not in the wilderness."

"She knows what she's doing out there, Payne."

"Aye." More so than Payne ever would. "But this is spring in Ramaj Ariye, and Ariye is always hungry for blood." A knot of messengers cantered past, heading north. He glanced at the barrier hedge from which they carefully kept their distance. There were eyes in those bushes, eyes that watched irritably while the caravan passed. Every hunter clung to the shadows, waiting for the forest to return to its natural state, waiting its chance to strike. His sister was out there among them.

He cast a silent prayer to the moons. At least bring her to the Grey, he told them, but he knew a sinking sensation. Even if the wolves accepted Nori into the pack, they would be a precarious safety. She couldn't know if the wolves would protect her or turn on her like a swarm of lepa when they sensed what was deep in her mind.

Kettre watched the worry flicker across his face. "It's Test time, Payne. Almost everyone's on the road. Maybe she simply saw someone she knew and stopped to trade news."

"Aye," he agreed shortly, though Kettre didn't know the half of it. Nori was a mobile way station for anyone passing things on to their parents. She'd received half a dozen messages just since they'd left Sidisport from their parents' web of informants. Her own reports were not unimportant, either. Trail conditions, predator patterns—sure, she reported those things like every other scout. It was the other notes that were beginning to raise some eyebrows. The movements of unusual riders on backtrails, the signs of meetings held out beyond towns, cryptic messages that were intercepted, and fragments of code collected while doing tower duty. With Payne's council notes in there, her scout book would be an interesting read for more than one set of merchants.

He frowned, thinking back. There had been that night spider in Nori's sleeping bag, and the mold in their trail food last ninan. If Nori's nose hadn't been as sensitive as a badgerbear's, they'd both have been stuck in some healer's clinic, sick in bed for months. They had chalked it up to the usual travel hazards, but perhaps Nori had grown suspicious. She might have tried to look into something alone. For all that she let him lead in town, she was two years older, and as protective of him as he was of her. She didn't always tell him everything.

He felt a cold finger on his spine. Beyond the verge, the wilderness now stretched its arms into full darkness. Somewhere out there, his sister had vanished like a chill in the sun. If she had fled there deliberately, thinking it was safer to lead a danger away than toward him . . . "Arrogant, moonwormed idiot," he muttered.

Kettre hurried her dnu to catch up. "You're not going to call a search, are you?" He merely glanced at the woman, and she scowled. "Moons, Payne, you don't always have to know where she is and what she's doing."

He shrugged.

"At least wait till we reach the camping circle and can check with the other trains."

His jaw firmed, but he refused to answer. Instead, he spurred ahead.

"You'll catch hell from the Hafell," she called.

A moment later, she reined in again beside him. This time, she didn't try to dissuade him. She just eyed him with a frown. If she hadn't seen the deep concern he'd let slip a few times when he'd lost track of Nori before, she would have suspected him of being unhealthily possessive of his own sister.

They had passed only four wagons when a hunting bolt tore into the black brush in front of them. Kettre's dnu shied, and Payne reined back abruptly. "Godsdammit to all nine moons," the woman snapped. Ed Proving was shooting the palts again. She glared back at the older man and got a half wave of satisfaction in return as Proving set his bow back between his legs and pulled out a small leather flask. The two shadows of night birds that had circled overhead were out of sight, and a single black feather fluttered down in their wake. "Why the hells does he do that?" she demanded.

Payne chuckled at the exasperation in her voice. After three days in the caravan, he'd have thought Kettre would be used to it. "He says they poop on his wagon top."

She glanced angrily back at the man. "He's going to shoot some *chovas* someday."

"Only if he's lucky."

As if Proving's bolt had been a trigger, Payne wanted to snap at each wagon driver they passed. But the men and women were content to urge their tired teams on in their plodding pace with clicks and low commands. Merchants rattled behind family wagons, and families sang softly to children. The scent of hay and grain clung to the feed wagons and clogged Payne's nose so he couldn't test the air. The cold-storage transport smelled of sweet insulation. That cleared his nostrils of the hay scent only so they could be filled again with the dark, dusty odor of the herb wagon. The entire line rumbled down the glowing road like a massive centipede writhing through the dark, uncaring, unstopping for anything as trivial as a scout out late on the trails.

When the Hafell, Brean, saw them coming up at a canter, the lanky man took one look at Payne's face and pulled away to the side of the wagons. Brean muttered a quick curse. NeBentar was young, but still the son of Aranur of Ramaj Ariye, and he rode with two men who had decades of judging and dealing with threats that Brean could only imagine. The Hafell wasn't about to ignore The Brother and, through him, the Wolven Guard. The best he could say for the uncles was that Payne spoke for them as much as Payne did for his sister. Brean rarely dealt with the uncles himself. Now he barely waited for Payne to rein in. "Well?" the man said irritably.

The younger man didn't bother with preamble. "I'm calling the search."

The Hafell's lean hands tensed on the reins, and his dnu chittered uneasily. He muttered a curse at the six-legged beast. If he didn't know better, he'd have accused the dnumaster of slipping dried choudi weed into half the feed to make them as antsy as their riders. He pulled his beast irritably back. "Godsdammit, neBentar, we're still an hour from Chileiwa Circle."

Payne shrugged tersely.

The Hafell looked at the set of Payne's chin and knew the young man wouldn't change his mind. "Moonworms on a rabid dog," he snapped. "I'd like one day, just one godsdamned day without some kind of emergency. One day without a broken ankle or axle. Twenty-six hours without some harebrained scout getting lost."

"Nori would never intentionally—"

The man cut him off abruptly. "Intentional or not, it's one more chak-driven delay. Of all the *chovas* whose bids we accepted, I'd have thought you two—" He jabbed his finger at Payne. "—would be the least of my problems." ·

The words stung. The cozar weren't nomads, but craftsmen who, during the trade seasons, traveled in family groups and shared road duties, knowledge, trade skills, and profits. They thought of their wagons as rolling homes, or rather as rolling stockades that kept their goods and families safe. The *chovas,* or hired-on guards like Kettre, rode escort in exchange for meals and the safety of the caravan.

Payne and Nori weren't *chovas,* they were *keyo.* Technically, they were also hired-ons or *chovas,* but since they had been raised with the cozar, they had guesting or *keyo* berths, not *chovas* berths with the wagons. They were like distant cousins, not strangers to the cozar. They were expected to do cozar duties like any family member, but that was no hardship. Most duties were as simple as washing dishes, watching the children, sharpening tools, or currying dnu—mundane tasks that anyone could do. With Nori now on the trade rosters as an animal healer, and both she and Payne in the lists as scouts, the Ell and Hafell had been happy to accept their bid for the train. For the cozar, who feared to leave their wagons, two fully ranked scouts were more than welcome, especially the children of Aranur and Dione.

It was also the reason the Hafell was furious that Nori was now missing. For any scout to be so careless as to run trail without leaving word? Brean would have her up at fireside the minute she got back, and the Hafell would be doubly harsh because of her skills. To lose a scout, let alone the Wolfwalker's Daughter, from a caravan spoke poorly for a man. Payne forced himself to say steadily, "She's been gone almost eight full hours, Hafell."

The lean man snapped, "I know how long she's been godsdamned gone. You've been asking every outrider, driver, and child down the line if anyone has seen her. I just heard from Giveaway Gaesel myself."

Payne clamped down on his retort.

The Hafell closed his eyes for a moment, took a breath, let it out, and rubbed his forehead. "Call your search. Take whom you need, trail riders, *chovas,* whomever. And neBentar," he added, as Payne turned away. "You may not like Ed Proving, but you'll want him with you. He was a damn fine tracker once."

Payne nodded curtly as the Hafell cantered back to his post.

Kettre looked uneasily up the line toward his two uncles. "You'll tell them?"

The young man snorted. "You think they're not aware? They're just waiting for the word." His uncles were nearly as protective as he was. They had always been uncomfortable around their mother, the Wolfwalker Dione, but Nori had wormed her way into their hearts with the acceptance only a child can give. It would be different when she became a wolf-walker, since such scouts were often used to track raiders down for trial, a fact their uncles seemed to see every time they looked at Dione. But until that day, Wakje and Ki could ignore Nori's lineage and think of her as a daughter.

Kettre glanced forward toward Wakje's wagon and hid a shiver. Payne and Nori treated their adopted aunts and uncles like best-loved blood relatives, but the Wolven Guard were cold men and women, hard-faced, old with killing and maiming. They had a way of watching people that made one think a man was a threat first, a target second, and third, a walking corpse.

"Take the front of the line, but I'll tell my uncles," Payne told her. "I'll take the rear of the line till then."

Behind her, as she spurred ahead, she heard Payne tell the first driver, "I'm calling the search." He was terse in the cozar way, and the other man nodded slowly and answered as briefly, "I can spare Brenna to help."

"With my thanks." Payne pulled away and headed down the line.

He would have talked more with the message master, but the old woman was looking for a note she must have misplaced. Yesterday it had been two of the carved message sticks; today it was a thin piece of paper. The white-haired woman told him curtly that no ring-runner had seen Nori. Even before Payne rode away, the woman had gone back to sifting futilely through the notes with her thin, bony, blue-veined hands, like a spider knitting paper.

He nodded at the outriders posted by Cy Windy Track and Nonnie Ninelegs's wagon, but didn't stop. He didn't envy that riding post, not with the fanged animals huddled inside the wagon walls, glaring through their cages.

Cy nodded back as he passed. "You want our *chovas* to help?"

Payne shook his head. He wanted the outriders on the twenty-year lists, not the youths whose gear was still so new it shone with fresh layers of varnish. The wilderness wasn't kind to the inexperienced. Scouts like Nori might continuously map the counties for danger spots to the human settlements, but changes happened quickly. A map made three months ago could be obsolete today. Ring-runners disappeared every spring on supposedly well-traveled routes, more this year already than in any other recorded. Raiders attacked out of new game trails and disappeared into areas that had fallen into disuse. Worlags and badgerbears and bihwadi still worked their way through the barrier bushes. And then there was the forest itself. Every year, at least a dozen gatherers were lost when they simply stepped off of the trail.

His hand tightened on the reins. It was now near midnight, but his sister was out on the trails, in the thickening dark, poking her nose where it didn't belong. Damn girl might be two years older, but she sure as hells needed a keeper.

He reined in at Proving's wagon, and the man's driver, One For Brandy, gave him a sharp look. "It's on, then," the older woman guessed.

There was a quiet belch from the man beside her, and Payne glanced across. Ed Proving had his bow tip balanced on his toe, a quiver of light arrows at hand. The string of wing feathers strung across the front panel swung hypnotically by his knees. The man glanced at Payne, lifted his flask, and, as Payne watched expressionlessly, took a sip, held it a moment, then swallowed. Even with the light breeze, his breath stank of parskea.

Payne kept his voice steady. "I've called the search. If you're willing, I could use a tracker."

Ed Proving didn't answer immediately. Instead, he raised his bow and took aim at a dark shadow that angled out from the trees directly for his wagon. He let the light arrow fly. There was a faint squawk, and the palt veered off. The man grunted in satisfaction.

Payne waited, but an outrider cantered up and said Kettre had sent her back. "Fifteen minutes," Payne told the woman curtly. "We'll meet at the end of the line." The cozar woman nodded and trotted away, and he turned back to the tracker.

Ed Proving looked after the cozar. "She's steady. Doesn't know the first thing about tracking, but she's got good eyes. She can learn."

"Good eyes are all I've asked of her." He got a warning look from One For Brandy and tried to make his voice less sharp. "I'm grateful for her help."

"She won't ride with your uncles."

"Few will," Payne said dryly. "That's why we'll be in two teams. Wakje and Ki and you, if you're willing, will ride out with me from Four Forks and track Nori north. Kettre will take the others and work the frontage trail back from one of the crossings, in case she's gone ahead."

"Won't be able to start till morning."

"We can get to the trailhead tonight."

Proving didn't look at him. "There are other trackers among the *chovas*."

"Aye. I'll be speaking to them, too. But from what I hear, it's you I want with me."

"From what you hear?" The older man laughed outright, swirled the flask deliberately, then lifted it again, watching Payne over the rim as he sipped. "Been a while since I've been out."

Payne smiled sardonically. "Brean recommended you."

"You must have made an impression on him." Proving belched again, a soft sound nearly lost among the wagons, and tucked the flask under his thigh. He raised his bow as a pair of palts flew across the road ahead, then lowered it as he lost the shot. "Why the rush to call the search? You worried about your Test, boy?" Payne tried not to bristle, and Proving added, "It's only been eight hours. She can't have gone more than fifteen kays, two dozen by dawn on foot. Trains like this move slowly. We could take five days to find her, and you could still reach Shockton on dnu."

Payne snorted. "Sure, by riding four days straight. I'd be the only one at Test with a butt shaped like a saddle. Payne Saddlebutt. Now there's the rep-name I want."

Proving chuckled, then gave him a surprisingly sharp look in the faint light. "You're damn protective of that girl. Overprotective, some say. You ever cry wolf?"

"No." The word came out flat and hard. Payne forced his jaw to relax. "Eight hours gone without a word, near worlag hunting grounds?"

Proving fingered his bow. The boy was right: the girl could be hurt or worse. In a bad-luck spring like this one, she could be cut off from the road by a dozen things, from flooded creeks to poolah. "There are old raider haunts back in there, hunter meadows, dozens of loop trails, and Black Wolf doesn't usually leave much sign. You'll need the luck of the moons to find her." He caught movement out of the corner of his eye and studied the darkened canopy for wing shadow. Then he reached for his flask again.

"Help me make that luck," Payne said softly.

Proving's hand arrested, then he took a deliberate sip, got to his feet, stretched stiffly, and disappeared into his wagon.

Payne glanced at One For Brandy.

"He'll go," she replied to his unspoken question.

Payne's voice was flatter than he thought as he thanked her and reined away.

VII

Run fast, for night runs with you

—Randonnen saying

Nori ran loosely now, well into her second wind.

Wolfwalker? Rishte called out faintly as the wolves picked up her scent.

They were moving fast, and in spite of her fear, in spite of the need for safety, a flash of joy hit with his voice. The bond she had tasted so faintly through other wolfwalkers, it could be hers now if she wanted it. The grey was almost leaping at her, stitching itself into her mind.

The yearling caught sight of her and howled. *Wolfwalker!*

She grinned ferally. It wasn't the title *Wolfwalker* that she heard from him, but an image of the Noriana half of the Nori–Rishte bond. It was a pulsing thought, filled with a human–wolf power. It was tentative, but it was feeding on their fear and urgency like a starving man on bread. Every kay the two of them ran, the yearling's voice was stronger.

She sent her answer: *The worlags should be crossing downstream by now.*

The rest of the wolves flooded out of the trees and turned to flank her. She tried to think as they ran. With raiders, she'd have to go around the Bell Rocks camp and hope she wasn't seen. It would add time, too much time. The worlags would not be limited to those trails. They could cut right across to get her. She needed a distraction. The wolves, perhaps, to rouse the raiders? Or something else instead? She gripped that thought. Go around

66

or . . . go through? They were raiders, after all. Men who murdered, maimed, enslaved.

Men like her uncles.

The thought hit with a harder fist. She couldn't turn on her own kind. But the thought remained. The men at the camp were raiders.

Still human, her mind whispered back. What right did she have to lead the worlags into them like a stampede over a sleeper? To let others be killed in her place? Her uncles had been raiders once, when they ran the counties with her father. Now they were better men, men with ideals and convictions, or at least men and women who lived within law. That last thought caught. The elders of the trial block might send raiders to death for murdering messengers, but Nori was not an elder.

Cold, slitted yellow eyes seemed to flicker in the back of her mind. Bile began to roil in her stomach, and her gut clenched hard to quell it. The men at Bell Rocks had murdered, even if they hadn't murdered her. The wolves saw the trail clearly from corpse to copse, from ring-runner carcass to raider. This close to the source, it was sharp in Rishte's mind. Death, fresh death, right under her feet, all the way up to Bell Rocks. Another wolf pack had traveled this way hours ago, fleeing the gathering worlags. The odors had clogged the packsong. Rishte growled his agreement, and Grey Vesh echoed it hard. The one thing a predator always knew was the scent of death on another.

The cubs, Vesh sent urgently.

Nori shook her head. The choice didn't matter. There were only two ways past Bell Rocks: around the raiders or through them. If the wolves had made a mistake, if they were wrong, they would tell her when they reached the camp. If the men were other scouts like her, she could still call out the warning and wake them to shoot at the worlags. If not, if the odors of torture and death were on their clothes and gear, if the kill sense was in their minds, then the men at the rocks were raiders. Killers. Murderers. Not her kind, not even like her uncles. Scavengers, like bihwadi.

She made her decision and felt her stomach twist. "Moons forgive me," she whispered.

Rishte didn't understand the guilt she tried to swallow, but her sense of purpose was clear. He raced ahead on the trail.

She figured her speed, the worlags' pace; the distance to the raiders. Not far. Not too far. Just two kays now. She could do that. Only two more kays to run.

Black trees rose out of blackened ground. Night did more than blind her: shadows taunted, branches grabbed. She used her own fear as leverage.

Speed. Urgency.

She hadn't realized that she'd slowed. She tried to pick up the pace again, but her legs were breathlessly numb. What strength she had caught from her rest by the creek was gone again like wind. She could use the bond to pull strength from the pack, her mother had told her once. But Nori wasn't yet bonded. The beginning of the bond was there, aye, between she and Rishte, but it was just a thread of grey. It took time to build the kind of link over which she could focus the grey. Time to learn to interpret the packsong, time she didn't have.

The wolves had no such problem. Rishte felt her need, felt the weakness in her legs and the threat to the pups. He howled into the pack. Grey Helt snarled back, and the wolves closed in around her. Grey energy surged. It hit and flushed through her body like angry blood that suddenly boils.

"Rishte," she gasped. She didn't question why he'd done it. She simply ate the wolf pack's strength as a starving man sucks at a broth-soaked crust of bread.

A dip, an open stretch, a tangle of vines, a washout. The trail turned, this time south around a small, crumbling ridge. South, toward the worlags. In the wolves, tension spiked and Vesh snapped, and Nori put on speed. The trail would turn north again, but not for half a kay.

Hurry. The pups. The voices of the other wolves were a steady, blinding rhythm.

She didn't answer. She just sprinted toward the beetle-beasts. In the gloom, she imagined she saw them: leathered arms in the shadows, purplish claws in the brush. She couldn't feel where they were, couldn't tell how close. Twigs snapped to her left.

Gods, they were right on her—She jerked, stumbled. Sucked in air to scream—

It was only a pair of jackbraw. The scrawny birds were locked in their three-day mating tussle, and they scuttled away like a two-headed crab, staring in all directions.

Closer, every step took her closer to the beetle-beasts, while the worlags raced up the trail. By all nine moons, by all the Ancients, she prayed without conscious thought. If she didn't reach the turn in time where the trail forked back north . . .

Her legs burned. The water-weight of her trousers dragged on her legs and stuck sloppily to her skin. She sucked in gnats and choked and spat, and the sixth moon broke over the eastern ridge. She was counting the trail in tens, not hundreds of meters now. Her hand clenched again instinctively, empty of her blade, and she barely noticed the clumps of fireweed that began to line the trail. Her only thoughts were of the armed men camping out at Bell Rocks and the worlags racing toward her.

By the moons, they had to be close. She could hear them underneath the howling wolves, the rhythmic pulse of beetle-beasts where their limbs struck the packed earth sharply. By all the idiots in the first silver hell, she was running straight toward their jaws.

There—movement, just at the edge of that hill. She caught it through lupine eyes, not her own. A moment more and she saw the leathered beasts for herself. Now her own vision could clarify the bone-and-black contrast of wolf-sight. She could see the beetle-beasts through a gap in the trees as clearly as could the wolves.

Wolfwalker, hurry—

Somewhere in muscles she thought were numb, she found more speed to burn, but the stitch in her side stabbed baldly. Rishte gathered the snarls of the packsong, shoved them toward her, filled her with more speed. The tenuous bond became sharp. The turn, there, where the fireweed ended at an old shale slide. Where the trail forked back steeply north, away from the beetle-beasts.

The wolves flashed ahead. Like a black tide, the worlags swept forward. Nori judged their speed and kept her pace to a steady sprint. She didn't dare panic, not yet. There was still one kay to the camp. Six, eight minutes. That's all she had to go. She didn't even hear herself curse as a wet boot turned loosely beneath her.

She hit the turn with a skidding run. Caught a green branch and used it to sling her body around like a whip. She threw one wild-eyed glance over her shoulder, half bounced from the force of the branch whipping back, and flung herself up the trail.

The camp. A ring of boulders. Some scrawny barrier bushes. Safety.

Rishte felt her relief and snarled in her mind. *Death-scent. Blood-scent. Danger.*

Were the men killers or just scouts who had found the bodies? She tried to shout the question into the grey. She didn't understand the answer.

The worlags gained. Wolves seethed around her. She felt every inch, every dip, every rock and puddle as they did, before her own feet touched it. The stinkweed patch—she jumped it before she realized it was there. That hanging vine, she ducked before it grabbed her hair. A forest cat hissed from an overhead branch, and she snarled so savagely as she charged its tree that it leapt back and fled in the darkness.

How far? she gasped out to Rishte.

The wolf's answer was urgent and sharp: an eerin, wounded, running, staggering, going down.

Half a kay? Less? She skidded down a tiny cut in the earth, vaulted a boulder, felt another branch snap on her ribs. She charged up the other hill. The wolf cubs whimpered helplessly as she pressed them too hard to her chest. Gnats stuck to her sweat-slick skin and gritted like grains of sand.

Two wolves now ran behind her. Rishte was ahead like a grey guide in her mind. Half a kay, maybe less. She kept that goal in her head as her father had taught her: Focus. Never give up and you'll never lose. Never slow, and you can't be caught. Don't stop and you'll never die. But he was Aranur of Ramaj Ariye, and he'd brought his mate back from the moons themselves. Nori was only his daughter.

Worlag claws snapped like ticks behind her as they clipped

through the shrubs with ease. She put on another burst of speed. Half a kay. Less. She couldn't see the campfire yet, but it was there; she could smell the wood. Idiots, she thought in the back of her mind. A fire at night was like a calling bell to a venge. To her, it was a beacon.

Her boots burned on her feet. Her arms were streaked with blood from shallow weals and scratches. One end of the sling flapped loosely, and she grabbed it in her fist before the pups could slip out. The camp was almost visible.

A tiny rise, a knee-deep creek, a patch of mud, a tree.

Danger, killers, Grey Vesh snapped into her mind. *Not-pack. Lobo. Protect the cubs.*

I hear you, Nori returned. *Are you sure? Are you sure?*

Helt's voice cut across Rishte's with the territory scent. Nori almost gagged. Urine. He'd smelled the raiders' urine, and the kill sense in their minds. Blood-scent, decomp, urine, sweat—it was all there. She felt as if she'd licked a dead body. Her stomach heaved, and she staggered two steps, clenched her jaw like stone, and found a tiny burst of speed. Killers. They were the killers. There was no doubt of that in the wolves.

Light flickered. Rishte snarled. Instinctual unease, learned terror. The light, the blaze, the heat, the burning that could eat the bones of the forest. *Fire.*

I see it. Go. The Grey Ones obeyed like a shot. They raced away into the dark, leaving her with their young. Deep in her mind, behind her fear, the alien yellow eyes flickered. Call out, warn them, the thought rose up. We don't turn/attack our own kind. She bit it back with her teeth. Danger, death-danger running behind her. She didn't cry out the warning.

Worlags closing. Eighty meters. Sixty. She bolted toward the small patch of light. The wind shifted, and the smoke-scent was suddenly stronger. It was a banked fire, a small fire. They were upwind, and they didn't know she was coming.

She sprinted now without thought. The yellow eyes narrowed beneath her mind. Her stomach clenched. She could see the flickering ring of the raiders' camp, the circle of rough stones. Years ago, a ragged line of barrier bushes had been planted along two sides of the camp. Thin logs now created a rude corral to the left. A trail of sparks coiled up between trees. The man on watch was alert, not dozing, and another man sat nearby, working on some papers. Two others were down in their sleeping rolls. A pile of supply bundles, a stack of message tubes, some nondescript packs, an open pannier . . .

She flung herself toward the circle. She had no breath to call out, and didn't realize how silently she still tried to run.

Slitted eyes glared in the back of her mind. (*Warn/call*) *them.* (*Death/death*) *follows you. Warn them.*

Nausea twisted the edge of her stomach. Fear punched through her gut. But still she did not cry out.

Behind her, the chittering fell silent as if the worlags, too, saw the men and saved their breath for the kill. Or else the sounds of wind and fire and fear filled her ears and blocked out their hunting.

Ahead, the riding beasts in the corral shifted restlessly. One dnu jerked its head and chittered. The guard raised his bow and stood in one fast movement, nocked a war bolt, and stepped close to one of the boulders. The other man thrust papers under the edge of a sack and did the same. All the dnu were chittering now, and two of them stamped their feet. The first man murmured to the other. The second one shook his head.

Like a demon, Nori burst from the shadows. For the barest instant, the two men were caught by the sight of her violet eyes glinting in the firelight. Then the first one shot instinctively. The bolt missed by a hairbreadth and was snatched up by night behind her. She leapt a boulder into the ragged circle. "Incoming," the guard shouted. The other man lunged for Nori's arm. The two sleepers woke instantly.

"Worlags," Nori screamed, letting fear take voice. She almost wrenched free. The raider heard the unmistakable terror in her voice and flung her toward the others. Both guards whirled to face the beasts, and Nori staggered into the bags and papers. The woman raider threw off her covers, snatched up a bow, and grabbed for Nori with her other hand. The other man leapt wildly out of his own sleeping roll, tangled for a moment, and missed Nori's arm. She scrambled across bags and bedding. The raider woman was right behind her. A bony hand caught her ankle and yanked. Hard fingers dug into her knee and threw her expertly to the ground. Loose papers scattered like leaves. Nori rolled, jackknifed, and slammed a hard-knuckled fist into the back of the woman's wrist. The raider's hand spasmed open. She kicked the side of the woman's jaw and tore free, but tripped on the edge of the fire. Sparks seared her arm. One moccasin crushed coals. Wet leather sizzled. The other raider caught the edge of her jerkin, and she skidded on sheets of paper. Her fist was a blinding hammer on the man's elbow, his ribs, his kidney. He stumbled, caught himself, and the first worlag sprang into the circle. Nori didn't wait. She grabbed what she could in her fist—a handful of notes, half torn, no more, lunged up and, clenching the papers, threw herself through the smoke. She jumped a saddle pack and fled as the beasts turned on the raiders. She was into the shadows, back in the night, when the first man screamed behind her.

VIII

You think you can see threat?
Search where you will,
You'll never find it.
It's always where you forget to look,
Behind you, right at your heels.

   —from *Stealing Time,* by Lansa neHoare

Wakje wasn't surprised by the news of the search. The older man simply tossed the reins of his dnu to Payne, then murmured to his driver and climbed back into the dinged-up wagon. A few moments later, he emerged fairly dripping with weapons. His sword was belted on. A double quiver of war bolts was slung across his shoulder, and a compound bow was slung beside it on a tipstrap. Like Payne's father, Wakje preferred the maneuverability of the compound bow to the draw speed of the recurve. It was one of the first lessons the ex-raider had taught the boy. When shooting in close quarters or in the forest, it was the ability to shoot from any position, not the speed of the draw that mattered. There was no advantage in shooting a faster bow if one had to spend seconds positioning its length before getting off each shot. With worlags, badgerbears, and raiders, the difference between the recurve and the shorter compound bow could be the breath between life and death. The other debates, of distance shooting and careful releases—those discussions were for competitions and lie-and-wait hunting, not for fighting worlags.

Kettre watched warily as the older man slapped a war cap on his greying head and plucked yet another knife from a rack behind the driver. The ex-raider already had two knives—one long, one shorter—sheathed at his belt. There were two more strapped onto his thighs. The fifth he tucked into the slot in his left boot. Kettre wouldn't have bet that there wasn't a sixth blade down the back of the man's collar. With the pouch of throwing stars at his belt, Wakje could have stood off a pack of raiders by himself. He added a travel kit and two small botas, then stretched his arms twice as if that would loosen his body sufficiently for any action.

Payne watched Wakje adjust his sword, and didn't even feel like smiling at the wealth of weapons as Wakje stepped neatly from seat to saddle. At a glance, the only sign of the man's past life was the long scar that ran from chin to cheekbone on the left side of his face. But with a thread of fear tightening Payne's gut at the absence of his sister, he had never been more grateful that his uncles had lived a different, darker, more violent life before they had joined Payne's parents.

Like Wakje, Ki was already geared up. Kettre nodded to Ki's two sons, also ready to ride. Payne threw an absent, worried smile at Ki's daughter, who was to remain behind with their driver. "Nori's been uneasy since this morning," he told his uncles, and both men gave him a sharp look.

Kettre couldn't quite keep the accusation out of her voice. "She didn't tell me that."

"It wasn't anything she could pinpoint," he explained. "Just a feeling."

Ki's voice was sharp. "Here? Among the cozar?"

Wakje exchanged a look with the other man. Nori had been "uneasy" for a while in Ramaj Tume, too, a couple of years ago.

"She knows this area like a mountain goat," Ki murmured to Wakje.

"Aye," Wakje returned. But she'd been away for years, and the Ariyen hills were webbed with game tracks like a well-veined leaf. A summer here and there couldn't make up for a long absence. Landmarks shifted, the earth could change, and there were always raiders. He should know. He'd been one.

Payne thought of Nori's scout book. "A lot of *chovas* joined us in Sidisport."

Instinctively, Kettre looked back along the line. Neither Wakje nor Ki turned his head, but Wakje said softly, "The girl was feeling itchy?"

"Lots of mishaps," Ki pointed out in a low voice.

Wakje flicked his gaze meaningfully at Payne. "Think on it," he told the other man.

Ki nodded. A drum of hooves grew loud over the rumbling wagons, and they looked to the other half of the road. It was yet another ring-runner, laid low on his dnu as he passed, heading south, with a stained bandage around his arm.

Wakje rubbed at a deep scar on his cheek. Nori's instincts were among the best he'd seen in the forest, but still undeveloped when it came to humanity. If she bonded with the wolves, she might be able to sense that kind of danger better, like Dione did. Nori's mother had often been able to sense the intent in men before they struck. It was the predator sense of violence that the wolves could pick up from human minds. It was a thought that Wakje shied from. He dreaded the day Nori reached through the grey and felt the killer that lurked inside him. As old as she was now, it wouldn't be long before she started drawing the wolves to her instead of chasing after the grey. Until then, he thought more easily, if she was wary, it had to be something she'd seen or heard herself, something within the caravan.

As Wakje watched with his hard, flat eyes, extra riders all along the caravan peeled away from the wagons and rode toward The Brother. Half the riders didn't even know Payne or Nori except through gossip or as they'd met in this train, but they split off anyway. Cozar custom, Wakje thought. Lose one, lose all. As loyal as family.

Payne tried not to snap at the two outrider youths who grinned at him as they reported in for the search. He caught Kettre's frown, took a breath, let it out, and muttered, "It's Test time."

Aye, and that was half the problem, Kettre agreed silently. Payne had been chafing to Test for years, but his parents had held him back. Now—and probably only because Nori was at the end of her own Test age—he was being allowed to go for the rank he wanted. Two ninans, and he'd have his rank and be away on Journey, larking through the counties like the other youths he'd envied for the last three years. Kettre had already heard rumors that the elders had him up for an assignment thought "worthy" of the son of Aranur.

As for Nori, gossip said the elders would take this chance to try to convince her one more time to Test and Journey away from Payne. So far, the elders had had little luck in separating the brother and sister, and they wanted two legends, not just one. But Nori had been careful to stay on the trade lists, not the council duty lists. Trade duty, backwoods scouting, vet work, crafts—they weren't the skills the council could justify coercing. What irritated the elders was that they also weren't the talents that usually made a legend. For all Nori's skills in scouting and defense, in six years, the elders had rarely gotten her in front of the council, let alone convinced her to take on a council project or work for a specific elder. What jobs Nori did accept were for relatives, and no one mistook those as anything but favors to family. Kettre suspected the elders would have had better luck trying to hire the Wolven Guard.

Payne raised his hand, but it was Wakje scanning the riders with a cold look that brought them quickly to silence. Payne tried not to notice. But when he explained the search plan, more than one of the *chovas* spoke out. "She is a fully qualified scout, neBentar," said Murton. "Three ranks higher than you. And Ironjaw Trail is well traveled. Aren't you jumping the gun?"

Payne squashed his irritation. It was only fair to question a search that started out at night, but it was typical of Murton to point out that Nori's scout rank was already among the highest in the county. He kept his voice steady. "Eight hours is six hours too long to be gone without a word."

Another Sidisport outrider frowned. "But Ironjaw Trail runs halfway to Deepening Road. Why would she go all the way out there?"

Payne shook his head. "Nori collects plants, herbs, even soil samples. She could wander almost anywhere. And she knows Ironjaw Trail. If she's cut off from us, from Willow Road, she'd try to take that trail all the way across so she could send word back to reassure us."

He caught a flicker of what he'd swear was satisfaction in Murton's face. His violet eyes narrowed at the *chovas,* but another Sidisport rider broke in. "I can't see Black Wolf running all night," the burly man put in, "even if she is on that trail. She's probably setting out right now in some scout camp with a brace of pelan on the coals."

Even the cozar were nodding now, and Payne took a breath and held it for an instant before answering calmly, "If she is safe in a camp for the night, we'll laugh about this tomorrow, and I'll stand all of you up for an ale at the next wayside tavern. But I don't feel like laughing just yet. She's gone without a word, and that just isn't like her."

Wakje pulled out a piece of jerky and chewed it thoughtfully. Nori and Payne had been dependent on each other since they were children. Too dependent, according to some. Although— and Wakje hid a flash of dark humor—it was a deceptive partnership. Payne was the obvious troublemaker, the one more visible, the one who covered for Nori, but it was often Nori who planned the way. She was the more elusive half, but the one with the sharper knife. As much like her mother as a mirror, he acknowledged, though she would hate the comparison. Still, some of the best raiders he'd ever known had gone down in the wilderness.

Beside him, Gallo Cantaway Soon caught the ex-raider's expression. The cozar tried to hide the fear that settled into his own gut. For a cozar, there could be no greater moment of tension than when the wagons rolled out of sight. The wagons were a cozar's home, his family, his safety. Away from them, Gallo was just another soft-fleshed piece of prey, waiting to be someone's dinner. He couldn't help saying, "She's Journey age, twenty-three in a few months, and every scout takes time alone to run the forest. With the wolves . . ." The older man shrugged.

Payne shook his head. "She's not bonded with the wolves yet. She can't hear them any better than you can." Nor could she count on the Grey Ones to protect her, but that wasn't something he could tell them. The wolf pack dogged Nori, like ghosts tangled at the edge of her mind, but it was an edgy sort of contact. To them, she was like a young lepa. Not lethal, not yet, but a creature who would be deadly once the talons within her sharpened and matured. She said she couldn't tell sometimes if it was wolves or worlags on her heels. He suspected that, when the bond did occur, it would require the approval of all the pack, not just of the partner wolf.

"If you're willing—" He spoke the cozar request phrase automatically. "—Proving, Murton, and my group will ride south with me to Four Forks where Nori was last seen. Kettre will take the rest of you north to one of the crossings and work back along the frontage road in case she's trying to come back over." He glanced up at the moons to judge the time. "Ride in to the trailhead tonight and start your search at dawn. Stay together, leave message rings at the cairns in case you miss her, and keep your ears open for the foxhorns." He reined into the lead position. He glanced back at the *chovas* to watch them fall in, and prayed that Nori didn't have half the worlags on her trail as he seemed to have at his back.

As they reined after Payne, more than one rider studied the darkening shadows. Once into the trees, the trails would be dark as a bitter man's heart. Kettre murmured a quick prayer to the moons as she took her group north past the wagons. She stared at the thin shield of thorn-spiked shrubs that stood between her and the wilderness. That barrier would repel most predators, unless they had the scent of blood. Predators, like badgerbears and worlags. It would be one or the other, she thought. Badgerbears or worlags. She didn't realize she'd spoken out loud until Gallo, beside her, shivered.

IX

Bind yourself,
Blind yourself to your fear;
Bind yourself to your strength.

Find yourself,
Bind your thoughts with your will;
Wind yourself into strength.

Find yourself,
Align yourself like a blade, like a knife;
Wind yourself into life.

    —from *Resist the Mist,* by Mari maDeenan

Nori didn't stop running when she fled the raiders' camp. She tried to close her ears to the shrieks as she ran, but they echoed like foxhorns trapped in her head. The nausea was rising hard. But she wasn't sick, she wouldn't be sick. She refused to let herself vomit. She kept on, finally remembering to stuff the handful of papers into the sling before she lost them. Then she pressed the sling close to her body while the pups mewed with the pressure.

The darkness, the blackened trees, the ring-runner bodies and odor of death . . . With the wolves in her mind, it was a nightmare mosaic. Plague fevers flushed through her thoughts, while the smell of decomp clogged her nose. Worlags chittered endlessly while they slashed apart the raiders. She didn't realize that her own horror had strengthened the death sense. The taint deep within her and the fresh link to the wolves both opened her to images her mind could not interpret, and they warred for her consciousness. For the engineered wolves might run with humans, but it was the birdmen who owned the world, and it was the telepathic birdmen who lashed out at the wolfwalker when she turned on her own kind.

The slitted eyes flashed icily deep in her mind. She staggered, then fell to her knees, retching among the ferns. "Gods," she whimpered. Tears mixed with the bile on her chin. She wiped her face with grass. The scent of the crushed stems mixed with the heavy, acid odor of the vomit. She felt her stomach try to heave again and cursed at the fear that crippled her. For the daughter of a weapons master, for the child of a wolfwalker, it was the ultimate in shame.

Close. Too close, Rishte sent worriedly. He snapped at her heels. *Get up. Get up and run.*

She dropped the soiled grass and forced herself back to shaky feet. She took one unsteady step, and then stretched that into an even shakier trot. The other Grey Ones loped before her. She could not see their eyes and couldn't hear their directions except as an insubstantial wavering. Much stronger was the sense of those other eyes, watching and silently judging. Those yellow eyes had a foothold now. She had opened to the alien when she had opened to the wolves, and the taint and the plague sense were stronger.

Plague. She focused on that as she ran. If she did nothing else this night, she must get word of that cliff seep to Payne. He'd make sure word reached Mama and Papa. More than her scout notes, more than the ring-runner deaths, more than the raiders at Bell Rocks, the news of a wolf sense of plague, no matter how old, must reach her mother and father.

But her brother would be on her trail by dawn, away from Willow Road. On the one hand, that would be useful. He'd find her scout book with the rest of her broken gear. Between what she'd grabbed from the raiders' camp and what would be left of her scout notes, they should be able to salvage enough for a credible report to their parents. Most of the information, the older notes, had already been passed along to the councils. At worst, she would lose some recent details and the ciphers she'd collected. The worlags would leave something, after all. They might tear the book because of her scent, but they sought human flesh, not paper. The beetle talons that had caught her back and ripped shallow flesh with leather . . . What had the raiders felt when she left them to the worlags? Slitted eyes flickered, and Nori swallowed hard.

Rishte gnawed uneasily at her thoughts. He was unable to understand her sickness at giving the worlags some other prey to kill. He'd sniffed her vomit and was puzzled. There was no food in it; it was a sickness, not a meal for a young pup. That her weakness was linked to the icy mind-taint disturbed him. It was like the scent of a lepa cutting through her thoughts. Through him, it created a tension in the packsong, like a raw claw that rags across silk. The older wolves knew she was bound in some way to the taint, not just to the Grey Ones, and they knew she would eventually seek out that taint, just as they sought her. They were not pleased about either bond. Oh, aye, she could go into the grey to reach the yearling, but she could not bring the cold with her.

The thought seemed to strengthen the faint, slitted gaze, and as the nausea rose again she staggered to a halt. She reached out, found nothing to support her, and almost toppled before she grabbed a thin tree. The headache was pounding in on top of the sickness now. Holding her breath didn't stop the bile from coming up, and she swallowed convulsively, over and over. She had never stood up to those alien eyes, but something in her stiffened as her stomach clenched again.

"They were raiders." She choked the words out in the darkness. "They killed six people on this trail alone. They'd have been sentenced to death on the trial block."

The slitted eyes were too hard, too sharp.

"If not me," she cried, "it would be someone else who must do it."

Beside her, Rishte growled urgently. Then Grey Vesh howled through Nori's thoughts. The stronger voice washed over Rishte's thin, young tones and, like an ax, slashed through that other, yellowed gaze. For a moment Nori was blinded. Then the ululations of Vesh's voice drowned out Nori's self-loathing and self-disgust. The fear, the gashes, the wobbling numbness of her legs, the needles that pierced her temples, the bile that burned her throat—all were swallowed by grey. She almost whimpered in her relief. The wolves were still helping her. Not for her or Rishte, but for their days-old pups. She dragged in a breath. "Gods," she managed. Her hands unclenched, and she pushed herself upright.

Within seconds, she was drowned again in the black trunks that held up the glowing sky. Beneath them, like a dark tabby, the trail alternated in patches of reddish white, then shadowed, black-grey earth. The colors were not reassuring. The night sounds were also louder than before, more immediate, more . . . threatening.

The third time she startled at a crackling in the brush, she nearly bolted from the trail. Rishte dodged instinctively and snarled at her sudden heart rate. It was a nightrail, already gone, hardly worth chasing at all. Nori cursed under her breath and tried to calm her pulse. It was the wolf-bond, she realized. It was strengthening and letting her hear just enough through Rishte's ears that every sound seemed closer, louder, caused by a larger beast. She had to get hold of herself.

Somewhere up ahead was the other group of humans, the small group, the one on Deepening Road. If she had interpreted the wolfsense right, they were five, maybe six kays away. They were a decently sized pack; there was enough sense of noise that there must be several riders.

Rishte's golden eyes gleamed at her. He had felt that thought, the way she had swayed toward the grey, and it pleased him.

She tried to focus on that, on the grey. The pack memory of the men came to her faintly: brash energies that flanked a deafening, slow-moving monster, like bihwadi around a bollusk. Nori found her lips quirking. That would be the riders and a wagon. The impression was the same as the one Rishte had had of Nori's own caravan, just smaller. As with the raiders, the group had been noted by another wolf pack moving its own pup east. Both that pack and Rishte's would have to restake their claims east of Willow Road. Rishte growled softly, agreeing in her mind. He flashed her an image of scratching and urinating to mark a new boundary, and Nori's bladder tightened. "I don't think so," she retorted. "That's for you to do." But she couldn't help the flash of image of herself with her pants down around her ankles, trying to pee on the rocks.

Rishte laughed in her mind.

It eased some of her tension. She looked down the trail, and their contact broke. A single wagon . . . Probably a fallback, delayed from the rest of its caravan. If she was lucky, one of their outriders would be willing to take a message up to a mirror tower, where it could be flashed across to Willow Road and ridden down to the Ell. Even if she didn't make it back to Payne before his search went out, the ring-runners would let the cozar know to sound the recall. That would keep him safe. He wouldn't reach the death-seep before the recall sounded. All she had to do was jog another five kays. She tried not to cringe at the thought. Five, six kays to the wagon? She could make that. She had little choice, she thought.

She picked up the pace again, slowed within ten steps, and tried to force herself back into the running mind-set. Two dozen steps, and she was back to a numbed jog. She cursed at her trembling legs. At this rate, it would be an hour before she reached Meridian Trail, and another hour to gain the tag end of the wagon group that rolled down Deepening Road.

Grey Rishte pushed up beside her. Like an adult prodding a child, he urged her to return to the trail-eating lope that the rest of the pack now wanted. The sense of firm command from the yearling made her snort. Rishte might be just one year old, but he was already trying to wield the assertiveness of a full-grown alpha male.

In spite of herself, she did shift to a slightly faster jog. She held that pace until her breath was in tatters. Still, she did not allow herself to slow much until she hit Meridian Trail. Only then—and she could not fully stop, or her muscles would collapse—only then did she drop again to a slow, loping jog, more long-legged walk than run, which the wolves paced easily.

She raised her arms over her head as she quick-walked to control what was left of her breath. Rishte dropped back beside her, and without thinking she gripped the hot, grey fur as she had done as a child with her mother's partner wolf. But the wild wolf twisted.

Trapped, slapped. The male snapped at her wrist.

Nori jerked her hand back. It was an unconcious move that instinctively yanked her mind away from the grey.

Rishte howled silently. He snapped again, this time to catch Nori's fingers in long, sharp teeth and drag her close. The fangs bit down. Nori cried out at the unexpected physical pain as the white teeth bit in. Sharp fangs jabbed into soft flesh, so different from the burn-pain of running. Rishte loosened his jaw almost instantly, but did not let go. Instead, the young male now barely bit against Nori's hand, his teeth a steel trap not quite closed.

Wolfwalker, the grey voice growled.

Vesh and Helt had stopped and turned. They watched with unblinking eyes.

Hesitantly, Nori tugged her fingers free. Then she reached out to the sweaty scruff. This time, the wild wolf suffered her touch. Oddly, it soothed them both. Nori let her breath out carefully, reveling in the oily feel of the fur. She barely noticed the loose tufts that clung to her sweaty palms. She crouched and carefully picked two burrs from his hair where they had tangled in his ruff. The wolf twisted to face her.

Their gazes met. Golden-to-violet, mind-to-mind. Human, lupine thoughts met and merged. Images shifted, shattered against each other as patterns clashed. Vision, too high for Rishte; for Nori, too close to the ground. Body heat, too hot for Nori. With the wind chilling her bare skin, it was cool-clammy for the wolf. In the wolf's mind, harsh lines crisscrossed and twisted. They had human colors without lupine meaning. Contrast without movement. Images, concepts from a society that meant nothing to the beast. In Nori's mind, nightmare creatures shifted and took shape like writhing fangs. She gasped, gagged on the tastes that seemed to run down her throat. The grey creature snarled like a feral dog. She choked out a cry of disgust. Then their minds began to shift around each other. Closer. Then closer again, like tumblers starting to mesh.

Dirt, soft beneath blackened pads. Musk-sweat, hot breath, gritty soil on tongue.

Breathing too fast, still sucking air, she thought. Cool breeze, lifting. Thank the moons, this is an old, packed trail . . .

East, rising light. Old trail. Rabbit den that way—smell it. Cold water up ahead.

Stone Ridge is behind me. Water, stream? Payne must be more than twenty kays south and east . . .

Human pack is moving, moving away.

He'll be worried . . . Got to get the cubs to a new den. It will be morning before I can get back. Cold water? I have to wash. Have to get my sweat-scent down. Fourteen days to Shockton . . .

Sun-nights running, running trails. Wide trails? Man-trails.

Man-road, she clarified mentally. *Willow Road. And wagons. Behemoths that deafen the pack.*

Chimera-bollusk, she agreed with a laugh.

She broke off midthought.

The wolf stared into her violet eyes. *Chimera-bollusk. Wagon.* He seemed to roll the concept around in his mind, tasting it from different angles. *Wagon,* he agreed. *Noisy.*

"Aye," she whispered.

The wolf's golden eyes gleamed, and he probed toward her mind again. *Wolfwalker,* he sent softly.

"Grey One," she breathed. She touched the musky fur again. "You honor me." Rishte's lips curled back. Nori didn't realize that her own had done the same.

Even with the pack's wariness, need was developing between them. This was not just a fleeting attempt to link. The bond had truly begun. The idea of absence was already painful as they started to find and fill in the holes in each other's minds. Soon, in days, maybe even in hours, even if Rishte understood how deeply the alien taint was set in her mind, he would not be able to leave her.

She stared into his golden eyes until she could feel him wrapping around her thoughts, making himself fast in her mind even as her head throbbed with the strain between the yellow slitted eyes and the golden gaze of the wolves. She pressed her fist to her temple, and the grey seemed to surge in answer.

She knew what to do with that lupine strength. She had been drilled in its use since she was a child. She hadn't had a grey partner of her own to practice on, but she knew in theory how to do it. How to draw energy out of herself and focus it through the wolves to help them or heal herself. It was the Great Trade made by the aliens and Ancients: Ovousibas, and land to live on, in exchange for the barriers that would protect the birdmen's offspring.

With Rishte, Nori could use that kind of mental focus to fix her own aches and pains—if she dared. Ovousibas, the internal healing, was forbidden. In the centuries that had passed since the aliens sent plague, internal healing had become a myth, carried only in the memories of the wolves. There were perhaps two dozen people who knew it was real. Only one—Nori's mother—had mastered the technique. To do it now, without having the control to keep from being discovered by other wolves and, through them, by other wolfwalkers, was to chance being hunted down and killed. But oh, it was tempting.

Strain her thigh? Just reach for the yearling and heal it up. Break a leg, and knit the bone as neatly as melding clay. With internal healing, she'd be able to touch the packsong and seal muscles back together like book-matching a grained veneer. It wasn't quite that easy, but it could mean the difference between life and death, between dragging a leg to get away and limping at a run. She'd never have to worry about gelbugs or weibers again. Not that she usually did—the taint had some advantages—but there were times when even those slitted yellow eyes did not protect her. But the grey wolves hated the taint in her, and the yellow eyes hated the wolves.

Rishte growled softly.

Choose, she thought, between yellow and grey. Choose her form of protection. She was tempted . . .

Wolfwalker, no.

She blinked. For a moment, she stared unseeing at the yearling. Then she sat back on her heels. "Aye," she said softly. She was too tired, too unfocused, too distracted by fear and the newness of what was happening between them. "You are right. This is not the time."

She shifted, felt the papers crinkle in the sling, and pulled them out to study them while she caught her breath. She'd grabbed what she could, but the bag with the message tubes would have been a better catch. Those tubes probably contained the letters and contracts of every ring-runner dead in the past two ninans.

The first was exactly that, a contract from one merchant to another. She moved to a brighter patch of moonlight and smoothed it out. She recognized the guild seal even if she couldn't make out more than half the spidery writing. That could be passed on intact. Then there was a torn report from a caravan guide on the status of trade along a particular route. It would have been more useful if there had been more than the halves of the first two paragraphs. The third was a letter, this one written in symbols that looked like a Tamrani House code. If she'd had her scout book, she might have figured out enough of it to know which one. Ariye kept close tabs on the Houses, and there was almost always someone who could be bribed.

There was little enough on the last torn piece. She'd interrupted the raider before he had written much down, but the three irregular lines made her sit back on her heels abruptly. Code, and not a House or guild code. She couldn't read it; it was new, but she recognized the structure. At least four other scouts had brought in samples like this one over the past year and a half. She knew, because she'd been birded just three ninans ago with a message from her mother. Six Ariyen scouts had gone missing after reporting to the council that they would try to get more samples. It was one of the reasons the Test council would be bigger than usual this year. The Ariyen Lloroi wanted to hear directly from the elders in the outlying towns. Something was coming, something was building up against Ariye; they just didn't know what it was.

Nori was no elder, but even she recognized that raiders didn't bother with code unless they were part of something much bigger than a single raider band. "Crap on a stickbeast," she whispered. If the raiders at Bell Rocks survived the worlags, they could be on her trail even now to retrieve their code and silence the one who took it. She jammed the papers back in the sling.

She had to get this to her parents, but staying on Deepening Road would be a mistake. It was the first place the raiders would look for her. And although she knew both scouts and ring-runners assigned in this part of the county, she didn't know how to locate the contacts her parents used. Payne, not Nori, kept track of the web of informants, and people found Nori, not the other way around. There was an old weaver woman in Ayerton, but it would take Nori at least a day to reach her. With Test coming up next ninan, the woman might not even be there. On the other hand, Nori could make it back to Willow Road by morning if she managed to borrow a dnu. Then Payne could send the code by fast rider north to Mama and Papa.

The irony of what she was doing made her snort. The elders were so anxious to get her to do duty, but she'd been doing exactly that half her life. It was visibility they wanted, another Dione in the ranks, and that's what she denied them. If she had a choice, she'd stay in the background forever.

Puzzled, Rishte stared into her violet-grey eyes. *The trail? The two paths?*

Nori caught the image of the wolf at a fork in the trail. It was the same image she'd had since she was a child, of the choice between yellow and grey. She smiled wryly. "Choice," she agreed. "Of that, too. Soon enough."

Rishte stared back into her violet eyes. He didn't understand, but he recognized the sense of the slitted eyes, the sense of power that seemed to crackle around the image of her mother. Tendrils of that power had already seeped into Nori, but not through the wolves. The sense of Ovousibas didn't bother the yearling, but the sense of the taint touching Nori's grasp of power made him growl, as if he would challenge the yellow eyes. The slitted gaze seemed to flicker open.

Grey Vesh snapped.

Nori and Rishte jerked.

Vesh bared her teeth and glared. *Tainted. Alien.* The thought grated on the pack. It was why Vesh and Helt were so reluctant to let Rishte bond. A wolf–human link was an intimacy that clung to every level of thought. It would echo through the memories of the telepathic wolves. Accepting Nori meant accepting not only another human in the packsong, but also the things attached to the taint.

"No harm," she breathed. "I meant no harm."

Vesh backed off, but didn't stop snarling.

Nori's sweaty skin prickled. She shook it off, but her lips were still curled back with Rishte's own, lower growl.

Wolfwalker? Rishte nudged her uncertainly.

She stared down at the yearling. Even under Vesh's protectiveness, she could feel his need for the bond like her own.

Blood-scent, he sent. *Sweat-scent, breath, hot breath, your breath, Nori-breath. Wolfwalkerwolfwalkerwolfwalker . . .* Rishte's voice was a simple song, the need for affirmation.

"I am here," she whispered, projecting the words into his mind. *We are together.* She touched the grey fur again and let her finger run slowly along the ruff. Rishte's shoulders rippled. Wild as he already was, he could allow only the edge of that contact, but she could hear the longing in his mind for the close touch he didn't understand.

Human-thing, Nori-thing. Nori-mind. Mine. Wolfwalker, wolfwalker.

Vesh snapped irritably, and Rishte's ears flicked at the pack mother. The yearling turned his golden eyes away from the wolfwalker. Contact broke. Her breath caught at the loss. The Ancients had engineered the bond to trigger off the optic nerve. With the link so new, the abrupt cessation of intimacy was like going blind at noon.

In front of her, Rishte turned to face the pack. His chest seemed to gain breadth as he growled at his pack mother and father. *Nori-mine,* he sent. *Wolfwalker-mine.*

Helt snarled. *Human-thing. Tainted. Not-pack. Not-mine. Lobo.* His ruff rose like a brush.

Rishte's hackles rose in return. *Nori-mine,* he insisted. His lips wrinkled back like old skin. His white, curved teeth were bared.

Slowly, carefully Nori stood.

Vesh watched her with that unblinking gaze. Finally, the female snapped at Rishte's shoulder. The yearling's ears flicked back. Vesh snapped again, and he submitted with another snarl. The mother wolf glared at Nori. *Danger. Danger-you. Old death, new death. Danger.*

Slowly, Nori nodded. The other wolves were older and stronger in their minds than Rishte. They could see the taint in her like blood on the grass. Rishte could not see that danger clearly, not through the excitement of first-bonding, but the taint in her mind had brought the pack's sense of nearby plague to the foreground.

"That kind of death is long gone," she tried to reassure them. She let her voice help focus her words through her mind. "I'll mark the place. My mother will check it out, but it's just a memory. You have no need to fear it."

New death, Vesh growled angrily. The female glared at Nori. *Danger-you.*

Nori didn't argue, not with a full pack of wolves with teeth bared right in front of her. She understood completely: the mother wolf wanted the human-thing gone as soon as her pups were safe. She took a breath. Distance, she told herself. Focus on that, not the taint. "The men on the road," she said instead. "They are still kays away. Are there any humans closer?"

This, the wolves could answer. There was a sense of Nori's voice falling, falling away. Then a din of snarling grew far back in her mind. It thickened, blended, split apart. It came back more darkly before it tightened, like loose strings being slowly twisted into a thin cord. Moments later, the young wolf bared his lips as he gazed back into Nori's eyes. *No men. Poolah hunting to the east. OldEarth deer moving away to the west back to their night hideouts. Bollusk bedded down beneath the thickest blackheart trees. Nothing else on the trails. Men on the trail. Closest.*

· Two more kays, then. Maybe three to reach the road. She rolled her shoulders to ease their tightness. Three kays, max. She could do that.

Grey Vesh, impatient to get going again, pushed up beside Nori. The wolfwalker opened the sling. The mother wolf sniffed her pups, then looked up, met Nori's gaze, and growled. The older voice was harsher, wilder than Rishte's. It reminded her coldly that her link to the yearling was not yet set. It was barely clay or hard-packed sand, not twisted silk or stone.

Nori stared unblinking, unwilling to risk breaking that contact as she caught the depth of images and grey law that lay behind that voice. She suddenly realized that this was to be a lesson, the teaching of the young. For to the wolves, Nori was still young. She was not yet on her own, away from her pack, her family. Instead, she clung to the freedom of youth that her mother had fought to give her. It would not last. Eight ninans, and she would turn twenty-three, the final age of a Journey youth. It was the age at which even the Wolfwalker Dione must admit that Nori was grown. The wolves could read that point in her as clearly as if they counted the days to her birthday. Until then, as a yearling, she could still be influenced, could still be swayed toward the grey. Vesh had begun to realize that Rishte was already well caught. The pack mother had only this night to change the human-thing to better protect her child.

Nori sucked in her breath. *You honor me,* she sent reverently.

Vesh merely snarled more loudly. Behind the rough voice, the packsong seethed. This was not what Nori had seen through Rishte. That had been a wash of sound, like a hundred wolves howling from beyond the hills or the sound of surf near dunes. Vesh's mind was deeper, clearer, more distinct. It was like looking at a painting and seeing the individual brushstrokes instead of mere shapes and shades. In its own way, it was as strong as the taint that twisted her guts together. She and Rishte would be like that someday—if they stayed together.

Nori stretched her mind toward that packsong, using Rishte as a focus. Like light in a lens, voices shifted from a din into lupine growls. Needs and urges broke against each other like children crying out, laughing, hitting each other in play. Distinct images swept past: field mice digging desperately down, away from the wolves who pawed at their bolt-holes. One pack, then another, hunting eerin and deer into the brush. Packmates tumbling at a den, splashing across streams and nosing through sparse meadows for rasts and moles and rabbits.

The memories stretched back from yesterday, from last ninan, from years ago. Passed from one grey generation to the next, these were the images that formed the base of the packsong. Any wolf could tap into that ocean of memories. They could see from other wolves the trails that had become too deadly to run, places of predator fights, places the wolves avoided. They could see other memories, too: humans they had bonded with, humans scouting, human-things that had little meaning to the wolves. Old images were faint as smoked glass, but the recent ones like Nori's run and the death of the messengers in Gambrel Meadow were sharp as heavy crystal.

Curious, Nori deliberately tried to ease into the image of the death-seep near the cliff that had reminded the wolves of plague.

Vesh growled louder.

Nori did not flinch. Slowly, she sent her question again. *When was it there?* she asked. *What was it that formed the danger?*

Uneasy, but caught by Nori's violet eyes as much as the wolfwalker was by the grey, Vesh pierced the packsong with her question. The seeking swept out reluctantly. The answer came back with a snarl. Wrongness, unease, old danger burning—it was a jumble of need to avoid the area. It was also crisp, as if the urgency from Nori's run had pulled it into the foreground and given it more focus. There was more than one seep at the cliffs. The wagon track was the remnant of only one memory where men had dug in the earth. Six other swamps had begun to stretch north along the ridges, and the wolves were getting nervous. Nori frowned. The wolves were shifting north and east, not just to escape the worlags, but also to avoid the ridge, to avoid places where men had been near the cliffs. Places men had died.

Show me, she sent.

There was a flash of fear, the scent of sickness, the odor of decay. In that instant, Nori saw trees, flat walls, charred wood in piles. Fear-sweat. Terror in men. Death, burning death, sick death, and something too deliberate.

She felt a chill. *Take me in—*

Vesh leapt back with a snarl. One wolf snapped at Nori's leg with a vicious bite that had her stumbling away. Grey Helt's fur was bristled like a hedgehog, and another one's lips had curled back so far that its mouth seemed to drip red off its teeth like the open maw of a poolah. Even Rishte stared at her like a badger-bear, caught up in the defense of the pack.

"Easy. Easy," Nori breathed. She swallowed her sudden fear that it was she, not the seep, that was the greater danger. She edged back, automatically letting the hum rise in her throat. She kept her gaze on Rishte. "I mean no harm to you."

Vesh growled without stopping, and some part of Nori's brain wondered how wolves could do that while still breathing. The other part focused on that sense of deliberate death. It had been recent, like a hunting trail a few years old, not faded like the Ancients. It crawled like cold steel up her spine. She could almost taste the dread in Rishte.

It was Helt who nipped at his mate's shoulder, glared once more at the wolfwalker, and indicated the trail.

Nori understood. There would be no more memory-walk. Not with her. What she didn't know was whether their rejection was for any wolfwalker who sought that danger, or for her alone, the scout with the taint in her mind.

X

Look closely, the signs are small,
Like spider prints in dust.

—from *Tracking the Moons,* by Vergi Vendo

Wakje watched and chewed on a stalk of grass as Payne paced the edge of firelight. This close to the trailhead, the verge was wide. He had room to jog if he wanted.

Mye, Ki's son, turned over again in his sleeping bag. "Moonworms, Payne, are you going to pace all night?"

"If I have to," he said shortly.

"You might at least try to sleep." Mye tried to restuff his shirt under his head.

Ed Proving belched softly, and one of the *chovas* rustled his bag of jerky, trying to get the last pieces. Another outrider was snoring like a bollusk. Payne's voice was dry. "I'm more likely to sleep in a full-blast furnace than with all this peace and quiet."

Ki glanced over from his watch post. Like both his sons, he was a lean man, incredibly fast in spite of his age. It was Ki who had taught Nori the knife and the guitar, with his fingers flying equally well over steel or strings. He'd taught Payne and Nori to ride, climb, shoot, splice rope, how to judge a man's moves by his balance and the way he set his muscles. Ki had eyes like a lepa watching the grass, seeking any movement, yet he'd never lifted his voice to them in all the years he'd taught them. Payne's father had said more than once that, if it hadn't been for Nori and Payne, Ki would have gone back to his raider ways within a year of joining Payne's father. It was why Ki avoided their mother as much as Wakje did. The Wolfwalker Dione was a constant reminder of how they'd been caught and sentenced, of the killers who lurked inside them. When Payne bonded—if he bonded, Payne reminded himself—Ki might turn away from him, too.

Now Ki watched Payne with an unreadable brown gaze. "You won't be any good tomorrow. You'll need sharp eyes to catch her trail."

"I know," Payne returned too shortly. He was trying to stay controlled, but it had grown harder as every hour passed. Nori might be older by two years, but Payne had looked after her since he was twelve. No one had asked him to, but he'd been there when they'd brought her back from Sidisport. Payne and Nori always slept side by side—she'd had nightmares since she was born, but after Sidisport the dreams were worse. In the months it took for her to recover, he'd become a shadow-guard. He'd followed her until she got so used to it that she stopped looking over her shoulder to find him. Mama had been furious when she learned that he'd been challenging the older boys, but Papa had taken Payne quietly aside and shown him a few more techniques. With what Wakje, Ki, Weed, and his other uncles had taught him, he'd lost only three of those fights. He'd also earned a strange, unconditional approval from his uncles, as if, even at twelve, he'd suddenly become a man, one whom even they could rely on, almost an extension of the Wolven Guard. It had been exhilarating, and he'd been cocky as a preening chak until he'd been caught by six boys behind the packing house. If his uncle Weed hadn't come along, he'd have had every bone—not just an arm, a wrist, and a nose—broken well into the second moon.

And Nori, well, she could fight, but she rarely did. She was terrified of something inside her. He'd seen her freeze up a dozen times rather than strike first, as if some demon could tear physically out through her skin if she lost control of herself. And then afterward, the blinding headaches that could put her down for a ninan. She could barely be trusted to defend herself until after she was actually attacked.

Payne rubbed his jaw and stared at the camp with its small, lonely fire in the midst of the tramped-down clearing. If Nori had been uneasy, if Wakje and Ki thought someone was stalking her in the caravan, perhaps she had fled willingly to protect herself or to draw the danger off.

Dammit to the ninth hell and back, he cursed silently. Out here, away from the caravan, she'd have no one to watch her back. He wanted to snarl at Murton as the *chovas* pretended not to watch him. One of the other *chovas,* Gretzell, raised Payne's hackles also. There was something far too jovial about the man, like a fatty veneer over a rigid, vicious core. Even maSera, the slender young outrider with the long brown braid, felt like a threat right now. "Idiot-brained bollusk," he cursed himself.

"Payne," Ki started.

He whirled and slammed his fist into a tree.

The small camp went silent.

He stared at his own hand. He hadn't known that was in him. "Moonwormed ass of a cave bleeder," he muttered. He closed his eyes and rubbed his bruised knuckles. Two of them were already welling out blood. He wiped them on his leggings and met his uncle's gaze. His voice was low. "My apologies." But he couldn't help adding, "It's just that she could be anywhere. She could be—" He shrugged angrily.

Wakje waited a minute. Then he said simply, flatly, "Payne."

The warning was clear. The ex-raider had never tolerated a man who lacked control. Payne took a breath, let it out. "I know," he returned finally. "But I can't sleep. I can't sit still. I just need to . . . move." He resumed his pacing like a badgerbear in a cage.

Wakje's cold eyes followed the youth, but his thoughts flew after Nori. The two were close enough that the one sometimes unconsciously felt what the other did. They both admitted that they could sense the wolves on the edge of their minds. If Payne was this restless, perhaps he reflected the girl through the Grey Ones who never quite left either one. Wakje remembered more than one grey dusk with gleaming eyes, a carcass shredded by long-jawed fangs, the smell of blood and musk . . . Wakje felt a chill in his bones. He had never trusted the grey.

XI

"Rest a while," said the Tiwar.
"Why?" she asked, puzzled.
His voice was soft. "Because you are still bleeding."

   —from *Wrestling the Moons*

By the time Nori saw the barrier bushes for Deepening Road, she was barely doing a walk-jog. The wolves had judged the wagon's speed well; it wasn't far ahead. But instead of relief at catching up, she was getting increasingly jumpy. She finally realized that it wasn't her, but Rishte's growing sense of fear as the wild wolves approached the humans. Bad enough that he'd had to trail the behemoth-wagons all day to get her attention. Now she wanted him—and the pack—to nip at the giants' heels. She had to dig deep for the discipline to hold the wolf-link open and still lope toward the wagon sounds.

The odor of the shrubs began to hit her like sharp, jabbing slaps. The fireweed, blackthorn, and roroot that made up the hedge were usually faint—just a mild, pithy scent easily dulled by the herbs planted inside the border. For some reason, the stench of this stretch was stronger. She wrinkled her nose and tried to breathe shallowly. It took her more moments to realize that, with their link as open as a gossip's mouth, Rishte was sending her the odors received by the entire pack. The nasal assault was from the Grey Ones. "Rishte—" Abruptly, she closed down on the link. Her last sharp sense of the wolf was an echo of lupine laughter.

She crossed the first wide lane, stumbled over the tree-lined meridian on knees made of gelatin, and forced herself onto the other side of the road. It seemed to take forever to catch up those last few hundred meters to the trailing wagon guards.

There were no dogs to warn of her approach, for which she was grateful. The wolves would have killed any guard-pets. Still, the wolves stayed in the rootroad trees as she loped up behind the city *chovas*.

Instinctively, Nori had stayed in the shadows until she was close, and the one outrider who had looked over his shoulder hadn't seen her. She didn't have the voice to call out to them, and with the wolves in her mind she couldn't force herself to do it. The pack was on the edge of attack-panic already as she took their pups among humans. She simply drew up beside one of the riders and, numbed, waited for him to realize she was there. She was not disappointed by the reaction.

"Buk piss!" one of the younger ones cried out. The youth jerked the reins and actually startled his dnu into his partner's mount.

"What the—" The young woman's mount skittered into the meridian, nearly unseating the girl in the soft edge of the roots. "Hevre take you—" she snapped.

The first youth drew a sword so shiny that Nori could see its engraving. His thoughts—and his sudden spike of fear—were transparent: the beasts he saw behind him were a pack of the pink-eyed, doglike bihwadi, slavering at his heels.

There was a commotion in the front of the wagon as the lead guards reacted to the noise in the back. Nori didn't have breath to reassure them, but it didn't matter. Already the third guard, the one who had been alert, was putting his half-drawn sword back in the scabbard. This man was no youth, and he'd read her in an instant. Quickly he whistled the signal for a ring-runner, then nudged his dnu closer to Nori.

She didn't greet him. She just extended her hand. He caught her sweat-slick wrist with a firm, callused grip and swung her up as if he didn't even notice her weight. He settled her more firmly behind him before he realized her whole body was trembling. Rishte dropped back to the pack with a low, mental snarl.

"Vidon, did you see that?" the young woman guard said excitedly, wheeling her dnu around.

"They're not bihwadi," the first youth returned eagerly.

"They're wolves." He yanked his dnu carelessly back to the center of the road and twisted to peer back at the Grey Ones.

Nori glanced at the two city guards, and almost slid from the dnu as she did so. She was straddling the edge of the saddle's flange, just in front of the dnu's belly segment. She scooted closer to the older man, but it didn't help. Her balance was off, precarious, as if she were unsuited for riding. She grabbed the guard's belt to steady herself and cursed at her undisciplined mind. Again, it wasn't her; it was Rishte. Four legs, not two. Low balance, not tall. Ruthlessly, she clamped down on the fragile bond. There was instant relief for her body. She ignored the frustrated howl that rang through her mind. Now her muscles knew what to do, and she slid easily into the riding beast's rhythm.

The first youth wrenched his dnu around so that he could see the creatures behind them. "It's an escort," he guessed, forgetting to keep his voice low. At a hard glance from Nori's rider, the youth reined back into position, but he was unfazed by the discipline. "I'm Vidon neBerum," he introduced excitedly. "Subrank student to Gankira and Lee, Tamrani Ser, of the Third House, Liegtha. She's Gariala maStura, subrank student to Gankira and Lee, Flint-dau and Glass-dau. You're riding behind neLivek."

With her mind caught in the wolves, the titles washed over her without meaning. She recognized only the sense of the words, that the woman was high guild, and the young man Tamrani, and that both were out of Sidisport. They were anathema to Ariye, then. She nodded a tense acknowledgment and searched her memory for the more familiar name, neLivek. He was perhaps eighty or ninety, thick with aged muscle, but not yet showing the thin white hair of someone well over a hundred. She'd felt the twisted scar on the palm of his hand when he'd taken her wrist. Along with that, he wore a southern-style harness with a double rack-quiver.

"NeLivek of the Two Seeds?" she asked over the man's shoulder. Her voice was hoarse and dry from running and too much snarling at Rishte.

"Aye." He was surprised, and he spat the seeds he'd been

sucking to the side of the road. "Though it's been a while since anyone called me that. I go by Tysil neLivek in the trade lanes." He'd gotten the other rep-name forty years ago as an outrider with a Diton caravan. It was a wry reminder that the cozar remembered a man's reputation long after he himself had misplaced it.

NeLivek glanced over his shoulder, then lost the beginnings of his grin. Up close, the blood streaks were clear. He made a subtle signal at the man who was cantering back from the front, but kept his voice casual as he untied his bota bag and passed it to Nori. "This is Hunter," he introduced. He ignored Vidon's look when he didn't bother with the formalities. "He's in charge of this spit-poor excuse for an escort. We're outriding the cozar family of Rocknight Styne. They broke a wheel and fell behind the train."

She nodded as she uncapped the bota bag. That explained the number of outriders. An Ell wouldn't usually hold up an entire caravan for one disabled wagon, but he would dispatch as many guards as he could to escort a fallback till it rejoined the safety of the line.

The taller man, Hunter, judged the way her legs kept twitching as if she were still racing the black road. She was jumpy as a Grey One. He half expected her to startle back into the dark at the sound of his voice. "Warm night for running," he commented.

Nori jerked another nod. Her breathing was still hard, and she did not trust her voice.

Hunter scowled as he realized just why Vidon was staring so blatantly. That sling barely covered her. "Vidon, Gariala, ride forward," he ordered curtly. With an arch look from Gariala, the two reluctantly obeyed, leaving the rear guard to neLivek. The tall man stripped off his overvest. "We'll stop in ten or fifteen minutes at the Clever Springs wayside." He held out the garment. "This should do for now, unless you need a shirt before you wash."

Nori glanced down and wanted to roll her eyes. As casual as scouts had to be with each other, one still had to make allowances for teens. "I'll wait," she said shortly. She shrugged the proffered vest on over the sling.

Hunter nodded his approval. As with most experienced ring-runners, she didn't put prudishness ahead of safety. Besides, the treated leather wiped off like chancloth, although—and Hunter hid a grin at the thought—his mother would swoon if she knew how her expensive gift had been baptized. Considering the state of this ring-runner's skin, had the woman asked for a shirt, it would have been stained beyond saving. "Raiders or worlags?" he asked.

"Aye," Nori answered obliquely.

"Both?" He was startled in spite of himself.

She nodded and drew the vest in more closely. It was body-warm and well softened, and it smelled of man and dnu. It wasn't standard *chovas* gear, not with that fancy edging and tooling as fine as any she'd seen. Her family was well off, but even they didn't wear things like this on the trail. This vest would cost two months of scouting wages. Rich, then, she thought, but riding guard for a fallback wagon? She slanted Hunter a look.

He knew what she saw: a man maybe five, six years older than herself, with the typical broad shoulders and muscular build of a southern Ariyen. His hair was so dark it was nearly black, and long enough in the Ariyen style that he braided it back and tied it with a leather thong for travel. It wasn't an affectation, as it would have been on Fentris the Fop. He just hated the bother of getting it cut.

In the sunlight, there would be hints of red and gold in his hair, and his eyes would be a sharp, clear green. In the moonlight, his face looked angled and planed, cold, perhaps even harsh. His mother had told him more than once that he could have been as handsome as his brothers, except that his chin was too square, his eyebrows too thick, and his nose too arrogant to appeal to any woman. When he'd escorted his sisters to events, he made them look as delicate as three-thread lace. His face hardened at the thought of his sister, and he fingered his layered belt again. Jianan had almost paid with her life for the notes that Hunter now carried.

Nori's eyes flicked to the fingers that tapped the thick belt, and Hunter's hand stopped abruptly. His green eyes narrowed at Nori. Only four hours ago, Fentris Shae had caught up to him and handed over Jianan's notes. Now this woman came out of the night with a tale of outrunning worlags? Fentris knew the city like the back of his hand, but knew nothing about the forest. The fop would never have noticed if he'd been followed. That left Hunter here, late in the night, with seven untried city youths at his side, two years of reports on his person, a possible murderer at his back, and all of them kays from the caravan.

Nori caught the sudden sharpness in his gaze and went still.

From behind, Rishte bristled. *Danger. He watches. Bare your fangs.*

Hunter started to speak, then stopped himself. She was poised not for the kill, but to flee. She had reacted as if he was a threat to her, not she a danger to him. He said softly, "We mean no harm to you."

Nori tried to smile, but her lips curled ferally instead. Rishte's instincts were too close.

Someone called back from the front, and Hunter didn't look away from her as he ordered sharply, "Hold position. We'll stop at the wayside."

Nori forced herself to sit back. He had an unconscious authority that reassured her more than his words ever could. Her father had the same manner, as did her uncles. Great, she thought. He was one of the perfect ones, like Payne. Tall, skilled, confident, strong—his arm muscles were corded like twistwood. He probably couldn't even spell *fear.* Even his clothes were perfect: full-cut for easy movement, dull colors, and varied patterns to deceive the eye in the forest. His riding boots were tesselskin. Tough, light, breathable, and with just enough give that they never seemed to bind. Expensive as oldEarth fox, and not usually worn on rough trails. He was either too ignorant to realize just how badly they could be gouged up, or too wealthy to care what they would cost to replace.

Hunter watched the emotions flicker across her face, and the way she shifted to protect the sling. "It's usually riders, not trailrunners, who carry bulk," he prodded casually.

The grey growled in the back of her mind. Protect. Defend.

Nori tried not to snarl back. *I will not let him harm them,* she answered. But she adjusted the borrowed vest carefully so she could slip the papers out of the sling and into the vest pocket before showing him what she carried.

Hunter leaned to look and sucked in a breath. "Wolf cubs," he breathed. He'd never seen any before. He resisted the urge to reach out and run his finger along one of the blind balls of fur. Somehow, he knew the Grey Ones who slunk behind would not have allowed that contact. No wonder she was so defensive. "How old?"

"Four days. Birthed over near Stone Ridge." Her breath was still shaky, but she grinned suddenly. "And snatched from the jaws of a worlag pack with all the luck of the moons."

With the smile, her face was transformed. From a smudged, shadowed visage, she suddenly seemed to glow. Hunter felt his jaw drop. He closed it with a snap. Up on the wagon box was Rocknight Styne's niece, a shapely girl who would become a sultry woman. This lean creature would never be called something as simple as beautiful. Her chin was too strong to be piquant. Her eyes were dark and slightly slanted, as if she were more wolf than human. The scratch that marred her left cheek made him want to lean in and lick that thin line of blood, taste the salt and heat of her. His loins tightened. It wasn't her features that arrested his gaze. It was the way her eyes danced when she smiled. There was an intensity about her that made the other girls in his group seem pale and fatigued. A moonmaid, he thought with an odd bit of whimsy. His thoughts crystallized abruptly. Dark eyes, black hair, strong chin, and high cheekbones. Moonlight and night, and wolves on her heels?

She was the image of the Wolfwalker Dione, if one imagined Dione without scars, and if Dione were thirty years younger. Competent as a ten-year scout, though, if she'd run up on ne-Livek without the man even knowing until she was right beside him. Experienced, yes, and brave—or stupid—enough to run trail alone under worlag moons with a wolf pack at her heels. He could think of no wolfwalker other than Dione who could come close to this girl's description. Then again, when wolves Called, men Answered. Dione had had a daughter.

He kept his voice casual. "Wolf cubs, snatched from a pack of worlags? They must have been right on the den."

She didn't notice his expression. "We got the cubs out of the den site, but the worlags didn't give up. They cut us off before we could reach the Chimneys."

He nodded in turn. The Chimneys weren't really channels in the stone, but rather an ancient façade of fractured basalt that led to a mesalike ridge. There was speculation that the caves that once riddled the ridge might have been home to Aiueven before worlags—and humans—came to the world. Now its shallow, collapsed depressions were a safe haven for anyone who could scramble high enough to be out of the beetle-beasts' reach. "How in the name of the First House did you stay ahead of them?"

Her voice tightened. "I didn't. I tried blackthorn thickets, Ironjaw Creek." She had to talk now, had to get some of the adrenaline out of her system. "Nothing worked. They had my blood-scent. They wouldn't give up the chase. So we led them to some raiders camped out at Bell Rocks."

"How did you know they were rai—"

She cut in flatly, "I found the bodies before I got there. The kill-trail led to the camp."

NeLivek frowned over his shoulder. "Moonworms, girl. Let me get this straight. You outran a worlag pack for thirty kays—"

Nori stared at him, then burst out laughing. Thirty kays? Now, that would add to the legend. Sure, she could do that distance at a jog, on good trails, in the daylight without a pack, and if she felt like a marathon. But at night, with panic in her blood and tripping on every root? He must think she was her mother. "Not hardly," she corrected. "I was already at Stone Ridge. I took the shortcut over Small Hill. And I rested at the creek, and again in a hunters' meadow." She lost her smile abruptly. A meadow that had held human bodies. Bodies of men who had died for what she now hid inside Hunter's vest.

The *chovas* snorted. "Alright, so you sprinted ten or twelve kays to Bell Rocks, then deliberately led the worlags through a raider camp? Didn't they try to stop you?"

Nori looked away. "I didn't hail them. I just jumped the

perimeter, called a warning inside their camp, and ran on through. It was enough to wake them for the worlags. They started in on each other. I . . . I kept running."

Hunter nodded at the long weals on her shoulders and neck, the line of blood on her cheek. Another track of red dribbled down from under the edge of her hair, and her arm was scabbed with blood. He wondered if she knew. "Something got close enough to mark you."

"Just a brush whipping. Thorns and branches."

"One of those looks deep."

She met his gaze but didn't answer for a moment. In the moonlight, her dark eyes were flecked with something not quite human. "One of the worlags got close before I went up the rocks." Her hand clenched involuntarily. Her bow had snapped like a straw, the wood as flawed as a politician. Without her arrows to hold them back, the worlags had leapt at her like starving dogs on dinner. The images rose in her mind like screams. Purple-black claw-fingers had slashed up. She'd parried with a knife, thrust down with the shards of the bow. The knife had broken. The tip of a claw had caught in her sleeve, raked the length of the back of her arm—

She sucked a breath, held it, slowly let it out.

Hunter watched her control her fear and nodded to himself. Dione's daughter would have learned early on to swallow such emotions. Moons knew there were three ways to deal with being born to a legend: embrace the myth, rebel like a raider, or sink into weakness and shadow. That this woman was here, now, proved that she had chosen the first path. He wondered if she had accepted a Journey assignment yet. With parents like hers, she would be snapped up like salvation once the elders tagged her for duty.

She stiffened suddenly and looked over her shoulder. He whipped his dnu around. He didn't even question her sense of danger. "What is it?" he snapped out.

She shook her head. "Rider." She relaxed and faced forward again, but her hand gripped neLivek's belt near the outrider's knife. "Ring-runner, most likely."

Interesting, he thought. She was more instinctive, more quick to react than he'd heard. She had almost drawn the outrider's weapon as her own. She'd also, he realized, heard the rider at least ten full seconds before Hunter himself caught the hoofbeats. Ears like that were wasted on a trail. He made the guest offer casually: "You are welcome to ride with us as long as you have need."

But she surprised him. "I'll rest with you, if you're willing. But I'll go on tonight."

In front of her, neLivek scowled. "All the way to Ayerton? That's a full day's ride."

"Not to Ayerton. Back to Willow Road."

The guard twisted farther to scan her scratched face, as the ring-runner pounded past, his city crest gleaming in the night. "What's so important that you can't rest now and travel on with us in the morning?"

Nori shook her head in answer to neLivek. She couldn't tell them she had stolen raider code and didn't dare stay with their wagon. Raiders could be thorough—her aunts and uncles had taught her that. They weren't above killing an entire group to make sure that the one they did want died.

But that wasn't her real fear. What chilled her guts was her brother. Payne knew she would not have left the caravan without him for more than half an hour. If he called the search before she returned, he would end up heading straight for the death-seep. Knowing him, once he neared the cliffs, he'd bypass her trail and head right for the rocks where she would have tried to climb out. Normally, that was a safe bet, but this time it could mean his death.

She couldn't even warn him to stay away from the cliff. The word *plague* caused a terror equal to seeing Aiueven. To give that signal by foxhorn, where everyone else could hear it? She'd start a countywide panic about something so deep in worlag hunting grounds that no one would likely go near it for half a year, long after her mother could check it out and, if necessary, post a quarantine.

And how could Nori explain why that signal should sound? She should not have recognized the sense of it; the wolves knew it simply as burning death. To them, it could have been anything from spring fever to pogus flu. She could never admit that she'd actually had plague or been cured by her mother, not when the cure had been through a healing technique that was forbidden to everyone. Her entire family would be hunted down like witches.

On the other hand, Nori knew where her trail had taken her. She knew how to shortcut back to it once she got to Willow Road. If her brother was too far into the hills to hear the fox-horns from the road, she could blow the recall signal herself from one of the ridges, and bring him back before he was exposed.

"At least wait till daybreak," neLivek tried again. "We can give you an escort then and make sure you get back safely."

"No," she said flatly. "But my thanks for the offer."

But Hunter had seen the flicker of fear when neLivek demanded she stay. He glanced back at the wolves, then out at the black forest. There was something out here she feared more than the beetle-beasts they'd run from. He felt a chill. He'd heard that the Wolfwalker's Daughter refused to Test, but never that she was a coward.

NeLivek scowled again. "It's already past midnight. You can't make Willow Road by dawn. It's almost fifty kays by road."

"It's barely twenty-five by the cross-trail," she countered.

"On an unlit trail," the older man returned sharply. "You'll ride faster in the light than at night, no matter how many moons are shining. Moons, girl, if it's a matter of sending word to your caravan, we can send a couple of guild-ser to ride the black road. Once they reach the main circle, they'll send a night runner on to the Tendan Ridge tower. They'll pass the word to your Ell that you're safe tonight with us."

"If you're willing, I thank you for it." But it wouldn't be in time for Payne. She'd left the cozar around Four Forks. That was fifteen kays from Chileiwa Circle. By the time neLivek's ring-runner reached the circle up ahead, transferred her note to a tower rider, and that man reached the tower . . .

She bit her lip. This part of Ariye was wrinkled with ridges and gullies like a dried-up apple. Bound on one side by the canyons of the River Phye, and on the other by the edge of Fenn Forest, it had only two tower communication lines. One tower line ran the length of the river ridges. The other ran up the Wyrenia valley foothills to the icy northern mountains. The land between valley and river was rough. She should know; she had just sprinted through it. It would take hours to get a message to Payne by the normal ring-runner route. It would take the duty rider two or three hours just to climb to the nearest tower. Then the message would have to be mirror-flashed along that ridge line till it could cross over to the other tower line. Then it had to be transferred to paper or carving stick. And then carried by another rider down to Willow Road, and south to Chileiwa Circle. At least another two hours to do that, she figured, possibly even three hours. It would be well into morning by then.

And someone would have to ride back to Four Forks where Payne would have started the search, and into the forest after him if he didn't respond to the recall from the road. Payne could move fast when he wanted to. He wouldn't wait for full light, and he'd know she would have left sign for him out of habit on the trail. What she'd casually hiked, he'd be riding at a trot or canter. By the time a rider got within hearing distance, he could be all the way to the plague-seep.

On the other hand, if she took the cross-trails back, she should be able to beat any ring-runner to Willow Road by at least an hour, maybe two. That meant the recall signal would be sounded only two or three hours after dawn. If Payne didn't respond to that signal, she could take her shortcut toward the cliffs and sound her own recall. If the moons were with her, he'd hear that before he went over Stone Ridge. She had to reach him. If she didn't, she could be burning his body in days.

"Twenty-five kays, in the dark." Hunter motioned with his chin at her bloody arms. "Under worlag moons."

She ignored the chill that fingered her spine. By all nine moons, she knew there were worlags. She'd just outrun a hunting pack. She'd thrown four men to their claws. Screams echoed in her head, and she swore she could suddenly smell blood. It had to be hers but with her imagination heightened by night, it was the blood of the men she had killed. She started to shiver violently.

"Here now," neLivek said firmly. "You're safe with us." He

reached back and rubbed her thigh firmly. It was a strong, non-sexual touch, as impersonal as a healer's, and Hunter watched her stiffen, then steady under the strength of neLivek's hands. He said, "You insist you cannot stay?"

She nodded mutely. With the slitted pain still throbbing in her head, she was unable to articulate her growing urgency.

NeLivek snorted quietly. "Crazy ring-runners."

Hunter made a soft sound, and Nori gave him a sharp look. The grunt had not been an affirmation of neLivek's statement. She braced herself for his argument, but none came. Instead, the tall man asked casually, "Have you needs, *bande'inna*?"

It was the cozar way of asking, terse and to the point. She hid her frown. She had not given any cozar signals, but she'd been raised with them; her speech was peppered with phrases she didn't even notice, and she had not offered them her name or title. If he realized she was cozar-raised, he might have guessed more about her than she wanted known. The offer of aid was almost deliberate, like a test. But courtesy required her to answer in kind, so she said simply, "Water, clean cloth for the wounds, access to your healer's supplies. I'll need chamomile, cotton-wood, and curcuma root in a tincture. Shirt, jerkin, socks, and something clean for a new sling. Belt knife—I'd prefer two. Matches, bota, war cap. A forty-pound bow and two dozen heavy hunting bolts if you can spare them. A map and a dnu, returned to you in Shockton."

By the way she answered without qualification, Hunter knew she would return or replace everything, not just the dnu and gear. He rode back to the lead thoughtfully. If neLivek thought this girl was just a ring-runner, Hunter was a spotted worlag. He doubted the girl knew that, when neLivek was arguing for her to stay, her lips had curled back like a wolf's. Black hair, lone running, and a pack of Grey Ones on her heels? She spoke like a cozar but dressed like a scout. And her skin was torn like a bad-gerbear's prey, but she didn't seem to notice. Any normal ring-runner would be screaming for gelbug wash by now, but she was content to wait till they halted at the wayside. He knew of only one other scout who was so blasé about being scratched up, and that was the Wolfwalker and Healer Dione. The arrogance was right, too. The girl had asked for temporary safety and the gear to continue her run, but she had accepted their help as if it was her due. He glanced at the wolf shadows that loped far behind their dnu. The songsters said it was only a matter of time before she bonded with the wolves. Hunter would bet his weight in gold that that time had finally come.

He resisted the urge to look back at her. He had wanted an Ariyen scout on contract, but he'd jump at the chance to have a wolfwalker instead. It was said they were more perceptive than others, that they had eyes into men's minds, even that they could hear through walls. He could use someone like that if what he suspected was starting to erupt. It had been sixty years since the last House War in Sidisport. With spies in every guild, eyes in every House, and now knives on every road, every House leader was watching his friends too carefully, not just his traditional rivals. Somewhere in the center of the city, the webs for a war were being spun. The movements his sister had been tracking, before she had been stabbed, had implied exactly that: that alliances had formed between enemies, and that power was gathering in unseen hands. The odd thing was that most of the hints were coming from outside the city, from county scouts and traders. They were seeing the shifts first, as if power was gathering outside the city instead of building up inside. It was why he wanted an Ariyen scout to help him investigate.

He fingered the belt where Jianan's notes were hidden. If the power shifts were spreading north, a war could engulf the trade lanes like fire in brittle grass. Ariyens had no love of Tamrani or any others from Sidisport, but even Ariyens would give up a Journey scout when their own interests were at stake.

He glanced back at the grey beasts who shadowed the woman and cubs. "Black Wolf," he breathed. "Jangharat." He'd bet the sixth moon on it.

XII

Quarry mine, blessed am I
In the luck of the chase.
Comes the deer to my singing.

—oldEarth Navajo hunting song

The wayside was typical, grown out of what had once been a small grazing field. It was too small to boast fountains and bathhouses, but large enough that it had a freshwater spring, corral, tack shack, and wagon posts, all of it encircled by the ubiquitous barrier bushes. Three cozar families were already bedded down in the small spaces. A lone guard stood by the fire, armed with a bow as they turned into the circle.

As they reined in, Nori started to slide off the dnu, but realized too late that her legs weren't yet working. NeLivek caught her arm as she sagged, then lowered her easily, holding her weight till she could stand. "I've seen more than one ring-runner run his legs off," he said easily as she managed her thanks. He dismounted and shook out his own long legs. "Give us a few minutes, and we'll have the gelbug wash warmed up. Hunter or I will give you a rubdown to keep you from cramping up."

A few minutes later, she had settled the sling and pups into a crude nest in the darkest corner of the wayside. Nori hid a smile as Grey Vesh stalked onto the remnants of the shirt. The female glanced at Nori like a disdainful queen. Then the pack mother sniffed her pups, lay down, and waited while the two blind balls of fur squirmed instantly toward her teats.

Nori stood and tried to ignore the gazes of the Test youths who watched from the corral. She rubbed her throbbing temples. There were too many eyes on her here, and not just from worlags and raiders. She tried to reach out past the spikes pounding her brain. Payne, she thought, be patient. I'm alright. *I'm alrightalright . . .*

Rishte slunk to her side, and she opened her eyes. In spite of the headache, she smiled faintly. After barely ten hours, the yearling's voice was an easy grey, as soothing as her humming was to a cat. Vesh's was still salt on glass, and Helt was a coarse file on her thoughts. The other wolves were like pumice on Nori's skin. To them, her voice must be similar, a raw foreignness that made them jittery and defensive. And they weren't beyond showing it, she realized, as Vesh growled at her from the nest.

She carefully backed away. "Come," she murmured to Rishte.

He slunk a handspan after her into the light, but the sounds from Hunter's group made his ears flick constantly, and his teeth were partly bared.

She stopped and squatted down. She ignored the sense of her leaden limbs as his golden gaze met her violet eyes. Like a waterfall, wolf and human fell mentally toward each other again. They hit, clashed, then meshed out into a smoother weave. Nori reveled in that sense. Rishte was snarling, but it was like a purr, not a threat to her. She was snarling back, but it was a hum of pleasure, not just a projection of need.

He stretched his nose to touch her thigh. Her hand floated at the tips of his ruff. There was still tension. With the other humans near, the instinct to leap, run, snap at her hand was like twanging a wire. At the same time, there was an eagerness to touch back, to snap and wrestle.

"We are bonding," she breathed in wonder. She kept her voice soft and let it slow into the rough humming that came so naturally. "Easy, grey. Pretty grey." She met the golden gaze, sucked in a breath as his voice became abruptly clear, and let her hand descend toward his fur.

The yearling's growl lowered into an almost continuous sound. There was a sense of fire in her mind, like a blindness of heat and smoke. There were the human smells: sweat-scent, musk, a thick, cloying perfume, soap-scent and lotion, oils and warming food. In the back of her mind, she could hear her own breathing through the wolf's ears. Payne, she thought, you should feel this. Her hand lowered till finally, like the lightest breath of wind, she touched the tips of the fur.

Rishte bristled, but suffered it for the second time that night. Suffered it, and let Nori move her hand along the ruff, smoothing the rising scruff. Suffered the urge to bite and taste blood, and fought that to revel in the pressure of the petting like a two-month pup playing with Pack Mother. "Yes," Nori breathed. "Just like that." She shifted her fingers, and the young wolf lost the battle.

You are mine, Rishte snarled. He twisted to catch Nori's hand gently in his teeth.

Nori almost laughed at the possessiveness. She gripped the Grey One's muzzle, wrestling him until he jerked his head free. The creature snapped at her wrist, and though he didn't break the skin, he marked it clearly with indents.

Nori grinned. "Possessiveness" was too simple a word for what was growing between them. Rishte now clung to the inside of her skull like a tick on the haunch of an eerin. She could not breathe without taking in air from lupine lungs, could not move without feeling lean, ropy muscles flex. Every movement of every leaf near the circle caught her eye so that the entire circle danced. Her brain was too full of vision.

Her mother's words came to her: "It will ease. It will overwhelm you at first, but then you will sort out the grey."

A bare scuff of leather on leather, and she whipped around in a fighting crouch, one hand protecting the vest pocket. Rishte was gone, snatched up by shadow.

"Easy," Hunter said quickly, freezing in place. "It's just me."

Nori slowly dropped her hands and sank back on her heels.

He kept his eyes on her face. "I'll rub down your legs," he offered. "Rocknight Styne's daughter, Lispeth, will help wash the scratches. In the meantime—" He held out a bundle, a carving knife, and a blank message stick.

She nodded her thanks, then slashed a quick message into the soft wood: all well; back after dawn; Black Wolf. She could have written her terse note on paper, but wood was more durable. If the message had to be left in a cairn, better it was wood. Beetles ate paper like candy, but wouldn't touch wood for ninans.

She finished as voices rose behind them, and Hunter glanced back at the Test youths. "They're choosing a rider," he explained dryly.

Nori kept a straight face as she handed back the knife. "A difficult decision."

He snorted. "Three days on the road, and they have yet to do any duty, including care for their own dnu. I caught them paying a couple of cozar boys to do it for them at the last two camping circles."

Nori's lips twitched. "There is a simple solution to that. Let them go a day on foot in their fancy riding boots."

He chuckled. "Now, that's something I want getting back to my mother, that I made her darlings walk."

"Why you?" she asked. It wasn't as idle a question as it sounded. He was too comfortable with his wealth to be riding guard for a cozar.

"One of them—that one, with the sorry mop of hair—is a cousin of some sort, according to my mother. The son of my grandmother's half sister's daughter." Or was it her aunt's half sister's cousin? He shook his head. "The others belong to my mother's friends." He wasn't about to leave them unsupervised, not with a shapely cozar girl trying just about every trick he'd ever seen to get up in the saddle behind both Nefsky and Vidon. He'd bless the moons nine times over when they reached Shockton and he could turn them over to the martial masters. Nine more days with those spoiled youths and he'd be ready to kill someone. "You should eat," he said abruptly.

She tapped the stick. "This first, if you're willing."

He nodded. As they approached the argument, he narrowed his green eyes and cut in, "Vidon, Eteli, what's the problem?"

"We rode all day," Vidon returned sharply. "And we're already unsaddled. Besides, she's cozar. One of the cozar should take it."

"They'd be more polite about it," neLivek said mildly from the side where he was currying his own dnu.

Two of the youths flushed, but Vidon gave the *chovas* a dirty look.

"We're trying to decide how to cast lots," Hunter's cousin explained defensively.

A blond youth had been studying Nori as she approached, and something flickered across his face as he caught his first real look at her. But his voice was diffident as he said, "Hells, if it's that much of a burden, I'll do it." He stepped toward the wolfwalker and held out his hand.

Nori looked into his steady blue eyes. She didn't know she'd started to shift into a fighting stance until Hunter's tanned hand closed over hers. The shock of his warm, callused skin made her jerk back. Hunter firmly slipped the stick from her grip and handed it to the ring-runner. "Still jumpy?" he murmured into her ear.

The familiarity made her yank away. She stopped, let out her breath, and stepped back more casually, only then realizing her other hand was on the vest pocket again. She dropped it abruptly.

There was a knowing look in the young man's eyes as he lashed the stick onto his belt. "The circle below the Tendan Ridge hub, right?"

"Aye." NeLivek answered for her as he handed up the young man's bow. "You don't want a riding partner?"

The youth grinned as he vaulted onto his dnu. "Don't need one on Deepening Road, and I won't be riding the ridge route. Duty rider will take this on."

"Ride safe, then," neLivek told him.

"With the moons." He spurred out of the circle.

Nori stared after him. NeLivek took the rest of the youths back to the fireside, but a slender man, the one dressed even better than Hunter, gave her a thoughtful look as he caught her expression. "What is it?"

She shook her head, and Hunter paused to study her, too. She said uneasily, "He's not as young as the rest of them."

On her other side, Hunter snorted. "You mean he's not as spoiled."

"You know him, then?"

Hunter gave her a sharp look. "No. My cousin picked him up on the way out of Sidisport. He had no Test chaperone, and my cousin offered him a *chovas* berth."

"And you?" She glanced at the slender man.

The man called Fentris tilted his head to study her. "I am not familiar with his family name." He nodded toward the road. "But he seems to be making himself useful."

Hunter bit back words: Unlike you, fop.

Nori frowned at the hint of derision. She stared down the road for another minute. Then she shook her head at Hunter's silent question and returned to the bundle of clothes.

Fentris left them as they passed the fireside while Nori shook out the shirt and jerkin. "My thanks for these," she told Hunter as they returned to the shadowed area outside the firelight. She would have known they were his by the scent alone, but the cloth was another giveaway. They were as finely made and finely dyed as her borrowed vest, not the typical mottled, un-bleached blend that she and Payne wore for scout work. She fingered them covetously. The shirt was smooth and tightly woven. The jerkin was beautifully tanned, green and grey. Either one alone probably cost as much as her entire riding outfit. She looked up, caught a thoughtful look on the tall man's face, and said merely, "There was no one smaller?"

The tall man shrugged. The noise suddenly toned down behind them at the fireside, and he glanced back and snorted to himself. Fentris the Fop had spoken. Vidon and the others might push Hunter to the limits of his patience, but none of them had gone so far as to antagonize a man rumored to be a murderer. Even Styne's niece, Civi, was more circumspect around the fop. Raised with the best the city had to offer, Fentris Shae had given the girl no more than a few mildly amused glances when she tried slipping her blouse off her shoulders to give him a glimpse of her blessings. Now Hunter stifled a laugh as Vidon refused a quiet order. Fentris simply slid two languid fingers along the hilt of his knife. Vidon stiffened and quickly turned back to his dnu. Hunter lost his humor abruptly. The hilt trick had been something Shae had learned from his older brother, the one Shae had supposedly murdered.

Hunter looked back at Nori, then into the shadows. He couldn't see the wolf. It was gone, he realized, as remote as the young woman before him. For she was withdrawing even as he stood there. It irritated him. He'd offered her *bande'inna,* unconditional aid—a ride, a dnu, a guesting berth, even a full wagon if she needed it—but she seemed to see him as little more than a threat. It only confirmed that she was hiding something serious enough to keep her from accepting more than the barest of her needs. Even now, she hardly glanced at his shirt. She probably didn't even care that it was his; only that it was warm, that it was her due. But he would ride with her tonight back to Willow Road, and with the image of her in his mind, naked inside his clothes mere meters away in the dark.

He brought his attention back as she frowned at him. He nodded at her legs. She hesitated, then sat down and stretched out. He began rubbing one down hard.

Nori grimaced and braced herself against the ground, but made no sound as he stretched and pummeled her tight muscles. He had large hands, she noted, and he knew how to use them. He fairly imprinted his palms into her thighs. She almost asked him why he was heading for Shockton, but when she looked up, he was studying her silently. She looked away, hiding the growl that rose to her lips, and merely thanked him when he was done.

He turned her over to Lispeth, the cozar girl, to help with the gelbug wash, and the girl shielded her as Nori carefully shrugged out of the vest. She couldn't hide the crackling sound the papers made, but Lispeth didn't seem to notice. Instead, the girl pressed the first wash-soaked rag on her back.

Even though Nori was expecting it, the first touch stung enough to make her hiss. It quickly grew to a burning as the girl worked it down her back. Nori didn't complain. Gelbugs were indigenous parasites that bred in open wounds. Once in the flesh, they passed blood through their maggotlike bodies the way mining worms did stone. In the indigenous eerin or dnu, it was a cleansing of certain toxins in exchange for a warm breeding ground. In humans, the parasites turned blood into a thickened gel. It was said that a single gelbug could kill a man in two ninans. Nori had seen it more than once. It was an ugly death.

Lispeth started on another welt. "Vidon called you cozar, but you don't look cozar."

Nori smiled. She knew this game. "I'm Randonnen," she returned. "But I was raised in a wagon like yours."

The girl cocked her head. "You could be a raider."

Nori's smile widened as she scrubbed at the blood on her arms. "Aye."

"Or a lost miner who's chasing one of the Ancients' metal maps."

"That's true." She injected a note of speculation into her voice, as if she was seriously considering being lost as a career path.

"Or a moonmaid disguised as a ring-runner, come to test our *bande'inna.*"

"It's possible," she agreed as she wrung out the rag. She sighed heavily. "But I am only a bead maker, far from home and alone." And carrying raider code, she added to herself. And hiding a knowlege of plague, and pretending she wasn't bound to the wolves. She stopped her thoughts abruptly, shifted, winced at the burning in another gash. She was still bleeding. The wash wouldn't burn so badly if the gashes had fully clotted. Still, the wounds should be closed on the surface by morning. She felt a deep satisfaction at that. Wolfwalkers healed quickly.

When Nori donned Hunter's shirt and tunic, the girl giggled. "It's too big. You should have taken one of Gariala's or Civi's, or one from the other Tamrani."

Other Tamrani? The girl had to mean Shae. The tall, slender man was the only other one with clothes that cost a fortune. Nori looked back at fireside to find him idly watching her. She scowled. One Tamrani at an Ariyen council, perhaps, but two? Something serious had to be up for that. She caught Hunter's gaze in turn as she reached for his discarded vest. Suddenly fearing that she would expose the raider papers, she stilled. Then Lispeth shifted so that she shielded Nori from the fire. The wolfwalker glanced sharply at the girl. Lispeth nodded deliberately at the vest while she kept her hands busy folding the rags. Nori smiled faintly. Quickly she stuffed the papers into a crude packet and tucked that inside the jerkin. She noted with satisfaction that Hunter now was frowning.

Lispeth followed her gaze. "He's been thoughtful since you joined us."

Meaning he'd seen the papers? Or did he realize she'd held something important back when she was explaining her arrival? She studied the cozar girl. "What about Shae?"

"He hasn't been here long, but he watches everything."

"And you?" she asked Lispeth slowly.

The girl straightened as if insulted. "Cozar business is silent business."

Nori hid a smile. "Aye, it is." She hesitated. Her voice was gentle as she asked, "How old are you, Lispeth?"

"I'm of age," Lispeth added. "I know the laws."

Nori touched her hand to the jerkin pocket.

Lispeth raised her chin. "I chose the secret freely, and so choose the silence, too." Then the girl spoiled it by adding, "Besides, they're Tamrani."

Nori grinned faintly at the disgust in her voice. "They are indeed." She folded the now empty vest and handed it to the girl. "My thanks, Lispeth Shepherd Night. I will remember you."

The girl flushed darkly. It was her first rep-name, and it was no insult. Shepherds were small, discreet night dogs that made little sound and kept their nests so well hidden that it was rare to find one in use. She bobbed her head with embarrassed pleasure at the wolfwalker.

As they returned to the fireside, the girl almost leapt to get Nori a plate. Then she trailed Nori toward the corral as the wolfwalker tried to keep moving to keep her rubber legs stretched. Nori was about to thank her and tell her to tend to her own needs, but at the first bite she stopped and raised her eyebrows. "Tamrani eat well," she murmured. "Almost as well as they dress."

Lispeth giggled. "They eat like that at every meal. Papa says they'll be too heavy to ride their own dnu by the time we get to

Shockton, and their pretty shirts will be rags from splitting at the seams."

"Perhaps I should hire on." Nori tasted a piece of spiced and sautéed pelan, and almost sighed. There was no bitterness, no aftertaste, just sweet juicy meat, as if it had been shelter-grown. "To help use up the extra food, you see, and keep them from splitting their clothes."

Lispeth giggled again.

Rishte growled softly, and Nori looked to the road. This time, she didn't startle at the sense of drumming hooves. She smiled to herself. She was getting used to the lupine alert.

A few minutes later, the ring-runner cantered into the circle. In the shadowed moonlight, his face looked deformed at first. It took her a moment to realize he was as bruised up as she. She knew him, too. NeLivek wasn't the only one to move quickly to the corral where the messenger reined in.

Lispeth's brother ran past Nori to take the dnu. "Have you needs?" the older boy asked quickly.

Kuwurin swung down. "Water and a quick meal. If you're willing, I've two coppers for a rubdown for my Hermes." He patted the lean neck. "Be quick, though. I'm for Tendan Ridge tonight—" His voice broke off as he caught sight of Nori. He blinked. "Well, hells of the second moon. My first piece of luck tonight."

"Aye, runner," she said softly, using his title, not his name.

Kuwurin glanced at the others, then nodded. "Aye, runner."

Hunter cocked his head at their tone. They knew each other, it seemed. He nodded at the man's face. "You look like you could use more than a quick meal." The lanky rider sported raccoon eyes, a massively bruised cheekbone, a scrape on the chin, and what looked like a recently broken nose.

Nori's lips quirked. She didn't figure she looked much better. "You are rather . . . pretty in color," she told him.

The man grinned sourly. "I was set on when I stopped for lunch. There were two of them, waiting in the stables." He started to rub his stubbled chin, hit the scrape and winced, and shook his head sourly. "They took all but two message tubes, and only left me those because they fell under the saddle and were missed. I've messages for you." He nodded at Nori.

She glanced at the others, then stepped away with the ring-runner, leaving Hunter and the rest to watch curiously.

She kept her voice low. "It's good to see you, Kuwurin. There were dead ring-runners just off the Ironjaw Trail. At least six over at least two ninans. I couldn't stay long enough to search for more." She quickly described what she'd seen.

He took in her own scratches and scrapes. "Then I'm more than glad to see you also, and not just because I expected to have to send your messages across to Willow Road. You're a hard one to keep track of, Black Wolf."

"The gossips always know where to find my brother. You can leave messages with him."

He snorted. "That troublemak—" He broke off as she tried to hide a flicker of anger. He said quickly, "He's, uh, young for it, I thought."

She forced herself not to snap. The wolves were jittery, too close in her mind, and she had to work to say, "He's been doing this duty since he was eighteen."

"Aye, well." The man shrugged, winced, glanced over his shoulder toward the fire, then dropped his voice. "*Madaka Dione*, this duty is for the Lloroi."

She didn't blink at the code phrase. "Word or written?"

"Both. The first was a two-page report, sealed, from the Kiebba lab. You'll have to send back to them to get another copy."

"Any idea what was in it?"

"A sealed report from an underground lab? Not a clue." She cocked her head, and he smiled wryly. She was too much her mother's daughter. She knew full well that a long-term council runner like him would have a fairly accurate guess.

He admitted, "I'd say it had something to do with a new strain of luminescence, one that your mother brought in last year. It's brighter than they expected, and they've already sent samples on to Ricton and Shallow Ridge. Dione wanted to be kept informed."

"But you wouldn't have a clue, of course."

Now he grinned. "I've been riding this stretch for six years with my Hermes. I have more than one friend in that lab."

"And the second message?"

"Short and sweet: The Beo rabbit is riding tall."

She nodded. It meant that scout Purjik, grandson of a man named Beodan, was taking the ridge routes to Shockton, since he was late like the white rabbit in the oldEarth tale. She wondered why. Purjik was one of the most conscientious scouts she'd ever met. If scouts ever wore watches, Purjik would have worn four just to make it to the meetings. If he was taking the ridge routes—the tall road—then he was willing to risk poolah and bihwadi and worlags as Nori had, to get to the town on time.

But she said only, "My thanks, then, and my duty."

"Your duty," he nodded in turn. It would take hours to recall and write out all the other messages he'd been carrying. At least these two had been delivered.

Nori stopped him before he returned to the fire. "One thing, if you're willing." She hesitated, then nodded toward the Tamrani. "I've not given them my name."

He was surprised. "They've seen you."

"Aye, but it's dark, and I'm smudged and dirty."

He glanced at the far shadows, where he could see the wolves waiting, then gave her a sharp look. It was in her eyes, the wildness of the pack. "So that's how it is," he said softly.

She flushed. "I just need a few more ninans."

Before being called to council duty, he guessed. "You have my discretion."

"Till after the Journey parting?"

He nodded. "As you wish."

He left Nori at the corral. She looked back at fireside, then leaned on the rails and stared blindly at the dnu. Ring-runners dead on the trails, it happened. But messengers set upon in the stables? She wanted to check the jerkin pocket where she had hidden the code.

She knew instantly when Rishte slipped up beside her. *Fire. Men. Too much noise. Danger-scent. Not safe.*

"Aye," she said softly. The yearling was right. Best to leave quickly now. She hadn't missed the curious looks on the Journey youths' faces. There had been rumors for years of her parents' network, and Tamrani had sharp eyes. Between the wolves, Lispeth, and this messenger, she'd probably compromised the last of its subtlety.

XIII

"Confess," he cried.
"I already did."
"But you see, I don't believe you."

　　—from *Playing with Swords,* traditional staging

Hunter met her at the corral. "That looked serious."

She met his cool gaze with a bland expression. The moment she'd done so, she realized her mistake. The Tamrani's lips curved in a faint, knowing smile. She turned away quickly, but he continued to watch her. Wolfwalkers rarely had good poker faces, and new wolfwalkers were the worst. She'd probably just given away more than she had with Lispeth.

She picked out a dnu and let Hunter get its tack, while she made her way to the other end of the circle to settle the two pups in a new sling. Grey Vesh snarled as Nori took the pups again, but the wolfwalker took no offense. They all wanted away from this stretch of land with its worlags, raiders, and plague.

The ring-runner rode out a few minutes later, and Nori waved as she made her way back to the corral. She frowned as she saw Hunter saddling another dnu for himself. A moment later, Lispeth's brother brought two cozar hackamores, not one, and neLivek was behind the boy, carrying his own gear. "I need no escort," she told them quickly.

He merely continued tightening the cinch. "I wouldn't let anyone go alone on a cross-trail, let alone a scout who's already run her legs off."

Her violet eyes narrowed. For all that he moved well, he was still cityfolk. He had no business riding the black road. "It's twenty-five kays to Willow Road. Moons only know how far you'd have to ride then to catch up to your caravan."

"They're not a fast group," he said mildly. His gaze barely flickered as it took in Lispeth and her brother. "We'll make up time out of Maupin."

"You have Test youths here."

He shrugged. "With four wagons and ten outriders, there are plenty of bows to keep them all safe."

She said more strongly, "The cross-trail is rough, and I'll be moving fast. It's not a road for citymen or *chovas*—"

He put his hand on her arm, but she shied away, and neLivek stirred uncomfortably. Hunter stilled. He knew what the *chovas* was thinking: Touch the wolf if you dare. The man was right. Too much fear still lurked in her dark eyes. He made his voice quiet. "Do you really want to ride that cross-trail alone?"

In the dark. With raiders and worlags hunting.

Nori stared at him. The flush that crept into her cheeks made her want to turn away. He continued to regard her steadily. Finally, cursing herself under her breath, cursing her parents, cursing the moons for her gutlessness even if it came from the wolves, she found her voice. It was stilted and formal, but she managed, "I welcome you—" She broke off as Hunter's gaze went over her shoulder and his expression suddenly hardened.

Fentris had approached, and Hunter's face darkened to see him leading his own well-bred dnu. He stopped the slim man with a sharp gesture and said flatly, "You are not coming with us."

Nori glanced at Fentris. When she'd first noted the second Tamrani, she'd seen the languid movements that the wealthy of Sidisport sometimes affected. But this man's movements were not so much studied and practiced as naturally smooth, like a serpent's. He was surprisingly lean and hard under the fancy clothes, and he gave off an impression of wiry strength—the kind that would surprise a man who believed strength had to show more visibly. In fact, she gave him a thoughtful look. Hunter had slung his bow like most travelers would, out of the way for wilderness riding. Fentris had slung his like a raider, for pulling out at a gallop. She cocked her head, and he caught her speculative glance. He'd said almost nothing to her all night, but she could swear he was challenging her now behind those blue, inscrutable eyes.

The fop turned and gave Hunter a sardonic look. "There's more traffic on Willow Road than on Deepening," he said blandly. "I'll have an easier time getting a guest berth the rest of the way into Shockton."

Hunter's eyes narrowed. "If I leave, they'll need you to watch the youths till they catch up with the caravan."

Fentris grinned without humor. "Come now, Brithanas. They might fear my knife, but they don't respect my sword. Leave ne-Livek behind in my place. You'll be a happier man when we continue on separate roads."

Hunter glanced at Nori. He lowered his voice. "The wolf-walker might prefer other company, Shae."

"It's just scout, not wolfwalker," she said sharply.

Fentris kept his voice mild. "Why don't we leave that up to her?" Deliberately, he turned his back on Hunter and asked her the silent question.

Nori looked from one to the other. She wasn't short in stature, but between the two tall men, she was beginning to feel it. She bit her lip. She didn't want to accept either of them, but they were forcing her to make the travel oath to both, or judge one man by another's antipathy. As Hunter started to smile in grim satisfaction, she said finally, "You are welcome with me. You are welcome as my brothers. Ride and eat and fight with me, and your children shall be as my own."

Fentris raised an elegant eyebrow.

"Uh, look here—" neLivek started.

Hunter broke in. "Shae, you can't—"

"We join you," Fentris cut in. "And take your burdens as our own."

Hunter turned on the other man. "You snake-headed lepa. You have no right—"

"We're not in the city, Brithan—"

"Do not," Nori cut in sharply.

Both men broke off. NeLivek raised his eyebrows. Between the Tamrani, ring-runners, worlags, and wolves, this was better than a play.

Nori ignored him. "Not here," she said flatly to the two Tamrani. "Not here, and not with me."

All three men stared down at her as if she had sprouted talons.

She gave each one a hard look in turn. She did not consider their age or experience, or that the Tamrani wielded power in the cities. In the forest, except with twenty-year scouts or wolfwalkers like her mother, she had always led.

Fentris raised his other eyebrow at Hunter. He inclined his head graciously to Nori. "As you say."

Hunter's jaw tightened. He motioned sharply for the cozar boy to finish saddling Nori's dnu. Sley had been watching with carefully neutral eyes, but Hunter suspected the rumors would fly as soon as they rode out. He stalked back to the fireside to get his gear. NeLivek, after one amused glance at Nori, followed the tall man more calmly.

Fentris mused, "I don't think either of us has ever been spoken to like that."

Nori snorted. "By a mere scout, you mean. If I've offended you—"

"No, no," he reassured her. "It was an . . . intruiging experience." He hesitated, then said, "I am curious, though. Did you know who I was before you offered the travel oath?"

She cast him an irritated look. "No."

"Do you know who I am now?"

She repeated, "A snake-headed lepa named Shae?"

He choked, caught his breath, and managed, "And that means nothing to you?"

"Should it?"

"You have no idea who he is, either, I suppose?"

Now she was exasperated. "No, and I don't care."

The man's lips quirked, and he turned away quickly to get his own gear, but Nori heard him laughing.

As Fentris reached the gear area, Hunter put his hand out and stopped the other man. He kept his voice low—this was Tamrani business—and accused the other man flatly, "You forced her to make that offer."

Fentris kept his voice even as he reached down for his saddlebags. "I, too, am heading for Shockton."

Hunter jerked the strap tight on his own saddlebags. "Just what do you expect to do if we encounter worlags on the trail?"

The other man hefted his bags over his shoulder. "You knew me for years, Brithanas, and you know how I was trained. Do you really think I didn't do what I could for Jianan?"

Hunter gave him a sober look. "Just as you did for Joao?"

"Ah, yes." Fentris stared at him out of those unreadable eyes. "I let my brother die. Let him or did him myself," he corrected dryly, "depending on the story."

"I'm not looking for a confession."

"Damn you, if I'd give you one."

Hunter laughed without humor. "You've kept that, at least, your stubborn streak. I hope it serves you well."

"I've needed it," Fentris retorted. He nodded after Nori. "You'd do well to develop one yourself if you think to catch that one for a scouting partner."

"So you recognize her."

"Hard not to, with those looks and the wolves. What's amusing is that she doesn't have a clue who you are."

"Titles aren't as important out here. Reputations count for more."

"I wonder what she'd say if she knew you were heading for council with some very interesting notes. With her parents, the Wolven Guard, and that reputation of hers, she might know more than you think about the patterns we've been seeing."

Hunter didn't seem to move, but he was suddenly closer. His voice was soft. "Say anything of that to her, and we'll have a serious problem, Shae."

The other man stood his ground, and his voice was uncharacteristically hard. "I'm not a boy anymore, Brithanas. I don't scare the way I used to."

Surprise flickered in Hunter's cool gaze. "I never thought you scared easy."

Fentris snorted.

As the slender man started to turn away, Hunter found himself asking, "Just how much do you know about the wolfwa—about our scout?"

Fentris halted, hesitated, then finally turned back. Like most merchants, his family had several spies on the duty lists. They watched the other houses, intercepted messages, sometimes even killed. Out in the county, they reported regularly on the councils and prominent families. With Brithanas gone so long from the area, it didn't surprise him the other man was asking.

His voice was flat. "I know that Black Wolf—and her brother—report to the scout masters every month. She never speaks in front of the councils, but she's been in closed meetings with the Lloroi, a man who conveniently enough, is one of her uncles—a blood relative, not one of the Wolven Guard. And she's far too wary and nervous for simply wanting to return to her brother."

"There are the wolves."

"That's not what I saw in her eyes, nor what you saw there, either."

Hunter gave him a sharp look. "You always did read people well."

"Actually, I learned that from you."

Hunter hid his surprise.

Fentris nodded toward the corral. "If I were hiding something, I'd be wondering how much she really does know, how much she's guessed by seeing us together. I'd be wondering how much more she'll realize on a long, slow ride in the dark."

Hunter gave him a hard look. "I'm wondering the same about you, right now."

Fentris met his gaze steadily. "If you're worried about prying eyes, you should think about switching caravans."

Hunter straightened slowly. He'd already arranged with the cozar to watch the youths the rest of the way into Shockton. Then he'd quietly packed his essentials. After skimming through Jianan's notes, he'd understood instantly why she'd become a target. His own sense of being watched might not be imagination, either. It disturbed him what Fentris might have already guessed: Hunter was taking this chance with Black Wolf to change caravans. "If I was worried about prying eyes, should I be worried about yours, too?"

"You mean, especially since some of the trade-route property that's changing hands is titled to your family and to you?"

Hunter stepped close. He lowered his voice further. "Exactly what do you know, Shae?"

The other man regarded Hunter with those dark blue, clever eyes. "Where do they keep their dry meals around here?"

"You mean rations. Trail rations," Hunter corrected sharply. "Back of the wagon, grub box. Shae—" He caught the other man's arm. "What have you seen?"

The other man waited a heartbeat, as if to see how far he could push the taller Tamrani. Finally, he said, "As much as you. Maybe more. You've been west too long, Brithanas."

"While you've stayed at home in the city." Hunter could have sworn he saw pain flicker deep in the other man's gaze before it was shuttered again.

"As you say," Fentris agreed. He turned and began rummaging through the grub box for what the cozar apparently called trail food.

Hunter glanced over at Nori. Her dnu was saddled, and she was lashing on her pack. He said slowly, "Perhaps we could exchange information."

"Exchange." Fentris's voice was flat.

"You're still Tamrani."

"Of course. I must have forgotten. We trade in information."

Hunter picked up a discarded bag of dried fruits and tucked them back in the bin. He said mildly, "Sarcasm doesn't suit you."

"Actually, it seems to be wearing well this season."

Hunter snorted. He hesitated, then asked abruptly, "What happened, Shae, when Joao died?"

Fentris stilled. Then he went on packing his gear. "I'm sure you've heard every version that made the rounds. Likely, one of them is true."

Hunter murmured, "He always said, if he died by violence, it would be your hand on the blade."

Now Fentris did turn and stare at him. "And you believe that?

That I'd stab my own, my only brother in the back, just to get the title?"

"Did you?"

"Go spin a chak, Brithanas." Fentris turned his back, and didn't see Hunter frown thoughtfully at him. He made his voice carefully bored. "What kind of information do you have to offer?"

Hunter glanced at Nori again, then said quietly, "Land is changing hands, and not in traveled districts. Businesses are being bought where they can't possibly make a profit. There have been too many convenient deaths in town this year. I know of six myself, and have heard rumors of others. I've had word of others now, among property owners, people who would never have sold their land, but whose land went up for auction after they died. The lots are all along the same two lines leading in and out of the city." Fentris looked up at that, and this time Hunter caught a flicker of surprise. "But you knew that," he added softly.

Fentris nodded slowly. "You keep a closer eye on the family stores than I thought."

Hunter shrugged. "It's a shortsighted man who doesn't watch for power shifts near home."

"And land is power," Fentris murmured.

"Someone is readying the land for changes that will reach across the county boundaries."

"And you're going to the Ariyens?" Fentris's voice was dry. He lifted the edge of a towel from a rack to see if there was something useful behind it. "Since when do Tamrani alert others that there's money to be made?" He dropped the towel and looked around in exasperation. "Aren't there any fresh meatrolls?"

Hunter's voice was equally dry. "Trail rations are exactly that, Shae: rations. Try the jerky."

"Damn stuff is addictive," the slender man muttered. But he had noticed that the wolfwalker was ready to ride, and he quickly filled his pouch with the smoked meat and another packet of trail mix. He glanced at Hunter. "You're worried now," he murmured. "Worried enough that you're not just going to council to pick the elders' brains. You're actually thinking to ask the Ariyens for help."

Hunter reached over to secure the grub box Fentris had left unlatched. "Yes," he admitted. "Whatever is going to happen will center in Ariye. There's no other reason to buy up the land around the county outskirts."

"You want a partner," Fentris guessed. "Someone who knows the middle counties, who has contacts across the trade routes. An Ariyen with ties to the council." He followed Hunter's gaze toward Nori. "And you've got your eye on the Wolfwalker's Daughter. On Jangharat. On Black Wolf."

Hunter didn't deny it. She'd be perfect for what he wanted. Raised among the cozar, she had an unquestionable reason to travel wherever and whenever she wanted. She had contacts across the nine counties to rival a forty-year trader. Hells, her parents could not have created a better county spy if they had planned her life from the womb. The young woman was practically an undercover elder. She ought to be, he thought. For generations, her family had held positions in the councils, the guilds, and included some of the most competent weapons masters in decades. She was as close as one could get to being born to a council seat even if she avoided those duties like plague. All of which meant that she had knowledge of which she wasn't even aware—knowledge that he could use.

Fentris had been watching his cool green eyes, and recognized the look. "She won't agree to go with you," he said softly. "They don't call her Nori No-Elder for nothing. Rumor has it she's been denying her own council for years, and you're as close to being a councilman as Sidisport ever spawns."

"She might change her mind if she thought the information worth it."

"She's more likely to walk away. She's apolitical, Brithanas. She ignores alliances like a rock does the sand. If she's seen any unusual shifts through her scouting, she's not likely to share them with you."

He straightened and studied the slim Tamrani. "What was it that caught your attention, Shae? That made you notice the shifts?"

Fentris hesitated. "A man's death."

"Someone important?"

Something flickered in Fentris's dark eyes. "No," he answered in a bored tone. "No one at all. Just a clerk who supported his mate, his three children, his crippled brother, and that man's son."

Hunter had the grace to look uncomfortable. "I see."

"No." Fentris suddenly sounded tired. "I don't think you do, Brithanas. But that's really not the issue. I'll be gone in a day, on Willow Road, and you can go back to your games with Black Wolf." He stalked away to finish his business packing up his gear.

Hunter's green eyes narrowed as he watched the man walk away. Then he thought of the wolfwalker's father, of that cold, chiseled face and watchful grey eyes. Of her mother's stubborn defiance in keeping her last two children away from her own council tasks. Hunter could read between the lines: the council could have the parents, if they left the children alone. Fentris wasn't wrong. This young woman would do almost anything before taking on an elder's duty. Yet she'd dealt with four raiders as casually as if they were roasted rasts on a stick, and she'd spoken to Hunter and Fentris as if they were bickering children. Right now, as she waited impatiently, she had pulled out her borrowed map and was studying it intently, and for what? Trail notes? He had nine days, he figured, before they hit Shockton. Nine days to get into her head.

He watched her for a long moment. "Jangharat," he murmured. If his family had any influence at all among the Ariyen elders, she'd be working with him before the Test ninan was over.

*

At the corral, as Sley adjusted the stirrups on Nori's dnu, the boy glanced at the two Tamrani and took the chance to prompt Nori, "You haven't told us your name or title."

"I have not," she agreed shortly. Her headache was dulled, but not so much so that tension, like that between Fentris and Hunter, couldn't spike it. Her neck also prickled with the wolf-sense. Rishte had circled the camp with her until he now lurked in the shadows by the road, making her want to growl at the city youth who lurked by the rails, trying to be inconspicuous as he listened in.

Sley asked, "You said you were a scout, but you're a wolf-walker, aren't you?"

Nori ran her hands down along the legs of the dnu, checking for burrs. She kept her voice low. "One doesn't have to be a wolfwalker to run with the wolves."

"But the pack brought you here," Sley persisted. Lispeth poked her brother, and he shushed her as he said to Nori, "The Grey Ones out there now, on the road, waiting. I can just see them from here in the light." He waited a heartbeat. "Are you? A wolfwalker?"

"Sley," Lispeth hissed.

He shook his head at the girl, but he kept his voice low. "You heard her before. She holds to the courtesies. She's cozar enough." He turned back to Nori. "Three questions."

Nori straightened and regarded him in an uncomfortable silence.

By the fire, Hunter glanced over and swore under his breath. Nori was looking at Sley as if she was about to strike the youth. Fentris noted their posture at the same time and started to hurry his steps, but then both men stopped themselves. They glanced at each other, then waited to see what the wolfwalker would do.

"Three questions," Sley persisted. "Are you Dione?"

With long practice, she kept her face expressionless. "No. That's my mother."

The boy nodded slowly. "Then you're Black Wolf."

Nori adjusted a long knife at her waist and shrugged.

Sley watched her carefully. "They say you won't Test to your rank. That you haven't for six years. Why not?"

Lispeth winced. The cozar girl entertained notions of Two Silence, which the wolfwalker could invoke at any time for asking inappropriate questions. Two days of absolute silence, in which they could not even confess their discourtesy. But this was Dione's daughter. Everyone would know what they'd asked.

Nori regarded Sley for a long moment. Then she smiled, slowly, but the expression was somehow chill. "Because I have only eight ninans to live."

"Then what happens?"

"Sley," Lispeth wailed quietly. Four Silence would be a shame they would not live down for a year.

Nori continued to smile. "Then my world ends, and my mother's world begins." Her voice was quiet as she caught the girl's wince. "It's alright, Lispeth Shepherd Night."

"Are you—" Sley started.

Nori cut him off with a small gesture. "Three questions, three answers."

The young man caught sight of the Tamrani watching them and felt his neck darken. His questions may have been within cozar law, but they had not truly been courteous. On top of that, the taller Tamrani had been obvious enough about the wolf-walker, and one didn't cross the Tamrani. The boy handed Nori the reins, and his younger sister grabbed his hand and towed him angrily back to the fire.

Nori leaned her head against the warm dnu. Eight ninans, she thought. Two months till she turned twenty-three and was formally out of the Test ranks. Till she began to walk in her mother's footsteps, trying to cure the plague. Sley wanted to know why she wouldn't Test for rank within the county like the other youths her age. She shook her head to herself. In two months, when she turned twenty-three, she would face much more than a simple Test. She would face her mother-mother's people, the Aiueven of the north. She took a breath and straightened. Payne and youths like Nefsky and Sley worried about Test and their Journey assignments. Nori worried about survival.

She looked to the shadow where Rishte waited. He growled in her head, and her lips curled back. It was all about strength, she told herself. She had better find some soon.

She mounted and waited impatiently for Fentris and Hunter to join her.

"Ride safe," the cozar driver told them as they wheeled their dnu.

"With the moons," she returned. Then they urged their dnu to a smooth, six-legged trot onto Deepening Road.

*

At fireside, one of the Test youths could barely contain himself with what he'd overheard. "That was Black Wolf. Dione's daughter," the young man repeated to the others.

Sley dropped down beside his father as the older man murmured to neLivek, "The Heart of Ariye runs true."

Neither man asked the boy to leave, and Sley tried to sit straighter beside them, but his eager words spoiled the effect. "They say she doesn't run alone. She's always with her brother. How much would you bet that she doesn't tell Dione what she's been up to tonight?"

Rocknight Styne raised his eyebrows. "Dione would find out if she doesn't know already. A mother always does. It's Aranur the girl wouldn't tell." He tossed the dregs of his drink onto the coals and listened to them hiss.

"True enough," neLivek agreed. "Aranur, now, I've met that one a few times."

The city youths listened avidly. NeLivek had been up and down the counties for six decades, while Rocknight had been driving a wagon for more than a hundred years. Both men could tell tales that offered more than one spike of fear.

Rocknight refilled his mug with hot rou. "Aye, he's a dark one, Aranur is. Dark and dangerous."

"Remember one time in Ramaj Eilif, he rode into a raider camp by himself and came out with their hostage. Not a shot fired, and twelve people dead on the road behind that band. He never said what he told them, but those rasts rode for the Bilocctar border like they had a Tumuwen winter on their heels." He shook his head. Each time neLivek had met Aranur, he'd come away thinking he was more than relieved the man was not his enemy. "Always was dangerous, that one."

"As you say," the driver agreed. "Even before the Wolven Guard. Bred true, he did, like Dione. You could see it in her eyes." He indicated the night where Nori had disappeared.

The other cozar nodded in turn.

"Worlags," one of the Test youths breathed. "And right through the raiders, and all to rescue two wolf cubs." He grinned at the others. "Now that's worth some gold to a songster."

"No." Rocknight Styne's voice was sharp, and the town youths looked at him in surprise.

"She is cozar," Sley said firmly.

"If she wants it told," his father explained less curtly, "she will tell it herself. We have no right to spread her stories, except amongst ourselves." He let his gaze travel around the circle. "Remember that," he said flatly. The city youths met his eyes uncomfortably, but finally nodded.

"Cozar custom?" one of the youths asked hesitantly.

"Cozar right." The other man's voice was unyielding. He gestured for the youths to prepare for bed, and they left the fire for their bedrolls.

NeLivek murmured, "She's not really cozar. She's always been Randonnen."

"She was raised with us till she was sixteen."

"Except for that year in Ariye."

"Aye, but that wasn't a good year or she wouldn't have come back to the wagons." Styne kicked a log and sent a spiral of sparks up into the night.

NeLivek grunted. "Warm still for the hour."

"Aye, that it is." Rocknight settled back on the bench.

The other man chewed on his toothpick. "Heard that a small pack of raiders hit Winn's train over near Black Bottom Creek. Killed four people, including two elders who were heading north for the Ariyen meetings. The whole train will be delayed for a ninan. Might be the same bunch Black Wolf saw at Bell Rocks."

The driver murmured his answer, and the fire crackled down in the night.

XIV

If you must work against your reputation,
Perhaps you should try working on it.

   —Randonnen proverb

It was two hours past dawn, and Payne's group had just reached the base of Stone Ridge. There wasn't much left of the wolf den that had once been safe for the pack. The earth was dug out; the smaller boulders had been turned and tumbled as the worlags clawed after the scent of newborn wolf. The remains of some of those worlags testified to Nori's presence. She might not have hurried on the way to the den, but she sure as all nine hells had been sprinting to leave.

Payne wrenched her longknife from the midjoint on a worlag carcass. A few minutes later, he found one of her boot knives in the rocks. It was dark and sticky with dried ichor. She had been close when she'd shoved that in. Too close. There was blood—human blood—on the handle. A moment later, there was a shout as Ki's oldest boy found half of her bow beneath another dead worlag. Wakje found the other half jammed between two boulders, with the torn remnants of her belt pouches.

His uncle pulled the splintered wood free as Payne picked up the pouches. Most of the pouches had been clawed in half; the contents were scattered among the rocks. Herbs, matches, a shattered signal mirror . . . Payne shoved a small boulder over and jerked a small book from beneath the loose rock. It was Nori's scout book. It was whole, for all that the cover had been clawed. He turned it over in his hands. The claw mark matched the one in the pouch where she'd kept the book. Both had been on her person when that tear had been made.

139

Of all things to leave behind, that small book spoke of panic. There were names in that book, descriptions of messengers who had slipped past the main roads, notes from other scouts she'd met on the ridges, even fragments of code from the towers. Along with that were his own notes: names, places, council gossip, rumors of private deals. Payne had risked his neck for some of that information. Nori had done the same. Nothing was truly secret, but the book was still valuable, not just to the Ariyen elders, but also to those who might have wished that their activities had gone less remarked. It was always on Nori's person. To leave it behind? He almost glared around the clearing, daring someone to find her bones as he stuffed the book into his jerkin.

Wakje's hand on his shoulder startled him, and he blindly accepted the broken bow the ex-raider handed to him. The break was ragged, as if it had twisted before snapping in half, and there was darkness in the core. More blood? He tortured himself by imagining her terror.

"You'd know," Wakje said flatly.

Payne's jaw firmed. "Aye, I would." He threw down the shards. Nori had never liked the bow anyway. He couldn't help wondering as he stalked away whether he would be able to sense it if she died. Even if he had a bond with the wolves, he might not be able to sense her. His mother said that the wolves passed on only the sense of the living. The dead were silent ghosts. He stared at the shattered remains of the area. If he felt nothing from Nori now, did that mean she was dead or just that the danger had truly passed? Moonworms, but he could go crazy second-guessing himself like that.

Behind him, Wakje stooped and picked up the wooden shards and studied the break with a frown. The darkness in the core was the wrong color for ichor. Wakje peered closely at the break, turned it in the light. It wasn't a dirt stain, nor was it blood. "Payne," the man called.

There was a note in Wakje's voice that made Payne move quickly.

Wakje turned the wood for him to see. "Rot," the older man murmured.

Payne glanced at his uncle's face. The ex-raider wasn't joking. "That doesn't make sense. No rot would survive the initial tests of the wood, and Nori's had this bow for three months."

"It might not have come out on the first couple of uses."

"Nori would have felt anything like that long before she bought the bow," Payne returned flatly. "You can't get an inner knot past her when she's going over the woods."

"Even Nori-girl could be fooled by something she can't see."

Payne set his jaw stubbornly. "Have you ever known her to pick a weapon with bad wood? If there's rot in there, it's new."

"Can't be new. There's too much here, all along the center." The older man ran his fingers along the rest of the wood.

"I'm telling you, Nori would have felt it."

"Maybe. Maybe not." The thickset man slid a knife from one of his scabbards and began prying at the break. "Well, well," he murmured, more to himself. "Looks as though something pierced the wood." Wakje glanced at Payne. "I'm thinking of that archery competition in Ariye, two years ago, when Nori-girl walked off with last place."

"It wasn't really last place," Payne protested absently. "Her spacing was perfect."

"She hit the bull's-eye only once."

"She made a spiral with her shots, from center out. It was beautifully done. Even Gamon admitted it later."

Wakje picked at the spot of rot. "It lost her the prize."

Payne grinned. "You're too goal-oriented, Uncle. Besides, she didn't lose her reputation."

"That's what I'm talking about."

He finally caught his uncle's drift. "You mean the Great Broken Bow Debacle?" He thought back to the way she'd replaced every screw in the compound bows with a pulp plug. The bows had fallen apart the third or fourth shot each archer had tried to draw. "Sabotage. Okay, I get your point." He frowned at the older man. "You know it was a joke, Wakje. She didn't actually break the bows."

The older man ignored that. Wakje flicked his knife in again, exposing the black spot of rot like a surgeon. "The line goes all the way to the outer wood. It's just hidden in the design. Now look back at the center. It's an almost perfect circle, straight in through every line of grain, as if something was injected into the wood."

"An insect?"

He shook his head. "Borers twist along the grain before they go through a growth line. This was deliberate." He looked up. "Ki," he called.

"A moment," the other man returned. "I've got something here you should see." Ki pointed to a dark smear on the short cliff as they joined him. For a moment, they stared up at the stained stone.

"Human," Wakje murmured.

Payne nodded. Only human blood would attract black gnats and blue-biters like that. He studied the marks. There wasn't really enough blood to scare him. The stains could have been from anything—a scraped palm, a torn nail.

Payne forced himself to turn to watch Proving dissect the rest of the scene on the ground. He might dislike the man, but he had to admit he was more than glad Proving was there. It had been Proving, not Payne, who'd caught that second set of prints where Nori had turned off the main trail.

The *chovas,* Murton, had started it. They had paused to rest the dnu when the guard had shouted that he'd found Nori's sign and that it was fresh. Murton had mounted and charged off, and no one had questioned the man. They'd simply jumped up and spurred after the outrider like a horde of stingers to water. Proving had cursed them all from behind, but the entire line had followed the outrider, trampling whatever sign had been there before they realized the *chovas* had been wrong. It had taken more than a kay to realize that the guard had been following the marks of a stickbeast. Murton had been shamefaced and devoutly apologetic, but Payne had had little sympathy. If it hadn't been for Proving, they might never have recovered the trail. As it was, they had wasted precious time, and Proving was furious. The cozar had cursed them all for idiots and promised to slap the eyes from the skulls of anyone who trampled his tracks again. Murton was assigned to the rear.

Up to that point, they'd hadn't been sure if Nori had been following the tracks of the wolf or the Grey One itself. Half a kay

later, they were sure she had been with the wolf. There was only
one explanation for that, and Payne felt a twinge of envy that
the wolves must have Called his sister. That was why she'd left
the wagons, why she hadn't awoken him. With her background
and sense of duty, a Call would have been too strong to refuse or
even hesitate to Answer.

Speed, urgency . . . He pictured the scene in his mind. She'd
arrived before the worlags, but he didn't know if it was in time
to save the wolf cubs. She'd fought there, with her back to the
cliff, had lost her weapons, and had climbed out, while the
wolves ran north to get away. From the top, though, which direction had she taken? Southwest, toward the Chimneys, or
north and west, toward the wolves? Worlags could run a man
down like hounds after a deer, but if she climbed the cliff, she
would have had several kays' lead. Payne could go around with
the dnu and pick up her trail again at the top, or they could simply climb after her. The climb wasn't difficult; the crack in the
cliff ran halfway to the top, and there were plenty of holds above
it. He looked at the blood smear again, then asked over his
shoulder, "Have we got all the arrows?"

Ki answered, "As many as we can salvage."

"Alright. We'll leave the dnu with maRaya and Kahrl. Nori
went up, that's obvious. It would have gained her twenty, maybe
thirty minutes while the worlags went around. We'll signal from
the top to let the other parties know if she went south to the
Chimneys or north."

He yanked off his gloves and stuffed them in his belt. Then he
fit his hand into the cracks in the stones. Tightening his hand
into a fist, he jammed it in the rocks so that he could hoist himself up, then up again. There was another smear at eye level on
the stone. They were finger tracks: she'd brushed the dust from
the cliff as she climbed and left her blood behind. He eased
himself back down. It took him only a moment to get the rope
from his saddle, hand his sword, bow, and quiver to Wakje, and
toss the bulk of the line to the broad-shouldered *chovas* Murton.
He tied one end of the rope onto his belt.

Payne set his fist into the gap between the columns, then
glanced over his shoulder.

"Ready," Murton told him calmly. He'd opened the rope loops so that they wouldn't tangle as he fed them to Payne. "Climb on."

The youth started grimly up the short cliff. Judging by the smears on the rocks, Nori had left enough blood to mark her trail that even a headless worlag could follow her.

He was halfway up the short cliff when he heard the distant foxhorn. Instinctively, his gut tightened. He waited for the repeated signal. When the sequence came again, he leaned his head against the stone. Recall. Successful recall. The signal came a third time, and Payne breathed a moonsblessing.

Murton called up. "She must have come back at the north crossing, just as you suspected."

Payne grinned down as Ki's son pulled out his own horn and blew the response. Trust Nori-girl to turn the world upside down for a day. He tried to ignore his anger at her carelessness. She'd be paying the sixth moon to Brean for a ninan for the trouble she had caused.

He looked down, shrugged the rope off his shoulders, and let it fall. Down below, Murton started coiling it up for the saddle. A few more minutes and Payne joined the others on the ground and took over the coiling from Murton as the others readied to ride. He'd almost finished when his fingers noted a change in the rope's thickness. He paused, ran his hands along the length, then finished coiling the rope. A minute later, he casually walked over to Wakje.

"Here," he said softly, indicating the stretch of rope. The older man ran his hands over the loop. The thin spot was like a gap in an old pillow. The rope sheath was intact, but the inner cord—the braid that gave the rope its strength—was so thin that only a quarter of it was still holding. "Good thing that recall came when it did."

Wakje's face, impassive as it usually was, grew subtly harder. "Someone fell on that rope. Or misused it."

"It's mine and Nori's rope," Payne answered flatly. "No one climbs on it but Nori and me."

From the side, Ki murmured, "It's a classic damage pattern."

Payne agreed. He tucked the thin loop carefully back in the

coil and prayed his hands didn't shake to show his temper. He kept his voice low. "You think someone deliberately damaged it?" He looked from one uncle's set face to the other's. "You think someone's trying to kill her before we get to Shockton?"

"Or you," Wakje agreed. "When was the last time you climbed on this?"

"Midterm break, on Irregular Rim. We did Kingpin, Spongen, and Whisker Face. Simple climbs, Short columns—two pitches each. Neither of us fell or strained the rope."

Ki's voice was dry. "Angered any cozar fathers lately?"

Payne gave a short laugh. "Two, but I brought both a quarter eerin just before we hit Sidisport, and all was forgiven."

"You're sure?" Wakje asked.

"They invited me back for dinner."

Ki barely nodded at his son when Mye joined them. "And afterward?" Ki prodded Payne.

"Moonworms, Ki. It's not as if the girls didn't want the attention. They've been following me around ever since we joined the train."

"And you indulge them both."

"It's just dancing."

"In the moonlight," Mye said slyly.

Payne grinned now. "I, too, have a reputation to maintain."

Ki handed him back the rope, and Wakje murmured, "Might not be the reputation you want, not if it's bringing you this. Perhaps you should think about jealousy and old boyfriends."

Payne looked at the top of the cliff and slowly lost his grin. If he'd tied off the rope for the others to walk up the face, the line could easily have snapped under a man's weight. With that jumble of boulders at the base of the cliff, any fall would have been nasty, if not fatal. Wakje was right. It was time to think about enemies. The problem was, he didn't know where to start.

He glanced over the group. He knew his uncles, he knew Ki's sons. He knew Ed Proving and Murton and the others only by reputation. Murton, for all that the man knew which end of a sword to use, sure as hells didn't know the forest. But why would the outrider want to hurt Nori? Murton seemed pleased that his friend B'Kosan was interested in her. That was the problem with everyone Payne could think of. Everyone liked Nori, reserved as she was. It was Payne who irritated people.

He fingered the rope as he lashed it behind his saddle. It didn't make sense, he thought. They'd done nothing but graduate and head to Ariye for Test. If someone just wanted Nori's scout book, it could be stolen—perhaps not easily, but certainly without the effort of sabotage. Unless someone didn't want them to Journey, there was no reason to cause them harm. He thought on that as they filed onto the trail and cantered back toward the road.

XV

If you build the target around yourself,
You have only to wait for the arrows.

    —Randonnen saying

Morning on the grazing verge, on the side of Willow Road . . .

Nori opened her eyes from dozing. There was something she should hear . . . She closed her eyes and concentrated, but Rishte was far away, up on a ridge, out of reach of anything but the faintest of impressions. There was nothing nearby except for small birds that twitted the brush and wind rattling through waxy leaves.

The yearling had hung back when the rest of his pack had split off. He'd waited for Nori to follow the pack east. When she didn't, he'd slunk back until he could overlook the verge where his wolfwalker stubbornly settled. He had howled unhappily more than once, startling Fentris, then Hunter as the sound rose from first one hill, then another. For the last two hours, he had been silent, more and more cautious as traffic thickened and his pack grew ever more distant.

Nori had with difficulty let him be. She could have slipped away to meet him, but both Tamrani had wanted her close. The pair of poolah last night had been nothing; they'd passed easily. The bluewing moths, though, and the swarm of night sprits that had devoured the hatching moths like a blizzard—those had unsettled the men. Nori couldn't quite work up the energy to argue with either one. Her entire body ached, her eyes burned, and she could barely stay awake enough to tell Rishte she had to sleep.

Besides, it had to be the Grey One's choice to stay with her, instead of returning to his pack. She would not coerce the bond.

Right now, he snuck along the edges of her thoughts with a warning. Dnu, she realized. That was the sense of fast-moving dnu. It wasn't the thin pounding of a single rider, or the rumble of a caravan, but a thick thunder, as if a herd of six-legged eerin were running on summer-hard ground. She smiled as she got to her feet. She caught Hunter's attention. "The searchers are coming in."

He shaded his eyes and peered down the empty road. The front end of a caravan was coming into view from the south, and a pair of the Humbled trotted away, their dull black robes fluttering in the wind. There was nothing else on the road. He raised one eyebrow when she shrugged and said, "It will be a few seconds."

He hid his satisfaction. She was bonding, that was sure. As the search group came into sight, he asked dryly, "Have you ever been wrong?"

She hesitated, frowning. "No . . . No, I don't think so," she said uncertainly.

He raised a dark eyebrow.

She laughed. "I'm kidding, Hunter. I've been wrong as often as I've been right."

Somehow, he didn't believe it. "You'd make one hell of a scouting partner."

Her face closed up. "There will be dozens of older, more experienced scouts in Shockton looking to pick up work."

"Of course," he said agreeably. But he watched her thoughtfully as she waved at the oncoming riders.

Kettre waved back and pulled up on the verge in a flurry of dust, just ahead of the others. "Where have you been?" the woman demanded as she slid from the saddle. She tossed the reins at the nearest man—Fentris—who caught them with a bemused expression.

Nori waved her hand at the dust. "Moons, Kettre, couldn't you get us any dirtier? What did you do, gallop back the whole way?"

Kettre didn't even pause. "We sent the search parties out last night, got started at first dawn. Payne was ready to chew up his scabbard when you turned up missing—"

"That sounds like him, but I am sorry. I didn't expect to be gone this long—"

"Sure, and the moons don't fly." Kettre glanced at the two men while the other searchers reined in. She lowered her voice abruptly. "Can't you go anywhere without finding some handsome man—or two—to bring you back?"

Nori grinned faintly at her disgust. "I didn't ask them along."

"You never need to." Kettre pulled her a few meters away from the others and lowered her voice even further. "So, spill. Who are they?"

Nori shrugged. "Chaperones for Test youth, out of Sidisport. Rich enough to afford fancy gear—"

The other woman fingered the fine, rolled-up sleeve of the overlarge shirt. "I can see that."

She swatted Kettre's hand away. "And idle enough to take a month out of their year to watch some relatives Test."

Kettre gave her a sharp look. She'd never heard Nori use such a dismissive tone for men she kept glancing at. Or rather, one man, she realized, as she caught Nori's surreptitious look toward the taller one. "But you don't know who they are?"

Nori sighed. "The slim one is Fentris, the tall one Hunter."

Kettre watched her curiously. "Hunter's a scout name."

The wolfwalker shook her head. "He's city. Rides with formal training, not loosely like a Randonnen."

The other woman glanced back toward the Tamrani. "What about the other one?"

"He's rigged right," she admitted. "But he knows nothing about the forest. They're both heading for the councils, but they're not friends," she added, surprising Kettre. "Fentris called Hunter 'Brithanas,' and he called Fentris 'Shae' when they were trying to irritate each other. Other than that," she said quickly when the other woman started to interrupt, "all I know is that they didn't do badly last night on the ride, and—" She ran her hands down the silk-soft sleeve. "they have excellent taste in clothes."

Kettre frowned. "Brithanas and Shae are family names, Nori. Old families. They're out of Tamrani Houses."

"The cozar said they were Tamrani," Nori agreed.

The other woman gave her a disgusted look. "You could have mentioned that first. It is just slightly, in the barest way, a teeny bit important."

Nori hid a grin.

"Brithanas," Kettre mused. "Moons, Nori, don't you know who he is?"

Nori shrugged. "Cityman, merchant. Arrogant and irritating. It's enough."

"Just once, could you use your brain for something other than badgerbear or stickbeast? Look at him. A Tamrani called Hunter in the trade lanes. Tall, green-eyed, well built, arrogant as old money, with a *chovas* hairstyle, but wearing tooled tesselskin boots?"

"I pick up the important things. I don't worry about the rest."

"You'll rest your mind all the way onto your funeral pyre if someone doesn't stay on your case. He's Condari," Kettre said in exasperation. "Condari Brithanas."

The wolfwalker didn't even blink. "Never heard of him."

"Payne will have."

"Payne hears all the gossip," Nori said, not quite under her breath.

"If you're going to ride with those two, you might consider listening to your brother. Even I have heard things about 'Noble Hunter' Brithanas."

"You live in Sidisport," Nori retorted. "You're supposed to hear the news."

"And Fentris Shae?" the brown-eyed woman warned. "You'd best be on your guard. He doesn't make for a good ally."

Nori looked at her with a raised eyebrow. "He's got a good seat, carries his blade like he means business. He startled a few times, but he didn't hint at bolting, even when we crossed the poolah."

"Poolah?" The other woman poked at one of the scabs on her arm. "You just can't leave the critters alone, can you?"

Nori shook her off. "You're as bad as Payne. The poolah didn't touch me. This is from the brush last night, when I was running from worlags."

"Worlags." Kettre's voice was flat.

Nori shook her head in silent warning. "I'll tell you later," she mouthed as the searchers began to dismount and greet her.

Kettre scowled. "Ask Payne," she returned cryptically.

Nori briefly explained the night to the cozar and *chovas* who had turned out to look for her. When Hunter would have added to her abbreviated version, she cut him off smoothly, leaving Fentris with a half smile on his face. Then she reassured the searchers, thanking them again as they left to catch up to the wagons.

Kettre stayed behind to wait for Payne and question the two Tamrani. Nori went back to her log pillow to close her eyes, not to sleep—she was too tired and sore for that—but to listen for the yearling.

She hadn't realized she had dozed off until the grey raked like a nail across her mind. She jerked awake. She was on her feet instantly, her hand going to her borrowed bow. Hunter was half on his feet at her abrupt warning, and Kettre and Fentris barely an instant behind. She poised, listening.

Wolfwalker, Rishte sent sharply. *Wake, alert. The pounding. Hooves on the ground like before.*

"Nori?" Kettre said sharply.

Nori held up her hand and shook her head. Rishte was close, and the sense of his warning was stronger. He was on edge, too, more twitchy since he'd crept closer to the humans. This time, she knew immediately it was fast, approaching riders. "Yes," she breathed. He'd keyed in to her need to listen only for a larger group, the one Payne would be with. He had ignored the other single and paired ring-runners who had passed while she slept. So soon into the bond, it was more than she could have hoped for. She sent him a joyful shaft of approval.

Wolfwalker! he returned.

Kettre, watching the change in Nori's body language, relaxed.

"It's alright," Nori told the Tamrani. Fentris gave her an odd look but lowered his bow, as did Hunter.

A few minutes later, a knot of riders pounded into view at a canter. Nori raised her arm, and Payne spurred his dnu into a gallop.

Payne barely came to a halt before sliding from the saddle, and he and Nori banged bows as they hugged until Nori shrugged hers off and thrust it at Kettre. Hunter noted the worry in both Nori's and Payne's faces until they exchanged some low words. Then Payne gave Hunter a look that didn't pretend to hide his protectiveness.

Hunter understood completely. He couldn't help glancing at Fentris as the other searchers arrived. He still didn't know whether to put a fist in the other Tamrani's perfect face for letting his sister get stabbed, or bring the man in to help, since Shae had information of his own that could help Hunter at council.

He looked back at The Brother. The height and lean, broad shoulders Payne had, Hunter suspected, came from the father's side. Hunter wasn't a small man, but he guessed he outweighed the youth by barely fifteen kilos. Also like his father, Payne's face was fairly sculpted. If the ladies thought Payne good looking now, they'd probably swoon over him in two years. No wonder he had a growing reputation as a troublemaker and rake.

Hunter had been expecting to see The Brother as spineless and jealous of his father's reputation and name. Instead, he saw a young man who moved with much of the controlled energy Nori had, as if Payne had already been seasoned enough to wear away much of the brashness of youth. It made Hunter study him much more carefully. The children of strong parents were often weak, as if they couldn't define themselves except as shadows of such visible roles. History repeating itself, he thought. The young man had been called a "miniature Aranur" and a "budding Rhom" all his years growing up. If it had been Hunter, he'd have dyed his hair, changed his name, and pretended he really was cozar.

After Payne's look, he was prepared for the once-over he got from two of the older riders. Those hard faces and trail-toughened rigs could never have been cozar. These, he thought, looking at Wakje and Ki, were part of the Wolven Guard.

Beside the three men, the wolfwalker seemed not just slender, but almost willowy. Hunter gathered his gear and tried not to remember how her muscles had felt when he'd massaged her legs. In the wind, his soft jerkin and baggy shirt pressed against her figure. He felt his loins tighten again. Slim she might be, but there was strength in that long, lithe body. He stifled an urge to run his hands inside the garment, over her smooth skin, and shock her out of her reticence.

Wakje glanced at Hunter, then studied his niece as she briefly explained again where she'd been. He didn't miss the tautness of exhaustion, or the long scratches and gashes on her arms and neck. She was leaving out a few details. Payne, too, gave her a sharp look, but accepted her story without protest. When she'd finished, the younger man turned to the rest of the searchers. "With our thanks, and if you're willing, you can ride back to the caravan. We'll follow in a bit."

Ki nodded to Payne and Nori, but Wakje made no move to leave; nor did Hunter or Fentris. The outrider, Murton, made as if to stay also, but Ed Proving simply handed Murton the man's reins and commented dryly, "They can manage, Outrider neKien. This road is fairly easy to follow, even for full-fledged scouts."

The *chovas* flushed, nodded curtly, and reined away, but not before Nori caught a flash of something cold in his brown eyes. It seemed directed at her, and she felt a chill. Rishte echoed it into her mind, and howled up on the hill. The other riders stilled, then glanced at Nori, but her violet eyes were clear, not unfocused as a wolfwalker's gaze often was. Still, there was speculation in their gazes as they waved their ride-safes. Uncle Ki studied her for a moment, then nodded to her and rode away with his sons.

Nori glanced at the Tamrani, then murmured to Payne, "Shall we?"

They walked away to talk in privacy. He glanced back and kept his voice low. "You're gouged up good, Nori-girl."

"It was an . . . interesting night," she admitted.

Payne heard the growl under her voice. His hand shot out and gripped her arm. "That howl. It's happened then? That's . . . is that your wolf on the hill?"

She couldn't help smiling. Payne's voice was so carefully steady that he had to be biting the insides of his cheeks. She disengaged his fingers. "The pack Called. One chose to stay."

Payne started to grin. With the wolves so wary of the taint in her mind, Nori had been terrified she would never find a partner. "It's happened," he murmured. "They Called, you Answered, and now you're really bonding."

"You would have done less, big brother?"

He mock-punched her shoulder and grinned when she couldn't quite hide her flinch. Served her right for adventuring without him. "Hells, you know I wouldn't have ignored a Call. Are you going to tell?"

"Not before we leave on your Journey assignment."

He nodded. What the elders didn't know, they couldn't control. Wolfwalkers weren't as rare as they had once been, but their skills were still in high demand. The Ariyen elders had been chewing their nails waiting for Nori to bond. Once she did, they could put more pressure on her to shift from the scout lists to the council lists. She could end up like their mother, drowned in county duties. Unless, he added to himself, she stood up to them or was already out on Journey.

He glanced back toward the Tamrani. "Do they know?"

"They suspect, but I don't think they'll tell." She hesitated, then asked more sharply than she intended, "Payne, how far did you get on my trail before you heard the recall?"

He said in disgust, "Moons, Nori, you didn't need to worry about me and the worlags."

But she surprised him. "I wasn't worried about that. You've never been afraid of them like I am." Rishte growled faintly as her thoughts turned back to that midnight run. She glanced back at the two Tamrani. "Let's walk a bit," she said softly.

She led him almost a hundred meters down the road before taking the papers from her pocket and handing them to Payne. "I took those from the raiders at Bell Rocks."

Payne unfolded them carefully. "They'd be more useful if they weren't torn."

"Aye, and I'd be more perforated," she said dryly. "The raiders were armed, you know, at the time."

He flashed her a grin. While she waited, she peered into the bushes and idly picked a few seedpods hidden back in the thorns. The pods had escaped the spring sun and hadn't yet burst, so they were both hard and aromatic. Payne handed her a belt pouch automatically as he read, and she dropped the pods inside. As with most scouts, it was habit to supplement their scouting wages. This time, they'd need the extra silver to help replace her gear.

Payne frowned as he studied the last sheet. "This isn't House code."

"No. One of the raiders was writing that when I ran through the camp. I think it could be the same as the other samples we saw a month ago."

He refolded the papers thoughtfully and tucked them inside his jerkin. "I'll find a rider and send these on after we copy down the code. The next contact I know is two days away, but he's solid. We can trust him with this."

Nori glanced back at the Tamrani and lowered her voice. "There was something else last night, Payne. At the base of Cotillion Cliff, a death-place, like the domes. Like the plague, but recent."

He stilled, his hand in his jerkin pocket. "So that's why you didn't want me following your trail, and why you don't want to confess the bond." He secured the pocket. "Plague." He said softly, "You're sure about this?"

"Sure as a rock set in stone."

He didn't doubt her. Mama had taken him to the same ruins as Nori. Like old sweat, a chill crept down his spine. Plague, and the wolves remembered it clearly enough to tell Nori before she'd fully bonded.

After eight hundred years, plague was still carried by the wolves. It was the reason their litters were so small, their pups often stillborn. It lay dormant in the Grey Ones until they did

Ovousibas—the internal healing—but then it erupted like fire. It was why Ovousibas was forbidden. The intense energies of the inner healing killed the wolves, and then burned out the brains of the wolfwalkers who tried to do it with them. Mama was likely the first person in three centuries who had figured out how to use the alien healing technique without killing herself or her wolf.

Nori had the same knowlege of botany and biology as her mother, and with her vet skills and the taint in her mind, Nori could be the perfect person to help find a cure for the wolves. But seeking such a cure wasn't a goal to admit to—not with the tombs of the martyrs lining the Ancients' roads. Any hint that Nori could recognize plague or survive it or, moons forbid, cure it, and she would be inundated with hopefuls. Even the Lloroi couldn't stop that kind of flood. She could be the death of hundreds who would try to return to the domes and die instead at the plague sites. Nori couldn't even know yet whether she could do Ovousibas at all, let alone do it well enough to survive the plague, as Mama had barely learned to do.

Payne's voice was low. "Did the wolves tell you how many died?"

She shook her head. "I couldn't get to any real memories. We're not that closely bonded."

"Not yet," he agreed. "It took Mama years to be able to read the Grey Ones' memories well. You could give yourself a few days." If she had managed to read any memories at all, her wolf must not be a pup. It would be harder for her, then, to stay among men if the Grey One was already wild.

The sound of drumming hooves reached them faintly from around the wide curve in the road, and both cocked their heads to listen. "Two riders," guessed Payne automatically. It was an old game.

"Three," she countered. "There's not enough distinction for two."

He caught the hoarseness in her voice and gave her a cross look. "You're cheating."

She grinned. She could hear the rustle of a dik-dik lizard, the flutterings of tree sprits as they swooped overhead, but she couldn't quite hear Rishte. "I would if I could," she admitted. "But your group scared him back up the hill. He can't see any better than you can."

"And I should believe you?"

"When have I ever tricked you?" she asked virtuously.

He raised his black eyebrows. Then he began ticking off the examples on his fingers. "Two months ago, when you slipped red pepper into my morning rou, told me I was late, and I gulped half of it down before I noticed. Then there was last ninan, when you got old Martonne with her sagging lips to say she was mooning after me in front of the entire fireside. And then there was the day after that, when you got me to challenge you—"

Her grin widened.

"—and chose puffballs for the weapons."

Her grey-violet eyes sparkled. "A man going up for Test should be ready for anything."

He snorted. "Anything like a weapon, okay. But puffballs? It was the stupidest challenge I've ever had. I looked like I'd been in a feather fight. Vina's brother has been calling me Featherhead."

"Payne Featherhead," she teased. "I like it."

"Aye, now there's a name I want to live with for a long time. All I can do is pray you get us into another scrape so I have a chance at another rep-name." An edge entered his voice. "And not another scrape like last night. Moonworms, Nori. Raiders, worlags, and plague?" He pushed her chin with one finger to get a better look at a long scratch.

She jerked her head away. "I wouldn't have done it, but Rishte—"

"Called," he finished shortly. It would have been strong, that Call. He'd seen it in other wolfwalkers, when their partners pulled them out of the cities. Nori was more sensitive than most, and if Rishte was at least a year old, his voice would be strong already.

The riders came into sight down the road, and Nori hid a grin at their number. "Well?" she prompted.

"Three," he admitted sourly. They were riding heads-down in a tight knot, hunched low, their features obscured as manes whipped around their faces. Two glanced over at Nori and Payne, then tucked their heads down again.

"Older sisters are always right," Nori said smugly.

"It won't be that way when I bond."

"You'll probably do it sooner than I," she admitted. "The Grey Ones have always liked you better."

"Maybe," he admitted. "But they hound you more closely."

"They want another Dione." They exchanged wry glances. "Here," she said, picking another set of seedpods.

"Here, yourself." He pulled out her scout book and handed it over. "It's a bit worse for the wear, but still usable. Best mark down the—" He automatically dropped his voice to a whisper. "—plague place." He watched her make her quick, neat notes. He forced himself to ask, "You think we should check out the site before we report to the council?" He dreaded her answer. They were still days from Shockton, the Test town. His Test, his Journey assignment—she could take them away with a single word.

She understood his carefully casual tone. No matter what her brother did, no matter which venges he rode, where he studied, how well he fought or scouted or worked, no one ever said, that Payne neBentar, he's a good man to have at your side. Instead it was, neBentar, he really takes after his father. Or, neBentar, bet he got that move from the Wolven Guard. Worse, Payne had had to look out for her all their lives, and it was her fault he'd been raised that way. Fear made her unreliable, violence made her sick, and both dogged her like the wolves. Payne had earned the rep-name The Brother because of her. If they weren't careful, they'd be tied together till the day she died.

She shook her head. "It's plague, Payne. If it's not just a memory, neither one of us could survive it. Mama's the only one who can check it out. We can't even risk sending word of it ahead. If the message was intercepted . . ." She shrugged. "There's time enough to tell Mama in person and let her take care of it."

"Someone else might find that spot accidentally."

"I doubt it. There was a wagon track in the area, but it was at least two winters old."

"Harvesters wouldn't go back in there till fall."

"Aye, and the trails in that area are years overgrown. If it wasn't for the wolves, I wouldn't have known where I was."

He snorted. She always knew where she was. It was one of the few things he envied about the taint in her mind.

She finished her notes and handed the book back. "My thanks for finding that. I was afraid I'd have to try to re-create everything. I borrowed a map from Hunter to mark the trails just in case."

"Looks like you borrowed more than that," he teased. He nodded toward the knives at her belt. "We found all your blades," he added, and lost his teasing tone. "But your bow is so much kindling."

She shrugged. "An easy loss."

"Maybe a better loss than you know," he said darkly.

She laughed, not understanding. "I never liked that bow."

"Neither did someone else."

"What do you mean?"

"The rope's been damaged."

She was surprised by the non sequitur. "You fell on it at the cliff?"

"Not me. But there's a flat spot, about ten meters in from one end."

Ten meters. Far enough in that it wouldn't be immediately noticed when knotted. She regarded her brother soberly. A flat spot in the rope wasn't a trivial problem. When someone fell on a roped climb, the falling body picked up momentum on the descent. When the climber hit the end of the rope, the rope stretched until either the fall was stopped and the body began to spring back, or the rope broke instead. Even when a rope held, a few strands usually broke inside the protective sheath. It was why one never used a rope—or other gear—that had taken a fall. One never knew how many strands were still good inside that sheath. But this rope was almost new, and neither she nor Payne had fallen.

"You're not curious as to how it happened?"

"Oh, aye, I am." She stared blindly at the ridge. "I've felt . . . watched in the caravan."

"Watched?" he repeated. "Not just uneasy? Watched like how?"

"Like that time up on Dizzy Ridge," she said slowly. "When the raiders were waiting at the cut." She hesitated. "I could swear someone has been in the wagon."

He stilled. "You didn't tell me that."

She looked uncomfortable. "It was a woman's scent on the gear."

"Moons, Nori, I'd never bring a woman back there."

She looked away. "Oliana is being fairly persistent, as is Arsala."

"Aye, so was Vina. But you know I'd never bring any of them into our wagon. You and I, we've always shared berth."

"Aye, but now you say that the rope's been damaged. And then there was my knife."

He frowned. "We found all three of your knives, and except for the ichor that you'll have to polish off, they all look fine to me."

"I've been carrying four knives, not three."

"Since when?" he demanded.

She looked even more uncomfortable. "Since a few days ago, when we hit Sidisport."

"You didn't tell me that, either."

She shrugged her apology. "That knife shattered like a dried noodle even though it barely pierced the worlag."

He nodded curtly. "Your bow was rotted, Nori. Uncle Wakje has the shards to prove it." They stared at each other. "There's someone in the caravan who doesn't want you hunting."

"Or either of us climbing."

"Or you using your knife."

She gazed without seeing down the road. "There have been accidents all up and down the caravan."

As one, they looked at his jerkin pocket where the thin scout book hid.

Nori cleared her throat. "Perhaps we should watch each other's backs more closely for a while."

"Aye," Payne said dryly. "I was thinking the same thing."

They started back, and Nori's mind whirled with exhausted thoughts. She didn't even notice that she continued to pick the seeds from the few vines that stretched through the barrier bushes. It wasn't until Payne poked her sore shoulder that she realized she was standing, staring into the shrubs.

She blinked. "Sorry."

"You can't get them," Payne said. "And we need to get back."

"What? Oh." She had been thinking about codes and raiders and something on the edge of her mind as she gazed blindly at a full set of seedpods that hung a meter inside the shrub line. "Actually—" She squinted. "—the bushes are fairly thin here, and two minutes won't hurt. I think I can get my arm through if you let me have your gloves."

Payne sighed and pulled them from his belt. "You're going to gouge the heck out of them."

"You need a new pair anyway. Besides, look at them. Totally in shadow and hard as rocks. They've got to be worth an entire silver by themselves." She pulled on the well-used leather. In the back of her mind, Rishte reached for her thoughts, curious as to what she was doing.

Payne watched her work her arm toward the ripe pods and cocked his head as he caught a sound of drumming himself. "Four riders," he stated quickly before Nori could speak. "Coming up fast from the south."

"Three," she returned absently. She grinned at his obvious sourness and continued to work her arm through the lattice of thorns. One lay in a new, long, shallow scratch, and she halted for a moment. "Dangit, I just need a few more inches."

"Nori-girl—"

"Hush. You'll break my concentration."

"You sound like Mama."

She rolled her eyes. "Shut up," she said instead.

He grinned, but fell silent.

Down at the bend in the road, the riders pounded into view.

Payne muttered a curse, and Nori hid a grin as he acknowledged that, yes, there were only three.

Nori's hand closed on the pods. "Gotcha," she said smugly. She started to withdraw her arm.

Payne glanced back at the oncoming riders. "You know, those riders seem like the same ones tha—" He broke off. "Dik spit, Nori," he cried out. "Get down."

She twisted to see. Thorns scratched her arm and she froze. The riders had suddenly spurred to a full gallop. Grey snapped in her head, and Nori saw bows come up, nocked like a midnight raid. They thundered toward her and Payne.

"Get down." Payne reached out to jerk her away from the bushes.

"I can't," she cried. "I'm not free."

Payne whipped out his sword. "Hurry, dammit!"

Back on the verge, Wakje and the others had idly watched the trio pass. When the riders' bows came up, Wakje didn't even hesitate. The ex-raider rolled to his feet and sprinted for his dnu as if he'd expected an attack from the get-go. Fentris, standing by the dnu, was three full seconds behind him. Hunter and Kettre, back on the verge, had to run to reach their mounts.

The three riders thundered down on Nori and Payne. Payne took a high guard in front of Nori, but it was a useless gesture. One sword on the ground, against three bows on target? Nori felt the yellow, slitted gaze deep in her mind watch the threat like a man tied down, like a man who must wait for the blow. Grey howls burst through in her head. *Wolfwalker*—

She saw the bows, the bent tension of each nocking, the lead rider's intense expression. She saw the instant in which each dnu hit that perfect moment of stability in its gait. She smelled the sudden fear in her brother as he shoved her farther behind him, almost thrusting her into the thorns. Then the riders' bolts released.

Time unstuck. Her mind broke free and submerged into grey and yellow. Like water, she slid Hunter's knife from her belt and slung it at the lead rider. The movement jerked her arm in the thorns, and they ripped shallowly across skin. Blood-scent filled her nose. Rishte howled. The knife guard caught on the lead man's bow and tumbled through his jerkin. It slashed leather, not flesh as the rider jerked himself back. The first war bolt tore past her shoulder. She twisted, left blood on the thorns.

The second man's bolt whapped toward them. Payne cried out. Nori stifled a scream as the third bolt slapped past her face. Rishte howled again as he raced toward her through the forest. She twisted and yanked, frantically now, bent and shoved at the thorns. Her heartbeat was a racehorse. She saw a bolt aimed. She shifted like water. The arrow ripped through shrubs at her hip. The lead raider drew again. She tucked, and a fifth arrow tore the mesh cap from her head instead of skewering her eye. She saw movement to the side and knew her uncle was at a dead gallop. The ex-raider jammed his bow tip in his stirrup and nocked it in a movement perfected with decades of raiding runs. He fired almost before the third wave of bolts reached their marks.

The grey sharpened in Nori's head. Her eyes hurt with black and white. Movement, angle. She saw Wakje, intent as a badgerbear coursing its prey. The lead attacker: a dark face, swarthy face, yellowed teeth and mustache. Another bolt that split the leaves between her arm and torso. Twenty meters behind Wakje, Fentris nocked his bow like her uncle. Far behind, Kettre leaned hard on her dnu, screaming her war cry. Hunter was already even with Kettre's tired dnu, nocking his bow and standing in the stirrups as he brought up a bolt. She saw the second raider: tanned, narrow face, and long, bony hands. She saw his eyes as he thundered past, terrifying eyes that burned at her: die, *die.* She reached and yanked at her brother. He slid with the motion. The bolt passed between her arm and his side. Payne twisted, ducked back, and the other cut across his back. The third raider: a tall man, heavy shoulders, jerkin old and worn, and his hands, steady, steady on the bow, and the bolt piercing air like lightning—

Wolfwalker! Rishte's iron legs flew across dirt, logs, long grass, ferns. Nori's hands grabbed for her other knife, but it wasn't there, wasn't there. Her lips curled back. Her free hand clenched. She didn't know she was snarling.

Payne jerked up his sword like a shield and threw his own short knife hard. It sank into the third man's gut and stuck. There was a cry, but the rider didn't fall off, and the dnu were away, away down the road, the riders hunched low for speed.

XVI

Sometimes the lesson hurts

—Randonnen proverb

Payne whirled. Nori yanked herself free from the last of the thorns. Her mind was still clouded. The grey had come up like a tide of animal reactions, and she shook her head, trying to regain her sight.

"Are you okay?" Payne snapped. His hands ran down across her shoulders, twisting her forearms until he saw that the blood was from new scratches, not arrows that had torn through flesh.

She jerked free. "I'm fine. But you were hit." She yanked his jerkin open in turn, pressed on his ribs to find the wound. The hole in the thick leather was smooth as a mine shaft, but she couldn't see the blood.

Payne shook his head, his eyes still burning with the adrenaline rush. He dug a finger into his jerkin and turned the hole out for her to see. "Skewered my—your—scout book like a shish kebab." He pulled out a bundle to show her the torn covers. The bolt had gone completely through both books and the packet of papers before stopping on his rib. The trickle of blood inside his shirt testified to that. "I'm barely scratched," he said quickly. "I'm okay, Nori-girl." He sucked in a breath with the realization. "Moonworms, they missed us," he said in wonder. "They missed us both completely."

She touched her hair where the cap had been torn from her head. But she could see that it was Payne's sleeve, not flesh, that had been cut where a bolt had slashed the leather. The back of his jerkin had a long gouge where another had cut across as

165

he ducked, and the jerkin now gapped open like a mudsucker mouth. Wakje pounded toward them, and Nori looked at her hip. She had a similar groove on the leather hip of her trousers. Her pant leg was barely hanging together, but there was only a welt on her skin.

Payne plucked her war cap from the shrubs as Wakje thundered toward them. The older man caught sight of the blood on Nori's arm, and his face went hard, but Payne shouted, "We're okay, we're not hurt—"

Wakje didn't bother to nod. He just wheeled his dnu in a tight circle and spurred it after the riders.

"Wait—" Nori cried. But Wakje was already gone. Fentris half pulled up a few seconds later. "Go with him," she cried. "Don't let him face them alone."

The slender Tamrani obeyed and spurred his dnu back to a gallop. He didn't have much hope of catching up with Wakje, but he didn't think the ex-raider would catch the attackers, either.

Nori jammed her war cap on her head and sprinted after Payne, back toward Hunter and Kettre. Hunter cut toward the wolfwalker and reached down. "Catch on."

She grasped his wrist, and he slung her up behind him. She slid into place like a latch clicking home. "Our dnu—"

"Your uncle," he snapped back, half jumping the dnu forward.

Her eyes flashed, but he didn't see it. She fisted his tunic. "Dnu first," she snarled.

Hunter glanced back, saw her expression, and cursed as he whirled his dnu the rest of the way around. At the same time, Kettre caught up with Payne. The Tamrani charged back toward the grazing verge with Kettre and Payne on his heels.

By the time they reached the nervous beasts, Wakje and Fentris were out of sight.

"Dammit to the eighth moon," Payne cursed, vaulting into his saddle.

Nori had one foot on the ground, one in the stirrup, when she slapped the dnu. She was on the rootroad before hitting the saddle, Hunter right beside her.

They'd gone only two kays when they passed the body. It was the one that Payne had sunk his knife into. The man was sprawled across the road, his dnu breathing heavily on the verge. The war bolt in the man's back would have testified to Wakje's shooting from the saddle, but the blood on the barrier bushes proved the attacker had been on the ground long enough to run before he was skewered. That, and the pool of blood that had spilled from his throat, was the statement of a knife.

They found Fentris and Wakje half a kay later, studying a break in the shrub line. The growling in Nori's throat was still choking her, making her words hoarse. Rishte was close, approaching warily.

"They've gone off-road," Wakje told them shortly, barely looking up as they reined in.

Nori slid from her dnu and tossed the reins around a branch. She could almost smell the trail through the wolf. She stared into the forest. "I could track them."

"Not this time." Wakje didn't even look at her.

"I can track them," she repeated, her voice half growl. She took a step forward to move past him on the trail. She sniffed the air like a wolf. It was Rishte's breath she sampled, and there was man-scent in his nose. She clenched her hands open and closed as if to stretch her fingers into wolf paws, then started to step through, onto the trail.

Wakje snagged her elbow. "Not by the second moon, Nori-girl."

Rishte snapped in her mind. In the tension, the thought was clear: *Male, strong, challenger. Fight.*

Like an animal, she jerked free. Her face twisted into a snarl, and her violet eyes were unfocused.

A flicker of shock hit the ex-raider. He froze. That wasn't the face of the girl he'd considered his daughter. What faced him wasn't human at all.

Fentris and Hunter looked from Wakje to his niece. Kettre's mouth made a silent O as she began to realize.

Male, sent Rishte. *Bristle, defend. Back him down. Back down,* he sent.

The words were a weapon in Nori's mind. It was the same kind of challenge Grey Vesh had made when Nori had approached their den. Her lips curled slowly back at her uncle, and her fingers started to clench.

Wakje read the wolf in her eyes and stepped back so quickly he almost hit Hunter. "Wolfwalker," he whispered harshly.

Hot blood seemed to burn in Nori's veins. Poised like the wolf, she nearly bit after her uncle to press the point. She breathed raggedly, too fast for her lungs. Then she shook her head, blinked, and let her breath out more slowly. The tension drained away like a creek.

"I'm sorry," she breathed. She closed her eyes for a moment and let the world settle back into focus. "My apologies, Uncle Wakje. I didn't mean to snap at you." She reached for his arm, but he stiffened. She halted.

His face was expressionless, but it wasn't his forget-it, it-didn't-happen, and don't-bring-it-up-again face. This was something else. Nori had seen this expression before on a venge, when he'd killed three raiders in their ambush overlooks. The three men had tried to throw down their bows, to give up. Wakje hadn't even twitched as he'd shot them out of their perches. She'd seen that expression again on the coast, when Wakje had broken a man's solar plexus. The mugger had drawn a knife on Nori. Uncle Wakje had disarmed the man with a slap, then had driven his fingers straight into the other man's torso. Then he'd walked her away, leaving the mugger to suffocate as his lungs forgot to work. She'd seen it, too, when Wakje put down a dnu, as if the creature was nothing. This time it was directed at her.

She tried to school her face to the impassive mask she'd learned so young, but Rishte snarled at the hurt from Wakje's rejection.

"Wolfwalker." Wakje said the word like a flat curse. "You've bonded, like your mother."

"Yes, Uncle Wakje," she said quietly. "I am bonding to the wolves." She had to force her voice to be steady. She knew he had always feared her mother. Papa said it was because he feared what Dione saw when she looked at him through the eyes of the wolves.

Payne stepped forward. "It happened last night."

Wakje looked at the young wolfwalker as if she had sprouted claws.

Nori saw the expression settle deep in his eyes. The rejection was a physical thing, like a fist to the gut.

Wakje had been with her and Payne almost constantly since their birth, guarding, teaching. He treated her as if she was blood-kin, not just the child of a man he followed. He was a second father to her, but he looked at her now as though she were a lepa.

"It's new, Wakje," Payne said quickly. "She's still getting used to it. She'll be better in a few days. You know that. By end-ninan, you won't even notice."

Bonded. To the wolves. There was a hole in Wakje's chest, as if a war bolt had struck through him without his knowlege. And fear—there was fear when he looked at the wolfwalker. He'd been a caravan guard for more than two decades, but a raider for almost three. It was wolfwalkers who had tracked him then, wolfwalkers who had scouted for the venges that tried to kill him for the rabid animal he'd been. The Wolfwalker herself, Nori's mother, had always made him uneasy. He'd always known that his Nori-girl would turn in time to the wolves, become a wolfwalker like Dione. Now he saw the grey in her eyes, felt the breath of the wolf curl her lips. She had become the one thing he feared, the thing that had judged him before and found him barely worthy to live.

He sucked in a slow, cold breath as he saw how she poised at the trailhead. Something tightened in his jaw, and he was surprised by a flare of anger. He'd taught her from birth, taught her everything he knew about tracking, riding, weapons, surviving. This was what she did with it? The fury that blasted over his fear surprised him as much as her bond. He savored it and let it color his voice till it was hard as iron. "This—this bond is why you think you can track them. Why you would start off now on the trail."

Nori nodded, keeping her face as expressionless as his.

He slapped her.

Her eyes widened before the blow struck, but she didn't block. His thick, callused hand was the flat of a shovel against her cheek. She actually hit the ground on her behind.

Payne sucked in his breath. Fentris and Hunter started to slam forward, but Payne grabbed Hunter's arm and jerked him back. Fentris halted uncertainly. "Don't," Payne said sharply.

"He just hit her," Hunter snapped. "For no reason."

Wakje ignored the Tamrani. Payne glanced at his uncle and said softly, "There's always a reason."

"A reason to beat a lady?"

Payne just tightened his grip. "She's a scout out here, not a Sidisport lily. Do not interfere."

The wolfwalker stared up at her uncle in disbelief. Then her lips curled back and she flew to her feet. Her eyes were blinded by lupine violence, and her mind was a tumult of snarls. Wakje waited until she was almost fully up. Then he slapped her again, reaching through her guard with the ease of a man who had spent five decades killing for a living.

This time, she half spun before hitting the ground like a rock.

It stunned her. Her uncle had shoved her more than hit her— he'd have broken her cheek if he'd used force—but her palms and knees were bruised from the roots and the small rocks on the side of the road. Her cheek burned from his hand. She got to her feet more slowly.

Hunter's hand had snapped to his blade. Payne had an even harder grip on the Tamrani's arm. "Don't," he repeated sharply, softly. "It is a lesson."

"He could kill her," Hunter snapped.

"He'd never hurt her."

"Are you insane?"

Payne shifted so that he was between the man and his uncle. "And he could have his sword in and out of your gut three times before you could draw that blade."

"You coward." Hunter almost hissed the curse. "You're her brother."

"Shut up, Tamrani. You know nothing."

Hunter stared at Payne. The young man had not backed down. In fact, Payne's face had lost all semblance of youth and was now as hard as his uncle's. The young man's fingers were digging so hard into Hunter's bicep that he'd need a prybar to get himself loose. Hunter forced himself to still. This wasn't his family. It wasn't his fight. Not yet, he promised silently.

Wakje ignored them both. He stared at Nori. "Idiot." His voice flayed the grey from her mind like a knife. "Pag-brained idiot."

The curse shocked her even more than the slap. "Uncle Wakje?" She formed the words uncertainly.

Her voice was still too low, too close to a growl. He hardened his eyes. "I'd rather be uncle to the brain-dead egg of an ass-worm than to a piss-minded bollusk like you." He pointed to the forest. "Track two armed men who have already targeted you. In heavy brush on an obvious game trail. With your eyes blinded by a godsdamn mutt of a wolf? By the spoiled curds of all nine hells, you show the judgment of an infant fresh from the womb."

Nori swallowed. She was beginning to understand.

"You've borrowed the few weapons you're carrying," Wakje went on in a hard, relentless voice. "You haven't reset your draw weight or rebalanced your blade, and like a boy green from the city heights, you left bow and blade behind—" He jerked a nod toward Kettre. "—as if your teeth and nails would do. Then you stuck yourself on the barrier line like a tin can in a target match, and trusted your reflexes to duck. By all nine moons, you missed the one knife throw you did get off when the raider was right before you."

A spot of color appeared high in each of her cheeks.

"By the piss of a dozen poolah, you can't even answer a question without reacting like an animal."

Her flush deepened around the pale marks of his hand.

He took a step forward until he towered over her like a brick wall. "Where is your trail kit?" he demanded harshly. "Your aid kit? Your rations and shelter? Where are your extra war bolts? By the seventh hell, you've thrown away everything I've taught you, everything you've learned from birth, in less than twenty hours." He was so angry his heavy bones were lined and white, and his cold eyes were like axes over his cheeks.

Nori's face burned, but she couldn't look away. She could see the killer in him clearly. She'd always known it was there inside him. But this time, it was full-face, bared, and stark, and all she could do was bite her lip and take it.

He gestured sharply at her. "Is that what the wolf-bond does for you? Makes you brainless as a hairworm?"

"I'm sorry—"

"Sorry?" He cut off her apology like a cook chopping rot from a carrot. "Will sorry save your life? Will sorry save Payne if he followed you down that trail? Out here, it's you who is responsible for the both of you. When the hell were you thinking of him? And wipe that sorry off your lips. Sorry never changed the act. It never grew back a hand or an arm. The best that sorry ever did was fill an open grave. By the spit of a two-headed lepa, I taught you better than that—"

The growl behind him made him whirl.

Danger, threat.

"No!" Nori cried out.

The yearling skidded to a halt and now poised, caught by the wolfwalker's cry. But his bristle was up and his fangs bared as he eyed the ex-raider like prey.

Wakje froze like ice.

The wolf edged closer like a bihwadi before it leaps.

Nori shoved herself between the wolf and her uncle. *No,* she snarled. *Back down. Back off.*

The yearling didn't budge.

Wakje stared at the wolf. In his fear, he didn't see its youth or the lack of breadth in its chest. He saw only his demon, but fear had always made him furious. His face tightened till the heavy bones now stood out like stone. "You call the animal to save you? You'd use the beast in your head instead of your brains— just like your mother. Just like Ember Dione." He said it deliberately, knowing it would sting. "And just like her, you'll need your brother and father and the Wolven Guard—" he spat the term. "—and even those Tamrani forever at your side to keep you safe, if that's how you'd use the bond."

"I'd never—I don't—" She felt a spark of anger herself. She drew herself up, refusing to back down. "You don't know what you're saying."

He leaned forward, heedless of the wolf. She could see him now, he thought. She could see the killer he really was, and the wolf would tell her to turn on him like a lepa. She was different from her mother, more feral since birth. She'd always been on the edge.

"I've watched your mother for twenty-three years," he ground out. "I've seen a dozen wolfwalkers. They all use the bond, but she's the worst. She relies on that link for everything from her sight to her strength to her reaction times. She's more wolf than woman, and she goes into a fight that way—like an animal, not the ranking master she is. She lets them in, and they fight inside her hands, and she doesn't *think*. Half her scars are from the wolves, because it wasn't a woman fighting."

"I'm not—"

"Your mother?" he cut in. "Aren't you?" He cursed her long then. "Were you thinking when you started down that trail?"

She stared at him while Rishte snarled through her head. She stared while her face burned like fire. He saw the instant she realized he was right. Her gaze changed, sharpened, as if the wolf had been thrust back.

The yearling snarled audibly, but Nori snapped back with her mind. *Don't interfere,* she sent harshly. *He is pack leader here, not me, and this is my lesson, not yours.*

Wakje waited.

Her voice was low. "I am not my mother."

"There is wolf in your eyes right now."

She seemed to straighten farther. "And I don't need him. I don't need Payne or you or anyone else on the trails. You're right, I wasn't thinking for a minute. But I am now. And I have not forgotten anything you've taught me, neither for me nor for Payne."

"Prove it." He glared at her. "Defend yourself." He struck her like a club.

She barely had time to slide the blow to avoid some of its force. She was only distantly aware that Payne and Kettre had thrown Hunter back. She barely had time to snap at Rishte to stay away before Wakje struck again.

It was an overhand right with a left hook to the head, blindingly fast. She didn't see it; she only felt it coming. She ducked inside, and his knee caught her in the gut just as her double fist hit up under his ribs. He grunted and brought an elbow down across her back. She staggered, but she was already into a twisted horse, and the blow slid off. His club-hands reached over her back for her throat, but she whipped around and caught the one and wrenched the pressure hold. Her heel snapped up into his inner thigh even as he spun her away.

They stared at each other. Wakje was balanced almost casually on the balls of his feet; Nori was half crouched before him. Wakje wasn't even breathing hard. Nori's heart was a hammer. The ex-raider nodded. "Better," he said curtly. "That was you, not the beast in your body."

Nori straightened. Rishte had slunk back to the edge of the barrier bushes, and his golden eyes gleamed with rage.

He cut her off with a gesture. "Remember," he ordered harshly. Deliberately, he ignored the wolf. He could already feel its fangs biting into his flesh, ripping his ribs free of his torso. He forced his voice to remain steady. "You'll know them again?" he demanded coldly.

She knew what he meant. "I saw them all clearly."

He glanced at Payne. "And you?"

"The lead rider only."

Hunter gave Wakje a hard look. "One of them was from my caravan. He's out of Sidisport. Name of Hoinse."

They looked at him in surprise, as if they'd forgotten his presence. He smiled grimly. He wasn't usually overlooked, and the feeling was irritating—almost enough to cover his sense of guilt at bringing this down on Nori.

Nori looked to the wolf, then the woods. "I could track them, Uncle Wakje."

He regarded her coldly. "Even without the wolf in your eyes, it's too dangerous. One rider as bait to draw them in, the other sets up the ambush. We did that all the time when we expected a venge to follow."

Hunter felt a chill at the ex-raider's expression. The man's voice was calm, but his eyes were still flat and hard. It was almost as if the attackers were already dead, and that catching them would be an afterthought.

"Mount up," Wakje said shortly. "We'll discuss this tonight with Ki."

Silently, belatedly, Nori pulled Payne's glove from her belt and handed it back to her brother. There were blood drops spattered on the fingers, and the scratches were deep enough that the leather would probably soon tear. It was the arrow hole in the seam of the middle finger that made him shiver. He made his voice light. "I should make you replace these. Do you know how much a good pair of gloves cost?"

She smiled faintly. "Good thing they weren't good gloves." She untangled the reins of her dnu and swung up into the saddle. She was still twitchy from the attack. *Follow,* she sent to the wolf.

Rishte snarled in her mind but loped onto the frontage trail.

Fentris and Kettre reined in after the three. Hunter brought up the rear with a thoughtful expression. He wasn't sure which had angered him more: being an afterthought to Nori, or being ignored by the Wolven Guard. What he was beginning to realize was that the Wolfwalker's Daughter was more tightly bound to her family than even he had suspected. In some ways, it was reassuring. In others, it made him uneasy. If Payne or Wakje or someone else she cared for was threatened, Hunter suspected that she would throw away every secret she knew to save her family. Absently he fingered his belt. For the rest of the ride, he was silent.

XVII

*"If it startled you,
Then you really weren't watching
    well at all, now,
Were you?"*

—Grasp's mother in *Playing with Swords,* traditional staging

They caught up with the caravan in the early afternoon. Nori let Payne give their report and her apology to the Hafell while she headed for her sling bed. They didn't tell Brean of the attack, and even Nori agreed with that. Admitting that raiders wanted them dead wasn't likely to make them more welcome. And it wasn't all that surprising, not with parents like theirs. The Ell and Hafell would have taken that into account when they offered the *keyo* berths.

In spite of her exhaustion, she didn't sleep easy. Every ring-runner who cantered past the caravan made her flicker awake with her heart pounding and her hand grabbing for a knife. Wagon sounds that had been lullabies to her as a child—the snap and creak of leather, the sighing of wagon springs, the stressing of wall panels as they slipped and eased back into position—were now startlingly loud. Like watchers themselves, she could feel Wakje and Payne, then Ki and Liam, taking turns riding close outside, beside the cozar wagon. That, and her dreams were haunted by snarls.

She woke again fitfully to darkness. The wagon had been parked; she could hear the sounds of fireside, smell the rich blends of stuffed hostina baking on the lids of the ubiquitous stew pots. She could smell the spicy Diton cooking and hear the nasal voice of an evening teacher above the conversations.

It disturbed Rishte that she had not leapt away from the humans now that he'd finally awakened her. He pulled like a tether, and she had to fight not to jerk to her feet and race to him. All afternoon, he had loped along the ridges to keep pace with the caravan. By evening, he was twenty kays away from his pack, and uncertain of Nori so far below in the wagons.

I'm here, she returned, but he howled again, as if he couldn't hear her. She closed her eyes and focused her thoughts into a single spear. *I'm here. I'm hereimhereimhere.*

Lonely, he seemed to send. *No pack. No trees or dirt or warm darkness. Come to the ridge, wolfwalker. Lonelylonelylonely.*

Trees? Dirt? There was a possessive note to the sending, as if he'd lost land or, rather, the sense of safety of known territory. *Soon,* she returned. *Soon, soon.* But the noise of the evening cookfires intruded. Cutlery clattered, voices clumped and rose and subsided, dnu chittered in the stables. She lost her focus. She fought to find it again, squeezing her eyes shut to see and hear only the grey. For a moment, she thought she had him.

—wolfwalkerwolfwal—

Then it was just the faint sea of the packsong, subsiding and seething at the far corners of her mind.

She winced as she swung her legs down, stood, and turned up the lantern. She had bruises on her knees and thighs, and she bit back a groan as she pulled off the shirt she'd slept in. She was alone, but still couldn't help glancing around surreptitiously before slipping Hunter's shirt from under her pillow. Quickly, she pulled it on. Its softness was a sin over the scabs that tightened on her back. She reveled in it for a long moment. Then she stuffed a knife in her waistband, caught up a towel, some clothes, and her toiletries, and jumped stiffly down from the gate.

Outside, Payne straightened. "You look like the second hell."

"Hell is as hell does," she returned automatically.

"And we'll be there and back before dawn," he finished the quote. "Heading for the showers?"

She nodded, and he fell into step beside her. In spite of the overcast night, the circle wasn't really dark. Lanterns hung at every other wagon, yet the shadows that lurked beneath the wagons were like monsters under dozens of beds.

There were few who preferred a shower to dinner, and Nori

had the bathhouse to herself, while Payne waited discreetly outside. As usual, she washed quickly, scrubbing her skin aggressively and dressing quickly in clean clothes. Then she washed out Hunter's dirty shirt and her own soiled garments.

"Ready?" Payne asked as she met him at the door.

Both of them studied the aisles warily as they walked. With three wagon trains, the circle was crowded. As usual, half the outer wall was a series of corrals, open-air stalls, stables, and firewood bins. The second half was a line of fountains, bathhouses, washhouses, and waste and fire pits where debris and trash were dealt with. Payne raised a hand in a silent wave at the repair pavilion as they passed. It was still busy, which wasn't unexpected, given the number of mishaps they'd had.

Inside the circle, the wagons were lined up in double rows in loose groups of four. This close to the Test ninan, the quads had been crushed together until there were only narrow aisles between them. One access road led in to the circle on one side, and another one led out. Both gates were always guarded. Aside from the gates, there were only narrow channels through the spiky barrier bushes that created the circle's outer boundary. Nori scanned the two breaks she saw by the firewood stacks. If she was careful, she could slip out later to the yearling, and no one else need know. Once the firewood bins were closed, this part of the circle was unused till dawn.

All three firesides were hidden by the crowded wagons, so the aisle they went down was barely more than a black column of lowered gates, sling beds staked out like sagging fishnets, and a line of posts from which dangled the guild and family markers. Besides the sleeping dogs and a single woman who climbed down from a gate in the distance, there was almost no movement. There wouldn't be, Nori knew, not till dinner was over.

There was a murmur of voices to the left of the stables, and Nori listened before dismissing them. Elder Connaught was always being hit up for favors, even while he tended his dnu. "Is Uncle Wakje at dinner?" she asked Payne.

"He and Ki went into town to ask around. They took Mye and Liam for color." Instinctively, Payne kept his voice low. "Most folk won't go into town till after dinner, when the festival really fires up."

"Speaking of dinner, I can smell the pelan from here."

"Leanna is saving you a plate. By the way, I traded off your tower duty today for one tomorrow."

"With my thanks." Her towel bundle loosened, and she rolled the clean clothes up more tightly, then stretched her shoulders to keep them from stiffening up. "I don't think I could sit a saddle if my life depended on it."

Payne refrained from pointing out that it just might. "Don't thank me yet. Brean's got a list of *andyen* duties for you to work off for disappearing." He hid a grin at her mutter. He could have sworn she'd said he should do them with her since it was he who'd called the search.

She said instead, "So what did you find out about Hunter?"

"Hunter," he frowned. "That's the shorter one, right? The skinny one?"

She raised one eyebrow, then looked down at her legs, her arms, and finally at her scratched-up hands.

"What are you doing?"

"Just checking to see if I was born yesterday."

Payne gave her an old-fashioned look. "Alright, so I talked with Memory Dahl."

She hid a smile of her own. The most important people in a cozar train weren't the Ells or Hafells, but the memories, the people who had inherited the engineered genes for perfect recall. They had become the walking libraries on whom the fortunes—and lives—of a caravan could rest. Payne almost always bid for their caravan based on the memory talker, just as Nori bid based on route.

These days, Payne was always bargaining for a position on the memory's wagon seat. Kettre said it was to learn as much as he could file away in his far-too-organized brain. In Memory Dahl's case, that was considerable. The woman could recite the structure of four of the original nine counties, from Lloroi to elders, to guild and trade leaders, to merchants and craftsmen, even to the outlying farmlands. Memory Dahl even understood the tangled hierarchy of the Houses of Sidisport, where House leaders juggled status the same way young boys juggled excuses.

This year, Payne had bribed Memory Dahl with a fine-tooled, leather-backed comb, a packet of eastern tea, and an oddly wrapped package from Nori. It was the latter that had made the old woman's eyes light up enough that she granted Payne two full afternoons, not just two hours, for their scheduled travel. He scowled at his sister. At the time, he'd have given two fingernails to know how she'd found out that the old woman's driving seat could use new shocks. When he'd said that to Nori, she'd bargained him first into doing her fireside duty, and only then confessed that old bones were like those of tree sprits, brittle and easily rattled. Memory Dahl always needed new shocks. Payne had been stuck on fireside cleanup for two days while Nori lounged on the wagon gate and plunked on her dinged-up guitar.

He knew he shouldn't complain. By the end of the fourth day riding, he'd had a list of merchants and fighters who had bid and lost out on berths in Ell Tai's caravan, a gossip tally of the ten Sidisport *chovas* who had won this caravan's guest lottery, descriptions of five raiders supposedly causing trouble in this district—not that he expected to see them himself, what with the crowd of outriders in the train—and the detailed history of a pair of frauds. The last two had earned *bok'vah* among the cozar several years ago for abusing the aid they were offered.

"So, what did you find out?" Nori prompted.

Payne gathered his thoughts. "Condari's out of Wyakit, one of the first Tamrani Houses, but you knew that. If you didn't," he added dryly, "you deserve another Wakje-slap." He nodded at her flush. She hadn't bruised, but that was only because it was Wakje giving the lesson. Had it been Aunt Oroan, she'd have been marked far into next ninan. "The short take is that your Brithanas has been in the western counties for the last four years, is well respected among the traders, and is said to be a fair hand in a fight."

"He's not my Brithanas," Nori said sharply, but she was disgruntled. "A fair hand—did you get that from the memory or from one of your new girlfriends?"

He shrugged. "Does it matter? City gossip has it that he came back to Sidisport on a summons from his mother. Now he's heading up to Shockton, and he's already got two slots in the council meetings, early in the ninan. That means he's offering or proposing something, and that he wants the answer fast, before he goes back to town. It also means he's powerful. Two slots early on gives him a chance to go before the council again if he doesn't like the answer. That's two slots more than most elders get."

"It's amazing," she said dryly, "how much you learn from your doe-eyed liaisons."

"If you'd try a few liaisons once in a while, you might learn something of interest yourself."

She ignored that. "First House, first century," she murmured.

"Aye. They're not as rich as some, but they've been around, well, forever." Payne pulled her to a stop, glanced around the deserted firewood bins, and lowered his voice even farther. "They're powerful, Nori-girl. You want to know how he got his rep-name? Three years ago, he was taking a trade caravan across Bilocctar. He'd gone ahead with one of his people to negotiate a crossing, and the wagons were hit by raiders. For some reason, Brithanas had no gold to his name at the time, but he put together three different venges on favors alone and started hunting raiders. He tracked down every one of the attackers within two ninans, and then he hit their backers—and you know that caused some ripples. He said it would make them think twice before looking at his cargo again. He's had almost no trouble since. He used to be called Noble Hunter. Now it's just Hunter." Payne shook his head. "Nori-girl, he's got ties to half the councils in half of the original counties. You might as well have asked an elder to guard your back as ride the night with him."

She hid her growing unease. "I'm starting to realize that—" She broke off. As the noise from the fireside got louder, she had been absently straining to hear the softer night sounds. Now the sense of what she'd not quite heard finally filtered up to her consciousness.

Payne's hand went to his knife at her stillness, but she held up her hand to freeze him. She turned, listened, and took two steps back toward the stables. It had been a small sound almost lost against the distant noise of fireside, but it had not been a natural one. She cocked her head. A flurry of small scufflings came from the right. Her violet eyes narrowed, but as realization hit, her feet were already moving.

Payne didn't waste breath to curse. He was on her heels when she skidded around the stable corner. He had a single glimpse of the struggling figures—one tall, grey-haired, gagged, and wild-eyed, with his arms bound behind him; and the other, just as tall but built like a stevedore, hauling the first along. Nori launched herself like an arrow. Silent as she was, the husky man sensed her. He whipped his head around, had time to shift. All three went down in a tangle of flailing limbs. Nori grabbed for the elder. Payne saw the attacker's arm rise, the sheen of steel, the knife begin to fall. His heart froze even as he felt his legs bunch and go. Then Nori twisted off the elder, slammed her knuckles into the thick man's gut, kicked his knee out, and bared her teeth like a wolf. In the darkness, her growl shocked the man for the hair of a second. Then her claw-hand struck the inside of his arm and tore deep into muscle, and she slammed her other elbow up under his knife wrist. The raider jerked. His blade cut cloth instead of flesh. She stiff-fisted his gut as the blade slashed back, and jerked away just in time. He missed with the knife, but not with his other fist. She tumbled back, and he lunged to his feet.

Then Payne tackled him like an ax on a log. The kick meant for Nori missed, and the man's knee smashed into Payne's hip; a fist glanced off Payne's cheekbone. The two men broke apart, scrambled back to their feet barely long enough to leap for each other. The knife cut jerkin and scored Payne's ribs, and Payne grabbed the man's forearm. Nori lunged in for his wrist. Her hand slid over a meaty fist, caught one thick finger, and wrenched it back hard. She felt the bone tear free through tendons and tissue. Then his elbow hit her ribs. She missed the full pressure hold, and staggered back to her knees, unable to catch her breath. Payne's other fist slammed again and again up into the man's gut. The knife finally dropped, and the two men crashed into the barrier hedge.

Well-shorn bushes cushioned their fall, but spikes inside the hedge grazed Payne's scalp; another pierced the top of his shoulder. The other man jerked as thorns cut his face. Neither cried out. The thick man thrust Payne sideways and scrambled to his feet, bleeding from his cheek and hand. He pulled a second knife from his boot and threw it at the bound form of the elder even as he turned to run. Nori shoved the old man down hard. The elder fell awkwardly to his knees, and the blade split the air between them. Payne struggled out of the shrubs, and Nori lunged back to her feet. The raider pulled a third knife and poised, ready to throw.

On the balls of her feet Nori stilled. Payne froze. The raider backed carefully away. He didn't want to throw his last knife, but if he had to, he would. Nori slid one step toward him, and he shifted menacingly.

"Nori-girl, no," Payne breathed. In the dark, he couldn't tell if her violet eyes were clear, but he could almost see the growl deep in her throat, not quite under her breath.

Challenge. Fight, Rishte snarled.

Her lips curled back. *I want him. Want his flesh in my teeth. Want his blood for my brother's.*

The man stepped back again and found the shrub channel. His dark expression found hers with grim promise. He threw himself into the dark.

"Dik spit." Payne scrambled to his feet. "Is every raider in the county coming down on the cozar? What the hell is wrong with everyone? Nori-girl, are you alright?"

His words were loud—too loud. Her ears were filled with her pulse, her breathing, their breathing, their sounds. She stared after the attacker.

Human-thing, running. Feet hard on the ground. Blood, hot. Close, still close.

She wanted to chase, to taste skin and blood.

"Nori?" Payne said sharply. "Are you okay?"

She didn't turn, but her lips moved. She caught the snarl before it got out and formed the human words, "Aye. Just bruised." Her jaw ached and her ribs were burning. "You?"

"Scratched, and I'll have a sore knee tomorrow." He helped

the elder to the man's feet while she stared down the barrier bushes. It was Rishte's ears, not hers, that heard the soft, quick steps. The attacker wasn't some bumbling idiot green from first rank. He'd been trained enough to be able to dodge both Nori and Payne without blinking, to let go rather than risk getting caught, and to run quietly on dark, uneven trails. She didn't even suggest that they chase him out onto the bridle path that ringed the cozar circle.

Rishte eased closer in the forest, so that Nori could almost feel his fur on the ferns. *Challenged, triumph. Pack safe, safe.* His satisfaction with her was clear.

She snarled her agreement mentally. She started to turn, but realized her teeth were still bared. She took a breath, cleared her expression, then stalked back to the elder.

Payne had brushed Connaught off, but the older man's eyes were still wide. The elder jerked his head toward the shrub line and mmphed at them both. Nori shook her head. "It's too late to raise the alarm. It's full dark. He's already got his dnu, and it would take time for us to saddle up and follow—if we could."

Payne scanned the bushes. "I agree." He looked back at the elder. "Also, we've three wagon trains here, dozens of individual families, and the town crowd in and out of the circle like juice through a sieve. There'd be a full panic at the fireside with all the parents screaming for their children. He'd get away in the confusion alone, or be able to try again. And the cozar won't go out in this darkness. Not with children in the train. That's just asking for hostages. Considering—" He glanced at Nori, and said instead, "—other things, it might be just what they want."

The elder mmphed at him as Nori tried to loosen his gag. The knot was tight enough that it had cut the old man's mouth. His lips had already swollen around it, and his breathing was restricted and labored. The wolfwalker's eyes narrowed at the knot. The attacker had had no intention of ever removing the gag. Connaught had been destined for death, not ransom. "Stay calm, breathe slowly," she told the older man. "This will take a minute." She could almost see the thin pulse in his neck.

Payne snagged a lantern from one of the darkened wagons. He lit it, then squatted to study the tracks.

Connaught's bony fingers trembled as they jerked futilely at his bonds. "Wait," she told him. "Be still. This may cut a bit." She drew her blade and worked it sideways under the leather. A moment later, the gag was free, and she started in on his wrists.

"Damn raider spawn." The older man choked out the curse around bloody lips. "Black Wolf," he managed belatedly. "NeBentar. Moonsblessing on you both."

"You're alright, then?" she asked.

"Yes, although a few more minutes, and it would have been a different story. If I were ten years younger—"

"You did alright," Payne cast back. "If you hadn't slowed him down enough to make some noise, you'd have been outside the barrier bushes and dead before anyone knew it."

Nori nodded. The elder's wrists were puffy around the thongs. "Payne, give me a hand here."

His eyes were still on the shrubs. "Can you hear anything?"

She knew what he meant. "He went west along the bridle path, then up into the woods. That's all I can tell. He wasn't one of the arch—"

"Aye," Payne cut in quickly. "I didn't recognize him, either. Take this back." He handed her the lantern. "I'll get the thongs off."

"I was in the stables," Connaught explained. "Sharkun—Sharkun Backhills—had just left for the fireside, and I was going to follow as soon as I checked the tack." Payne nodded as he worked at the leather. Elder Connaught had traveled long enough over the years that he double-checked his gear every night. "That man came out of nowhere. One minute, I was alone, the next, I was down in the straw with that rag in my mouth and my hands behind my back."

Nori thought back to her night run, the bodies, and the ring-runner who'd been set upon. "Did he say anything?"

"Yes." The elder's voice was dry. "Not to struggle if I wanted to live. By the way he tied the gag, I thought that was a bit moot." He added unsteadily, "He couldn't have picked a better time to take me. Everyone is at fireside or in town at festival. With three caravans here and all the Test traffic, there's good trade going on in both places. Lots of riders in from the roads, songsters in from the other trains. There might be ten people still trying to sleep, but the rest are staying out." He shivered. "Makes me wonder if Thella really did ride away at all."

Payne frowned down at the bonds as he worked the blade under gently. "You mean the elder who left back at the Chain River?"

"The one from Bitston, yes." His voice grew sharp. "You know that no one actually saw her go. Her gear and dnu were simply gone when the morning count was taken. If she didn't leave on her own, if this happened to her, too . . ." His voice trailed off ominously.

"Damn lucky we were near," Payne muttered.

The old man nodded tersely. "I'd have thought, with the Tamrani among us, you two would be at fireside."

"Nori didn't wake up till a bit ago," Payne explained. "She wanted to . . . hang on, I've almost got it. Clean up first," he finished. "There. Easy," he warned as the older man eased his arms forward. "You should see the healer. Those are pretty bloody."

"I'll see the Ell first," Connaught stated flatly. "This wants action." But the old man was cradling his wrists and clenching his hands at the same time. Nori could imagine the needles of pain that pierced those old, stringy muscles. The elder gave her a shaky grin as he saw her worry. "It's a fine way to start your council duty, Black Wolf—saving a council leader."

Nori's eyes widened as she realized what she'd done.

"Here now," the older man said. "What's the matter?"

She almost backed away. "Oh, hells, I didn't mean—"

"Black Wolf has other duties right now, Elder Connaught," Payne cut in smoothly, stepping in front of her. He brushed at some of the blood that had dripped on the older man's tunic. "And Noriana maDione is on the trade lists, Elder Connaught, not the council lists. She will take up her council duty in time, when our parents approve it, but not before the Test ninan."

"Of course, of course. Your Test." The elder nodded, winced, and touched the corner of his torn mouth.

"Besides," Payne added, "any council duty Nori takes on would have to be approved by the Lloroi."

"Handy to have him as an uncle, eh? Lets your family get first pick for your skills?" Connaught tried to chuckle, but he was still shaking, and the sound came out more like a gasp. It frightened the old man. He took a couple of breaths and blinked. Payne and Nori looked far too serious for the comments he'd just made. "Ariye has always looked out for her neighbors," he told them slowly. "I consider this no more than the same." Interesting, he thought, how relieved Black Wolf looked. He took two steps, sucked in a breath, and started to crumple. Payne grabbed his arm, and Nori caught his elbow. For a moment, he sagged in their grip. Then he straightened. His wrinkled hand trembled as it went to his head. "Must have hit me harder than I thought."

Nori ran her hand over his scalp and found the goose egg.

"Can you walk?" Payne asked in a low voice.

"He was hit in the back, not the front," Nori told him. "It'll be nausea and eyesight, not walking to worry about. The lump doesn't look too big, though, and he was only out for a moment—"

Connaught's pale eyes sharpened. "How do you know that, Black Wolf?"

She shrugged. "I heard you talking a few moments before."

"You heard me being attacked?"

"No. We were down here, too far away, and he must have been very quiet going in."

"Or quiet while he was waiting," suggested Payne.

The other two looked at him sharply.

Payne shrugged at the old man. "You go to the stables every night. You stay late to tend your gear." He nodded at the elder's swollen, bloody hands. "You might want to watch how much time you spend alone in the future, Elder Connaught. Or at least change the pattern of your daily tasks."

The older man nodded slowly. "I will do that, neBentar." He glanced at Nori and said to Payne, "If I thought you'd take the duty, I'd hire the two of you in a minute to ride *keyo* for me." He smiled wryly at Nori's expression. "Don't worry, Black Wolf. I won't insist." He started to turn away, but stopped. "You might want to watch out for Elder Mato, though. Someone's told him to push for duty from you, and he's never liked taking no for an answer. He thinks it makes him look smaller—as if he's not small-minded enough," the old man added derisively.

Payne and Nori exchanged puzzled glances. Who would tell an elder to hound Nori for duty? The cozar knew it was more likely to push her out of the caravan, not into a council job.

A couple of cozar wandered down the aisle toward them. "Aye, Elder," one called. The other waved, then peered toward the little knot. "Everything alright?"

The older man started to open his mouth to answer, but Payne put his hand on the elder's arm. Connaught stiffened. Payne shook his head slightly. Even in the dim light, his warning expression was clear.

Connaught cleared his throat. "Fine, thanks," he called back. "Just a late negotiation."

The cozar chuckled and climbed up in their wagon.

Connaught turned to Payne. His voice was low but curt. "Explain yourself, neBentar."

"Elder Connaught," Payne said formally, "I respect your position. But I must ask that you remain quiet about this until we discuss it with my uncles."

The older man's gaze slid to Nori, then back to Payne. The wolfwalker watched him warily, and Payne's violet gaze was as sharp. So, he thought, they were up to something. He wondered if it was for their parents or the Lloroi. "What about my attacker?"

"Speak to the Ell and Hafell, privately. We'll warn the gate guards, and we'll keep a watch for him ourselves. I doubt he'll try again."

"Doesn't mean someone else won't."

"You've got three outriders assigned to you."

Connaught snorted. "Sidisport *chovas*. One does nothing but crack sour jokes. I caught the second one eyeing my lockbox like a worlag does a crippled hare, and the woman is small enough that she couldn't fight off a stickbeast, let alone protect me from half a raider."

Nori raised her eyebrows. "Where are your own guards?"

"I always loan them to others when I'm riding with Ell Tai.

However—" He gave his wrists a sober look. "—I believe this time I'll ask them back."

Payne cleared his throat.

"Don't worry, neBentar. I'll keep quiet for a night. You've asked, and I owe you that, at least."

Payne let out his breath. "We'll walk you back."

"I wouldn't turn you down," agreed the elder dryly. "Though you might want to change before you attend fireside."

Payne looked down at his dirt-stained knees, front, and elbows. Then back at Nori. Her knees were splotched with dirt from the stable path. Judging by the way she stood, her right knee ached as much as his did. Her sleeve was torn, and the hem of her shirt was ripped. "Aye, and shower again, as the moons would have it." He did a double take, then frowned at his sister as they fell into step. "Nori-girl," he said slowly, "is that my shirt you're wearing?"

She looked down. "Uh, yes," she admitted guiltily. "I needed to wash mine."

He muttered a curse. "Just once, could you steal your clothes from Wakje?"

XVIII

In the forest, hide the worlags,
In the long grass, hide the rasts.

   —Nadugur saying

Payne and Nori dropped Connaught off at the healer's wagon, then headed for the gate guard. The *chovas* B'Kosan and another outrider were doing the guard duty, and they gave Nori and Payne a sober once-up, once-down look while Payne described the raider. When Payne finished, Nori added only, "He had long fingers and thick bones. He'd ridden or walked through clove bush recently, and he had spicepot and ale, not wine or grog, at dinner."

"Hells, Black Wolf," said B'Kosan sourly. "Two dozen of us had spicepot, and half of everyone drinks ale. I'd be taking in some more in myself if I wasn't standing guard." He nodded down the road. "Besides, almost everyone will come back at the same time when festival's over. We could miss a bollusk in that crowd."

Payne hid a scowl. Some *chovas* never took duty seriously if it was only for berth and bread, not pay. "Do your best," he said shortly.

As they strode away, Nori said softly, "We should tell Brean about today."

"The raiders on the road? No." Payne shook his head. "We need to think about this first."

When they got back to the wagon, Nori felt like a stiff old woman climbing up beside her brother. Her entire right side felt like it had been hammered, and her hip and jaw had new bruises on top of old ones. She could still feel the weight, the mass of the raider. If Payne hadn't tackled him off her when he did, she would have been dead beneath him.

Her brother caught her expression. "It's alright, Nori-girl."

"Aye, for now." They politely turned their backs to each other to change, and Nori added over her shoulder, "We will have to tell Uncle Wakje and Uncle Ki."

"Aye. Raiders at Bell Rocks, raiders on the road, and now raiders inside the circle? Something's bringing them out like wind on flames." He scowled as he rummaged through his half-empty duffel, tossed it aside, and dragged out his extra gear bag. He finally emptied his gear on the gate, found his extra clothes, and yanked his bloody shirt off over his head.

Nori sat down on the gate, but she couldn't relax. She started when Payne plopped down beside her. At least she wasn't the only one. When three girls tried to sneak past the wagon, Payne almost grabbed for his knife. "Girls," he said sharply.

The three jumped, squealed, and whipped around, clutching each other.

"Best get back to fireside," he told them. "It's not safe in the circle tonight."

"It's The Brother," one whispered. "And Black Wolf."

Nori resisted the urge to roll her eyes.

"Aye?" he prompted.

"Aye," they chorused. They scurried back between the wagons. Nori's voice was dry. "Why not just tell them about the attack?"

He twisted and tossed his toiletries bag back into the now cluttered wagon. "They get the picture now."

"And the myth of The Brother grows."

He grinned, stuffed his gear bag behind him, and leaned back.

Like most cozar wagons, this one could collapse down to a buckboard or be expanded into a shipping transport, or even a trade stall, in six configurations. Empty, it was light enough that four dnu could pull it at a trot all day and hardly know it was there. Payne knew that for a fact. He'd driven harness all his life and even won a few times in the races. Unfortunately, light weight meant little padding, and he shifted uncomfortably as a corner of something poked into one of the new bruises on his back.

Nori didn't notice. She was thinking back to Hunter's words, that he'd recognized one of the raiders on the road. "Tell me more about Hunter," she ordered as he settled in on the gate.

He slanted her a glance. She'd already asked more questions about the Tamrani than he'd known her to ask about anyone. "Before he went to the western counties, there was a bad patch for the family," he finally answered. "Lots of scandal, a fire, his father dead of a heart attack, and him taking off for the west. His mother's now in charge in Sidisport. She's sharp. She's expected to last six or seven more decades before she thinks about bowing out. It's speculation as to why Brithanas hasn't taken the family name as First Son, but he's not lost anything by doing so, not judging by the cost of that shirt you hung up."

She scowled and wished she'd shoved Hunter's shirt back behind another one to dry less visibly.

Payne tugged a handful of undergarments from the bag behind him, then the offending pack of sharpening stones. He tossed both carelessly over his shoulder.

"Moonworms, Payne. Can't you put anything away?" She leaned back and plucked his unused underwear off a box of swords. "Uncle Wakje will use these as polishing rags."

"They go in the second bin."

"I know where they go. Why don't you?"

"Because," he drawled, "I was distracted by a nice little raider you decided to play with after your shower. Before that, I was busy saving your butt on the hedge line on the road. And before that, I was leading a search for a missing sister. I didn't have time to worry about cleaning up the wagon."

Nori swallowed her retort and climbed silently back into the home. Holding the offending garment by two fingers, she pulled his duffel out from behind him and started to repack it.

Payne tossed a pair of rolled-up socks at her feet, along with a bota bag. Silently, she put the bota in its slot, but she stuffed his socks in by his fuel bottle. It would serve him right if they rotted. At the very least, it might teach him to put them away himself. "If Condari's so good," she said, "why haven't I heard of him like his father?" With her back to him, her voice was muffled. She barely caught the water filter he tossed in her direction.

"Because—" Payne explained as if she were a child, knowing it would irritate her further. "—you've a blind spot when it comes to men. Because Brithanas has been out in the western counties for most of the last four years, and because they still talk about Ranakai Ao as if the old man walked on water." Nori gave him a dirty look at his overly patient tone, and Payne hid his grin. He tossed his moccasins into her hands. "Because you never hung around with the city snooties like I did, scooping up the council gossip. And because you're so afraid of what comes out of Sidisport that anyone who lives there is less than a rast in your eyes. Hells, Nori-girl, if the Ell called me on it in council, I'd have to swear by the second moon that you couldn't tell a man from a mudsucker."

Nori flushed. "I'm not so blind that I can't tell a man from a mudsucker, worlag, or lepa."

"No," he answered. "You don't worry whether they're mudsuckers or lepa. You just reject them all."

She stilled.

"Oh, hells, Nori. I didn't mean that the way it came out."

Her voice was quiet. "I do have friends, Payne. Kettre, Surah, Zdravko."

"I know. You just . . ." He shrugged helplessly up at her. "You just don't have very many. Once in a while, try meeting someone new."

"The friends I have think of me as Nori, not just the Wolf-walker's Daughter. And they rarely get me into trouble, unlike some people's friends," she added archly. "Who help them into enough hot water that they're known to half the councils."

"My friends aren't that bad," he protested. "Besides, I can't ride with just one person a year. I'd go batty."

"To each his own, big brother." She dropped back down beside him and let her legs swing absently as she chewed her lip. She stilled as someone paused on the other side of their wagon, but whoever it was moved on. She thought she was hearing Rishte again, too. She poked her head around the side of the wagon and looked toward fireside. She'd have to sneak dinner while others were cleaning up, then snag some scraps for the Grey One. She could take off then, meet the yearling, and work her way back into the forest. "Tell me about the other one, Fentris Shae," she said. Two young women tried to catch Payne's eye from the end of the aisle, and he waved jauntily at the women. She added dryly, "You can flirt with the elders' daughters later."

"Don't think I won't." He grinned slyly. "Those girls can teach a man a lot. I could lecture Papa on politics now."

"Sure, it's all about politics."

He poked her shoulder. "You could take a few lessons yourself, Nori-girl."

She swatted him aside. "Not while you're there to do it for me. Fentris Shae."

He answered obediently, "Fentris Shae, also known as Fentris the Fop, also a First Son, out of Kamaikin House. Memory Dahl says she's seen his men as far east as the territories. He's still here, by the way."

She shot him a sharp look. "I thought he was going on to Shockton with whatever riders he could hook up with."

He shook his head. "He's made some sort of a deal with Brithanas. They'll probably join a faster group once they rest up for the day. I wouldn't have done it, the deal," he added darkly. "The fop is supposed to have stabbed his own brother in the back to become First Son. It never came to the trial block. Rumor has it his father bought him out before disowning him. He's refused every challenge over the insults. Memory Dahl says he's probably twice as rich as Brithanas, but he'll never be able to flaunt it. His wealth makes him acceptable in city society, but half the county thinks he's a coward."

Nori frowned. There was something in the Tamrani's movements that made her think of her uncle Ki. Fentris had killed, she agreed, but she doubted it had been his brother unless his brother had tried to kill him. There was more darkness than guilt in him, as if he'd lost his faith, not his ethics. But she said only, "Let me have my scout book? I want to put in some of our notes before fireside breaks up."

He handed her the punctured book. She gave it a wry look as she poked her finger through the hole left by the war bolt. "That's a lot of rewriting just to make up for saving your ribs."

"And here I thought you loved me like a sister." He grinned faintly. "Besides, I'd say we're even, seeing as how I tackled a raider for you."

She got out Hunter's map and began making the detailed notes she hadn't had time for before. Coordinates, the cliff, the surrounding trail, the bodies in the meadow—everything she could remember as she referred to the map. Then she gleaned what she could from the papers she'd stolen from the raiders, and copied down the raider code. Or rather, she copied what was left of the three lines after the war bolt had punched through them.

Payne watched her for several minutes. "Nori-girl, is there any chance the raiders at Bell Rocks could have survived the worlags?"

She kept her hands steady as she finished her notes and erased her faint marks from Hunter's map. "All three were armed and jumping up as fast as the fourth moon. There were only six or seven worlags. They could easily have lived."

"They would have seen you clearly."

"It was night and firelight."

"There were four moons, and you look like Mama, just younger."

She didn't answer, but he noted that her fingers tightened on the pen.

"Nori-girl," he started.

"It's done, Payne," she said flatly. "There's no help for it."

"And if they come at you again?"

She tucked the papers back in the book. "They weren't the archers who attacked on the road. Besides," she added, "Hunte—I mean, Condari, recognized one of them from his own caravan."

Payne blinked. "You think they followed you to get to Brithanas, not us?"

"I don't know, but Hunter is protecting something. He was too cautious when we met, as if I would be a danger to him."

She glanced around and lowered her voice. "He said Fentris had joined them only a few hours earlier last night. Why would Fentris, a Tamrani rich enough to afford a dozen council ring-runners, ride so urgently himself to meet Condari if he didn't carry something so secret that it had to be delivered in person?"

Payne finished slowly, "And then Brithanas left his group in the middle of the night with the Wolfwalker's Daughter."

She nodded. "It was as if he was just waiting for an excuse to escape someone's prying eyes. Today—"

"Today, you and I, or rather a man and a woman, were attacked on Willow Road. We're both tall, Brithanas and I. We're both dark-haired. We're both wearing scout clothes, even if his cost half a fortune more than mine, but they wouldn't know that until they were close. The timing fits." He nodded to himself. "You hit Willow Road at dawn. You had to have been seen by any number of riders while you waited on the verge. I didn't catch up to you for three more hours. There was plenty of time for someone to figure out that you two were out on the road, alone."

"But we weren't alone," she pointed out. "Fentris was with us, and you, and Uncle Wakje and Uncle Ki, Kettre. There were two entire search parties."

"They couldn't know when we'd reach you after the search was called off," he countered.

Nori shook her head. "We're guessing out to the sixth moon, Payne. Condari's been with his caravan since they left Sidisport. Why follow him to kill him here if they've had him in their sights for days?"

"Shae hadn't caught up with him yet."

"Neither had I." She frowned down at the scout book. "And then there's the attack on Connaught. And the rope being ruined. And now there's the raider code—" She broke off abruptly as they heard a muffled, "My apologies. I didn't see you."

"It's alright," came the low reply. "Just tightening the laces."

Nori's mind sharpened like a knife. With Rishte still on the edge of her mind, his attention speared back with the predator's single-minded focus. She'd slid her knife from her sheath and slipped off the gate in a single movement. Payne was right beside her. Like two shadows, they moved around the neighbor's wagon toward the other aisle.

They moved swiftly, but in the dark, by the time they took those several steps, they couldn't tell who it had been. A burly man and a slender woman were standing together, their heads bowed toward each other, their fingers linked as if in intimacy. The man was in *chovas* gear, but the woman with him was cozar. They broke apart as they noticed Nori, nodded in embarrassment at the wolfwalker, and wandered away toward the food line. Nori frowned after them.

Payne's voice was soft. "Listeners?"

"Who?" she whispered dryly in return. A pair of men were walking away in one direction, a mixed threesome were going the other way. Two women stood near Repa Ripping White's transport, and three outriders threw stars and moons by Nonnie Ninelegs's cook post.

"Do you know any of them?"

"With three caravans camped together and fireside just broken up?" Nori peered through the elongated shadows thrown by the cozar lanterns. "That one there, on the left, walking away. That's Felor Fasthand. No one else could move that way. The others . . . I don't know. The man on the left greeting Denby Handsome—I think he's Tika's friend."

"Tika Reading?"

"Tika Long Way 'Round," she corrected. "She's been hanging out with a couple of the Sidisport *chovas*."

He slipped his knife back in its sheath. "I'll talk with her tonight, and with Felor, and see if they saw anyone near us."

Ki's daughter saw them at the edge of the quad and waved, and Nori waved absently back. The girl quickly put down her pitcher and took a plate from the pile of freshly washed dishes. Nori muttered as they returned to the wagon gate, "So much for a few quiet moments. What did you do, tell Leanna that the minute I woke up, she should feed me?"

"I never said a word," he protested virtuously.

She snorted. "You wouldn't have to. You probably just gave the poor girl that wicked grin, then said how much you envy Mye and Liam for the days when it's her turn to cook."

"It worked for Papa when he was sparking Mama."

"Mama wasn't that young or gullible, and Papa was going to Promise her. Besides, Mama carried a sword, not just a kitchen knife. She could back up her own desires."

Payne glanced at fireside. "Speaking of weapons, after your bow and our rope, there's something I want you to look at." He went into the wagon, closed the door after Nori joined him, and turned the lanterns up high. Silently, he handed her his bow. She found nothing wrong with it, nor with Wakje's bow or quivers. She was on the last of the arrows when Payne handed her the quiver of war bolts he'd taken with him that afternoon. She examined the first one and ran her hand over the fletching. "That's odd. I'd swear . . ." She peered at the fletching. "This can't be right."

Payne watched her closely. "Last night, when I packed it, there was something I couldn't put my finger on, but I didn't find anything wrong with the glue or the bindings."

"It's not either one." She held the bolt close to the lantern. "It's the fletching itself. Look at the cock feather. It's from a left wing. The other two are from a right wing. These arrows would tumble in flight."

He let out a low whistle. "I see it now. Moonworms out of a poolah's ass, but the feathers are mixed on every one of these shafts. I'd never have noticed it by lantern light if I wasn't looking for it." He handed her the quiver of hunting bolts he'd taken with the war bolts. A moment later, she confirmed the same thing about those.

She fingered the last bolt with a thoughtful expression as Payne asked, "You bought these from Thrask, didn't you?" She nodded, and he said, "I thought so. You always did like the best."

She handed back the botched bolt. "I'm rethinking that right about now."

"You wouldn't believe that Thrask could have made a bad batch of war bolts?"

"And hunting arrows, too? One of the best arrow makers in Tume?" She snorted.

"I didn't think so, either." He slid the bolts back in their quiver. "So someone switched our arrows with ones that could pass for Thrask's."

"That would cost a pretty silver, Payne."

"Was there ever an ugly one?"

He met her troubled gaze. If the switch had been made after she went missing, someone had taken advantage of her absence to sabotage Payne. If before, it could have been aimed at either one. Either way, there were raiders inside the circle. Payne carefully hung the quivers back up. "Best not to let on till we can replace them," he said in a low voice. "We'll tell Wakje and Ki, of course. And Kettre. No one else."

She nodded, took the scout book from her belt, and started to tuck it away in her saddlebag. It might have been the chill from knowing that someone had sabotaged their gear, or it might have been the warning growl of the grey in her mind, but she halted. Then she turned, took a length of beading line, bound the book, and, while Payne watched, got some glue from the repair box and put a few drops on the back cover. Then she picked up her guitar, loosened the strings till they sagged like an old man's jowls, and slid the slim book inside the sound hole. She held it for a few seconds till the glue set.

"Won't that change the sound?" he asked curiously.

"Aye, but they'll just think I have dead strings." She tuned up softly, and Payne winced at the slides and wails as the strings were stretched back into place. With her ear close to the guitar, Nori didn't notice. "It'll stay sticky for days, so I can take it out when I want to carry it with me."

"You might want to start a new book, then, and keep that more visible." He opened the back of the wagon while Nori threw on an old jerkin.

Leanna was making her way down the aisle with two plates carefully balanced, and Nori asked in surprise, "You didn't eat earlier?"

"I did." He gave her a sly look. "With Vina at fireside. But Leanna knows I never turn down a good meal."

Her voice sharpened. "Did you eat from the common pot or from your rations?"

"You're kidding, right? With Vina's stuffed hostina on the fires?" He sobered at her expression. "What are you thinking?"

She lowered her voice. "I was thinking we should toss our jerky, trail rations, extractor roots—anything we've been storing. Anything that's been out of our sight. Get something fresh from stores."

"Damn," he said softly. "I didn't think of that."

"We'll need to change our water filters, too. And we'll need new arrows, perhaps other gear. Uncle Ki will have extra, but if ours have been switched—"

"His might have been also." Payne nodded. "We can pick up new gear in a couple of days, when we hit Wagontire."

"I'd rather do it now."

"There's that arrow maker in Greylog Laketon, a few kays off Willow Road."

"He's a gossip. Besides, I've never liked him." She hesitated. "Lantor Darklane is in Vallier's train. He'll have at least one or two quivers with the spine to match our bows—or your bow, anyway."

"His arrows cost a fortune."

"We have enough to buy them."

"Sure, if we skip meals for the next two months. We're supposed to be living on our scout wages, remember? Why do you think I was idiot enough to let you pick those seedpods while we were being attacked? Besides," he cut off her retort, "you'd have to appear at fireside during the contract hour when all the elders are there."

She looked away. "If you're willing, you could go for me."

Payne shook his head. "Not when they know it's you who lost your gear. We're both ranked scouts, Nori-girl. They have the right to ask *ben'chovas* from either of us if we want a fireside trade." He could see the tension that clamped her shoulders. He sighed. "I won't go for you, but I will go with you. I'll speak for us both, if I have to."

"With my thanks," she said quietly.

"You owe me."

"I always do," she said wryly.

They broke off as Leanna reached them. Payne put an easy

smile on his face. "Food from the gods," he teased as he took his heaping plate. "Served by a moonmaid." He grinned as the girl flushed.

"I thought you might be hungry again," Leanna stammered.

"Aye." He popped a whole rootroll in his mouth. "Nori would have starved me. Ah, Leanna," he sighed as the hot flavor settled in his stomach. "What will I do when you Promise?"

Nori rolled her eyes as Leanna hurried away. "You're going to have to be careful with her," she told him. "She's got it bad for you."

He cut at the bollusk steak with his belt knife. "She's too young to do more than tease."

"She's barely two years from the age of Promising."

"Which means she's a little girl with a crush."

"Not so little anymore. Let her down easy, Payne. First loves can be more than cruel. And," she added softly, "I don't think you can afford to let someone get attached to you right now."

He stared at her with an unreadable expression. It was so like their father's that Nori almost shivered. Then Payne turned his head and watched the slim girl walk away. "I see." He said nothing more, but his hand fingered the fork as if it were a knife, and Nori knew that he remembered.

It wasn't just Rishte pulling at her now that made her antsy. She was starting to feel trapped by the train. "Perhaps we should leave the caravan." He frowned, and she added, "We'd travel faster on our own. Hostages would be no use to them if we were out on the trails, out of reach."

He didn't answer for a moment. Instead, he chewed his lip while his mind raced, seeking the pattern. The ruined arrows disturbed him more than the attack at the hedge. That had happened before anyone knew Nori found the raider code, which meant someone wanted them out of the way for some other reason. He said slowly, "They'll be watching for us to do exactly that. In fact—" He thought back to Connaught's words. "—they may actually want us to leave the train."

"But here, they know where we are."

"And here, we can see them coming. Plus, there are six dozen cozar to watch our backs, and two of the Wolven Guard."

She was silent for a moment, "We should at least bird Mama and Papa. Tell them to be careful."

"Aye, but quietly, and not by bird or runner."

"Tower then. It's faster."

He nodded. If they were targets, it was probably to get at their parents, not really to get at them. It made more sense than Brithanas being followed from Deepening Road. It also made more sense than someone simply wanting Nori's scout book. Without the raider code, it just wasn't that valuable. That, and the archers on the road couldn't have known about the code she'd stolen unless they had contacts in every caravan. It was an ugly thought, and his jaw tightened. He'd start questioning the *chovas* tonight.

He noted the tight line of his sister's jaw. "Don't worry so much, Nori-girl," he said easily. "We've already seen seven raiders. There can't be that many left." He plucked half a roll from her meal. "It's your own fault," he told her when she swatted at his hand, too late. "If you'd eat faster, I wouldn't be so tempted by what was on your plate."

"If you'd bother to get your own seconds," she retorted, "I wouldn't have to fight for my firsts."

She rubbed the back of one fist at her temple. Sleep had dulled but not dissipated her headache, and the slitted eyes seemed sharper. She wondered what would happen if she simply asked them to make peace with the wolves.

Payne frowned. "Better get some new herbs for that."

Aye, she'd lost hers to the worlags. She dropped her hand. "After dinner," she returned. "The healer is at fireside now, and it's still too crowded there. Besides, I want to work out tonight."

He rubbed his bruised chin. His voice was dry. "I thought we already did."

She slipped from the gate, paused, and turned back. The grey in the back of her mind was gnawing now at her wariness, till it was beginning to feel like fear. She drew her shirt more tightly around her. Her voice was low. "You have realized that, if someone tampered with our arrows, and if that someone was a woman, the one who was in our wagon, then it's not just those archers to worry about. There's at least one more raider among us."

He stared down the dark line of wagons and nodded silently.

He watched her head for the message master, then dropped off the gate and stalked thoughtfully to the fireside. He paused often to talk with the cozar, kept his eye out for a *chovas* with a scratched cheek, but his attention wasn't on those he greeted. Instead, he watched those who watched his sister as she checked her duty log.

XIX

Demons hide in all of us.

—Nadugur proverb

Wakje and Ki returned as Nori and Payne were halfway through their workout. They weren't the only ones watching. Three Journey youths sat on the back of a gate across the aisle and looked on. At their feet, two young boys and a girl had sneaked out of their sling beds and were whispering excitedly as they watched. A couple of cozar and a lanky *chovas* had also stopped and now leaned on the gate, occasionally shushing the children.

Nori and Payne ignored them all. Near the Test ninan, everyone watched everyone else, hoping to pick up last-minute pointers. In the open circles, a good workout was entertainment. Next ninan when the Tests themselves started, Shockton would turn into a circus. Youths from at least three counties would converge on the town to be tested for their martial and survival skills, while their families looked on proudly. Rank would be awarded by the martial masters, and Journey assignments negotiated fiercely among the elders. And then the youths would be sent out in the county to look into a problem, sign on with a trade master, scout some obscure area, or, in the case of someone like Kettre, be assigned to one of the underground labs where the sciences were still kept alive. Payne would probably be sent to Bilocctar or Sidisport to keep an ear out for rumors and news. Having lived in their parents' shadows all his life, he was almost desperate for his own Journey and a chance to be known for himself. He'd jump at a duty to slip into Bilocctar and tease the worlag that chewed at Ariye.

Nori had been watching him gnaw at his frustration for the last three years. Although she'd taught Test classes for years for others, she'd still been surprised when, six months ago, Payne had asked her to start drilling him almost daily. He was good, too. Better than she'd thought. Now, in the night, the two moved fast, quietly, with only soft slaps and scuffs of boot on stone to mark their movements. The moonlight showed everything, like flashing black-and-white drawings. Soft blocks, sweep blocks, clutch blocks, throws. A murmured instruction, she attacked, and he fell back then turned it against her and lunged forward. She slapped him past, whipped around, and caught him in the kidney. He grunted, and they went at it again. Ten more minutes of that, and it was Nori's turn with attack drills while Payne tried to defend.

By the time Wakje and Ki stalked up, her speed had escalated, and Payne was starting to feel pressed. The ex-raiders watched silently as she attacked with punches, ridgehands, and claws. "Again," she said flatly as he started to tire. Payne was sweating, but he focused sharply when she came in again.

Strike, tear—

She forced the wolf back. She could almost see the attacker who had tried to take the elder. She'd struck here, high, high, low, at the side of the neck, back to the ribs, left, left, had driven in—Payne missed a block, and she pulled the blow. He still hissed when she struck his ribs. "Again," she said harshly. Her hands were blindingly fast.

Ki's eyes narrowed. She was still riding the high, the adrenaline and fear from the attack. He could see it in the intensity. She wasn't seeing Payne, but a target. She wasn't seeing her brother. It wasn't just the wolf-bond, either, that added speed to her hands. He felt a chill. He'd wondered how long she could hold it at bay and what it would do when released.

Nori didn't notice. The raider, she'd hit him there, but he'd brushed her off. He'd had a knife, and she'd clawed him eagle-hand, then hit right—

Claw, kick—

Overhand and a sweep so fast Payne had barely time to jump it. She struck there, and there, faster, harder. Payne missed again.

Ki said flatly, "Enough."

Nori caught her next blow before it landed, hung for a moment in her balance point. Her violet gaze was hard, and she eyed Payne as a wolf does a poolah. Ki's command had made her pause, but it hadn't really registered, and she held, breathing quickly, while the others were still. Then the tension drained, and she seemed to withdraw back into herself.

Payne straightened. He shook his head slightly, and she let out a breath. They saluted each other formally. Payne stepped back and grabbed his towel, wiped his face and arms, and slung the cloth around his neck. "Too damn fast, Nori-girl," he said.

"Not fast enough." She didn't smile in return. Her breath was controlled, but her heart was beating hard, and she could still feel the need to strike with something more than her hands.

Wakje glanced at the Journey youths and cozar. The three youths slid quickly from the gate and disappeared among the wagons. The cozar nodded and moved on. The children hung by the wagon for another moment, but Wakje turned his expressionless gaze on them, and they scattered after the others.

Ki set his saddlebags down by the cook post as he studied Nori's expression. "We spoke with the gate guard. You're alright?"

She looked away. "I didn't throw up, if that's what you mean. Can't say much for me other than that."

Payne gave her a sharp look. She had that tone again, as if she was hating herself. Ki's brown eyes narrowed. He swallowed the chill in his gut and stepped in front of her. "Hit me," he said flatly.

She didn't think. Her hand flashed out.

Ki blocked—barely, though she didn't know that—and turned it aside. But he'd slid his knife out at the same time, and the point was at her ribs. Her other hand was already striking his wrist to slap the steel aside, but it was too late, and both of them knew it. Nori went still, and Payne froze. In the lantern light, it looked as if they'd been caught in a portrait of murder.

Ki looked down at her and read her eyes. "How old am I?" he asked softly.

Wakje watched carefully to see how she'd answer. He'd caught the flicker in Ki's expression. The other man had seen something in the girl, and whatever it was, it had made Ki as wary as Wakje. The wolf? Or something worse? He'd never asked Aranur why he'd been so cautious about his child, why Payne had been charged with watching over his sister, why Dione had allowed a pack of ex-raiders to watch over her only daughter. Don't let her go north, that was all they'd said, and watch out for her headaches. But it wasn't pain in her eyes as the girl focused on Ki.

Nori didn't notice. The steel against her gut was an icy fang, not quite cutting her shirt. "Sixty-one," she answered Ki.

The man's voice flattened. "How old am I?" he repeated.

The point of the steel pricked skin. The flat of the blade chilled her fingers. It had gone in so fast, like a thought before it was formed. "Three hundred," she breathed.

"How old are you?"

"Twenty-two."

"Could you take me?"

She could feel the point against the pulse of the small veins in her skin. "Not this time."

He smiled without humor. She was better than she thought. Six months ago, she wouldn't have been able to touch that blade before the point had hit her gut. "What about the raider?"

She shook her head.

Ki let her feel the cold steel against her skin for three more eternal seconds. Then he stepped back and sheathed the blade. "He had years on you, as I do. Twenty, maybe thirty years of violence that you will never match unless you live as he does." He jerked a nod at Payne. "He outweighed your brother by twenty kilos, and you by more than fifty."

"He was built like an iron dnu," muttered Payne.

Ki's voice was dry. "Most men will be, compared to you, at least for the next twenty years. That's a density that only comes with age. It's the body's compensation for the loss of reflex and speed."

Payne glanced at the slit in Nori's—or rather, his—shirt. He said sourly, "You're both older than us by forty years, and there's nothing wrong with your reflexes."

Wakje smiled faintly, but the expression didn't reach his flat, black eyes. He'd lived in his own body long enough that every move was concise and direct and had his full power behind it. Most raiders achieved that, those who survived their first year. He'd lasted more than twenty before following Payne's father, Ki had fought for fifteen, and neither man was as fast as he had been. It was timing, not speed, that now kept them ahead of others. Even Ki, who had some of the fastest reflexes he'd ever seen, had slowed down with decades of age.

Nori's voice was low. "I know I should be grateful, but Uncle Ki, I hit him with everything I had, and I barely made him pause. I've trained with you all my life, and I still can't take one raider?"

Ki looked down with his pale brown eyes. She hated herself for failing, and more than that, she blamed herself for taking Payne into that danger. As a raider, he'd learned to recognize those emotions and use them to manipulate his prey. Here, it made him pause. She might be bonding with the wolf, but she had not yet fully turned away from him if she was asking questions like that. It gave him a strange feeling he didn't recognize, as if there were something wrong with his chest. He had the same feeling sometimes when he looked at his children.

He said slowly, "The jack had a knife, which didn't cut you. He outweighed you and hit you, but didn't break you. And you managed to take his prize from him and still get off with your lives. Was there something more you wanted?"

Payne murmured, "It's a damn sight more than I expected when I saw you tackle the man."

"You at least threw him into a bush," she retorted.

"And you got off scot-free," Ki said sharply.

She looked down. "My apologies, Uncle Ki."

Ki studied her. She was still tense, still reliving the moment, and he said, "If this had happened eight years ago, what would have happened to you?"

She met his cool gaze. Eight years ago she hadn't been put

through the intensity of training daily with half a dozen ex-raiders. They had handled her in monthly shifts, sending her off to the next Wolven Guard as she went through each town with her parents. She had trained before that, but she'd been a child then, and most of the lessons had been in the martial rings. The ex-raiders' lessons were different. Where the ring-trainers taught her form and finesse, the ex-raiders taught survival. "Eight years ago, I'd be dead."

"And four years ago?"

Four years ago, she'd been nearly nineteen. She'd been fast then, but not confident. She'd been afraid of the demon inside her, of letting it out through her hands. A knife looked too much like a claw. "I'd probably be cut," she admitted. "Perhaps dead." She forced her hands to relax. "I understand," she told them flatly. "I'm smaller, less experienced, and I'll never have your fists—"

"For which we are truly grateful," Payne put in.

"—I've only got speed, training, and a couple of elbows, and that's got to do for me."

Payne looked at the blade that was back in his uncle's sheath. He murmured, "Don't knock the training, Nori-girl. It kept you alive tonight."

It shouldn't have had to, not inside the circle. Nori looked at her uncles. "With tonight and what happened back on the road, we were thinking to leave the wagons. Go the rest of the way on the backroads."

"No." Wakje's voice was flat.

"But if the circle isn't safe anymore—"

"No." He cut her off. "There are rumors of raider action up and down the county. If that is what's going on here, they'll be ready for you to leave. Cut the prey from the herd, then run it to ground—it's exactly what they want you to do to make yourself an easier kill."

She looked down at her hands. Her fingers had clenched again. An easier kill. She'd always been that. She'd never stood up to anyone except when someone else was in danger. She looked at her slender bones for a long moment, then dropped her hands as if she despised them, as if they were wrong for her, and turned to climb into the wagon.

Wakje stopped her. The thickset man didn't speak for a moment, then finally growled, "You'd never have made a good raider, girl, but I've seen worse out on the trails."

It was as much a compliment as he had ever given, and Nori stared at him. She almost reached out to see if it had been real, but he stepped back. Wolfwalker. The word hung between them. She didn't try to touch him again. Instead, she simply nodded, then turned and climbed into the wagon.

Ki loosened his braid as he waited for them, then fast-combed it and tightly rebraided the silky curls. As a raider, he'd worn his hair loose. In the counties, he kept it braided. It hadn't been a conscious choice; he'd simply found himself doing it the day he chose to ride with Noriana's father.

Wakje scowled as he finished, and Ki glanced at him. "She still turns to us," he murmured. "Maybe the wolf won't be as strong in her as it is inside Dione."

"Did you look in her eyes?" Wakje spat to the side. He braced himself on the gate and toed off his boots so he could pull on his moccasins. He never slept barefoot, not since he was a boy. Old habits. A man never knew when he needed to jump up and fight.

"Aye, I saw her." Ki said slowly, "But there is something other than wolf in her now."

Wakje's voice was flat. "Maybe that will make her stronger."

"Maybe that's what is holding her back."

Wakje gave him a sharp look.

The other man nodded toward the wagon. "She'll have to face herself, sooner or later. She'll have to accept what she is."

As they had. Ki didn't have to say it out loud. Wakje muttered instead, "Wolfwalker."

Ki snorted. "If you believe that, you're an idiot."

"Aye," the thickset man agreed shortly. His voice was almost wry.

Nori waited till Wakje, Payne, and their driver were asleep before trying to slip away to Rishte. She needn't have bothered trying to be quiet. All three men woke when she sat up, their hands going to the weapons under their pillows or slung at the edge of their beds. She murmured "Just a walk," but Payne muttered "I'll take care of it" to Wakje before the ex-raider could bite out a command.

Nori sighed as she snagged a cloak from the wagon. Then she buckled on a weapons belt before Wakje's watchful eyes, and added a tiny trail kit, just in case. Then she and Payne strode quietly toward the stables.

Payne opened his mouth, but Nori beat him to it. "Don't say it," she warned.

"You know the rules," he returned flatly. "You don't go off far on your own, not with raiders around, and especially not to the wolves, not when you've started to bond."

"Aye, but I feel safer out there, with Rishte."

"And that's a problem, isn't it?" he retorted.

"Payne—" she started.

He cut her off sharply. "If I can see this much in your face when you think you're in control, how much are you feeling inside?"

"I—" She broke off. He might be younger, but he had clear eyes, whereas hers were clouded with grey. And he was right. She could smell the rich scent of warm dnu, the thick dust of hay, the heady odor of manure. The camp was like a complex bread baking slowly in the night. Her nostrils flared to catch each scent that Rishte smelled. Her eyes strained to see contrast and movement, and her skin seemed to ripple as if it had fur, not a few hairs to sense the wind. "I feel more," she finally whispered. "It's strong, Payne. Like a river that tumbles boulders."

He said nothing for a moment. "Can you call him to you or does he just respond to the pack-threat?"

He meant the attack on the road, and she hesitated.

"You'd better find out." He tried to make his voice light. "You go feral on me, and I won't have to worry about Wakje. Papa will scatter my bones himself."

She answered slowly, "Rishte can't come to me here. He's a yearling. He's already afraid of the men, of the wagons."

Payne said softly, "So are you, and not just because of the raiders." She looked at him then. In the dark, he wasn't sure if her eyes were focused or not. "Nori-girl, be careful. You can get pulled in too far, too fast, when you first bond. You might never find your own voice or stay . . ."

"Human?"

Her voice had been carefully even, but Payne knew she was feeling fear. The slitted, yellow gaze of the alien that watched over her thoughts—it had influenced her before. With the telepathic aliens so close to the settled counties, it was a wonder they hadn't all mutated four degrees past human. Worse, the wolves had to be pulling hard on Nori against the taint inside her. The temptation to escape into the grey must be strong as an avalanche. It could make her want them badly enough that she forced the wolf to bond.

"You can't stay with him," he said finally. "Not for more than a few hours at a time. He has to come to you," he said firmly as she tried to speak. "He has to choose by himself."

As do I. She wasn't sure she'd spoken out loud, but Payne nodded, apparently satisfied. He motioned for her to lead the way through the hedge.

She didn't look back as she knelt and scrambled through the hole hidden behind the stables. It had been made by some determined child years ago. After more than a decade of use, it was now big enough for a careful adult.

Payne didn't question her use of the unconventional path. He spent his time studying the shadows to see if anyone watched while they wormed their way under the hedge.

On the other side, Nori led unerring in the dark. First to the bridle path that circled the camp, then onto a game track that led up the ridge. Twenty minutes later, they were hunkered down on the edge of a small broadleaf meadow. The fuzzy stems were still shedding, and Nori shook, then bent the leaves into a quick shelter before crawling inside. Payne crawled in beside her, closed his eyes, and went back to sleep. Nori grinned faintly. Her brother could sleep almost anywhere, but for all that, he would know the moment the wolf came close.

She closed her own eyes and concentrated. *Rishte. Rishte.*

The answer was immediate and strong. *Wolfwalker.*

Her eyes flew open and she smiled. They had learned enough

of each other's languages that, even without the eye contact, the images of each other were almost clear. *I am here,* she told him in her mind.

Alone, not alone.

She nodded. *My brother is with me.*

Rishte hesitated, but she could feel him slink closer. She waited. And waited. It took twenty minutes before his nose nudged Payne's boot.

Payne didn't bother to open his eyes. "Tell him not to gnaw," he murmured.

The voice made Rishte leap back and snarl.

"Spooky mutt," the young man muttered. "I mean it about the boots."

Nori looked at Rishte and met his eyes, violet into golden. It had been hours since they were together, and their minds hit hard.

Fear, aggression, threat. Threat? Attack. Run. Run away.

Brother, packbrother, she sent urgently. *Trust him. Trust me.*

Threat. Come, come away.

"It's alright," she said out loud. The sound made Rishte flinch back, but he held. Nori continued, murmuring so that he could get used to her voice. "He is my packbrother, Rishte. You must meet him and accept him if you are to bond with me."

Wolfwalker, Rishte wailed.

She held out her hand. "Stay, Rishte, stay with me. Stay with us." She waited, but he did not move. Finally, she lay back. She heard the wolf panting, but could not tell if he eased closer. A moment later, she put her arm over her eyes to keep the fuzzy debris of the broadleafs off her nose. There was a frantic jerk back near her feet. "It's okay," she soothed. "It's alright." She closed her eyes. "Pretty grey, handsome grey. Just put your head down and sleep."

Payne had almost dozed off when she murmured, "In the old-Earth plays, the scrawny girl always gets to beat up at least half a dozen villains."

His mutter was dry. "Let me know when you're in one of those plays."

She rolled onto her side. She could still hear the slap of steel by her side as the raider's knife slashed down . . . She clenched her fists, then relaxed them. When she finally dropped off into her dreams, she knew that Rishte's golden eyes watched over her with unblinking wariness.

XX

Nori woke on the edge of dawn, when the faint grey began lightening their shelter. Her warm legs were suddenly cold, and she knew Rishte had been curled against her till she shifted. "Payne," she murmured.

He sighed. "I know."

She smiled faintly and wormed out of the shelter. She stood for a moment, listening to the tree sprits as they swooped between the trunks, and for gaps in the forest sounds where other birds ought to be. She didn't see Rishte until he snarled at her back.

Wolfwalker.

Her smile widened. She turned to meet his gaze. Their minds slammed together and meshed almost instantly. He would never be human, and she would never be wolf, but they were learning to hear each other. *We are alone?* She projected the sense of the words.

His golden gaze was unblinking. *No hunters,* he agreed. *Too close to the stink line.*

Barrier hedge, she corrected softly.

Stink line. Hedge.

She filed away the lupine definition as Payne wormed out of the shelter after her. "Moons, Nori-girl," he muttered. "Traveling with you is like being with an infant. I never get more than two hours' sleep." He scratched the sleepsand from his eyes. "That the wolf?"

215

Rishte's fangs were bared, his ruff up, and the snarl growing deep in his throat. Payne hid his grin and let his gaze meet the golden eyes soberly. Blurred images blinded him. The yearling's fear-aggression almost made him stiffen. He held himself still with effort. *Grey One. Rishte,* he sent carefully. *You honor me.* He could sense the easiness between his sister and the wolf, and for the first time felt his own voice as the rough one in the grey.

Rishte growled for another second, asserting his bond with Nori. *Packmate,* he finally acknowleged. *Packbrother.*

Payne nodded mentally, then broke the contact. "Wow."

"Aye," Nori agreed.

"It will be like that for me," he said quietly, watching Rishte slink back.

"Yes," she agreed. "Just not with him."

He glanced at her. Her words had been almost harsh, and her eyes unfocused. He said sharply, "Nori."

She stiffened, blinked, and lost the tension in her face. "Sorry."

"Dik spit, Nori-girl. Don't let him pull you in that far." He glanced after the wolf and added more worriedly, "You're too new in the bond. If Wakje hears you do the possessive thing, he'll—"

"—tan my hide like an eerin. I know." Rishte was watching her from the edge of the trees, and he pulled her to run after him.

"We should get back."

She sighed and shook herself. She looked again at the trees, but Rishte was gone.

They made their way carefully back, not by the same track to the hole in the stable hedge, but by a different path that led around to the access road. Payne didn't question her caution. They both knew not to repeat a trail when hunters were about.

They were almost back to the circle when Nori snapped up her hand. Payne froze. Rishte was a kay away by then, digging in the moss for woodmice, but his golden eyes seemed to burn into her mind as he caught her sudden tension. Even at that distance, the grey sharpened her senses.

She eased back behind a bulge in the hedge. Payne did the

same, ignoring the twigs that stuck in his back and the sharp odor of roroot that released as he pressed in. A moment later, he heard the murmuring. He strained his ears, but could distinguish nothing. He glanced at Nori, but she shook her head. When the sounds faded, they waited a few seconds, then Nori peered through the edge of the bushes. Two men were walking away toward the camp. She froze as one of them looked back over his shoulder, but he didn't see her. The man did it again a few meters later, and once more before they disappeared around the bend in the access road.

"Two men," she reported softly.

Payne kept his voice as low. "Talking outside the circle at dawn?"

"They weren't the dawn guards."

"They weren't cozar at all if they were outside the circle," he returned flatly. "I wish we'd been closer."

"Closer and they'd have seen us. They looked back all the way down the road."

"Then I wish you had Rishte's ears."

"Now that would be lovely. Every day I could wash my face, brush my teeth, and comb my ears."

He grinned impishly. "Might make Brithanas take more notice of you."

"He takes notice enough already." She said softly, "They're far enough ahead now to follow." She loosened the thong over her knife.

Together, they toe-heeled it toward the camp, their feet almost silent on the ground. At the edge of the last turn, they dropped to a casual walk and came into sight of the gate guard.

"Aye, Ubo," Payne greeted the pudgy man.

"Aye, neBentar, Black Wolf." The man said speculatively, "Didn't see you leave."

Payne answered easily, "Went out the other way and took the bridle path around. Lots of traffic," he added. "Never knew so many merchants to get up this early when they didn't have to."

"You've the right of it there. Night guard said there's been *chovas* coming and going like rasts in a fat bin."

Payne looked past the guard. "Shouldn't *Chovas* Murton be standing with you?"

Ubo shrugged. "He didn't show for duty. Dirvan is getting his backup."

Payne exchanged a glance with Nori. "We thought we saw a couple of outriders come in right before us."

"Aye. Two *chovas* from Vallier's train. They wanted to catch an early ring-runner on the road before we turned out for the day. Don't know their names, but they were headed into our quads, not their own wagon lines." Ubo gave him a thoughtful look. "That stuffy Rezuku and one of his *chovas* were asking after you two a bit ago." Nori stirred, and Ubo glanced at her. "Not you specifically, Black Wolf, but they wanted to know who was out. They seemed unhappy with the answer, as if they were expecting something different."

Payne shrugged nonchalantly. "They probably wanted to pick our brains for fireside."

"Probably," the guard agreed. "Best watch yourselves, though, even on the bridle trails. It's a bad-luck spring all around."

Payne grinned wryly. "You've the right of it there. My thanks."

"Anytime, neBentar. Black Wolf." He waved them into the camp.

There were too many people already moving within the circle to see where the two men had gone. They started down the first wagon aisle just in case, noting who was up. A dog growled briefly as they approached the wagon he crouched under, but fell silent when Nori shushed him. Payne gave her a wry look, and she shrugged.

They slipped past the message wagon with the rookery. The message master was already perched on her box. Her eyes were half closed, and her bony, two-hundred-year-old frame was wrapped in a thick blanket of chancloth while her great-great-grandchildren prepped the harness. She nodded to them and closed her eyes again, trying to recall the messages she'd somehow misplaced.

"Split up?" Nori asked in a low voice.

"Are you crazy?" Payne retorted. He took her hand to pull her along. They caught curious glances as they passed fireside, where five women were huddled around their morning mugs of rou, and Payne murmured, "Let's stroll. Better yet, let's argue."

Nori eyed the wagon line. "About what?"

He snorted. "I still think you ought to Test."

She stiffened.

He grinned. "That'll do it."

She hid a sigh, but said obediently, "We've been over that a dozen times."

"A hundred, and it won't change my mind. If you don't Test, you can't Journey." He nodded toward another stovefire where the breakfast meal was already going strong.

She caught only the usual scents of food and dnu and sleep sweat, and she shook her head slightly in answer. Aloud, she said, "Test is to find out if you can survive on your own, and I've taught those classes myself for years. There's no point in Testing myself."

"Without Test, you can't get rank, and without rank, you're offered only the worst of the county jobs." He looked sharply left at a snapping sound, but it was just a sturdy woman in nightclothes struggling with a stiff window latch.

Nori tested the air again and listened for a second as they passed another wagon. Almost automatically, she returned, "Journey is not some sort of religious quest, Payne. It only started as a way to keep the gene pool diverse. Now it's just a way to make us leave our homes and spread our skills around."

"I suppose you'll say next that rank is just a knot on the line, not anything important."

She shot him a glance. It had been hard for him, watching his friends Test for rank before him. He'd had to endure a dozen challenges a year from youths who taunted him about it, others from men who pushed him as being only a poor copy of his father. It was Nori's fault. The one year they had been separated hadn't been a good one. After that, Payne had been held back from rank so that he wouldn't Journey before she finished school, passed her third bar, and was free to travel with him. She said lightly. "Rank isn't status, Payne. It's just a recognition that you've got enough judgment to leave home without putting others in danger. It's supposed to prove that you've learned enough, that you don't need a host of friends to save your rear end from some stupidity every time you set out on the road."

"Ah, now I see why you avoid it."

"Oh, spit in poolah's eye."

He hid a grin. It might be a forced argument, but her voice was growing sharp. He glanced between a quad of wagons, then ducked his head and looked underneath them to see who was walking on the other side. He motioned a small circle with his finger for her to continue. "If I want rank, I have to Test."

"Hah. Test has never been required for rank. I've been offered rank without Test since I was twenty. Last year, the elders were begging me to take it—" She broke off and looked narrowly at a wagon, then shook her head shortly and moved on.

"I just want you to have your own Journey." He twisted, then walked backward a few steps to see who was up and around behind them.

"I'd rather tag along on yours," she muttered.

"Fat chance the elders will let you do that."

"Fat chance you'll get rank if you don't practice more—" She broke off.

Kevinel Runitdown opened his wagon door to the left, and shook out a blanket. "Aye, Black Wolf, neBentar," he greeted them cheerfully. A few wagons down, the caravan healer came out of Ed Proving's wagon, glanced around, nodded to the two scouts, then made his way swiftly back toward the cookfires. The curve of a bottle was clear in one of his pouches.

Payne spat to the side. "There's an easier treatment for hangover. Just stop drinking."

But Nori said slowly, "I don't think Proving's as much a drunk as you think." That healer had had uldori with him. The pungent painkiller was best taken orally, but it didn't go down or stay down well. Some healers mixed it with parskea or rootie or some other strong alcohol to make it more palatable, which would go far in explaining the flask Ed Proving always carried. "You said he was good on the search."

Payne nodded reluctantly. "He's half the reason we stayed with your trail."

"We should talk with him. He's still got sharp eyes, and he knows a lot of scouts. He might have seen—" She broke off and flicked Payne's sleeve. The slight movements two slots away had stilled as another cozar called a greeting. A second later, the people in the wagon began moving again, but almost too deliberately.

Payne walked closer, adding as if they hadn't paused, "I'd practice more if you'd stop running around by yourself in the forest. The Hafell was fit to flog you for that stunt."

She caught his determined gaze. "I had other things to do," she retorted.

Payne shot her a warning look.

"—And as usual, you were sleeping," she amended. She scuffed her moccasin, then stopped, bent down as if to adjust the lace, and looked along the undersides of the wagons. She nodded slightly to Payne.

When the *chovas* B'Kosan stepped out around the back of the wagon with his toothbrush, they broke off as if uncomfortable. The outrider looked at Nori with undisguised appreciation. "Out walking?"

Payne shrugged. "Wakje prefers that we argue elsewhere when he's still trying to sleep."

The outrider looked at Payne but spoke to Nori. "I'll be riding duty for Rezuku's wagon today. Perhaps Black Wolf would like to keep me company?"

She looked away.

B'Kosan grinned and made his way jauntily toward the bathhouse.

Nori muttered, "He knows I don't like him."

"Aye," said Payne with a frown. The gate guard had mentioned Murton, and Murton had been assigned to Rezuku since the merchant joined them. Now B'Kosan was riding guard for the man from Sidisport. Payne looked after the *chovas*. "Could you tell anything?"

She shook her head. "The cookfires are going now, and the scents are too mixed."

"So B'Kosan has Murton's duty for the day," he murmured. "And Murton didn't show up for gate guard."

"Who would want to take out a *chovas*?"

"No one." He kept his voice low. "Unless the *chovas* in question had seen or heard something he shouldn't have seen or heard."

"Murton could have jumped caravans," she countered. "He wasn't making friends here, and we've traded off at least half a dozen *chovas* with the last three trains we've camped with."

Payne noted the way she was focused on Rezuku's wagon. He said firmly, "You're not getting in there." Not, at least, without him.

Her violet eyes sparked with sudden anger, but she kept her voice low. "They came after us, Payne. They could have—should have—killed us on the road yesterday. What if they'd hit you? What if Rishte had been with me?" She looked back at the wagon. "He's got one of the few wagons you haven't been invited to, and Kettre could get me in there."

"Sure, if she wanted to risk a trial block. Besides, you think if Rezuku is involved, he's left his plans lying around for someone like you to find them? There's no way in the fifth hell. Either Rezuku or his driver is always near the wagon. If not them, his guard stays close."

"Like Murton?"

He scowled.

"For someone who isn't carrying ores, this Rezuku seems awfully careful."

"That's too easy, Nori-girl. Lots of merchants are protective of their cargo."

She said slowly, "Aye, but he's not greedy enough."

Payne turned. "How do you figure that?"

"I watched him before at the lunch fireside. He might have been there for the business, but he didn't watch the trades as carefully as the others did. He watched the people instead."

"The mishaps started before he joined us."

She studied her brother. "But you're thinking about it now."

"Aye," he agreed again. "Now that the gelbug's in my head. I wonder how many messages he's received."

"There were two waiting for him at the message master when I checked the tower log last night."

"Two messages isn't excessive."

"No," she agreed. She waited half a heartbeat. "They were in code."

Payne gave her a sharp look. "What kind of code?"

"I only got a glimpse of it."

"But not the raider code."

"Not that I could tell."

It was frowned upon, but some scouts kept code fragments in their scout books, and pieces of messages they'd run across. They were puzzles that occupied the mind while they ran trail, rode long distances, or simply waited for the next job. Nori was no different in that respect. Over the years, she'd collected fragments from more than a dozen sources. Few people realized there was such a brisk trade in tower codes. Fewer still knew the places a scout could set up and read the signals freely. Long shields on the mirrors kept the signals focused toward the next tower and provided reasonable privacy, but decent scouts knew a few high places where they could read the signals. Nori had once gotten a bloody nose from two scouts who were fighting over a vantage point. She'd broken it up, sent them away with a threat of calling a badgerbear to the rock, and taken the vista point for herself. Payne had sat a few of those ridges with Nori. Gods, they had been some of the most tedious days he'd ever survived. He'd gladly gone back to council duty and had been grateful ever since that he'd never been assigned to the towers.

Tower teams had no days off during their duty. Two mirror-men, one to send, and one to receive, had to be on duty twenty-six hours a day, nine days a ninan, four ninans a month. Although some of the tower folk hunted or trapped on their off-shifts, most stayed close to home. The remote ridges made dangerous country in which to be out alone. All of which meant that scouts like Nori who brought in fresh meat or delicacies could trade for almost anything they wanted. Most traded for free messages sent to their families. Nori traded for code.

She followed his thoughts. "I've got tower duty for the next two days, and Jezeren is working one of those towers. I was going to send our message to Mama and Papa through him. I can check with him at the same time to see if he's seen any code like ours."

She knew she'd won when he said, "It'll be tricky, Nori-girl. Rezuku is more careful than some."

"Just let me know when."

"We might have to go to the Ell," he warned. "To arrange some sort of general search."

"That kind of defeats the purpose, doesn't it?"

"Depends. It would be interesting to see Rezuku's reaction to anyone getting into his wagon."

"Aye," she said softly. "It would."

XXI

"Tower duty, that's when you leave the groomed roads
And comfortable towns and better taverns—
    With fine ales, I might add—
To ride muddy, rocky trails
Up jagged mountains,
While being chased by bihwadi, worlags and poolah,
    To reach some hermit sitting on a mirror,
Who's going to hand you some sticks and tell you to
Go right back down."

— Grasp, in *Playing with Swords,* modern staging

An hour after dawn, the caravan was rolling. Nori had
avoided both Hunter and Fentris at breakfast. She'd seen
Hunter, but he'd been talking with some elders. When he'd gestured her over, she'd merely waved in response. The tall Tamrani
had scowled after her, but had disappeared into the meeting
wagon with Fentris, leaving Nori to stay with Wakje's driver on
the wagon seat as the caravan rolled out.

That lasted barely two hours, until her legs had stiffened up in
new and interesting ways. She went back to the saddle almost
willingly to start working off her *andyen* duties, or debt chores,
as Kettre called them.

She looked down the pale rootroad as she trotted. It was a
dirty yellow-white ribbon under a thin canopy of branches that
arched overhead. The forest would be much thicker and safer
with its shadows and brush and soft trails. Here, where the
sun hit, everything was exposed. She could even see the seams
between the individual roots that made the planks of the road.
Impact flattened and hardened the roots so that well-traveled
roads were like warm stone. Only the edges and shoulders were
spongy. She wished she could run on it barefoot. Her toes

225

twitched in her boots. Her stomach growled, and she caught herself just before she snarled.

It was the wolf again.

She tried to blank her mind.

She was passing Ed Proving's wagon when the line of palt feathers fluttering against the footbox caught her attention, and she reined in. Proving glanced at her, belched softly, pressed a hand to his stomach and closed his eyes for a moment, then gave his driver a nod. One For Brandy quietly handed over the reins and disappeared into the wagon.

Nori didn't speak for a few minutes. Without looking at him, she finally said, "You have good eyes, Ed Proving Trail. Did you use them last night when you were up?"

Proving raised a scraggly eyebrow, then sloshed his flask. "My sight's not so good by the end of the day."

She slanted him a look. "You don't sleep so well, either, but your ears are better than ever."

He gave her a sharp glance, then looked away. His voice was flat. "You know."

She shrugged. "My mother . . ." She let the word trail off.

He nodded shortly. Raised with a master healer and as a vet herself, Black Wolf would know enough to recognize the signs. He struggled with his humiliation. Bad enough folks thought him a drunk. Now he'd be pitied for the pain, for the splitting headaches the slightest sound caused, for dying like the withering husk of a weakening man who doesn't know how to let go. A palt flew out of the tree line, and almost viciously he jammed the reins in the wood grip, raised his bow, and shot. The arrow flew true, and the bird tumbled suddenly, then plunged over the barrier bushes.

Nori politely didn't look at him till he set the bow back in its holder and picked up the reins again. He looked at her grimly. His eyes were already slightly bloodshot, the skin around them tight as he tried to hang on to some shard of pride. She said quietly, "A healer's silence is a patient's right."

"You're not a healer."

She gave him a lopsided grin. "Animals, humans, what's the difference?"

He regarded her for a long moment. Then he snorted. "To you, perhaps none," he agreed. He stared down the road. Finally, he said, "Aye, I was up. You'd left already with that brother of yours, probably to see that young wolf who's been hanging around."

Nori winced.

He said dryly, "It's not me to worry about, Black Wolf. But I'd be more careful next time I go out after dark. Someone was watching your wagon."

To get at the scout book? She'd taken it with her, and her hand itched to check its pouch. Her voice was carefully expressionless. "Did you see who it was?"

He smiled without humor. "It was the end of the day, Black Wolf. My eyes . . ." He shrugged, took a small sip, belched, and tried not to reach for more. Take too much in the morning, and he'd not be able to keep the rest down in the evening to make it through the night. He kept his voice steady as he added, "Whoever it was stayed smart. Disappeared before that uncle of yours got up and took his walk-by. Didn't slip back into place till after."

Nori nodded. Wakje often got up and walked the camp in the middle of the night. She wondered sometimes if his dreams were as bad as hers. "The watcher, he was over by Rezuku's wagon?"

But Proving shook his head. "He was eight wagons down from yours in my direction. And he was relieved by another man at the second watch, and by a woman just before dawn." He caught the determination in her violet eyes. "I wouldn't go looking for them, Black Wolf, not without a passel of armed folk at my back. They all moved like your uncles, sure and quiet."

"But you heard them."

He chuckled without humor. "I heard the rasp of their leathers every time they moved."

And every snore, rustle, and murmur around him. No wonder the man couldn't sleep. But she said only "My thanks" as she rode forward again.

Kettre was waiting with the message master. Nori shook her

head almost imperceptibly as she greeted the old woman casually.

"Eight messages, prepaid," the message master told her, handing over a bundle of message rings and a thin roll of paper. "Your duty."

Nori glanced at the three carved and painted sticks, then slid them into her pouch. Regardless of shape, the wooden messages were all called message rings. They weren't the most efficient way to communicate, but they were one of the most personal. The emotion and style of the carver went directly into the wood, the messages couldn't be accidentally changed in travel without the damage showing. They'd been used since the sixth century for almost all formal agreements between merchants, Houses, guilds, and counties. They were like promises, she thought. Or like code. The nuances, implications and even hidden messages in the carvings were often invisible to any but the person who would receive them.

She checked the five paper slips, then rerolled them and slid them into their tube. Then she met the message master's pale eyes and said softly and deliberately, "Nine messages, my duty."

The old woman opened her mouth to correct her, then halted. "Nine messages, aye." She squinted at Nori. "I can't quite remember who brought in that last one, though."

"Ah, it came in with a ring-runner last night. Not the usual rider."

"Of course." The thin woman made a note in her tally book. "I don't know what's getting into my brain these days. Bad tallies, messages astray." She shook her head.

Kettre asked in a low voice, "Did you ever find those missing rings?"

Nori gave her friend a sharp look, and the old cozar gazed at both of them for a moment. "Not a hair of them," she finally answered, equally softly. Two *chovas* trotted toward the wagon, and the message master said more loudly in a sour voice, "That idiot Mato actually accused me of claiming they were missing just so I could still charge them for the sending. I'd have bitten his head off if I had your teeth, Black Wolf. My birds never come back empty-toed without me seeing it, you can bet the sixth moon on that."

Nori and Kettre hid grins.

The old woman waved for the *chovas* to wait, and picked up a small stack of books with her thin hands. "If you've got company on the ride, you can take this up also, if you're willing."

Nori glanced at the three books. "Ah, the monthly trade-off." They were well worn, but they'd be welcome at the isolated tower. "What titles?"

"Two classics and one modern: *Landfall,* by Lurien, *Who Hunts the Wolves,* and *On the Edge of Aiueven,* by Reveven."

"I've been avoiding that last one," she admitted as the cozar handed them up to Kettre.

The old message master grinned toothily. "As have I."

"I hear he still claims it's based on my mother."

"I'd say he wishes he *were* your mother, saving the world and all. But what does an old woman know?" The message master shrugged her thin, bony shoulders. "It's a fast way to silver to mention Dione. On your way now, Black Wolf." As the waiting *chovas* took their place, the old woman called after them, "And don't forget to bring back the other books they've finished."

They waved over their shoulders.

They were well ahead of the caravan before Nori told Kettre about the watcher Ed Proving had seen the night before.

Kettre scowled. "Watchers, kidnappings, and attacks on the road? Someone's got to be communicating constantly to put that all together."

Nori nodded. "We'll start watching the ring-runners and message master more closely. If messages are going missing, someone might be intercepting or stealing them so she can't keep a record. Uncle Wakje says they did that sometimes to make it harder to backtrack them later."

Kettre slanted her a look. "I don't see how you're going to be able to tell anything from that old spider. She just added a nonexistent message to her tally simply because you asked. You might as well call her a tally ho."

"Moons, Kettre." Nori looked around quickly.

"Don't worry, she didn't hear me," the woman returned sourly. "Besides, it's true."

"It's completely different," Nori returned sharply. She scowled at Kettre's knowing look. "I'm different," she said finally. "She'd tell me if anyone other than the Ell or Hafell asked her to do the same thing."

"Of course. MaDione."

"Moonworm crap," Nori muttered. Kettre was right. As usual, the message master had assumed that, if Nori asked for help, it was really for her mother.

It was quiet as they started up the narrow path. Even the jackbraws seemed subdued and lazy in the warming sun. Small goldencups grew out of the bark on the sky side of the trees, and the scent of lemon and cloves was heavy in the air. Nori noted it all, saw and smelled and heard it all, but she'd left the cozar behind in her mind. Her senses stretched now for something else. She didn't have long to wait.

Forty meters up the trail, Rishte slipped out of the brush. Kettre stiffened in her saddle, but Nori grinned. The yearling bared his teeth. He was poised with eagerness. Nori didn't even look at Kettre. She simply leaned forward, spurred her dnu, and jumped the riding beast forward. Rishte turned and pelted away. He seemed to laugh in her mind, and she felt her muscles loosen with speed. Up, up—

"Damn you, Nori!" Kettre belatedly spurred her dnu after the wolfwalker.

The trail wasn't yet steep, and the dnu charged up the trail after the wolf. Rishte leapt a half-cut log, and Nori sailed after him. Her dnu landed with bunched legs. It bucked itself up, then bounded over the next log, and Nori threw her head back and laughed out loud. Rishte howled in her head.

She finally pulled up at a switchback where the trail began to steepen. Kettre caught up a moment later. "By the molded cheese of a forgotten Tumuwen herder, you might give a girl a warning."

Nori laughed. "You never used to have trouble keeping up."

Kettre made a face. "Wait till we're back in the city. Then we'll see who falls behind."

Nori grinned. "Speaking of the city, did you see Surah before you left?"

"No, but I heard she's now down on Silverheart Street."

"That sounds pretty, at least."

Kettre sighed. "It's a whore street, Nori."

"Oh." Nori felt like an idiot. She glanced at the wolf. He stood on the switchback, panting easily and waiting for them to go again. Up? he seemed to ask.

At least there she knew what to do. She nudged her dnu after him again. The riding beast was used to wolves and didn't blink at the command, but Kettre had to urge her own dnu hard.

It took two hours to reach the ridge. From there, they could see the message tower that squatted one hill over. It was a newer stone structure, fully enclosed, poking out from the trees like a multieyed monster. A set of massive, tubed mirrors were mounted on the top, two facing south, and two facing north. Each was covered with lines of shutters to close it off when not in use.

"Predator flag is up," Kettre murmured.

Nori nodded slightly. "It's a hungry spring."

As they watched, the shutters flickered, and a mirror began to flash. The light flashed on the edge of the cylindrical shield, and Nori's eyes narrowed as she squinted at it.

"Anything interesting?" Kettre asked.

Nori watched for a moment, then shook her head. "Nothing that affects us. The bridge is still out on the lower Raine River, so those elders will be late to council."

"What a tragedy." Kettre laughed at her expression. "You can't claim you're thinking otherwise."

"What I think and what I'll admit are two very different things."

"As always, Black Wolf. As always."

Following the wolf, they clambered down the next stretch of trail. Rishte stayed ahead of them, turning every now and then to wait. Up two more switchbacks, a steep stretch that would have had their calves aching if they had been jogging . . . Rishte was trotting ahead, looking back, trotting ahead again. Nori felt her lips stretch in an answering grin. Not even the threat of predators could make her feel trapped out here.

When Rishte paused and growled softly in her mind, Nori pulled up. Mudslides, rockfalls, and old trees had broken most of the barrier bushes. What was left was a ragged line of pitiful shrubs clinging to the side of the hill in a desperate attempt to stay rooted. She nocked her bow with a borrowed arrow and kept her eyes sharp.

Kettre followed suit. She'd learned long ago that the wolfwalker had sensitive ears and eyes. When Nori eased forward, Kettre kept her distance so both had room to run.

They had almost reached the tower when Nori pointed. Kettre saw nothing, but ahead, Rishte's bristle was up. Their riding beasts were uneasy, and starting to chitter with fear. Kettre could feel hers tremble. Like Nori, she crooned to soothe it.

Someone in the tower noticed them down on the trail. A small face appeared, disappeared, then leaned out, pointed to the right, and waved another red-striped flag. "Watch for . . . ba . . . ," he shouted. "Ba . . . bear . . ."

Nori raised her hand in acknowledgment. She waited a moment listening to the trees. Then she nodded at Kettre, jabbed her heels in the sides of her trembling dnu, and loosed him. Kettre reacted instantly. Both creatures jumped. Somewhere behind, the women caught a glimpse of reddish brown fur, but Nori yelled wildly and charged the tower. Kettre was on her heels. They didn't even try to dismount and open the gate. They simply hunched down, sailed over, and skidded into the courtyard.

"Moons!" Kettre burst out as they reined in.

Nori was laughing. She pushed her braid back over her shoulder and grinned at the other woman. Frustrated, the badgerbear flowed near the gate, stretched up and clawed the top of the beams, then padded back along the wall. Nori listened to it retreat. Then she tucked her bow back in its holder and dismounted.

The tower man called down, "Have a nice ride?"

The wolfwalker grinned back up. "Two hours of boredom for two seconds of fun."

"Come on up, then. I've got your packet ready."

Kettre just shook her head.

"Nine messages, none urgent," Nori reported to the lanky man and his partner when they reached the high message room. She had known Jezeren since they were children, but she didn't know the woman with him, and she didn't like the avid look in the tower woman's gaze. "Your duty," she said formally, handing over the packet. She let her fingers tap it meaningfully before letting go.

"My duty, acknowledged." The lanky man looked through the messages. He hesitated almost imperceptibly when the count came up short, but logged them in, and reached over to pick up his own packet. "I've got five going back down. Your duty, Black Wolf." He handed them over and logged them out.

"My duty, acknowledged," she accepted. She counted the four slips of paper, then rolled and tubed them tightly. The fifth message, the wooden message ring, was more formal: a small carved invitation hoop for Ell Tai, with beads, knotted line, feathers, and an ebony centerpiece. "Lovely," she murmured. She added slyly, "Although I hear the artist is a bit hung up on himself."

He chuckled. She knew he'd made the ring. "I hear the other carvers are jealous."

She grinned in return.

"I'm to mention that Bafaro's son is available to carve the reply. I don't think they really believed my competition," he emphasized, "would stay with one train long enough to do it herself."

Nori shrugged. Few knew she had been doing Ell Tai's message rings since she was seventeen. She took no coin—the old Ell had done her more than one favor, so the carving wasn't listed as council duty, and she was careful to work in private. The only reason Jezeren knew her work, and she his, was that they had trained with the same master carver.

Nori had been drawn to the work from the beginning. The patterns seemed natural, as if she could see through the wood as she worked. That, and the slitted eyes that watched her thoughts seemed to approve of the patterns she carved. With the wolf so close in her mind, she didn't examine the patterns too carefully as she tucked the formal ring back into its pouch and snapped it onto her belt.

Jezeren's partner looked as if she wanted to speak, and the mirror man glanced at Nori's small bundle of books and said quickly, "Are those the monthly trade?"

Nori nodded. "Two classics, one modern." She handed them over and tried to avoid meeting his partner's gaze. The woman had already called her the Daughter of Dione, Jangharat, Black Wolf, and The Sudden on the stairs up to the tower. Jangharat, she understood. She'd earned the Tumuwen name, "shadow of the forest," years ago when scouting with her mother. But how the tower woman had ever heard that last rep-name, The Sudden, was beyond her. She dreaded going back down, where she could be obligated to a meal and an endless half hour of gossip. Instead, she hopped up on the message table and leaned her shoulders against the wall as if settling in. "Tai's message master has always liked *Landfall*," she offered. "Thought you might not mind a reread."

The mirror man leaned back in his own chair. "Aye, it's a good one. I always liked that scene with the third alien, myself."

"It's alright," Nori answered diffidently. "My favorite is still the part where the wolves hit ground the first time."

"You mean the part where they scatter?"

"You know that wasn't a scatter," she corrected. "More of a loosing of the wolves. If you're willing?" She gestured at the water bota.

"As you like." He nodded. "No, they scattered, Black Wolf. They were so far gone when they hit the trees, it was three days before any one of them was seen again."

"Excuse me, maDione," the tower woman interrupted. "Would you like some tea or rou instead of plain water? We have some excellent brews down in the kitchen. We can talk more easily there, too, catch up on the news."

"My thanks, but water is fine." Nori barely glanced at her. "I have to disagree," she went on to Jezeren almost without pause.

"The Landers knew where the wolves were. That whole scene is an analogy of freedom: to be loosed on an open world after a year and a half on a colony ship, paying aliens to haul them across hundreds of solar systems, only to dump them on the wrong planet, where they couldn't know if they could make it."

"It's not freedom if you're still tethered to the landing site—"

"Which they weren't," she answered. "Except by their desire to remain together."

"That's not an analogy of freedom, but of the fear they had to overcome to spread out on the world."

The tower woman resisted the urge to roll her eyes. "Black Wolf," she tried again. "Perhaps you'd like to try some of the early roast? I'd be happy to serve you myself, perhaps find out what's happening in the pre-Test rounds?"

"Later, later." Nori waved her away and continued, "They feared nothing at that point that isn't always an issue on any colony planet. What were the dangers? What were the risks? They faced everything the moment they set foot down, and they didn't do it like timid mice, but in one fell swoop."

"One fell swoop is right. They had eleven years before the Aiueven came down hard enough to kill off more than a third of the population. And again, I'd say that that isn't an analogy of freedom, but a cautionary tale—"

The woman tapped her finger against her chair and tried once more to interrupt, but Kettre gave her a wry smile. "We could be here a while," she murmured. "They can argue this story for hours."

"You'd think the Wolfwalker's Daughter would have better things to do when she's riding tower duty," the woman said, a bit too sharply.

Kettre shrugged. "I'd be happy to try the roast and the rou. You know—" She leaned in conspiratorily. "—I was with the searchers who went out to find her when she left Ell Tai's train the other night."

The woman's eyes gleamed. "I'd love to hear all about it."

Kettre winked at Nori, who pretended not to notice. ". . . not until the end," Nori went on as the other two women made their way down the stairs. "That's when Sarro Duerr realizes what he has to do to buy the freedom they thought they had at Landfall—"

The lower door shut on the stairs. For a moment, there was silence in the tower room. Nori and Jezeren looked at each other. "New partner?" Nori asked finally.

"Aye, out of Sidisport. Moons, but I thought she'd never leave." He stood up. "When she saw the Daughter of Dione riding in the courtyard, she just about tripped on her own pants to meet you." He pulled a book off the shelf, bent the spines back, and eased a flattened roll of paper out of the gap between the covers.

Nori hopped off the table. "So what have you got?"

Jezeren was all business now. "The usual gossip, a few notes of interest. You'll want to check these."

Nori looked the papers over as he shuffled them out for her. She copied two into her old, punctured scout book, then showed Jezeren some of her own recent notes. He compared them to his message log, then looked at the large map that was painted on the wall. "There's been a lot of movement in that area," he murmured.

Nori nodded. "Payne thinks something's up. Raiders, maybe. We have a couple Tamrani riding with us now. They're not saying anything, but they wouldn't be heading for the Ariyen council if something big hadn't disturbed them out of their Sidisport lairs."

"I'll pass word to keep a sharp eye."

She turned to the page with the raider code. "Then there's this."

He studied it closely. "I've seen this before," he said slowly.

"When?"

Her question had been sharp, and he glanced at her before answering. "Not this exactly, but the form of it, and not through any tower traffic." He looked out the window, thinking. "Council meeting," he recalled. "Closed session, last year, early fall." He glanced at her. "This doesn't surprise you."

"I thought it was the same. I was asked to watch for it on duty." The tower man started to copy it down in his private book, but she stopped him. "It's dangerous, Jezeren. I was warned two ninans ago, just before we set out for Shockton. Scouts are going missing when they go after samples like this."

He regarded her thoughtfully. Then he nodded and turned back to the lines, setting them in memory instead. She knew he'd remember. He might not be able to tell a weed from a tree, but he could recall almost every message he'd ever seen.

She hesitated as she put the scout book away. She'd known him since they were children, but he was a man now. What did she really know of the person he'd become? And was it Rishte who made her more wary now, or the slitted eyes inside her mind that hated humankind? She shook both off and, watching Jezeren carefully, said, "That miscount—the eight messages? I need to send the ninth myself. Coded, falsified origin."

Jezeren looked over with a frown. Coded messages required a sender's name in the log. It was one of the ways the county made sure the towers weren't used by criminals to plan their raids and crimes. Jezeren fingered the large tally book, then tilted his head, closed the book, and stepped away to the window. There he turned his back to her and stared silently out at the forest.

Nori didn't wait for him to change his mind. She moved swiftly to the northbound mirror, checked the light level, then took the flash handle and began flicking the shutters efficiently. She sent the watch code, waited the scant seconds for the answering ready signal, then began her message. Begin, begin, begin; priority high; message to Dione. And then the coded portion: Check all gear. Watch for worlags. Avar Avan. End, end, end.

She signed it with her Sikinya scout name, one that would tell her parents that the danger could be subtle and deadly. There were only ten or twelve people who knew that name, and all were family. She didn't use the word *plague,* even in code; that would be something to speak of in person. She didn't specify a destination, either, just her mother's name. The towers always knew where to find the Wolfwalker Dione. They'd send the message fast.

When she finished, Jezeren turned and checked that the mirror was closed, then went to the tally book. "How do you want it logged in?"

"Ell Tai's train, via a night rider."

"You've taken care of that end?"

She nodded. "Hessa added a tally for me on the caravan board. She'll say it came in with some unnamed ring-runner."

"You can go one better than that," he suggested. She raised an eyebrow, and the man grinned slowly. "Trungon rode tower duty yesterday off young Ell Pero's train."

Nori frowned. "Pero should have been up in Bronton by now."

"They had some delays. One of their elders died in his sleep. Probably never should have been traveling, the old boot. Then some northern trader got drunk with his *chovas,* fell off his wagon box, and cracked his head. Twelve hours later, he finally died." Jezeren snorted. "The whole line was held up for two days while the caravan was searched front to back by a council Straker who was looking for a thief. You'd think they'd lost the county crest the way he tore into the wagons."

"It's a bad-luck spring," she said slowly.

"Aye. Pero will be lucky to lead a train again within his lifetime. But Trungon, now, he was riding fine. He'd claim the message for you without blinking an eye."

Aye, Trungon would. The scout knew Nori's parents well. He'd carried messages for them before. He also knew Nori and almost always left something with Jezeren when he knew she would be in the area. She rubbed absently at her wrist. "He didn't happen to have anything interesting of his own to pass along, did he?"

The tower man grinned again. "He said you'd ask that." He went to the tower door, opened it and listened to the murmuring from below, then closed it softly. Then he went back to his chair, reached down, and popped a spoke out of the legs. He drew a small scrap of paper from the hollowed tube. "He left this." There were no words on the scrap, just letters and numbers in two clumps of neat little lines.

Nori's violet eyes gleamed. "That's not what I think it is, is it?"

"Aye, and it's for the inner council only." She reached out, but he held it out of reach and grinned as she almost snapped at him. "It's council duty, so Trungon said there's no trade required," Jezeren added slyly, "but he also said you'd be willing to give him some token in return for making sure you and you alone get this."

She nodded impatiently. Her hands itched to take it. "I think I know something he wants."

"He said you'd say that, too." The tower man handed over the scrap and pointed to the top set of symbols. "It's in the same form as what you found at Bell Rocks. The timing implies they're connected. This first message went south around two in the morning after crossing over from the Deepening line two nights ago. The second set came back north from Sidisport just over an hour later. Someone wanted a fast reply, and someone else was willing to get up in the middle of the night to make it."

Nori felt a spike of excitement. Two nights ago, she'd been on Deepening Road. She'd just stolen the code from the raiders. That had been around midnight, and she hadn't seen the raiders in the hour afterward that she'd been on the trail. If they had survived the worlags, even if they'd ridden pell-mell for the second hell, they couldn't make the Tendan Ridge tower in time to send that message. But they didn't have to go to the hub tower itself. There were relay towers closer, if one was willing to ride trail in the middle of the night. In two hours, they could have made it to the Deeping or Elen Ridge relay. There had been that other rider, too, that Sidisport youth who had joined up with Hunter's nephew. He could have been set among the Tamrani to watch for news of trade. Watching Hunter meet with Nori would have been worth his while. Either way, if the answering message came out of Sidisport, she and Payne were right. There was more going on than a few raider bands harassing the Journey trains.

Jezeren pointed. "This is the to–from part."

She nodded. "It's almost the same in all of the samples. From what I remember, it's similar to what the council has, too."

"Aye. And these to–from sequences are a perfect swap. And here, the same T-sequences show up in both."

Nori fingered the scrap. T-sequences like those and another repeated pattern had appeared in each of the samples she'd seen. "I'll log the activity of that night and pass it along with these messages. The Lloroi's code masters should have enough by now to start pulling this code apart. Until then—"

"Be careful," he finished. "You also, Black Wolf."

She carefully copied both sets of lines into her book. Then she lashed the book closed, took the scrap to the waste bin, and burned it carefully. Jezeren almost protested as she destroyed the code, but she merely looked at him over her shoulder when he started to reach in to take it out of the flame.

He stepped back quickly. Her eyes had been cold, and her lips half curled back as if she would snarl. He waited till she had stirred the ashes before clearing his throat and prompting, "The token?"

She glanced at the map. "Tell Trungon that what he wants is near the junction of Triple Trail and Cata cross-trail, over on the east side of Teptich Cliff. I've placed a piece of shale, foot-sized, an hour down the cross-trail, around the fifth or sixth kay, near the base of a double-trunked pintree. The right corner points to a marker in some root moss two trees to the east. What he wants is growing in a patch thirty-two degrees, about seventy meters from that marker. Tell him to wear gloves. I trashed mine getting in there."

"Triple Trail, Cata. One hour down the cross-trail. Slate marker, moss marker. Gloves." Jezeren set the instructions in his head. "I'll pass it along when he comes back south tomorrow, and I'll warn him to up his message tally."

"How about you?" She was impatient to get this note back to Payne, but she glanced around dutifully. "Have you needs?"

"No, supply came through four days ago, and the calibration teams were here last ninan."

"Then I suppose it's time to rescue Kettre."

Jezeren grinned sourly. "I'd rather you rescued me."

"Your duty," she returned blithely.

XXII

Poolah lurk right at the ground,
When defending, crack their crowns;
Bihwadi circle, like the night,
Stand your ground or climb for height;
Badgerbears can flow like water,
Flee or you will be the slaughter;
Worlags pack and run you down,
Head for water or high ground.

  —first verse, *What to Do if You Run Into,*
                          an Ariyen teaching poem

Nori and Kettre left the tower as they'd entered it, in a burst of speed. The badgerbear was still lurking, but Jezeren opened a window on the back side of the gate and waved a slice of roast pelan. By the time the beast realized its prey was fleeing from the other side of the compound, Nori and Kettre were flying down the trail.

Since the caravan had stopped for lunch, they caught up an hour after they hit the road at a canter. Nori had time only to pass her scout book to Payne before she was swallowed back up by the cozar. She worked the meal wagon almost impatiently, checked in with the caravan healer, and got her scout book back from her brother just in time to receive more messages for her parents.

The first was delivered by the standard ring-runner, one of the dozens of messengers who passed during the day. The second was handed over by an older Randonnen scout who was taking two of her own students to Test. They exchanged gossip before the woman rode on, and the scout wished Nori luck. The wolfwalker wondered if it was for dodging the elders or for managing a Journey with Payne. She could barely wait to tell Payne about the code, but they had no time alone. She was scheduled for three more duty tasks for causing the cozar a search.

For an hour, she helped Mian with some of the exotics the girl was trying to raise. The vari birds didn't want to be sedated, and some noise outside spooked them into escaping their cages. The wagon was a shambles of feathers, fresh droppings, and clawed fabric before the three birds were recaged. Nori was still sneezing from wispy down as she left Mian to clean up while she went back to her own wagon to wash.

Elder Mato caught her there. "MaDione," he began as she stepped out on the wagon seat. "I understand you're on general duty today. I've been needing a scout and would pay dearly for two liters of fresh cassar root for an important dye present. I'd like to hire you to find a good growth stand before we reach Shockton."

Nori answered with careful courtesy. "My thanks for the offer of work, Elder Mato, but I have other duties to attend to."

"You don't seem to be doing any right now," the older man observed. "And I understand that you can climb well enough to reach the upper growths."

Climb on a damaged rope? She kept her face expressionless. "I'm scheduled for the teaching wagon an hour from now."

"After that, then."

"I also have extensive family duties. You should ask one of the other outriders. B'Kosan, perhaps, or maSera."

"I am asking you, maDione." A note of irritation crept into his voice.

One wagon up, Kettre looked back and caught the narrowing of Nori's eyes. She dropped back closer to Nori.

Mato didn't even greet the woman as he held his temper with difficulty. "Well, when will I have your answer?"

"I believe I have answered already, Elder Mato."

"The answer isn't acceptable."

The wolfwalker shrugged. She never stood up in council, but for some reason, perhaps because of the wolf in her now, it was almost satisfying to stand up to this man.

"I was told you'll be doing council duty in two months anyway, regardless of what else your parents have arranged."

"That's still two months away, Elder Mato."

"It's two months of laz—"

Kettre broke in. "My apologies, Elder. Nori, the Hafell has a question for you."

"Black Wolf—" Mato started.

Nori smiled grimly. "Please excuse me, Elder Mato. I'm still working off my *andyen*. I believe I know what the Hafell is waiting for." She nodded to the driver, stood up, and stepped neatly into Kettre's stirrup. She settled in behind the other woman as they turned and cantered away.

"My thanks," she murmured against Kettre's back.

The woman's voice was dry. "We've had enough mishaps in the caravan. I didn't want you biting his throat out."

"Then you have good timing." Nori's lips tightened. "Someone told him I could climb to the upper cassar root stands."

Kettre looked back sharply. "That requires a rope, and yours was sabotaged."

"Aye," she said softly. "I'd like to know who prompted him to ask. He's pushing me after everyone else has backed off, so someone is pushing him."

"I'm outriding only a few more hours today. I could look into that."

"With my thanks." She glanced down the line. "I take it Brean really doesn't have a question for me?"

"No, but we can make one up. The Hafell seems like a good sort."

Nori grimaced. "Good enough to have assigned me seven different duties."

Kettre chuckled. " 'You runs the trail, you pays the Ell.' "

They checked in with the older man, snagged a quick bite from the cookwagon, and headed back up the line.

"Oops," said Kettre. "Didn't take long enough." Mato's dnu was still up ahead. The elder had moved back to Rezuku's wagon and was now perched on the seat beside the merchant, complaining volubly.

"I'd curse," Nori muttered, "but it's just not worth the effort."

Kettre grinned over her shoulder. "You're boring when you curse, anyway. You really should take lessons from Payne."

From his outrider post, B'Kosan greeted them as they came abreast, but Mato's voice floated back clearly before he said anything else. "—can't get her to do a godsdamned thing. She's either working for the council or against it, dammit. And if she's helping at all, she damn well ought to do her duty when any elder asks. She has no right to withhold her skills." Rezuku's response was too quiet to hear, but Mato's sharp words weren't. "You heard those *chovas* yourself last night. She has to say yes eventually or shame her family. Arrogant little witch." He seemed to spit. "She's acting as if she can pass judgment on what I need and decide herself if it's important."

Kettre scowled, and B'Kosan raised an eyebrow at Nori. She shrugged. She'd heard plenty like that before.

Rezuku's voice was a soothing murmur, but Mato wasn't having any of it. "Cozar crap," he snapped loudly. "She's tight with those two Tamrani, but you try getting her to do the simplest task and see what I mean. I might as well try to talk to a stickbeast or pick a bouquet of redstick as deal with that . . . that . . ." Whatever he said was lost in a rattle of the wagon.

Nori's lips twitched. Stickbeasts were quiet, but they did speak, and redstick could be picked easily if one oiled one's hands and curled the leaves over the stingers.

". . . approach another scout?" suggested Rezuku over the wagon's noise.

"Because I want Black Wolf," Mato snapped back.

Kettre muttered bitingly, "What he wants is the status of the Wolfwalker's Daughter."

B'Kosan chuckled. "He's not the only one. I hear the Tamrani's interested, too. He was looking for you while you were doing your tower duty."

Nori frowned, but Mato's sharp voice cut through clearly. "—shortsighted, small-minded mountain rat like her mother whose only real value to the county would be in plunging to her death before she can breed more of the same."

For a moment, there was dead silence among the three riders. Then B'Kosan smiled at Nori. It was a strangely feral expression.

Deep in her mind, she felt the growl.

"Nori," Kettre began.

B'Kosan didn't seem to notice. "I'll challenge him for you, Black Wolf. It would be my pleasure."

At that moment, he reminded her of her uncles. "I thank you," she returned with difficulty. "But his sort has always used threats to get what he wants. I take no offense at his trying to manipulate your merchant."

B'Kosan's gaze flickered, but Nori didn't notice. Instead, she spurred Kettre's dnu to pass the elder quickly. The speed hardly helped. She felt the elder's eyes burning into her back.

Kettre spat to the side. "Whoever told him to push you for duty doesn't know the first thing about you. You'll have to watch him the rest of the ninan."

"I'm more likely to just leave and take some other route to Shockton." She paused. That was exactly what Wakje said someone might want. And Payne had been pushed, too, in his own way, toward a challenge from some of the *chovas.* If raiders wanted them out of the caravan, they were going about it the right way. "If you're willing, tell Payne to meet me after the hour," she told Kettre as the other woman dropped her off at the teaching wagon for the sixth of her *andyen* chores.

She spent the next hour dutifully explaining and answering the children's questions about the wilderness, but she couldn't help watching the outriders pass and note who was talking to whom. Mato, B'Kosan, raiders, plague—

The children broke back into her thoughts. "Black Wolf, tell us just one more."

"Aye, tell us about the poolah."

She sighed. She shouldn't complain. Teaching duty was one of the easiest things to do, especially for a bruised-up body. Since the teaching wagon was open, it was also one of the better places to be to watch the *chovas.* "I suppose there's time for a short one." She launched into the story easily, grinning to herself as they listened wide-eyed. ". . . so I punched it with the rock. Right on the crown. I was so scared, I actually hit it hard enough to stun it, just for an instant. Then I shoved the rock down its throat. Broke two fangs on the way in. My jerkin bunched up around its teeth—it's the only thing that saved my arm. It started choking, and I started stabbing it with my knife, and all the while its claws were tearing my pack, pants, everything it could kick. It finally chewed through my jerkin and started to rip into my arm—" She rubbed her forearm as if remembering. "So I punched it again, with the hilt of my knife. And found myself on my back, while it kicked out its death throes on my shredded boots."

"Were you . . . were you alright?" one child asked in the dramatic silence.

"Aye. I'd cracked its crown like an egg. My pack was in shreds, my jacket was in ribbons, and my pants . . . Well, let's just say they would have made fine netting for a Sidisport fisherman." The children laughed. "I packed my wounds with . . ." She let her voice trail off expectantly.

"Scofi moss," guessed a girl.

Nori smiled at her. "Aye, scofi moss mixed with wild angelica, two leaves for every handful of moss. I used flat-bark straps for my pack, which I softened by . . . ?"

"Scraping with a rock and rubbing with raw elbi nuts," put in a boy.

She nodded. "And I returned to the scout camp limping. There's just one thing." She looked at each of them seriously. "How big do you think that poolah was?"

"Three meters," said one boy quickly.

"Full grown," said a girl.

"As big as half a dnu," said another child almost at the same time.

Nori nodded as if considering their answers. Then she said quietly, "It was a baby poolah, not even weaned, and barely a meter long—including its tail."

The children stared at her as if she was joking.

"Had it been full grown, I'd be dead as a . . . ?" She looked at one of the boys.

"As a whipper lizard on shallow sand," he answered eagerly.

She nodded approval. "So what will you do if you run into a—"

"Poolah," the children shouted in unison. Nori hid a smile, and the children chorused obediently, "Poolah lurk right at the ground; when defending, crack their crowns."

Nori nodded to Payne as he reined in beside the wagon. "And for good practice, the second verse of the predator poem:

"Wildcat fights for den or prey;
Watch for tracks and stay away.
Bollusk trample, charge, and kick;
Climb a sturdy tree or cliff."

She broke off as Payne leaned over and said in a stage whisper to one of the girls, "I don't think she's remembering it right. The real verse is, 'Bollusk charge and like to trample; climb, or be a flat soil sample.' "

The girl giggled.

Nori gave her brother an old-fashioned look. "Payne, don't teach them that."

"Why not? You're the one who taught it to me." He winked at two of the boys. "Let's see, I believe another one goes like this: 'Dobo eels bite only once; let them nibble; don't be a dunce.' "

Even the boys were giggling now.

Nori clamped her lips shut to keep from laughing. "Payne, cut it out," she managed. "You're not supposed to corrupt the teachings during class hour."

"Oh, right. Not *during* class hour. I forgot." He slanted a glance at the small clock set into the wagon panel.

"The rest of the verse," she told the children archly, "goes like this:

"Badgers swarm out of the sand;
Talk and walk, don't run or stand.
Pritaries bite and bite again;
Kick and shout and run like wind."

Payne checked the small clock again. "Aye," he cut in. "Black Wolf never did get that last verse right. What she should have said was, 'Pritaries like to bite your ass; best to run away real fast.' "

One of the older children choked. The rest laughed outright.

"Payne, if you don't find something else to do—"

"Just being helpful," he said blithely. "And I did wait till after the class hour. I'm a firm believer in schooling. Why, I remember this one time—" He grinned at the students. "—when Nori and I were supposed to be learning history under old Master Hreggan, and Nori-girl got bored and decided to see how close she could call a pair of wild bollusk to—ow."

Nori had reached out, slid her hand down his arm to his ring finger, and started bending the finger back. "You'll excuse us," she told the children. "I believe it's time for your math teacher." She could see the reedy-slim woman already riding back to take over the class. She stepped across to Payne's stirrup, forcing him to kink back his arm as she kept her hold of his finger.

"Ow," said Payne a bit louder as she guided him away from the wagon. The children hid their giggles behind their hands. "Ow," they heard him say again. "Hey, Nori-girl, ease off. I can't hold the reins—"

Nori let him ride them out of earshot of the children. She finally released him to rub at his hand. "Is it possible," she said into his ear, "that I could do any of this *andyen* duty without you turning it upside down?"

He snorted at her. "Hells, Nori-girl, you scared the moons off their blessings with that poolah story. I was just lightening it back up before you bid them ride-safe."

"Right." She gave his back a sour look. "Now all they'll remember is, 'Pritaries like to bite your ass.' "

He gave her a lopsided grin over his shoulder. "Well, it is just as true."

Her lips twitched, and she looked away to keep from smiling. It would only make him worse.

She told him about the tower codes and Mato. She was telling him about B'Kosan's offer to challenge when she saw Hunter riding back. She broke off as she realized the Tamrani meant to rein in.

Payne murmured, "I'll check B'Kosan and Mato," and left her to get her dnu.

Hunter greeted her as she went to her last *andyen* duty, outriding another cozar. The Tamrani didn't seem inclined to speak, which puzzled her. She kept slanting the tall man glances, and she could swear she saw a half smile on his lips a few times.

"You were in the meeting wagon a long time," she finally remarked.

He glanced at her. "I wondered if you'd notice."

She gazed down the road to avoid his speculative expression. "I noticed that you've been talking almost nonstop with the elders."

"They mentioned you."

Aye, I bet they did, she thought. And Mato most of all. "I suppose they were after you to try to get me to do duty?"

"Yes, once. Yesterday evening."

"Just once? Yesterday?"

She didn't realize how disbelieving she'd sounded until he chuckled. "Just once."

Which meant he either told them to leave him alone, and they did, or else he had agreed to try again to convince her to ride with him. "Condari, why are you still here?" she asked bluntly.

"Call me Hunter. And I had business with your elders. Although I'll admit that I now have another reason to stay." He slanted her a meaningful glance.

She could feel her cheeks heat. But his jaw had tightened for an instant as he mentioned business, and she studied him carefully. "And Fentris?" she asked.

"He, too, has business with your elders."

"They're not my elders," she said, half under her breath.

He shot her an amused look. "No," he agreed. "But not for want of trying."

She snorted. She spent the next two hours chewing on her thoughts and studying the Tamrani while Rishte howled to pull her back into the forest.

Inns and taverns dotted the road at regular intervals, as did tiny wayside markets. That was one thing about cozar trains: they were slow enough that every family could shop, bargain, trade, and still keep up. Hunter wasn't the only one to stop at the waysides. Nori watched while he passed three written messages and a coin to one of the ring-runners who waited in the shade. Fentris did the same, as did several *chovas* and two of the Sidisport merchants.

Nori could feel Rishte watching from the forest. She wanted to be out there, on the trails. She needed to smell the trees, the ground, taste the branch water on eerin trails. And Rishte needed her. He needed the bond of the pack for company, for hunting, for defense. Danger that first night had tightened their bond, but they were not yet used to each other, and they gnawed in each other's minds. Yet when she tried to stretch into the grey, the slitted eyes deep in her thoughts seemed to blink open to stop her. Death and the smell of predators, of lepa, of Aiueven and plague were too close in both their minds.

Soon, soon, she tried to send. She needed to go now, into the wilderness. Feel the firm dirt on her heels, the soft leaves on her hands—

"Nori," Payne snapped sharply.

She jerked. She was heading right for the verge, about to spur her dnu across and into the forest on the other side of the grass. She hadn't even noticed her brother.

He leaned across and gripped her arm for a long moment. "Alright?"

"Aye," she whispered. She blinked to clear her vision. Color washed back in. The movements around her dulled. "Alright," she agreed shakily.

Payne watched her closely. "He's a year old, Nori-girl. There's already strength in his call."

She opened her mouth, cleared the snarl from her throat, and finally said, "I understand. I won't do that again."

"Damn right, you won't." But he scowled at a pair of *chovas* women who eyed them curiously. He drew her ahead and lowered his voice. "Why did he call? Was it . . . plague?"

"No. He's lonely," she managed. "Just lonely." She would go

to the ridges tonight to be with him. She'd be safe enough in the forest. Even the raiders seemed as inclined as the cozar to stay within the circle or on the main bridle trails.

He hesitated. "Can you feel it through him?"

He meant the plague sense, and she shook her head. "Not here, not right now. There was something earlier, when he was near the base of another ridge, but I couldn't tell if it really was plague or just something, like lepa, that reminded him of it."

"Best mark it down for Mama."

"Every time he's nervous?" Nori snorted. "Mama would end up chasing every poolah trap, badgerbear den, lepa cave, and lily swamp from Sidisport to Shockton!"

He gave her a sober look. "If even one of those sites is real . . ." He let his voice trail off ominously.

"And if it's just memories in the packsong?"

He shrugged. "Mama will sort it out."

"Aye," she agreed. Her gaze flicked to the hills. Even out of sight, Rishte was strong enough to challenge her. She had to remember that. If she forgot it, she could find herself riding blindly into the forest again, following the call. "Aye," she repeated. "I'll mark it down tonight."

She barely tolerated dinner when Payne and their uncles went to the circle tavern. It was a noisy place, large enough that the crowd was thick and volatile. Nori endured the laughter, shouts, clinking of glass, scraping of chairs on wooden floors, and the din of humanity for barely ten minutes before she fled. She made it back to the crowded kitchen, snagged a few meat scraps from a sympathetic cook, and slipped out with audible relief to the tree line.

Rishte was waiting impatiently. The yearling stayed in the shadows of the dark trees, unwilling to come close to the weathered inn, but growled at her to come with him. When she laid down the meat scraps, he edged forward, nipped each piece quickly, and darted back to eat in the shadows. He didn't meet her gaze till there was nothing left.

Come, now, he sent.

He turned, took a few steps, then looked back, waiting for her to follow. She had just risen when he startled, turned, and fled. Nori whirled.

B'Kosan and two other *chovas* spilled out the back of the inn with the light from one of the side rooms. The three outriders spotted her, waved, and staggered her way. She felt her lips curl back. She was alone against the tree line, and her hand crept toward her knife.

It was Wakje who arrested the motion. The thickset man appeared at the back door, glanced around casually, sat down on a nearby bench, and began to sharpen his knives. Nori found her lips twisting from snarl to humorless smile. B'Kosan must not have been as drunk as she thought, for he turned and staggered off with his partners.

They were barely gone when Payne poked his own head out the door. He murmured something to Wakje, then strode across the grass to Nori. "Fireside's going to start soon," he reminded her. "You need to be there to make your apology, and we need to trade for arrows."

Nori glanced back and noted the two Tamrani as they got their dnu. "Hunter said the elders hadn't bothered him about me."

"Well, hells, Nori-girl. They wouldn't bother you, either, if you stood up to them once in a while." He swung up in the saddle and grinned. "All you have to say is no."

"Mama never could." She reined in beside him. "Why do you think she avoided Ariye for so many years while we were growing up?"

He snorted. "You're not Mama—or so you keep saying."

She blinked.

He glanced behind them to make sure they were alone as they turned out onto the road. "You know the two men we followed and missed this morning?"

"Ye-es," she said warily, her thoughts still back on his other comment.

"The uncles and I were wondering if you wanted to use your wolf for a bit of human hunting after fireside if those two go out again?"

"Moons, Payne, you can track men, you can't hunt them with a wolf. I'd be blacklisted from ever getting rank."

He shrugged. "What do you need it for? Rishte will never care."

"Anyone I take contract with might."

"I doubt it. The elders would swallow a lepa whole if they thought it would help you take contract at all, and I'm beginning to suspect Brithanas would, too."

Nori flushed slightly and hoped the darkness hid it. "He said he had business with the elders. Has he left yet?"

"No, and it doesn't look like he will." Payne's voice grew bland. "He's asked for a guesting berth, as did the other Tamrani. They'll be with us all the way into Shockton." He chuckled. "Moons, you should have seen B'Kosan's face when he heard the news that Fentris the Fop would be staying. The *chovas* just about choked. And maSera, that outrider with the long braid, when she heard Brithanas ask for the berth, she went and changed into her best blouse and boots, along with a dozen other women." He shot Nori a look. "You didn't let anything slip on Deepening Road did you, to encourage Brithanas to stay? You know how you are when you're . . . anxious."

"When I'm scared out of my pants, you mean."

He teased ungently, "I would have said out of your shirt."

She flushed more darkly. She was wearing Hunter's blouse again. She wondered suddenly if that was why the Tamrani had smiled so often to himself earlier. Her voice was sharper than she meant as she answered, "I told him nothing about wanting to Journey or anything else."

"Maybe, but Brithanas has that look. He may be wanting a scout partner—" He broke off at her guilty expression. "He's already approached you," he accused. "He's already asked you to ride with him." His voice was suddenly hard. "You didn't commit to him, did you?"

"Of course not."

But her voice had been a bit too wistful. Payne cursed under his breath. "Moonworms, Nori-girl. The Lloroi would go along with a Tamrani request in a heartbeat if you even hinted that you were interested, and with the bond, you can't argue, not against the Lloroi. And every elder would back him, and not just because it's you they'd be getting on the council lists, but because you'll be a wolfwalker. You'll be welcome almost anywhere, especially with Brithanas. They always want to know what's going on in the Tamrani Houses."

"It's not as if I can Journey anyway, not if I'm to help find a cure for the plague."

"And who can you tell about that?"

She had no answer. He could Journey, but she couldn't. She could only tag along with him to hide her own work. "At least Rishte is still secret."

"For how long, with you snarling every hour? Ah, hells," he said sourly. "We can hide the wolf if we have to ride the backtrails to do it. That should keep the bond unknown for at least another ninan."

"Just keep me off the in-train duties as much as possible. I don't want some idiot like Mato saying I've promised to Test and take a Journey assignment because I've ridden duty for his wagon."

Payne nodded strongly. He was the last person to want her pushed into Test right now. The next ninan, with its Test and rank and Journey assignment, was supposed to be his, after all. "Don't worry," he told her firmly. "I give you my solemn, serious word, and you know how good that is—" She thwacked his shoulder, and he grinned. "—that it will be my goal in life to make sure you become the most unranked fighter in all of the first nine counties. After all," he added slyly, "how else can I force you to look up to me, unless I have the greater skills?"

"Rank, perhaps. Skill? Hah." She snorted. "Put the two of us on the same island with a knife, and I'll eat twice as well as you."

He swatted her away. "Only if you cheat." He lost his smile. "Talk to Brithanas, Nori. He's one of the bigger guns coming up in the counties. With his family behind him, he can pressure the

Lloroi in ways we can't imagine. And now that he knows you're a wolfwalker, he'll know just how to snag you."

"Alright." She sighed. "I'll talk to him again."

"Tonight," he said firmly. "You don't want to wait till Wakje or Ki gets involved."

She nodded soberly.

XXIII

The night has always had ears.

—Randonnen saying

Fireside was typical, with the usual business and requests for trade, after-dark complaints, and a dispute over *chovas* assignments that almost came to blows. The Solomon solution laid down by the Ell pleased neither man, but pride was in the way. Nori endured as usual. She was between Payne and Kettre, almost flinching each time someone jostled her. The smells of humanity clogged her nose, and her eyes seemed blind with movement: people shifting, getting up, edging past each row of legs. Colorful clothes like a visual whirlwind. The waves of murmurs that rose after each judgment or resolution. Her head seemed overfull.

Payne nudged her, and she tried to focus. A trader had discovered that his entire shipment of soft-leaf herbs was molding, and he accused the pack master of sabotaging his goods in favor of the cozar herbalists. Then the team master reported that half the lice wash had become tainted with a harsh bubble soap, as if someone had thought it would be fun to turn the insect wash bottles into endless bubble machines. Brean almost blew his temper over that, and more than one person glanced at Payne, not just at the other youths. Payne was equally angry. Soap in the lice wash wasn't a prank. The wash was absorbed into the dnu's skin to prevent lice from feeding on the beasts, and it would take the harsh soap with it right into the dnu's bloodstream. It could make the beasts sick for a ninan or more, delaying the caravan enough that they might not even make Shockton.

Then Nori flinched as an almost hysterical older woman rushed in from the message master and interrupted the meeting. Her grandfather had died, and the landholdings along a trade route that she'd inherited had somehow been sold instead of being passed along to her. She had four days to reach the assayer's office on the Eilian border while her family went on to Shockton. She needed a driver to take over her wagon while she rented some riding dnu. The woman was wailing curses up one side and down the other as she arranged the dnu for herself and her son and then galloped away in the night.

Nori had been aware of Hunter the entire evening. He hadn't spoken, but it surprised her that he'd paid such close attention when the woman's request was made. Fentris, too, seemed suddenly interested. In fact, she realized, B'Kosan and one of his friends were also watching the Tamrani. Nori almost missed the call for her apology as she frowned across the circle.

Belatedly, she stood up and turned in place till she had seen and been seen by the whole circle. She'd given Brean an informal apology earlier, but a search required one to the caravan. When she faced the Ell again, she began, "I offer my thanks for your support when the search was called, and my apologies that it became necessary. I did not intend to cause such worry, nor to take away the eyes and skills of the *chovas* who would otherwise have guarded you. All debt is mine and mine alone. *Jeferen keyo'andyen.*" She spoke the guest-debt phrase, bowed her head, and waited.

The old Ell nodded, pleased by the courtesy. Most *keyo* didn't bother using the cozar tongue even if they knew it. He studied her bowed head. Normally he'd have let Brean assign at least three full days of duty, but Black Wolf had already done seven debt chores. Considering that she'd tended their dnu freely since she'd joined the caravan, any guest debt she could accumulate had already been repaid. The *andyen* chores had been merely for form. The Ell waited only the required twelve seconds before saying firmly, "*Hashtik jeni sur'niloni andyen e'abran, Keyo* Black Wolf. The stones have fallen, no debt remains. Be at peace."

From the circle of elders, Mato seemed to pounce at the

words. "May I speak?" he asked quickly as Nori sat down in relief.

Payne looked over sharply, but Mato was already standing, barely waiting for the Hafell to acknowledge him. The elder gestured behind him. "This man, neDoshru, has need of a veterinary."

Payne's eyes narrowed at the hostler. With his lips barely moving, he whispered to Nori, "Stay alert, Nori-girl. That's one of Mato's cousins from his mate's side of the family. He runs three of the stables along this stretch, and he's after an animal healer."

"You checked him out today," she remembered.

"Aye, and I've used his dnu before. The man's always bragged about Mato and the other elders in the family." He listened as Elder Mato continued with his request. But Mato did not explain the relationship to neDoshru, and Payne was surprised. Family relationships were important to the cozar. Keeping an identity unknown during a trade talk was considered a breach of contract.

But Mato merely added, "The local animal healer is in the outlying district. NeDoshru has asked if the duty healer will come to his stable instead and treat the mounts for blue mange. There are several animals in need of attention. An hour or so of work."

"How many dnu?" asked Brean.

"Ah." Mato looked at his cousin. "There might be a dozen or more."

"How many exactly?"

Mato looked irritated. He answered finally, "Forty-three have been brought to that particular stable for treatment."

Brean's voice sharpened. "Forty-three beasts is a full day's work or more. That's a clear county duty, not just "an hour or so."

Mato looked directly at Nori. "I'm sure we can negotiate the terms."

Ten or more hours, away from the caravan? Nori didn't need to catch Payne's warning nudge. She tried to keep her face expressionless, but she could feel the snarl on her lips. She was not the caravan duty healer. She was a *keyo,* a guest. Technically, to outsiders, she was only a skilled *chovas*. The original duty belonged to a man who had skipped out on the train in Sidisport—or been done away with, she thought darkly. Since then, Ell Tai had assigned Vindra Twitch-Whickers to the position, but it was Nori who did most of the work. Here, if she responded to the call for a duty healer, she would put herself in the position of holding that position more formally. It was a small step from cozar to council duty. In this case, because the hostler was Mato's cousin, the elder could even claim she had done duty for an elder.

Kettre leaned toward Nori on the other side and whispered, "I saw that man ride in when I was putting up my dnu. His beasts have softhoof disease, not just mange."

Nori nodded almost imperceptibly. That would explain the need for another healer. Softhoof required constant attention.

From across fireside, Hunter was watching her curiously. She couldn't help raising her chin stubbornly at him as the Hafell glanced at her and waited a few seconds. When she didn't stand up, Brean turned back to the elder. "We have no duty vet with the skills you need, Elder Mato. NeDoshru should—"

"Excuse me, Hafell," Mato cut in.

Payne raised his eyebrows at the interruption. He wasn't surprised when the Ell directed a hard gaze at Mato.

The elder didn't seem to notice. "As of three months ago, Black Wolf is a fully ranked vet with three bars. She has extensive experience with both indigenous and oldEarth livestock. And rumor has it she began her training when she was twelve. She can calm crazed dnu with a word."

Brean's face was carefully expressionless. "This is not a gossip fence, Elder Mato. This is fireside. Requests for cozar or guest skills are made based on rankings within the caravan, not on rumors heard in town. As I have stated, we have no duty vet. Do you request the use of guest skills?"

Mato opened his mouth to protest, but hung up on a frown. "Guest skills?"

Brean nodded shortly. "Noriana maDione is not cozar, but guest in this caravan. A request for her skills must be made to her, not to me."

"Black Wolf is no guest here," the older man said flatly. "She was raised cozar. She lives like a cozar. You treat her like cozar, and even punish her like a cozar when she's wrong. Hells, she just apologized to you in the cozar language. You use her just as any county elder would."

Brean's face stiffened. "Nevertheless, she is a *keyo,* a close guest, not cozar."

"And I've been told that she is as cozar as you."

"By whom?" Brean said sharply.

Mato's gaze flickered, but he said quickly, "It does not signify, but you can't expect me to believe that she lives like you, speaks like you, and still claims she isn't cozar."

Nori had almost been enjoying watching Mato insult Brean, the caravan, and the cozar in general. Now her violet eyes went cold at Mato's assumption of her lineage, and she did not realize that, for an instant, her gaze echoed the chill of her father.

The Hafell looked across the fire, saw her expression, and hid a faint smile. Perhaps for once, she wouldn't need her brother. "*Keyo* Noriana Ember maDione," he summoned.

She stood reluctantly.

"If you're willing," he said. "Black Wolf, are you cozar?"

"No, Hafell," she answered truthfully. She started to sit back down, but Payne's words about standing up for herself came back to her, and she found herself adding, "To be completely honest, I believe—as someone pointed out so clearly earlier—" She looked directly at the elder, and her lips curled slightly. "—I am a stubborn, shortsighted, small-minded mountain rat whose only real value to the county is in plunging to my death before I can breed more of the same."

There was a collective gasp around the circle, and Payne was on his feet beside her.

Elder Mato's face turned beet red.

Payne made the gesture for an interim speaker and stepped slightly in front of her. "I apologize for my sister, Hafell," he said quickly. "She is overwrought from the events of the past few days." Nori kicked his foot, but he didn't turn a hair as he finished smoothly, "I believe she meant to say that she was a stubborn, shortsighted, small-minded, *Randonnen* mountain rat."

The titters around the circle couldn't quite be suppressed. Kettre turned quickly away, but her fist was stuffed in her mouth, and her shoulders were shaking. Mato ground his teeth, and the Hafell regarded the two for a long moment. From the contortions of the muscles on the sides of Brean's jaw, Nori had the impression the Hafell was struggling as hard as the others.

The old Ell spoke for him. "As you heard, Elder Mato, Black Wolf is not cozar. She is only another guest among us."

"A guest," Mato snapped. "So you give her the haven of the caravan, and expect no work in return."

Payne stiffened, and several merchants frowned. A wise man didn't insult the traders with whom he might have to negotiate later, but Mato was in his righteous robe and drawing his line in the sand. Nori stepped out from behind Payne before he could retort for her. Her quiet voice carried clearly as she faced the old Ell. "I have always appreciated the *keyo* berth the cozar have extended to me. I am pleased to perform any task that helps smooth the road for my friends. *Seye in 'stina in yo.*"

Ell Tai inclined his head approvingly. Salt and bread and water—it meant she had shared life with them and so was bound to them as a sister by all but blood. It was the travel oath for the cozar, as good as a contract in almost any circle. The old man turned sternly back to Mato, but Elder Connaught stood quickly instead. "May I speak?"

Both Brean and Ell Tai gave the elder a sharp look, but Brean nodded.

Connaught cocked his head at Mato. "I see that this is important to you, Elder Mato. Perhaps you would be willing to trade Black Wolf a dozen hunting shafts of Poorford Cedar from your Diton holdings, in place of the usual vet right."

There was another wave of murmuring at the suggestion of the rare wood. Nori and Payne both stared at Connaught. The elder winked subtly at the wolfwalker, and Payne felt the grin start on his face. Now, that was a payback favor. And while Nori was doing the vet duty, Payne could use that as an excuse to check in with the local council. If they did need to leave the caravan, this would be the perfect excuse to do so.

Mato stared in turn, then sputtered. "Poorford Ced—? But that's—" He broke off again. "Those are worth a fortune. Do you know how rare those trees are? We don't make three hundred shafts a year—"

"One silver for every three dnu is a bit steep for blue mange," Connaught agreed. He added smoothly, "Unless the animals are suffering other conditions that will require more attention once the *keyo* vet is on site. I hear that your friend's mount has a bit of softhoof. I understand that's quite contagious." Mato's lips thinned as Brean's expression went cold. Connaught smiled blandly. "And as you know, Black Wolf lost her bow and quiver at Stone Ridge. With her scouting duties, their replacement is as important to her as your friend's dnu are to him."

"You might as well ask for singing spruce," Mato snapped.

Connaught shrugged. "A dozen shafts of either, Elder Mato, would cover ten or twelve hours of a ranked vet's time."

"That's . . . that's blackmail," he sputtered.

Nori said diffidently, "If it would help, Elder Mato, I am willing to forgo charging your cousin for the medicines for mange and softhoof. Instead, I would provide any needed medications from my own supplies."

Payne hid a wider grin. He knew as well as she did that, although the herbs used to treat blue mange and softhoof were worth as much as the arrows, they could also be gathered fresh in spring—if one was willing to brave the wilderness to find them. That had never been an issue for Nori.

Mato started to speak, then caught Nori's reference to his cousin. "My cousin? How did you—" He caught the dawning expression on the Ell's old face and glared at Nori. "Four shafts, perhaps," he snapped. "No more than that."

Connaught had also caught the reference, and he glanced at Nori, then Payne. He raised one eyebrow. Payne nodded almost imperceptibly, and the old man turned back to the cozar council. "A dozen shafts," he said firmly.

Hunter was staring at Nori now, and Fentris was regarding both the brother and sister with a thoughtful expression.

"Six shafts," Mato countered.

"A dozen."

"You're not even trying to bargain."

For the first time, Connaught let a flicker of anger into his voice. "This isn't a negotiation. It's payment for vet services rendered to you from a fully qualified vet, who has extensive knowledge of the indigenous life on this world, and who is ranked in two related fields. You would be hard-pressed to find someone else as knowledgeable and skilled as Noriana ma-Dione on the road and available at this time of year. A dozen shafts, Elder Mato."

"Chak take you," he snarled. "A dozen shafts."

Connaught glanced at Payne for his approval, Payne glanced at Nori, and she nodded her agreement. The Ell held up his hand, though, before Payne could formally acknowledge the deal. The old man's face was hard, and he stared coldly at the elder. "You agree, Elder Mato: a dozen shafts of Poorford Cedar?"

"Aye," the elder snapped.

"You agree, Black Wolf: three hours of your healer skills?"

"Three?" Mato blistered. "We bargained for ten or twelve—"

The glance of the old Ell silenced him like a knife. "Three hours, Black Wolf?"

Nori didn't hesitate. "Aye, Ell Tai."

"Then this *bokat* trade is concluded." There was a darker murmur, and it took Mato a second to realize what the Ell had said, but even as he opened his mouth to curse, the Ell quelled him with a glare. The old man glanced at Nori, then back at the flushed elder. He didn't take his eyes off Mato as he said softly, "You may begin your service, Black Wolf, as soon as the *bokat* shafts are delivered. This contract is in effect from this moment through noon tomorrow. If the *bokat* shafts have not been delivered by dawn so that you can complete the service within the contracted time, this trade is annulled and your duty is considered done." It was another statement, one even harsher, since payments of unusual materials could usually be delayed for up to a year. The Ell knew Mato had not brought the arrow stock with him; it was unlikely he could come up with the payment before the contract time expired.

Nori didn't look at Mato as she nodded respectfully. "Aye, Ell Tai." She stepped back to take her seat again, but she was shaking. Payne rubbed her arm up and down to soothe her, but the wolf in her was bristling. She barely waited for fireside to be dismissed before stalking away from the crowd.

She snarled low at Payne, "He's not just being used to push us. He's with them."

But her brother shook his head. "Take a breath, Nori. He's a chak, nothing more."

"How can you say that?" She almost spat the words. "Every duty he's asked of me would remove me from the caravan, just as Uncle Wakje said a raider would try to do."

"Aye, but he's not from this part of the county. He couldn't know of the cassar root stands if he hadn't been told about them. And he's never met his cousin till now. Why would he seek ne-Doshru out unless that had been suggested?"

That stopped her.

"Look, Nori-girl, I had time to check into his background."

"And?"

"And he's nothing more than a midrange elder. He's never made enough of an impression on anyone to be accused of more than making his mind up too quickly and sticking to his position after that no matter how wrong he is. And," he added softly, "he wasn't a problem for us until after Sidisport."

She halted at their wagon. She was beginning to feel the ebb of her anger, and now she flushed that it had been so strong. It had been . . . animalistic, she realized. She'd wanted to tear at Mato. She took a breath, let it out, and managed, "B'Kosan joined us in Sidisport."

"As did Murton, maSera, Woraconau, Gretzell, and half the other *chovas*."

Now he really had her attention. "Chovas duty is perfect cover for a raider."

"Aye, but—" He broke off. "Heads up, Nori-girl," he said, softly. He gestured with his chin down the aisle.

She followed his gaze. B'Kosan and his merchant were heading their way. Rezuku lifted a hand to catch their attention.

"My apologies to you both," the blond man said easily as he came up, though his eyes were sharp as they took in the brother and sister. Nori belatedly slipped her knife back in her belt. "I didn't mean to startle you." The merchant nodded at Payne, then turned to Nori. "MaDione, I offer my sincere apologies to you in particular. It was in my presence that Mato insulted you so grievously both earlier and at fireside."

The man ran his hand through his thin blond hair in a gesture that seemed almost practiced, and Payne's violet eyes narrowed. He didn't think the merchant sounded displeased at all. In fact, he could swear there was a smugness under Rezuku's voice that made Payne's attention stand on edge.

The merchant, with his gaze on Nori, didn't notice. "Please," the man added. "Tell me what I can do to make amends."

"My thanks for the apology, Merchant Rezuku, but I take no offense." She started to turn away.

"Black Wolf, maDione, let me do something. I have many contacts up and down the county. Perhaps I can help you arrange some interesting stops on this trip or on your Journey when you accept it—" He broke off as Nori's face went carefully expressionless. He added smoothly, "Or perhaps something as simple as sharing a cup of Germeni wine with me to assure me you do not think so poorly of me." He smiled charmingly. "I admit freely that I have an ulterior motive, but I swear I will mention to you only this once that I would like to do business with your uncle, the Lloroi, and that I hope I can drop your name in the conversation when I meet him."

She looked down the darkened wagon lane for a moment. Lanterns bobbled with the strides of cozar who headed for bed, while other parties gossiped animatedly as they headed out for the inns. A pair of women had stopped nearby to murmur a last bit of gossip. It was normal; the entire night felt normal, but still she felt uneasy. She wanted more steel at her side than the belt knife and boot knife she carried, and this merchant made her wary. Yet Payne said nothing, and they did want inside the man's wagon. Slowly, she nodded.

Rezuku gave her a smile. "Tomorrow?"

This time, she couldn't help glancing at Payne.

"The next day then," the blond man said smoothly. "After fireside. My best Germeni wine. I've brought several cases for trade, and I would consider it an honor to sample a bottle with you."

She nodded again.

The satisfied merchant strode away down the line of wagons, and B'Kosan gave her a grin over his shoulder as he trailed dutifully along.

Nori muttered, "Probably thinks that if he steals some wine, I'll have a drink with him, too." She scowled after the *chovas*. "If I looked like Uncle Wakje, men like that wouldn't bother me twice."

Payne chuckled. "If you looked like Wakje, you'd have a chin like a butcher, hands like a meat grinder, and eyebrows made of bollusk hair, not to mention forearms like my thighs." He glanced around to see that they were alone for the moment, then nodded after the pair. "I think I'll tag along in the shadows and see who else he talks to."

"Good." She opened her trail pack on the gate to do a check of her gear. "B'Kosan was far too interested in Fentris's and Hunter's reactions when that woman's inheritance came up."

Payne turned to look at her. "That was about land on the southern trade route."

She nodded. "I've got notes on activity all along that route, all the way down to Sidisport and back up the Randonnen border."

He said slowly, "That would explain the Tamrani presence and why Brithanas wants the Daughter of Dione." He caught her expression and said quickly, "He probably never saw you as anything else Nori-girl. He is Tamrani, and you're—"

"The Wolfwalker's Daughter," she finished flatly.

"Aye. Noriana is just an animal healer and a backtrail scout. Those aren't the skills a Tamrani usually needs." He added, "He must be trying to get a jump on some kind of change in the trade lanes. It would have to be big, though. Tamrani don't move unless there's heavy gold involved." He rubbed his jaw and looked back toward fireside.

She snapped her pack closed, and Rishte growled again in her head. She growled her agreement back. But Payne put his hand over hers to stop her from slipping her pack on. "Don't go using that till after I get back, and till after you've had a talk with Brithanas. Get him to back off, but see what he knows, if you can. I'm going to follow B'Kosan."

She muttered a curse as she plopped her pack back on the gate. "Fine. I'll talk to him. Yes, now," she added before he could say it himself. She remembered B'Kosan's expression from that afternoon when the *chovas* suggested he challenge Mato for her. She caught his arm. "Payne, if you talk to B'Kosan, don't make any accusations. He's too much like Uncle Ki. He might challenge you, and it wouldn't be for fun."

He stared at her for a long moment. "I hear you."

The call of the wolf was a growling thing, deep inside her mind. It was yanking now like a leash. She tried to swallow her snarl, but she knew her voice was harsh. "Be careful, Payne."

His voice was dry. "Like Papa, Nori-girl."

"Aye, like Papa." Then he was gone, slipping after Rezuku. Nori looked down the now deserted lane, then reached back into the wagon, plucked an extra knife from the low rack, and strapped it onto her belt. She hesitated, then snapped a balanced blade out of the rack and tucked it into her boot sheath. Then she strode away to find Hunter.

XXIV

[*Grasp hefts his sword.*] *"Which one am I supposed
to kill, anyway?"*
"The one in blue." [*Chenshi spits to the side and
adjusts his sword belt.*]
[*Grasp peers across the stage.*] *"I don't see him."*
"That's because he is beside you." [*And Chenshi
draws his blade.*]

—from *Playing with Swords,* modern staging

The tall Tamrani greeted her with a smile. She looked uncomfortable, and he hid his satisfaction. This should be almost
easy. "Walk with me for a few minutes."

She cocked her head at him and gestured toward an empty
bench on the outskirts of the now sparse fireside. "We can talk
here."

He glanced at the small groups of colorful men and women.
Half wore plain, dark colors for travel and work, but the other
half were like vari birds at mating. Red shirts with black trim,
yellow-green cloaks edged with violet braid, and royal blue
pants with lime-green embroidery? They made a Tamrani ball
look dull. He'd almost laughed in spite of himself when Shae
had commented dryly earlier that his eyes almost hurt to see
them. He said simply, "I'd prefer the verge to the camp."

"Why?" she asked warily.

"I enjoy a stroll in the evening. After tonight, I'd think you'd
want one, too." She looked over her shoulder, and he added casually, "They've gone across to Vallier's train."

She shot him a sharp look. "Who?"

"Your uncles. Said something about talking to the other
scouts. Your brother went off that way. Shall we?" He motioned
for her to walk beside him.

She drew back. "I don't think so." It was too tempting to leave

268

the firelight, the flickering lanterns, the cozar noise. Safety in numbers, Payne had said. There were at least four outriders nearby, none of them Sidisport *chovas*. "Here is good enough."

"But not as pleasant as a moonlit verge."

Rishte growled in her mind, and she scowled irritably. "I'm tired and sore, Hunter." And ready to snap at anyone who came near, she thought. "I just want to sleep. We can talk here if we need to."

He raised one black eyebrow at her. "With a trail pack ready on your wagon gate? I'd say you were up for a midnight run."

"I said no. Not tonight. Not with you." She broke off, embarrassed. She couldn't believe she'd admitted that. She snarled back at the wolf in her mind.

The Tamrani's gaze sharpened, and his green eyes gleamed. "Are you nervous around me, Wolfwalker?"

"Of course not."

Hunter's voice was dry. "I'm flattered."

Her voice was sharp. "It wasn't a compliment."

He mock-sighed. "You were so nice on the ride today."

"You weren't so irritating then."

He actually laughed.

She nodded at a couple who greeted her, lowered her voice, and said, "Condari, I don't believe for a moment that all you want to do is talk." She took a breath and steeled herself. "You should know that I don't walk out with strange men. I'm also not in the habit of kum-jan, especially between bare acquaintances—"

He grinned at her unintentional pun. She might be a scout, but Randonnens were often stuffy about intimacy between friends.

She forged on. "And I'm tired and sore from the last two days."

"I remind you that I'm not half-bad as a masseur. Surely you noticed that before, when I rubbed your legs after your run. You weren't so tense with me then."

"Look, Condari—"

"Hunter or Con," he corrected. "And I don't even want my shirt back."

Nori blushed. She'd not yet returned either jerkin or shirt, and she was strangely reluctant to do so. It was almost as if she wanted the man near without actually being by him herself. "I'll return it—and your jerkin—in the morning after I've had a chance to wash them."

"I'd rather you kept them. And," he forestalled her. "Don't bother to ask why." That small smile played around his lips. "I think you know."

She refused to take a step back. "I know enough to ask again, what do you want, *Condari*?"

He tried to take her hand as he would if they were in Sidisport. "Noriana Ember maDione, have I offended you?"

She slipped free. "No, but—"

"Am I so badly trained that you were irritated or disgusted to ride with me?"

"You're competent enough on the trail."

"Don't slay me with admiration."

In spite of herself, she found her lips twitching.

"A walk, Noriana. I'm among strangers, here. I just want some conversation."

"You have Fentris."

He snorted. Although, he might have to start confiding in the other man if their interests were as parallel as he was beginning to believe. That woman at fireside, the one whose inheritance was sold? He'd heard of a dozen merchants who had lost properties in the past year the same way or something like it. But he said, "I want a walk, not a fight."

Nori hid a smile. She suspected that Fentris was deliberately provoking Hunter every chance he got. "You could go back to your own caravan."

"I'd have to be dead from a lack of curiosity if I didn't want to find out why you were so anxious to come back to this train. Half an hour, Wolfwalker. Down the road and back. You'll be in sight of the circle most of the way. You can even bring your wolf."

She regarded him so warily that he wondered if he'd sprouted fangs. Then she gestured abruptly. "We'll walk."

He didn't question her change of mind. Instead, he let her

lead him away from fireside, out the gate, and along the path that forked across the wide verge. Payne caught a glimpse of them as they passed the far quads, and Nori avoided her brother's gaze as he scowled after the pair.

There were other cozar stretching their legs on that length of road, and Nori seemed to withdraw into herself with every sly expression. Hunter, noting the rising flush on her cheeks, raised his eyebrows and gestured toward a darker side path. She gave him a long look, checked to see if anyone had followed them, then nodded in relief. They slipped away to the wider part of the verge where the others didn't venture.

Willow Road was the main way up the valley, with each lane separated and lined by a wide avenue of some of the oldest rootroad trees. In this area, the barrier bushes were almost six hundred meters apart, far enough that the verge was a small park dotted with watering troughs for dnu and stone benches set back in tiny arbors. The paths wound their way up the slight hill like loose white braids in an ancient knot. Still cooling from the day's warm sun, the air was heady with late scents from the clumps of pink and blue flowers, while pairs of pelan fluttered heavily down to settle for the night.

It was an old park, cleared in the second century. There was a sense of age trapped in the stone benches, like caskets holding the bones of the past. It wasn't just Hunter's imagination. Each bench was carved with the name of a martyr, each name a testament to a man or woman who had died bringing the last of the Ancients' technology out of the plague-ridden domes. Like the cozar pillars that marked events, the benches in the park kept the memories of the martyrs alive. He noted that the wolfwalker seemed unusually pensive as she touched a few of the benches.

Nori named each bench to herself as she passed it. The deathseep was days behind her now, but the sense of it was still with her. Even though Rishte had been nervous twice that day, she wondered if she had misinterpreted his impressions. Here, in this park, it seemed fitting that the wolves remember the plague through their memories, just as humanity did in its carvings.

Her tension faded the farther they were from the circle and the knowing eyes of the cozar. By the time they had walked silently through half the park, she knew no one was near. With the faint hunting cry of a badgerbear on the ridge, no cozar would venture this far from the fires.

They paused while Hunter splashed water on his face at one of the stone fountain basins. Nori looked east, into the thick forest. *Rishte?* she called carefully.

Wolfwalker, you come! Even with the grey little more than a blurred din in the back of her head, she didn't mistake that message.

Soon. Come to me. Come closer.

Wolfwalker, wolfwalker, the Grey One sang.

She smiled wryly. Rishte didn't hear her, not clearly. It was the contact, not the words, that he'd caught. She tried to stretch toward the grey as Hunter drank from the fountain. It was hard. The Tamrani was too close, too full of strength and presence. In the moonlight, she couldn't help noticing that his hands were rough-textured enough that the water caught brokenly across his tanned knuckles. It was as if reaching for Rishte made her more aware of everyone around her. Every movement seemed exaggerated, sharper, requiring a response.

She closed her eyes. Tried to sink into the grey. She didn't realize her hand stretched toward the forest. Grey din, blurred fog, swirls of images so faint they made no sense . . . Rishte . . . standing? Rishte moving, and the odors of the forest too thick to distinguish. But there was something in his voice that made her fingers curl.

"Nori?"

She opened her eyes abruptly. Hunter was frowning. Water dripped from his chin, and he dragged a sleeve across his face as he studied her.

"Unease." She didn't realize she had spoken out loud until she heard her own voice. She flushed at Hunter's silent question. A wariness or unease—that was what underlay Rishte's voice. It wasn't just eagerness for Nori to join him, it was the youthful fear of being kays away from the pack. For he was alone now, separated from the pack by distance and days, and separated from Nori by the other humans. The bond would grow stronger the more they had only each other to be with, but she couldn't help reaching out to the loneliness. She should not have heard it so soon in his voice, but the worlag run and her own tension had put a tightness into their thoughts that would have been months in building.

"You're dreamy," Hunter observed quietly. "And prickly at the same time. It's intriguing."

She was abruptly back to earth. "It is not my intention to intrigue you."

"And disconcertingly sharp as a knife."

She cast him a sidewise look. "I'll not answer that one, or I'd be forced to say where the blade would best be used."

He laughed.

She glanced around, made sure they were alone in the park, then took a deep breath. "I must ask something of you."

"Then ask," he answered easily. She'd used the cozar words stiffly, and he suspected that this favor was why she'd agreed to go with him.

She didn't look at him. Instead, she kept her gaze straight ahead on the ragged hilltop tree line. "Don't mention Rishte to anyone. Don't speak about my bonding. Uncle Wakje won't talk about it, nor will Ki, and Payne knows better. But you . . ." Her voice trailed off in a helpless shrug.

He walked on for a moment in silence. She hadn't used the cozar request phrase. If he didn't know better, he'd think that what she said had been an order, not a request. She was hiding the bond out of what? Insecurity? It was almost as intriguing as her prickliness. "Should I ask why this is so important?"

"Will you do it?"

He stopped, forcing her to face him. "Yes," he said softly. "Since you ask it." She nodded and made to walk on, but he caught her arm. She tensed, and he released her instantly. "It frightens you," he said, surprised. "I don't scare you, nor this night, nor the sound of that badgerbear out on the hill. But the thought that I might know you are bonding—that has you tense as a wire."

In the night, her violet eyes seemed to gleam. "You guessed before, back at the wayside."

"I suspected," he agreed. "I was sure after the trail to Willow

Road." He shook his head. There was a sense of wonder in his voice. Two nights ago, when she'd led them on that cross-trail, he hadn't known what to expect. The Wolfwalker's Daughter, five moons at night . . . They had been on a dark stretch, with the moons behind the clouds, and the Grey Ones gone ahead, when he got his first intimation of what it would be like to ride with a wolfwalker, not just with a standard scout.

Nori had pulled them up at the edge of the trees, just inside a meadow line. She'd held them there for a moment, then eased them back until they were well under the canopy, all the time not saying a word. Both men had watched her as much as they'd stared into the darkness. After a few minutes, the meadow seemed to lighten. It hadn't been the moon. It had been the moonthistles that were beginning to open. When two of the nine moons broke back out from the clouds, the thistles had started to glow. For ten minutes, they watched as the thistles burst out, feathery tendrils waving like grass in a sea. Then, just as their dnu began to get restless, the wolfwalker motioned. At first, it seemed to be just a breeze in the meadow. Then the thistles started to seethe.

Hunter's hand had tightened on the hilt of his sword before he realized that the wolfwalker was still relaxed. He had to force himself to let go of the hilt, although he didn't take his hand away. A few minutes later, the first bluewing moth had fluttered up from the thistles.

Hunter had sucked in a breath. He'd heard of this, but never seen it. Few scouts did. One had to camp for days—usually with spring worlags, badgerbears, and bihwadi hunting—to catch the bluewings hatching. He had watched intently as the first pale bluewings glistened and fluttered up. A minute later, two more had hatched. Then the entire meadow seemed to be ascending until the glow of spotted blue against the tendrils of yellow-white was a wavering palette of light.

Fentris had made the sign of the moonsblessing, and Hunter hadn't blamed him. With the bluewings curling up to the sky, it was an almost spiritual moment. He'd started to turn to Nori to thank her when she held up her hand to stop him. She pointed with two fingers, never taking her eyes from the meadow. Hunter had followed the motion.

He stiffened as the first black shadow struck. Within seconds, the night sky was filled with darting, swooping forms. Bluewings glowed brokenly in silent beaks that caught up the moths and cracked them. Fragments of glowing wings filtered down over the meadow in a ragged, luminescent rain. The thistles writhed, reaching for the torn blue. They fed below, while the tree sprits dove and tore apart the glowing, pale blue sky.

It took only five, six minutes before the meadow was still again. The last of the bluewings that survived escaped into the trees, and the tree sprits darted away in pursuit. The thistles, satiated, tucked in their tendrils and glowed serenely on their stalks, waiting for the dawn.

It took a growl from the dark before Fentris had broken that deadly quiet. His voice had been rough. "How many will survive?"

Nori stirred. "Enough," she'd answered. "Eight, maybe ten percent. It's been a good spring for moths."

"I hadn't realized."

"Most don't." Her voice had been dry. "You'll see it later, in the lumber you harvest for flatwood."

Fentris had given her a sharp look. He'd wanted to ask how she knew he had interests in the flatwood farms, but she had already begun to lead them out on the trail that cut through the meadow.

Hunter hadn't been able to help himself from tensing as they rode into that faintly glowing field. He felt no small satisfaction that Fentris's knuckles were just as white as the other man gripped his own sword.

Now Hunter studied Nori closely on the moonlit verge. "You knew as we approached the meadow that the bluewings would hatch. You knew it was time for a hatching."

She shrugged. "I picked it up from the wolf pack."

"You mean from one wolf in particular. You had that same look as now."

She looked away.

"Yesterday, when the rest of the pack went east, one of them stayed close to the road. You weren't wary then like you were before, and your eyes were often unfocused."

She found herself poised on the balls of her feet, as if he'd begun to attack her. "So Fentris knows also?"

"Probably. He's nothing if not sharp."

"And neLivek and the others, back at Clever Springs? Did they notice?"

Her voice was tight, and Hunter studied her before answering. "NeLivek might, but he'd say nothing. As for the others, they were too busy bickering about duties. They might have realized your name, but not that you were bonding."

"You've been around the Grey Ones before," she realized. "You barely flinched when Rishte came to the road."

"I've known a few wolfwalkers. You have that look, *Jangharat*," he said deliberately. He half raised his hand to touch her cheek, but let it fall when she shifted back. "And therein lies the problem, Black Wolf," he said softly. "You think I'm intrigued because you're the Daughter of Dione. But it wasn't the Daughter of Dione who ran out of the woods with a wolf pack on her heels. It was a woman with a handful of the Grey Ones' pups and the violet eyes of a moonmaid."

Her voice was low. "You speak like you're working toward something."

"Something," he agreed. "I was impressed with you on the cross-trail." He hesitated. "I'm curious, Black Wolf. How much do you know of codes?"

Nori tried not to stiffen. "I know the scout codes, of course, and the standard ring-runner cipher."

"You really have to work on your poker face." She looked uncomfortable, wary, and guilty all at once. "If I had to guess," he said softly, "I'd say you also know the council codes, the Lloroi's code, and your family whistle codes."

She shrugged irritably. "Lloroi Tyronnen is my uncle. I wouldn't be much use to him if I couldn't send him what he needed to know without—" Her voice broke off. "Damn you." How the hells had he gotten her to admit that? Did she trust him that much instinctively, or had she so little control now from Rishte?

Hunter nodded. "You've seen the trade codes, too, I'd bet. And probably some of the guild codes. What about the Houses?"

She didn't answer. She was watching him like a wolf now. If he asked about the raider code, she'd know.

But what he said next confused her. He regarded her with those cool green eyes and said quietly, "You love your brother very much."

She cocked her head warily. "Aye," she said finally.

"How much would you give up to keep him safe?"

She frowned. She didn't see where he was going at all. She said sharply, "I'd give up you in a heartbeat, Tamrani."

He chuckled without humor. "Very telling." He didn't explain that the flash of fear in her eyes said she'd already considered the question. She was worried about something that was coming to a head, he could feel it. He hadn't pushed her on the ride today. He'd thought her natural curiosity would keep her intrigued with his presence. Instead, she'd barely spoken to him. She'd spent her time with her brother, watching the men and women around them as if anyone could be a threat. Hunter was beginning to think that, if he wanted to get Nori to ride with him, he'd have to court Payne, too.

She eyed him carefully. "I might be willing to answer your questions if you told me why you are here, and why you are heading for council."

Hunter studied her for a moment. Then his voice lost all teasing and became firm and businesslike. "I've come north to ask your council for an Ariyen scout, but I'm beginning to think that a wolfwalker would suit me better." He didn't hide his seriousness. She had no idea what was at stake. The changes he and Fentris had seen were only the surface of a sea that was beginning to roil. If it was just a Purging of power, then only a few dozen, maybe a hundred would die. If it was a House War, then the entire city would erupt. Venges would hunt down families, and families would try to flee. It would spread to the southern Ariyen towns, then north on up the county. Whole villages could be slaughtered as the venge riders turned to raiding. He added quietly, "It's a duty that will affect Ramaj Ariye, and possibly all three of the middle counties."

Nori regarded him expressionlessly. So Payne was right again. It was Condari Brithanas wanting the Daughter of Dione. She didn't think for a moment that a scout request was the sole reason he rode to council, not with her uncle as Lloroi. Rishte began to growl in her mind, and she forced her voice to be steady. "I have other duties, Condari."

"Con or Hunter, Black Wolf. And I believe I can convince your elders."

"That's probably true, but I don't answer to the elders."

"You do answer to the Lloroi."

"You think to convince my uncle to go against my parents, when they're among his most important county allies?"

He smiled without humor. He'd sat his share of city councils since he was a boy. County intrigues were like cutting a child's puzzle. "Let's just say that I have some knowlege of how a council works and what he needs to keep it in his control."

Nori's violet eyes narrowed. Payne hadn't had the half of it right. "You're welcome to petition him, of course."

"For any scout except you?" He reached out and let his fingers trail along her arm.

She forced herself to stay motionless. But Rishte's growl was louder now, and her lips stretched in a faintly feral grin. "You're pursuing, Condari, but I'm not running. I'll turn on you if you close."

He gazed up at the stars. "I believe I'm tired of city lilies."

She stepped away and broke the contact. "Don't you understand? I don't want—" Her voice broke off as Rishte snarled sharply.

Hunter watched her tense. "What is it?" he asked sharply.

She shook her head. The wolf was closer, but she couldn't hear anything more than his growl. He'd seemed to send her a man-scent, but that would be Hunter. His scent would have carried on the slight evening breeze. Nori could feel her ears try to flick at the sounds of the park and the nighttime forest on the other side of the shrubs. Rishte didn't help. He was on the heights, pulling at her to come away. He was irritated and hungry, and the breeze blew west toward the wolf, taunting him with the odors of food and the noise of her humanity.

She didn't blame him for the call. After Mato, Rezuku, B'Kosan, and the watcher at the wagon, she was ready to bolt herself. And the wolf needed her running beside him. He rubbed roughly in her mind and growled at the man-scent, making her even more on edge, like a sword, unsure where to strike or parry.

"Nori?"

Wolfwalker.

Rishte howled the warning sharply. Hunter caught the flare of danger in her eyes, and his hand went to his long knife just as hers did. Her nostrils flared. She breathed shallowly, tasting the air. That hadn't been Hunter's scent in Rishte's nose. It was someone else. More than one someone else. Even with the faintness of the new bond, she could tell that now.

Her voice was almost inaudible as she warned. "There is someone coming down the verge."

"Payne?" he guessed irritably.

She shook her head.

"One of your uncles, then."

She held up her hand to stop him as she listened. She heard nothing, just the grey din sharpening in her mind and a pair of pelan settling down in the trees. "They're moving closer," she decided. "Not heading away."

"It's probably another couple of cozar, coming back from their evening exercise."

"No cozar would go so far from the wagons, not at night, not outside a group."

"You did."

"I'm not cozar, and you wanted to walk."

"I did." He smiled wolfishly.

She muttered something vaguely obscene. "It's two people," she added a moment later.

He studied her expression. This time, his voice was quiet. "You think they are a danger."

She tried not to snarl. She had her scout book in her jerkin, she wasn't carrying a bow, and she was out alone on the lonely verge with Hunter for company. If last night's watcher hadn't convinced her she was being targeted, this would do it twice over. She let her gaze rest just left of the path so her peripheral sight could seek movement. "Two men," she told him. "Not on dnu. On foot."

Hunter caught her arm. "This way, then." He started to pull her toward the road and the safety of the moonlight.

She slipped free with a twist. Her voice instinctively dropped to a whisper. "It's too bright over there. Too open. No cover." She gestured toward the trees and shrubs that hid the barrier bushes.

"Your way is into the shadows," he objected. "And you have no idea if they're friends or enemies."

She didn't bother to answer that. "Will you come?" she said impatiently.

He raised his eyebrows. Then he followed without a word as she stepped off the path and slipped between two tea shrubs.

A few minutes later, they were flat on the ground, their bodies close in a long pocket of roots with a low shrub to the side to distract the eye. They could see most of the path for forty meters, but the road was nearly hidden. Nori shifted off a root so that the knot of it pressed into her calf, not her knee. Hunter wriggled into a better position himself. It brought his thighs close to hers. He leaned and murmured, "This is where I wanted you, though I'm not sure how we got here so quickly."

"Moonwormed eater of dog breath," she retorted in a nearly inaudible whisper.

He grinned. "You swear like a cozar," he breathed back.

Nori rolled her eyes and tried to reach out to the yearling. It was a fairly useless gesture. Rishte was still too far away to be more than a blurred grey in her mind. At that distance, all she could read was that the yearling sensed her wariness on top of his own sense of danger. The grey shifted slightly: a different eagerness, sudden stillness, flared nostrils, pricked ears. The hunt. Her hunt? She almost cocked her head to listen to the impressions that swirled in the lupine fog. She could smell the sleeping scents of a flock of woodmice, the raw sap of a tree that had been scratched by a forest cat. She started to shake her head to clear it so she could smell the air around herself, not the wolf, but caught herself in time to stay still. Hunter noticed nothing.

In fact, she scowled, the man had just put his chin down on his arms and now pressed close to her side. She nudged him with her hip, but he didn't move. Damn Tamrani, she thought irritably. This wasn't even subtle.

Hunter, his face turned away, hid a smile.

The Tamrani's warmth kept her from shivering, and his long body was relaxed into watching, not tense as an inexperienced scout. It was almost . . . pleasant, she realized, as if she should feel safe, rather than wary from having him beside her. He certainly seemed content to lie there for as long as it took to wait.

They were silent for several minutes. The nightbugs began chirping again, and the tether vines settled down and refurled their delicate tendrils. Hunter started to ask if Nori had been wrong when a flock of tree sprits rushed up through the trees. He stilled further.

She used two fingers to barely motion to the left. A moment later, two men angled across the trees at the top of the small rise. They were perhaps forty meters away, and although they were armed, they were walking casually. Nori felt her cheeks heat.

"Very dangerous looking, indeed," Hunter murmured in her ear.

She recognized one of the outriders, and stiffened. "The *chovas* on the right, he disappeared from the wagons this morning—" She broke off. The other man turned and looked in their direction. It was the raider who had attacked Elder Connaught.

Hunter frowned. The wolfwalker's face had gone still and intent as a lepa. He could see the caravan guard more clearly now, and he shifted deeper into the shadow, a move that brought him even closer against her side. Her lips moved as if to curse him, but like him, she now made no noise.

The moons were bright enough that the shadows were a crisp black, not dull for easier seeing. Hunter's fingers pressed her forearm, but she'd already seen the two men turn to move closer.

Nori breathed slowly through her mouth into her sleeve so that there was almost no sound. Only the beat of her heart and the sense of Hunter's pulse through his hot skin filled her ears.

The grey din in her mind was so much a part of her thoughts that she didn't even hear it. No-thought, she chanted in her mind. No-thought. Nothing here. She kept her eyes downcast so they didn't gleam. She was small, nothing, of no consequence. A hint of shadow in darker night. Just a tiny creature, minding its business, settling down for the night.

In her mind, Rishte didn't understand at first. Then he realized she thought herself prey, not predator. He snarled, and Nori stiffened slightly. She hissed at the wolf in her mind. *No-thought,* she sent harshly. *No-sight, no-sound.*

Rishte growled back. He began to understand. Think like prey, be prey, draw them in, then leap and slash at the flanks, the knees, the heels. The sudden shaft of eagerness was like a slap, and Nori had to fight not to shake her head.

They would have remained unnoticed if it hadn't been for the pelan. The two men had actually passed their patch of shadow, ten or twelve meters away. They were moving away down the path when the four birds fluttered down toward the bushes. Both Harumen went still to avoid spooking the birds.

The lead pelan dropped, looking for a roost. It got its feet all the way around a branch near Nori's head when it realized what lay nearby. It exploded back up like a feathered bomb. Nori's heart stopped. The other three pelan hissed and scattered up, then winged back over the trees like wildly shot arrows. The two men whipped around. Their bows came up. "There," Murton snapped.

Rishte felt Nori's sudden fear like a kick. The grey voice clawed into her mind. *Danger. Flash to your feet. Run, escape.*

The other raider released his bolt a bare second after Murton's.

Nori started to roll to her feet, but Hunter slammed his arm down like a beam of iron. She barely heard him curse over the whip-by of the bolt.

Trapped. Run. Run!

She snarled, her teeth bared at Hunter. The Tamrani jerked back, then shoved her down again, sprawling across her to cover her. Murton drew another bolt quick as smoke, and shot slightly left, covering what he knew was there but couldn't quite see in the shadows. "Now," Hunter snapped, and released her. She fought free as he rolled the other way.

Wolfwalker—

"There, dammit," one of them cursed. The third arrow slashed by her face, so close that the waxy leaf it cut in half also cut her skin.

Lupine fury burst into her mind. She drew her throwing knife and poised half turned, half crouched against the shadow.

Hunter lunged back to shove her out of the way as she made herself a target. Murton couldn't not see him move. The *chovas* let fly just as Nori did. She didn't miss, but neither did Murton. Her blade sank into Murton's forearm as the man released, but his arrow ripped the top of Hunter's shoulder. The Tamrani cried out and jerked back. Then Hunter reached out one long, muscled arm and threw Nori down like a sack. She hit hard enough to bruise her back. As she fell, she drew his second knife from the tooled sheath on his belt. She twisted. The blade flew after the second man like a thought. Murton dropped his bow and turned to run like a hare. The blade splintered through his quiver.

"Go," the second man shouted. "Go!" The two men sprinted away.

Nori was nearly blinded by wolfish fury. She lunged to her knees when she was brought up short. The fingers that closed on her arm were made of steel. She wrenched free, but Hunter managed to catch her jerkin instead. "Dammit," she cursed him, caught his wrist, and forced his fingers open. "They'll get away."

He managed to grab two of her fingers. "Are you insane?" he snapped back, twisting her knuckles so that she had to turn with him. "Stay down. They don't want you now."

"Enough to loose four bolts—" She didn't even think as she wrist-locked his hand so that he was forced to let go.

"Four bolts at me, you idiot." He jerked her down by her belt. "Let them go."

"So they can shoot us again down the road?" Her broken bow, her scout book, Payne's rope, and the war bolts in the wagon . . . The attack on the road was just a warm-up. They weren't even bothering to be subtle anymore. She shoved back up, rolling her arm neatly free, only to find that he simply grabbed at her braid. She struck his elbow, hard enough to loosen his grip. "Let go, or I'll skewer you like a shish kebab and roast you when I return."

"You'll go nowhere without me."

"You're bleeding, you bollusk-brained dimwit. You won't make it ten meters, and they might go after Payne."

He dug his fingers into her elbow to yank her back. She countered, shoved him back. "Moonwormed fool," he cursed. "They aren't after your brother or you. And they're running hard. You'd never catch them. You can hear them on the road."

"Murton's one of them. He's right there." She yanked free. "Just there. He's hit the hilltop." Hunter grabbed the edge of her jerkin, then her braid again. She rolled his wrist so that he had to let go, but he grabbed her belt instead. "Dammit, Hunter. Let me go. They're getting their dnu. I can still catch them both with Rishte."

"There's a third man, Black Wolf. There has to be. He'll be the one with the dnu."

"I don't care," she cried out. "They could go after Payne."

"They'll be down the road before you can shout."

She jerked free. "Then I'll get my own dnu. I have to make sure. They must not come back—"

He grabbed at her one more time. "All you'll do is panic the camp and make it harder to catch them later. I know what they want. I'll find them myself when they try to hit me again."

She stopped struggling for an instant. She stared down at the wounded Tamrani. "What do you mean, when they try to hit you? They were after Payne and me." Her hand itched for her scout book.

"You're wrong. They were after me, not you." He pressed his free hand hard against his shoulder, then jerked clumsily at a belt pouch.

"Oh, let me," she snapped. She opened the pouch irritably and yanked out the roll of bandages. "You're the one who's mistaken. They were shooting at us, at Payne and me. Just like yesterday." She jammed the pad into his hands. As he released her, she took a quick stride away.

Hunter reached out one long arm and yanked her back. "Listen carefully, you little idiot. They're Harumen out of Sidisport, and if you think I'm going to let you go running after men like that in the dark, you're crazy."

"You're blind, not just bloody. I know who they are. I saw the second one attack Connaught last night—" She broke off. His face had twisted as if the pain was increasing. She closed her eyes for a moment to regain control. Then she stopped fighting his grip. Even now, she heard the sense of running dnu in the back of her mind. She'd be the idiot he called her if she took off after them now. If Uncle Wakje found out, he'd thump her up one side of Ramaj Ariye, then back down through Randonnen. After her lack of control that afternoon, he'd be justified. But she was furious. She could feel the attackers running. She could feel her legs tense to chase. Rishte growled eagerly in her mind, and she wanted to growl with him. Instead, she jerked the bandage pad back from Hunter's hand as he clumsily tried to fold it one-handed. It took her several seconds to realize that, beneath the lupine eagerness, something else lurked in her mind: fear. Now that she identified it, she could feel it breaking into her bones.

Was it that she knew who they were, or was it the scout book that had brought them down on her? Or was it the dead ring-runners she'd seen in the meadow? Or her sense of plague? It was the ring-runners who made it more than suspicious. She was swamped with the images of the bodies, and with it came the sense of the seep. Old death, burning death . . . Rishte howled, and she cursed silently.

She tried to clear her head, tried to think like her brother. She had to get back, get the scout book, get it off her person, hide it someplace better. Time must be important if they were willing to try for her twice in two days. The trigger point had been the night run, with the dead ring-runners and the raiders. Everything had started after that, after she'd gotten back to the road, when she'd finally returned to Payne. It had to be the ring-runners, not the seep, she told herself. It couldn't be the plague. No raiders could know of that place near the cliff. The wagon track had been years old, and that area had become posted long ago for worlags in spring. On top of that, the seep would be dry through summer and fall, the times when hunters went through there. But the chill that settled deep in her bones had more to do with plague. "Could they know?" She wasn't aware she had whispered out loud.

Hunter sucked in a breath as she pressed the bandage ungently onto the wound. "Know what?" he snapped. "That you're a wolfwalker? That's hardly grounds for murder."

She snapped back to the moment. "You think they want you dead just for leaving the city?"

"They want what I brought out of it—"

"Oh, aye." She rounded on him. "A hide so thick you can't get a thought through your head. They're trying to kill me, not you."

"This is the most ridiculous argument I've ever had. Do you actually *want* to be right?"

"Look—"

"They want the papers I carry," he snapped. "I've got four men and women, as well as my own sister, in the godsdamn hospital because of it."

Nori stared at him. "You've lost too much blood," she said with exasperation. She squatted beside him. She didn't notice the leaves or twigs stuck in her braid or the damp mud stains on her shirt. He was far too adamant about being right, about being the target. But it had been her bow, her knife, Payne's rope, and their arrows that had already been sabotaged. It had been Payne and she who were attacked on the road. And that raider had followed her out from the circle because she could identify him. Yet the Tamrani was still shaking his head as if he couldn't see it. "You're dizzy," she worried. "It must be worse than it looks."

"Dizzy, my foot." He clutched her arm as she made to rise. "And stay down in the shadows. The third one may not have been with the dnu at all. He may be here in the park."

"I'd know," she returned sharply. She tried to hide the note of fear in her voice. "There's no one left but us. And I suggest you get up with me, unless you want to bleed out on my boots." His fingers were starting to drip as he held the pad to the wound.

"How bad is it?" She pressed her hands over his to judge the heat in the blood.

"Ow, dammit. What are you doing?"

"Pressure. You have an open wound, you know."

"By all nine hells, you're supposed to be a healer."

"An animal healer, not a human doctor."

"You're supposed to have a year of human healing."

"It must not be my calling," she retorted.

"Moons." He sucked in his breath. "I'm likely to die from your touch long before I bleed to death on my own. I'd be better off as an animal than a human in your hands."

She grinned, but the expression was feral. "I specialized in wild animals, not in livestock like dnu and ass."

"Dik spit," he retorted.

She studied the wound. It was slowly soaking both shirt and jerkin. The gnats were beginning to flock to the scent. "It's messy more than deep. Tore the top, but doesn't seem to have nicked anything important."

"My body may not be important to you, but it certainly is to me."

"Don't be a baby. It'll ruin the manly impression you've been making on me all night."

He started to laugh and groaned. "Ow. Don't make me laugh."

"Seems like a good time for humor."

"For you, maybe, not for me."

"Then we'll walk. Can you stand?"

He slanted her a look from under his heavy brows. "Will you put your arms around me if I can't?"

"Now I know you're fine." She tugged at his elbow. His skin was cold with mud from the ground. "Come on, get up."

"You have the bedside manner of a badgerbear."

"I know. I practice hard."

He started to laugh again, cursed, and settled for keeping his balance as he stumbled out of the root-mass. He slipped again, and she caught him, one hand around his waist.

She brushed awkwardly at them both, dislodging broken

leaves and a twig from his shirt lacing. "It's not far," she encouraged.

He looked down at the top of her head. There was grass in her braid, and her cheek was smudged with his blood. But she was alive with adrenaline. Her violet eyes were sparkling, her body still balanced like a cat to strike. Her hand was like tinder, touching and firing the skin beneath his shirt as she slid along his ribs for a better hold. "Don't patronize me," he managed. "I've had worse wounds half the years of my life."

But his voice sounded weak, and Nori slipped both arms around his muscled waist, returning lightly, "I wondered. You're starting to look a bit hard-lived."

He draped an arm around her shoulder and let her take some of his weight. She was stronger than she looked. She didn't flinch at all. She simply fit her hips against him and adjusted her balance to his. Now her slim strength surrounded him, and her breasts pressed against his ribs. His hand clenched across her shoulder. She took it as a sign of pain and shifted to take more weight. She didn't seem to notice the change in his breathing. He could hear the concern in her voice. "Did I ever tell you about the time I took an arrow in the ribs? It was an accident. One of the hunters was too impatient and didn't wait for me to come back with the report on the herd. He thought I was an eerin. Shot me right through the shrubs."

Her breasts rubbed his ribs as he walked, and Hunter felt himself growing hard. "What an idiot," he managed.

"In more ways than one. He was too far away to do any damage. I felt the threat, turned around, and, pang, there was this arrow sticking out of my chest. It barely even cut the skin. Just left a tiny red mark, like the bite of a winter gnat."

Their strides weren't even, and her hips slid along his. "What's with the sudden spate of talking?" he demanded in quiet desperation. "I thought you were the quiet one."

Her voice was dry. "I was hoping to make sure you stay conscious. I didn't want to try dragging you all the way back by myself to the cozar circle."

He looked down at her face, noted the worry that tightened

her eyes, and gave himself up to the soft sensation of her body locked against his.

He made it all the way to the path before he stumbled again, but this time he almost fell. She barely caught his weight, and it took him a moment to regain his balance. She paused only to pick up the bow the shooter had dropped and Hunter's knife from beside the tree. She didn't see her own blade. Either Murton or the other man had carried it away, or it was lost in the shadows. Unless Rishte wanted to scent it out, she'd have to wait till morning. She stared at the hilltop as she listened to the sense of the dnu fading away in the distance.

He followed her hungry gaze. "You wouldn't have made it. They were already gone."

"I could have left you behind."

He grinned faintly. "You'd have felt too guilty."

She made a face.

"You throw well," Hunter commented as he rested against the trunk while she slung Murton's bow over her shoulder.

"I've had some practice," she returned noncommittally. She slipped her arms back around him and let him lean on her.

"Next time you think to put yourself in harm's way just to take a shot for me, I'll pin your arms behind you, truss you up like a roast pag, and beat that stupidity out of you. You'll think your uncle's hands are feathers compared to mine."

His voice was so mild it didn't register for a moment. Then she stopped dead. She stared at him as if he'd sprouted horns. "Excuse me?"

"You heard me." He tightened his hold on her shoulder. "Jangharat," he murmured. Then he turned her into his arms and kissed her.

She stared up at him as he did it. In the dark, her violet eyes flickered with sudden fear. Like a wild animal, she tore free and jerked back.

He thought he was prepared for her reaction, but he overbalanced. This time, she didn't try to catch him. He grabbed for a nearby sapling and stood for a moment, head down and cursing, as he got used to the new jags of pain. Finally looked back up.

She stood several steps back, breathing raggedly, her hand at her lips, watching him like a wolf.

In spite of himself, his voice was somewhat hoarse. "I won't apologize."

She dropped her hands and found her voice. "I didn't ask you to."

He straightened. He nodded at the trail. "Shall we?"

"You first."

He understood, and it angered him. If the shooters returned, they'd be behind them, and Nori would be first in danger. "Side by side or not at all."

She stared at him, but he didn't move.

"Together, Nori. I won't bite."

She licked her lips unconsciously. "What did you call that?"

He smiled, slowly, wickedly. "An introduction."

"Then you'll need no other."

"Now that's the arrogance I admire." He nodded toward the path. Reluctantly, she fell into step with him, certain now that he'd been faking his weakness. She cast glances every now and then at his face. It was tight, so she knew he was in pain, but other than holding the bandage to the wound, he seemed to not notice his shoulder. He'd had that bandage ready in his belt, she remembered. He hadn't argued when they left the path for the shadows, he'd been prepared for the raiders, and he'd thrown her around with ease. Oh, Payne had been right about this one. Cityfolk this Tamrani might be, but he wasn't at all a novice. She'd underestimated him badly. The thought was disconcerting.

Uncle Ki was at fireside, and Nori left Hunter on the gate of the healer's wagon to go get her uncle. She waited till she caught his eye, then raised her eyebrow meaningfully. Several faces turned to her, and there was more than speculation on some of them as they took in her dirty shirt and grass-stained trousers, the red-brown smudge that marred her cheek. Ki rose with sudden menace as he scanned the night for the Tamrani. "Get Payne," he murmured to his younger son. Liam nodded and strode away.

She said quickly, "It's not what it looks like, Uncle Ki."

The ex-raider nodded, but he didn't stop scanning the circle as he followed her away from the fire.

Nori barely waited till they had some distance. "He's hurt, Uncle Ki. He was shot. He's at the healer's wagon."

Ki's step didn't falter as he shot her a sharp look. "On the road? You raised no alarm. Report."

"It was Murton and the man who hit Connaught last night. They followed us—probably me—into the verge park. There was a third man in the distance, probably holding the dnu for them to escape."

"But it was the Tamrani who was shot?"

"By mistake, I think. Payne spoke to you?" He nodded, and she explained, "No other attack has been aimed at him. It's all been aimed at us."

They rounded the corner of the healer's wagon and could hear Hunter now.

". . . no reason to cut up this jerkin. It's the last one I have."

Nori felt a twinge of guilt.

But, "Put your arms down," the healer snapped. "Don't you realize how much you're bleeding?"

"I can judge that myself quite accurately. Let me get this off, dammit, before you leave me in cozar rags."

"Do you want my help or not?"

"He wants it, Healer Sastry." Nori cut off his reply as she stepped up. "He'll follow directions."

Hunter looked over. "Speak for yourself," he retorted.

Ki looked the other man up and down, and Nori wasn't sure her uncle had believed her till he saw that Hunter was more pre-occupied with the healer's hands than Nori's. "Shallow wound," Ki judged. "Messy."

Hunter indicated Nori irritably. "That's what she said." Ignoring the healer, he yanked the jerkin over his head, sucking in his breath as it pulled across the wound with more agony than he had expected. Silently, he finished the motion. Nori caught the soiled garment before he could drop it. "Did you tell him?" he asked, jerking his chin toward Ki.

"I was getting to it."

"They got off four shots—" the tall man hissed as Healer Sastry rubbed a numbing agent around the wound.

"Four?" Ki glanced at Nori, then hard back at Hunter.

"The fault wasn't his, Uncle Ki. He was preoccupied." Her voice bit. "He kept trying to shove my face through the ground."

"I was trying to protect you," he snapped. He met Ki's gaze with more than a lick of anger. "She kept trying to jump up and attack. I couldn't let her get hit for me." His jaw tightened ominously as the healer began to pinch the staples closed over the wound, and Nori knew the painkiller hadn't fully set.

She said sharply, "He was aiming for me, not you."

"You don't know that."

"The attack earlier was aimed at Payne and me. The accidents before then, at Payne and me. Why would they now follow you?"

"Because of you, Wolfwa—woman," he blasted back, barely correcting himself in time. "Because they don't want me meeting up with you. I carry information for the council. Information that, combined with a scout's notes, could help answer important questions. They can't afford for me to work with you."

There was silence for a long, strained moment. The healer continued to clean the wound, his ears closed to the discussion in the cozar way of distancing himself from things he should not hear. Hunter glared at Nori and watched the emotions flicker deep in her eyes. Distrust, wariness, puzzlement, and fear. He wasn't sure which had won out when she said quietly, "We've always been targets of some sort."

He stared at her, then hissed at Sastry when the healer pulled at his arm. "Dammit," he cursed. "You're worse than she is." The healer hid a smile. Hunter shot Ki a wary look, then spoke to Nori as if the others weren't there. "I can't tell you more, not until I know."

The wolfwalker's violet eyes narrowed. "Until you know what?"

He said harshly, "That you will do your duty to the county, not run from it like you have been doing ever since you turned sixteen."

Her face went expressionless.

Ki studied Hunter carefully. When he spoke, his voice was soft. "You've dragged my Nori-girl into your business, Tamrani. You've made her a target for your back."

Hunter glanced at Ki, then gave the older man a closer look. The ex-raider's face was still calm, but it gave him a chill. "I have," he admitted freely. "And if she'll ride with me—on Journey, as a duty, I don't care—I'll keep her as safe as I can while we deal with the changes coming to Ariye."

Nori felt a lick of anger. "I don't need you to kee—"

Ki cut her off with an almost imperceptible gesture. He gave the Tamrani a long look before turning back to Nori. "I'll check the road, follow the men if I find them. I'll take Mye and Liam with me. You'll stay with the caravan." His voice brooked no disagreement. "Wakje will watch your backs, and Payne will watch Leanna."

"Uncle Ki," she started. She glanced meaningfully at the forest.

"No." The word was flat. "Stay with the caravan. Stay with Payne. First thing a raider does to his target is cut him out of the pack. You almost gave yourself over to them already. Do not do it again."

She bit her lip. "Yes, Uncle Ki."

Hunter broke in. "They might not be raiders you're tracking."

Ki gave him a sharp look.

"They might be Harumen."

The ex-raider studied the Tamrani for a long, cold moment. "Harumen," he said softly. "I know them. They're out of Sidisport."

Hunter met his gaze without flinching.

Ki nodded toward Nori. "You have connected her to them, through you?"

"Yes. It was unintentional. But she is now a target."

"How much lead do they have?"

Hunter pursed his lips, thinking. "Fifteen minutes, maybe twenty, but the archer has a knife through his forearm. He'll have to stop to tend it."

"I never did." Ki's lips stretched in what was supposed to be a grin, and Hunter caught his first real glimpse of the ex-raider in those eyes. He glanced at Nori warily. This was the "nicer" uncle? She had six more of them to watch her like hawks, not to mention two adopted aunts who were said to be as venomous and cold-blooded as desert snakes. That didn't even count the blood-kin who had their own reputations as lepa. Perhaps it wasn't Payne protecting his sister at all. It might be her protecting the county from the rest of the Wolven Guard.

Nori's gaze flickered as her brother ran toward fireside. "I'll tell him," she said quickly to Ki, as she saw Payne throw a question at someone, then veer off toward the healer's wagon. She didn't look back at Hunter as she slipped away.

Ki looked at the Tamrani for a long moment. "You were . . . walking?"

Hunter started to shrug, but the healer gripped his shoulder in a vise and forced him to be still, and he sucked in his breath instead.

Ki gave him a long look for another chilling moment, then jogged away to the corral.

XXV

The knife at your throat is not the real danger;
The claw at your back is more sly.

    —Diton saying

The tavern was noisy as a concert of drunks. Even in the back room, Nori could hear more than she wanted. She looked at the map spread out before them, then around at the group at the table. She shivered. There was enough steel at this one table to take over half of Shockton. With Nori were Wakje, Payne, Hunter, Fentris, and Kettre. Hunter had given up his tooled but bloodied jerkin for a simple cozar one, and with the weathering he'd gotten in the last few days he now looked like a tall Ariyen. Fentris, with his embroidered tunic and tooled boots, his House ring and styled hair, was the only one who looked out of place, but all of them were heavily armed. With Ki and his sons away hunting raiders, the only one missing was Leanna. Wakje had simply said "No" when she made to join them. The girl had accepted it, but Nori didn't think that would last. Leanna was fifteen, with all the stubborn blindness of adolescence. She wouldn't tolerate being kicked out of the family meetings for long.

In spite of the privacy of the room, all of them leaned in to keep their voices down. Wakje looked around the table then said shortly, "Let's lay it out."

Nori glanced at the others, then picked up the pen and started marking. She didn't need to glance at the notes in her scout book. Every fear was sharp in her mind. "Two ring-runners, killed two days ago in Gambrel Meadow, a ways off Ironjaw

Trail. Four raiders at Bell Rocks. Yesterday, on Willow Road, three raiders in an open attack—"

"Three Harumen," Hunter cut in as he shifted his shoulder again. He just couldn't get comfortable. "I believe they were Harumen."

She glanced at him. "Harumen," she corrected, "in broad daylight after Payne and me, including one whom Hunter recognized. One Haruman at Cohenton Circle, after Elder Connaught. That raide—Haruman after Hunter and me in the verge park, with Murton, from our own caravan."

Payne picked up the pen and marked four ticks at the Cohenton Circle. "Possible listeners while Nori and I were talking. Two suspicious men at the Cohenton Circle at dawn, outside the gates. One of our climbing ropes was sabotaged. One of Nori's knives may have been deliberately fatigued. Our hunting bolts were swapped out for poor ones that would tumble in flight. And there was a woman in our wagon."

Fentris raised an elegant eyebrow at Payne.

He said impatiently, "Not that kind of woman. Someone who went in there without any of us around."

Nori added, "And then there is Rezuku."

Fentris cocked his head at her.

"Merchant," Payne explained. "Joined us in Adamstan. Nori doesn't like the feel of him."

"Then shouldn't Mato make the list?"

He snorted. "Mato's a buffoon. He'd never be smart or subtle enough to pull together so many threads. Besides, he's now *bokat* among the cozar, and I can't see a smart man pissing away so many potential allies."

They went down the list. Hunter added four people, and Nori waited for him to add a few more, but he didn't. She watched him carefully enough that he raised an eyebrow at her, and she quickly looked away. Fentris and Kettre added four names from the latest Sidisport gossip. Then they began listing accidents: Ell Tai's broken ankle, Rocknight Styne's broken axle, the weibers getting loose, and even older notes from Nori's punctured scout book. When they were done, the map was heavily dotted along the three main trade lines.

Payne murmured, "Either this is one hell of a bad-luck spring, or someone's declared war on the cozar."

Hunter studied the map. "Almost every caravan has been delayed one way or another. If this keeps up, the Journey youths will be scattered across the counties even at the end of the Test ninan, not to mention the elders who will still be on the road. Your Lloroi will be lucky to pull half a council together."

Kettre ran her finger along the trade lines. "All of us, so close together."

Payne nodded. "It's as if someone aimed a knife at the cozar's throats."

The hazel-eyed woman frowned. "Can you pass word to the Ells? If the cozar are being targeted, there has to be some way to let them know without starting a general panic."

"I could do that," Nori volunteered.

Payne nodded. As a ranked ring-runner for the council, she could get the message codes for any Ell or elder. "But there's no way to keep that secret. The Ells would tell their Hafells; the Hafells would have to warn the gate guards at each circle . . ." He shrugged. "It could drive the raiders—or Harumen—" He added with a nod at Hunter. "—underground before we've identified them all."

Nori frowned. "We should at least let the Lloroi know."

"Aye, if he hasn't heard already." He nodded as she raised an eyebrow. "Even allowing for the normal hazards of travel, we've had far too many accidents."

Kettre stared at the map. "But who would hit the cozar so consistently? I mean, look at us, we're just not that important—"

Fentris cleared his throat. "Excuse me, but you're not cozar."

Wakje gave the Tamrani a sharp look, and Payne frowned. "What?"

"You aren't cozar," the slim man repeated.

Hunter cocked his head at him while the others stared.

This time, Fentris spoke slowly. "None. Of. You. Is. Cozar." He nodded toward Wakje. "You and Ki, you're Wolven Guard, ex-raiders, out of Bilocctar, by way of Ariye. For all that you've ridden with the cozar for twenty years, you've never taken more than a *chovas* berth. You—" He nodded at Payne. "—are *keyo* or *chovas*—as you and your sister said so pointedly at the fireside. You might think of yourselves as cozar, but when it comes down to it, you're really Randonnen, with a bit of Ariyen thrown in." He nodded at their dawning comprehension. "Hunter and I are Tamrani. Elder Connaught is a Yorundan councilman. For all that he travels with the cozar every summer, Connaught also still takes a *keyo* berth, not a cozar place in the line. That other elder who left the train in Sidisport—I'll bet he wasn't cozar, either."

"No," Kettre said slowly. "He wasn't."

Hunter leaned back in his chair and regarded the other Tamrani with an odd expression.

Fentris ignored him and pointed to the list. "What about this woman, this Hael?"

"She's a scout out of Ramaj Diton," Nori answered. "She usually rides with a few of her students, but she's good enough that any Ell would gladly give her a *keyo* berth."

"As I said," he finished quietly. "A guest berth. None of you is cozar. In fact, I'd wager that at least half the names on your list aren't actually cozar."

"Dik spit." Payne stared at the slim man.

"But the caravans," Nori protested. "The accidents. Ell Tai's broken ankle."

"Oh, you're being harassed," Fentris agreed. "You'd be foolish to think otherwise. I just don't think it has anything to do with being in the wagons. You'd be traveling to Shockton one way or another—that's the one thing nearly everyone does do in a Test year." He glanced at Wakje. "In fact, the cozar have probably made it easier, not harder, to see that you have needles in the silk."

Nori shot Kettre a questioning look. "A rast on your tail," the other woman whispered. "It's a Sidisport thing."

Fentris looked around the small circle. "Let me ask one question: What would happen if all of you were delayed from reaching the Test town?"

There was silence for a moment. Payne snorted. "Nothing," he answered. "The meetings would be held without us, the Tests would go on, the Journey assignments would be handed out.

None of us is so important that the Test ninan wouldn't happen. In an extreme year, they might delay a few Tests so we could finish up late. That's about the worst."

Wakje watched Fentris closely. Even Hunter found himself considering the other Tamrani's words closely. Fentris ignored them both and persisted. "So there's no reason to delay you? To put you all out of action?"

Nori and Payne exchanged glances.

"What?" Hunter asked sharply.

Nori shrugged uncomfortably. It was Payne who answered. "Sometimes we're targeted by people who want to get to our parents, but that wouldn't explain Connaught or Hael or the others."

Fentris said softly, "Then what do you all have in common? What do you all know? What have you all seen?"

This time, the silence was longer.

"Think about it," Fentris told them. "Because that's what the reason is."

Hunter ran his hand through his hair. "Perhaps a better question is, what are we going to do about it, if we're now a set of targets?"

Kettre turned her bracelet absently on her wrist. "Three ways to deal with being hunted: siege up, go to ground; fight back; or flee."

"I'm beginning to be a big fan of fleeing," muttered Payne.

Wakje shot him a sharp look, and the younger man subsided. "We'll think on it," the ex-raider said flatly.

As Wakje rode away with Nori and Kettre, Payne paused on the tavern porch. He ignored Fentris and rested his arms on the banister to study the taller Tamrani. Hunter was watching the wolfwalker, and Payne's voice was soft. "What's your game, Tamrani? What have you dragged us into?"

Hunter didn't even glance at Payne. "Nothing you shouldn't already have seen," he answered. "Nothing that wouldn't already be considered your duty as the son of Aranur."

Payne's voice was flat. "You sound like an elder, Ranakai Ao."

"And you sound too defensive."

"I've had practice." The younger man straightened and

stalked down the steps. He took his dnu from the hitching post and mounted in one smooth movement. "Enjoy the rest of your evening, Tamrani. I doubt we'll see you much longer." He reined around sharply and spurred his dnu after Wakje.

Hunter watched them disappear with cool green eyes. "You might be surprised," he murmured. "I think we could share a few secrets."

"But you didn't," Fentris reminded him quietly out of the dark. "You kept it to yourself about the shifts of power we've seen."

"As did you," Hunter returned.

"I said enough." Fentris broke off as two men wandered out of the tavern and headed vaguely toward the stables.

Hunter rubbed his jaw and leaned on the wooden banister as Payne had done before him. Like the tavern, the wood was rough and unfinished, and somehow appropriate for their meeting. This whole trip seemed rough and unfinished, as if he was constantly looking the wrong way, blind to the real danger. "You think they'll leave the caravan?"

"Maybe. The wolfwalker seemed inclined."

"She's been inclined to do that since I met her."

Fentris shot him a look and Hunter actually chuckled. "No, I think I intrigue her in spite of herself. It's the uncle who's unpredictable."

"He's a raider."

"Ex-raider," Hunter corrected.

Fentris started to lean on the banister beside him, noted the stains on the wood, and changed his mind. "He's still a raider, Brithanas. He thinks like a raider, and he'll act like a raider when pushed. There were rumors about him in Tume."

In the dark, Hunter watched Fentris closely. Their deal was to share information, but neither one was comfortable enough to offer anything else. "Rumors?" he prompted carefully.

Fentris didn't meet his eyes. Instead, he looked out toward the darkness and spoke as if commenting on a neighbor's choice of dress. "About four years ago, the girl was stalked at the university by another scout. She nearly killed the man and herself in the process, and was unconscious for a ninan afterward. Then the stalker turned up dead. All the man's wounds were made by worlags, but they said it was rare to see so many gashes in one body."

"There was no proof, of course, of anything."

"Not against Wakje or his partner. Both uncles were accounted for the night the man disappeared. But it's said that, if you dangled a man in a worlag den, that's about the way he'd be hauled back out. That, if the Wolven Guard had their way, that's what they'd have done to him."

Hunter considered that. "Wakje won't want to leave the caravan until he's identified everyone he can. Then he'll send the boy and girl away, and start taking the Harumen out, one by one."

"Were you thinking to help?"

"The uncle or the girl?"

"The girl's prettier."

Hunter felt an unfamiliar roil of possessiveness.

Fentris strolled down the tavern steps, got his dnu, and mounted. He caught Hunter's expression and chuckled. "Don't knot your socks, Brithanas. But I'd watch her, if I were you. There are things going on in her head that don't make sense for what I know of the Daughter of Dione. She's afraid of something."

"Yes," Hunter murmured.

"A good look at that scout book of hers might tell you what it was. I think she has codes in there. Perhaps some we haven't seen." Fentris hesitated, then said diffidently, "We could alternate keeping watch on them. It would give us more of a chance to see when they're ready to run."

Hunter glanced at him. "That would put you at their backs, watching them, wouldn't it?"

Fentris stiffened, but went on doggedly, "I was going to propose that we also run when they do—in the opposite direction. Change clothes on the road and ride on as ring-runners to Shockton. The Harumen will assume we've gone with the girl and boy and follow them instead. It could give us a larger margin of safety."

"Safety. Yes. Of course."

Fentris stared at Hunter for a long moment. Then he spurred his dnu around tightly and cantered away.

Hunter cursed under his breath, unsure whether he was angry at the fop or himself. Maybe it was pride. He'd believed the worst about Fentris for months after he got word of the murder. After the first letter from Shae, he'd burned the rest without reading them. But somewhere in the past two years, he'd started to remember the Fentris he had known before, the young boy who had tagged along after Hunter and Joao when they went out to carouse the city. Fentris had been skinny then, just a thin boy determined to do better in his training so he could keep up with his older brother. Hells, it had been Fentris who had shown Hunter a trick or two in swordsmanship after he'd won the city's ranking league. Hunter frowned darkly. That had been just before festival, the year Hunter's nephew was killed. The year he'd put up his bow.

He looked at his dnu, at the weapon lashed onto its side. Then stalked down the steps angrily, started to raise his arm to untie his dnu, and sucked in a breath at the stab of pain. He pressed hard against the wound. It was sore as a loose tooth, and the staples were stiff and crusty. "Dik spit on a poolah's pelt," he muttered. But he stared down the road after Fentris and wondered about the man.

XXVI

Tethered by intentions
Bound by unseen law

—Tumuwen proverb

If the midnight meeting had been tense, night itself was a relief. Nori slipped away in spite of Payne and Wakje's watchful eyes, to meet Rishte just outside the circle in a small copse of breadbark. She spent the first hour copying notes from her old scout book to a new one. She rubbed dirt into the edges of the new pages, added some stains, smeared some of the lines with dirty fingers, and wrote twice in leaf ink. Then she ground dirt, nut oil, and bark debris into the cover. When the book began to look like her old one, she tucked it back in her jerkin.

She was tired, but she didn't feel like sleeping. Her shoulders prickled as if she was being watched, and even the yearling was uneasy. There were rugged cliffs to the west, with almost no trails along them, but when Nori suggested they try that side of the road instead, the yearling snapped at her hand.

Death, he snarled.

She stared at him. *There? Now?*

Death was all he would say.

She looked in his eyes and tried to read the impressions there. She could see rocks and swamp through lupine eyes, but the images were yellow-black, centered on movement, not shape. It was fuzzy, as if it had been passed along through too many wolves, or blurred by time. All she could tell was that there was a narrow split back into the cliffs where water trickled out, that it was to the west. The wolves associated that part of the rocks so strongly with the Ancients' domes that even the thought of it seemed to burn.

Death, he snarled again. *Burning. Then-now.*

"My gods," she whispered. She stared at the wolf. This was more than memory. *Plague. It's real?*

Burning, Rishte agreed.

She flipped her book back to her plague notes and entered a small code by the others. That made two spots where the pack-song remembered plague dimly in recent years, and two spots where it could be real.

Three eerin threaded their way down the slope and spooked as they neared a deadfall, and both Nori and Rishte stilled. Nori listened through her ears and the wolf, but the night breeze was soft enough to murmur in the leaves. Neither one heard anything. Still, Nori closed both scout books and wormed her way back through the brush, following the wolf.

Rishte snarled, and she looked down at him. If she felt this uneasy by herself, how much more intensely did the yearling feel without his pack? *Wait,* she told him. *I'll be back.*

She slipped into the circle, got her sleeping gear, and slipped back out by the firewood bins. This time, she moved farther away until Rishte was satisfied with their bed.

When she woke, it was quickly, with that heightened alertness in which every sound was a shot. It wasn't until the warm muzzle nudged her that she relaxed.

Dawn. Wet earth. The woodmice are moving.

The wolf nudged her again, then panted in her face. The stench of rotted meat was almost overwhelming. She gagged in spite of herself, then rolled out of her sleeping bag and got to her feet. The wolf dodged back, but held his ground a few meters away. Nori grinned faintly. He was getting used to her in spite of the taint.

When she slipped back into the circle, she studied the wagon for long moments before approaching. There was nothing amiss. Payne's mouth was half open in deep sleep. Uncle Wakje was silent enough that she knew he had awakened, but the ex-raider didn't move from the sling bed.

Nori nodded to her uncle and glanced at the sky. The stars

were washed out but clear enough for all that. Six of the nine
moons floated serenely overhead while the sun thought of breaking the tree line. In the shadows, Rishte's golden eyes seemed to
gleam in her mind. *Hunt,* he sent. *Hunger-hunt.* He turned away,
trotted a few paces along the barrier bushes, then paused and
seemed to stare straight at her. *Hunt with me, wolfwalker.*

She shook her head, not looking back at Wakje. *I cannot,* she
returned softly. *We'll be riding out in less than an hour. Come
with me instead. You can eat jerky and smoked pelan.*

The yearling trotted a few more steps away, then went silently
back into the forest. Nori listened for long minutes, but heard
nothing. He was still near, she could feel him, but he would not
come to her, not if she rode with men.

She slipped her knife onto her belt and rolled up her sleeping
bag with a slight frown. Rishte was wild enough that humans
frightened him badly, but it wasn't just the idea of men that
made him refuse to stay near her. That danger sense, the one of
old death, was growing stronger in his mind. She could almost
taste it now, like tension on her tongue, as if they rode toward it,
not away. She straightened, hopped up on the gate, and gazed
out at the brush line that marked the cozar circle. Trade shifting
south, ring-runners murdered, and Harumen inside the circle.
And over it all, like a balloon about to burst, she found out that
plague was real, not just a years-old threat. She shook her head
to herself. It made no sense, yet Fentris said the first three must
be connected.

She had tipped her head back to think as she watched the
stars fade when she sensed the presence nearby. Rishte had
slunk back to the forest as dawn approached, and Wakje had
gone back to sleep, but she needed neither to understand the
prickling in her shoulders. She didn't move overtly, but her left
hand slicked a knife from its sheath, and her voice was soft as
silk. "Move on, or I shall harm you."

There was no sound, but after a minute, she knew the man
had shifted away.

"Nori-girl?" It was Wakje, an almost silently breathed question.

"It was nothing, Uncle Wakje."

But when the sky lightened, she moved to the side of the wagon to examine the impressions. She needn't have worried. As usual, Uncle Wakje was ahead of her. He'd sprinkled a layer of flour on the stone paving on both sides of their wagon. Now he squatted by the wagon wheel with her to study the boot prints.

"Nice," she murmured, nodding at the flour. She pulled out her new scout book and sketched the prints onto a page.

He nodded shortly. "Scrub it out now. It's getting light."

They scuffed and blew on the stones so that the flour disappeared into the cracks. With luck, the watcher wouldn't even know he'd left his prints behind.

Payne was squaring away his gear in the wagon when she returned from an early breakfast. He glanced over his shoulder. "You look alright for having been shot at twice and dumped on the ground last night."

She nudged his open pack aside and hopped up into the wagon. "Twice missed, well blessed." She watched Wakje lead the wagon dnu by, then peered around the wagon at fireside. Hunter had already finished breakfast, and was talking with two of the young women. She got up abruptly and began securing her gear.

Payne followed her gaze with a sly look. "If Brithanas were smart, he would play up the gash and get Vina to serve him the rest of his meals."

"She's a good cook," Nori admitted noncommittally. Automatically, she plucked Payne's dirty clothes from his bin and stuffed them in the washbag. She didn't realize she used more force than necessary, or that her voice was a little sharp as she said, "I thought you were flirting with Vina."

Her brother hid a grin. "Why would you care who she flirts with?"

"I don't." She jumped off the gate. "Latch up, will you? I want to check with the message master before we go."

"Nori-girl." He caught her. "Watch out for Condari."

"He's no worse than any elder."

"You don't go walking out with elders." He caught her stubborn expression. "Crap on a brick and bake it, Nori-girl. At least the elders are old and grey and slow on foot. You can usually outrun them. This Tamrani looks a bit faster. I'd bet on all nine moons that he's got more than a simple partnership in mind."

Nori glanced up the line to where the two Tamrani were talking. "He's not the first, Payne."

"And he won't be the last to want your wolves and your reputation, not you."

"I know." Her voice was flat. "He made that clear last night."

But Payne persisted. "He knows things, Nori. I can see it when he looks at the *chovas*. He says he's heading for Shockton to make a proposal to the council, but he could send any flunky for that. He says he's carrying important papers, but he has no guards around him. Something's up, and for Shae to go along with it when they hate each other, it has to be more than big." He glanced around. "I've been talking with the elders, and they all say the same thing. He's interested in the trade routes."

Nori scowled. "Moons, Payne, why does that matter to me?"

"Because after fireside last night, I started wondering. I spoke to the ring-runners and felt out a few of the traders. There are rumors throughout the county. People are selling out along the southern trade routes, whether they want to or not, just like Piera's grandfather. There are rumors of blackmail, threats, even kidnappings, with the ransoms being deeds."

She gave him a sharp look. "You can't think it's Hunter who's forcing them to sell?"

"No. He's listening to the gossip with fourteen ears. I think he suspects the Harumen and whoever is behind them buying up the land."

"What does it matter who owns it?"

"You'd be surprised what matters to Tamrani," he answered. "But other than telling the council, that's not our concern. You've got a duty, Wolfwalker," he said deliberately. "And it's not to Sidisport. You can't afford to get mixed up in whatever House War he's involved in, not if we're going to track down the plague with Mama after the Tests. We have to keep to the family line, Nori-girl. Stay away from Brithanas."

She didn't look at him, but she nodded.

"He can't force you to ride with him." He watched her closely. "Unless you really want to."

She shook her head again. "We agreed. I can't. It would be nearly impossible to hide what I am—what I might do—from a partner."

"And you already have a partner." He tapped his chest.

"I was thinking that was Rishte," she retorted.

"You've been using him, haven't you?"

"Aye," she said quietly. She knew he was referring to her sense of the attack last night, and to her attempt to track the danger spots that made the wolves uneasy. She saw Bell Rocks instead. She saw the men who would by now be hollowed-out carcasses, scattered ribs, shreds of flesh in the mud.

Payne forced his expression to stay light. The relief that she had used the wolf, had been able to protect herself in spite of the curse—it was overwhelming. So was the envy.

Nori didn't miss it. "It isn't changing anything, Payne. Nothing's different. The fear, the sickness. The headaches. It's all the same. Moonworms, it's even stronger now because I can see it and smell it and taste it through Rishte's senses, not just mine."

A pair of cozar rode back along the line, and instinctively Payne waited till they had passed before continuing. "But three days ago, you led the worlags through a raider camp," he said in a low voice. "Last night you faced the raiders head-on. Brithanas said you went after them without hesitation. And you stood up to Mato at fireside."

"That was anger, not courage. And at Ironjaw Creek, I ran from the worlags like a blind rabbit. After Bell Rocks, I left my stomach on the side of the trail. I probably killed those four people, Payne, and I know I had to do it, but afterward all I could see was that I'd turned on my own kind." Her lips twisted with self-loathing. The daughter of the great Dione, cowardly as a nightkite. She swallowed and shook her head. "Last night, I don't know what happened. Maybe it was Rishte, not me, in my mind."

"You're not a coward," he said flatly. She gave him a warning glance, and he lowered his voice. But he frowned. Only three times had he known her to defend herself. Once, when she was fifteen, in Sidisport; four years ago in Tume; and one other time in Sciome. The first time had left her terrified of people; the second had left her terrified of herself. The third time, a blader had stepped out of an alley and demanded her silver. She'd refused. She'd let the man stab almost completely in before she'd finally moved. Moons alone knew how she'd been fast enough to avoid the knife, but she'd left that man flat on the ground, choking on his own blood. She could kill worlags, poolah, and badgerbears without batting either eye. She could best him in any martial ring. But every time she'd ridden with a venge, she'd been sick as a food-poisoned puppy.

They had hoped that, when she bonded with a wolf, her natural strengths would kick in, would give her a better defense against humanity. If they didn't . . . His jaw tightened. She would be even more like prey, more vulnerable, more easily taken. And the rabbit-fear he'd seen freeze her in place? That was like a flag to a predator. Raiders, muggers, Harumen—they smelled that kind of vulnerability like grease on a rising wind.

The Tamrani would have seen that weakness. Brithanas already felt protective toward Nori or, rather, toward the Daughter of Dione. If the Tamrani caught a whiff of her real vulnerability, he'd be on her like a mating bollusk. Even when they rode apart, Brithanas continued to watch her. It stiffened Payne's neck so that he found his own lips curling. Now that Nori was bonding, Payne wouldn't even be able to keep up with her to protect her from what she might face. He smoothed his expression with difficulty. "But you are bonding," he said, more to reassure himself. "It's just new. It will strengthen with time."

Nori regarded him curiously. Sometimes he seemed as stern as their father, and sometimes he sounded so young. "I'll work on it," she said gently.

"What is it like?"

She halted, closed her eyes for a moment, and opened them again. In the sunlight, her pupils looked almost black. "Moons, Payne." She reached out and rested her arm along his in a rare public gesture. "At first, I was almost dizzy, shocked, twisted inside myself. Then my thoughts seemed to straighten out—differently, but clear. It was a wash of clarity, a wrench out of the . . . the complacency of my own senses. It was a glimpse of grey in shadow. You know how your vision doubles when you look into their eyes? You see yourself through their eyes, not just out through your own. This was different. Deeper, harder. I swear my heart stops beating each time and yet doubles in pace. Time stops moving. I can feel teeth in my mind. I am torn apart and yet found at the same moment. And it grows. Look at me. I can't see or smell or hear him right now, but I can feel him even at this distance. Like a comfort that I can't touch, or the smell of hot rou and cinnamon steaming on a cold morning just out of reach."

"Is it . . . everything you expected?"

"More."

He swallowed his jealousy and lightened his voice. "More would give you Mama's touch, and you wouldn't be so sore."

"More of anything in that direction, and I wouldn't even have a bruise."

"Ah, but what's an adventure without a bruise to prove it? Besides, it serves you right for adventuring without me."

As if either of them could, she thought. The Tamrani didn't know it yet, but she was a losing proposition. She glanced toward the forest and felt a chill. Even if she was approved to Journey, she'd still have to follow Payne.

XXVII

When you struck him there,
Was it intentional?

—Question of the elders at the Test of Abis

Hunter nodded shortly as yet another cozar wished him a quick healing. They'd given out that he'd slipped, fallen, and gashed his shoulder on a branch. At least some of the cozar had suspected Hunter of something else, because he caught dark looks from more than one until Nori reined beside him and smiled a good morning.

Fentris's lips twitched as yet another cozar cheerfully wished Hunter good health, and Hunter was forced to thank them. "His pride is suffering more than anything else," Fentris told Nori as he hid a grin at Hunter's irritation. "They're not really wishing him a fast healing; they wish him less clumsiness."

Hunter's voice was as dry. "Yes, we Tamrani aren't known for our grace outside the ballroom."

Fentris lost his smile. Nori cleared her throat, but the slim Tamrani merely shook his head at her, brushed at his embroidered cuff where he'd already picked up a smudge, and said, "I believe I'll check in with the elders." He turned his dnu away.

Hunter frowned after the other man. Then he scowled at the wolfwalker. At least three Harumen had been planted among the cozar as guards, and almost no one had suspected. If it had been him, he'd have had still more waiting in the background to watch and report in case Murton and the others failed. He had reason to worry and more to be irritable. The skin around the healer's staples pulled with every movement, making him

311

sore as a twice-wounded badgerbear. "Aren't you the least bit tense?" he demanded.

Nori shot him a sideways look. "Three failed attacks are enough to convince anyone to withdraw. That, and Uncle Ki hasn't come back, so he's still hunting your Harumen. It's unlikely there's anyone else nearby, lying in wait or watching."

"You have a lot of faith in the Wolven Guard."

She sobered. "Don't call them that, Condari. They don't like to hear it, and it won't be good for you."

So she'd hear no bad words against her uncles? That was as interesting as her dependence on her brother. He inclined his head in tacit apology and changed the subject.

Nori didn't ride out to be with Rishte. It wasn't the need to give her sore muscles a break or any threat from attack that sent her back to the wagons when she tried to take the trail. It was Rishte himself who sent her packing. She had slathered on the liniment at dawn, and she stank to the wolf like a three-year mint field. He actually growled at her and backed away when she tried to meet his eyes. Then he rubbed his nose in the dirt and fled. Nori gave up, returned to Ki's wagon, and spent the next three hours dozing away in a sling bed while Leanna sang soft ballads with her driver. Rishte howled incessantly along the inside of her skull, and Nori tried at first to answer, but he refused to come close. She finally closed her thoughts to his gnawing, so she could close her eyes.

Kettre found her a few hours later, sitting on the back gate of Wakje's wagon, staring off into the forest as she plunked on her guitar.

The brown-haired woman tied off her dnu and plopped down beside her. They rode, legs swinging, for a while as Nori plucked idle tunes. It was an odd view, to watch the world pass by backward, with a team of hammer-headed beasts always five meters away, plodding toward them and never getting close. They watched a ring-runner canter by, then a small knot of riders made up of an older, dour woman and five eager, laughing guild youths. Journey youths, Kettre corrected. Their packs were thick enough to take them away from home, not just there and back to Shockton. Kettre would bet a tenth weight of gold that Nori would have given up her guitar to ride with any of them.

Nori ran through a sequence of particularly minor chords, then paused and said, "If you were a Tamrani, where would you carry your papers?"

Kettre glanced at her. "If you mean Hunter, probably in his belt. It's too carefully styled, even for him."

The wolfwalker plucked thoughtfully across the neck, then into a pattern of slides that sounded almost like moaning.

"Gods, Nori-girl. Can't you play anything in a major key?"

The wolfwalker grinned slyly, shifted into an insipid ditty, and laughed when Kettre groaned.

"I suppose I asked for that." The woman tucked a stray strand of brown hair behind her ear. "Fentris has three different belts," Kettre added. "He switches between them depending on which meal and which meeting he's attending. Hunter wears the one all the time and he's too careful about it when he's around some of the *chovas.* I'd bet that leather is wafer-thin so he can fold his papers inside it."

"Could you swap out what he has in there for plain paper, then switch them back later?"

Kettre shot her a sharp look. "Not unless the moons step in and he leaves that belt unguarded. But I'd have to know what kind and how much paper he kept in there. And he'd have to leave it unguarded a second time for me to return what we took."

Nori plucked a soft sequence up the neck of her guitar. "Fentris said the attacks weren't aimed at the cozar."

"Aye." Nori was thinking, and Kettre waited patiently.

"What if they weren't aimed at us, either?"

Kettre turned and looked at her. "You were nearly killed twice. Three times, if you count Elder Connaught."

"That's exactly what I was thinking of." Nori plucked a minor sequence that left Kettre's ear vaguely dissatisfied. "Did you know that the *chovas* Wora, the one built like Uncle Wakje, gets reports from every Sidisport outrider in the train, as well as a couple of others?"

Kettre frowned. "Wora is from Sidisport himself. Why

wouldn't he talk with the others? And how do you know it's reports that he's getting?"

"Have you watched Fentris?" Nori asked instead. "He goes around from one group to another, chatting, trading compliments. He's gathering information."

"That's what Tamrani do."

Nori nodded. "Wora does the same. He checks in with every *chovas,* or they go to him. He gets to every one of them over the course of a day." She played a sharp ditty that left Kettre almost on edge. "He never sends a message himself by the ring-runners. Three times, though, other *chovas* have sent a message soon after he's talked with them." She stopped cold and looked at the other woman. Her voice was soft. "Fentris asked what we all had in common, but there's nothing among us: no business, no allies, no enemies, no goals. I don't think that that's the right question."

"What is?"

Nori paused. In the silence, she said, "It's what could motivate so many Haruman to masquerade as *chovas*?" Kettre stared at her, and she ran a discordant scale. "They're Harumen," she added softly. "They work for the Houses. Someone has to pay them." Her voice grew even softer. "Someone had to tell them to try to stop Connaught from reaching the council. To stop us and delay the cozar."

"To do what? Delay the entire council? That would take dozens of Harumen in dozens of caravans. Somebody would notice."

"As we have?" Nori smiled without humor.

The other woman frowned and absently turned her bracelet on her wrist. "Have you brought this up to Brithanas?"

She shook her head and played a mournful, almost angry run. "I don't think he'll tell me anything. It took a war bolt to the shoulder to get him to admit he even carried the papers he got from Fentris. And he is Tamrani."

Kettre glanced at her face. "If he wants you enough for a riding partner, you could make a bargain with him. A few days' scouting for a read of what's in that belt. You've got two ninans to work on him."

"Aye, two ninans." Nori agreed quietly. "Till Payne gets his Journey assignment." She plucked a discord and didn't resolve it.

Kettre tried not to wince. "You wish that assignment were yours, don't you?"

"More than you know." Nori straightened and finally, to Kettre's visible relief, played out the sequence into a resolution. "But unless I make a deal with the elders, that isn't likely to happen."

When Kettre left, Nori stayed where she was, thinking. Then she got out her carving tools. She had felt whipsawed the last few days, and carving, like the guitar, was calming work that let her body recover and her emotions settle, while the smell of liniment faded from her skin. A few more hours, and she could run trail again with the yearling. In the meantime, she watched the *chovas*.

At noon, she took the chance to run the frontage trail with Payne and Rishte when the path dipped close to the road. At first, Payne had suggested the wider west trail, but Rishte refused to go, even though it was rough ground—cliffs and swamps—and no one would be using those trails for another month or two. The yearling almost closed his mind to Nori when she made the suggestion. His fear wasn't new, but it was still recent enough in the packsong, and through him, Nori could tell that many forest creatures had avoided the section of cliff. Nori didn't mention the reason to Payne, but they took the east trail instead.

They saw only two other scouts on the path, no *chovas*. Pleased with the quiet, Rishte finally began hunting, sniffing here and stopping there, disappearing for moments at a time, then reappearing like a shadow ahead. When a rabbit sprang up, Nori shot three bolts that cut grass, not fur; Rishte couldn't seem to snap on a limb. It wasn't until Payne started laughing at them that she finally realized they were influencing each other in subtle ways that affected their vision and balance. They had to draw back from each other just so Rishte could catch enough woodmice to fill his growling stomach. Nori left him in a meadow ahead of the train where he could hunt for the next few hours.

The pale roads were never empty this time of year. Riders passed on both sides of the caravan, and the verge was dotted with family wagons stopped for one reason or another. Small villages opened up, then closed again behind the wagons, while loose village dogs chased the dnu. Berque, Bustor, Lilly Camidon—the small grain towns were known for simple waysides and for some of the strongest liquor made in Ariye. There was Veragin, known for its oldEarth herbs, and Kalama for its smoked fruits. Turkinton was set back at the base of the western ridges. Nori was more than nervous when she slipped away to ask Rishte about the plague sense near those cliffs. Plague, near or even in a town? It would be the county's worst nightmare.

But they were north by kays from the last point at which the yearling had felt nervous. There was nothing near the Turkinton cliffs. Counting her midnight run with the worlags, Rishte had felt the death sense four times, each time near a cliff. It was a blessing of all nine moons that the ridges that bound the low hills were so rugged that few would ever go there, even in the scouting season. In spring, with the ground slick and treacherous, and the creeks swollen and hungry, even fewer would risk those trails. Turkinton and the other towns along Willow Road were safe.

Still, she had a hard time ignoring her chill as she looked toward the line of ridges. They ran almost due north, right up to the mountains, right into the heart of Ariye, exactly opposite the mapped arrowhead of raiders and Harumen that pointed to Sidisport. It was as if the one had been fired back out of the other darker, more subtle problem.

Nori was making her way back along the colorful wagon line to help Mian with the exotics again when she was distracted by two *chovas* women. At first, there was nothing she could put her finger on as the women trotted over to a pair of ring-runners who waited at yet another crossroads. One messenger had already been engaged by two traders, but the other greeted the women. It looked casual, but Nori suddenly became more alert. The ring-runner—he had that watchful stillness that spoke of anticipation. A moment later, the outriders handed over a message tube with almost no ceremony, wheeled their dnu, and trotted back to the line. On the verge, the ring-runner spurred away toward the tower trail. With the thick trees darkening even a daylight forest, he was out of sight in seconds. And the messenger hadn't been paid.

She started to guide her dnu back toward Payne to tell him about the two *chovas* and the ring-runner, when there was a flurry behind her. She whipped around.

"Look out!" cried Nonnie.

"Don't hurt them," screamed her daughter.

"Cy, watch out!" The woman ducked as two vari birds and a small, furred tano blasted out from the front wagon opening. A flurry of brilliant, chameleon purple-green feathers exploded from around a clump of brown-and-black fur. The two birds flapped frantically past the driver's head. Their clipped wings turned them into tangles of color as they struggled to stay aloft over the rootroad. Their wings were already fading to a pale yellow-white, and the black-and-tan predator behind them screeched and launched itself after the two birds. Like a handful of needles, the tano hit Cy's shoulder and clung for the barest instant. "What the—"

The tano sprang forward like a fist. Cy's hand closed on air. "By the moons—" Slitted leather wings stretched out instinctively, but like the vari birds, the tano couldn't take flight. It landed at Cy's feet on the footboard and clawed for a precarious grip. "The tano's loose," yelled Cy.

The shrieks of the vari birds startled the team, and Cy's young outriders cursed as their mounts skittered away. With a screech, the tano launched again, landed on the rump of one of Cy's dnu, and dug its hind claws into flesh. The harnessed beast squealed and started to buck. The tano was already jumping again, right onto the dnu's head. Its claws sank into thin ears, The dnu half reared in shock.

Cy fisted the reins and grabbed for the brake, but the team bolted—straight into the wagon ahead. "Free team!" shouted Cy. He braced his thick legs and hauled back on the traces, but the dnu were already out of control.

"Free team!" Nori yelled with the others as Cy's team plunged into the next wagon—Ki's wagon, with Leanna beside the driver. Startled, Hunter looked back just as outriders all along the line jumped their dnu out of the way.

Cy's wild team hit Ki's wagon like a stampede. Ki's rear wheels banged up and slammed down as the dnu crashed into it. The tano screeched as it was flung onto the gate. Its claws clung to the wood as the wagon shaft jammed forward. Ki's team leapt like sprinters as the post rammed against their legs.

"Free team!" shrieked Nonnie as she clung to her wagon.

Chase, run them down . . .

Nori was almost blinded by the rush of eagerness. "No," she cried out through clenched teeth. But she jumped her dnu after Cy's wild wagon before it tore through the rest of the line. Hunter saw what she intended—she could never hold that team by herself—and whipped his beast around.

Someone blew the running call, but the entire line seemed to unravel. One moment, the wagons were rolling, their teams trotting placidly along. The next, outriders were plunging off the road, Cy and Ki's teams were bolting right and left, and dnu reared and tore at the traces.

Nonnie clung to the wagon as Cy wrestled his team, but they hit the edge of the road, and the wagon tilted like a slide. Nonnie saw the trees, managed to grab her daughter by the arm. Then the team skidded up onto a root-bulge. The outside dnu shrieked as its middle leg caught between roots and snapped like a toothpick. The other dnu reared. Leather strained like a hair stretched too tight. Both dnu came down and bolted.

The wagon bounced over the mounded roots like a sled over knee-high boulders. Nonnie lost her grip on her daughter. Mian tumbled out and Nonnie fell back, scrambled to her feet again, and was slammed up hard on the wagon's hardshell portal. The woman clung for a second, blanking out. Then blood washed down her part line. Cy's team spooked off the roots. The front edge of their wagon clipped the back end of Ki's again as Ki's team hauled left to avoid another wagon. Wood splintered and Leanna cried out. Payne's head whipped around. Cy stood braced back against his footboard, fighting the maddened dnu.

"Free team!" he screamed. The wagon lurched like a bottle. And Nonnie Ninelegs lost her grip and flew forward beneath the hooves.

Nori watched it all in slow motion. She spurred her dnu, but she was meters away, the wheels were too fast. Hunter was in the way—

Payne blasted up like a badgerbear. He kicked his leg over the saddle horn, grabbed the edge of the saddle in one hand, and swung down like a hunting lepa. He snagged Nonnie's arm as the woman tumbled limply. For an instant, he thought he had her. Then the massive wheel of Cy's wagon caught the end of the woman's loosened shirt. Like a steel trap, Payne was jerked back and down. His grip almost ripped free. But the moons were watching, because Nonnie's shirt ripped like a leaf. Her torso slapped up against Payne's dnu, her legs dragging the road. Then thick hands plucked the woman from Payne's hand and swung her up and away. Payne spurred his dnu after the cozar, away from the panicked team.

Ahead, drivers had whipped their teams, pulling to the right, desperate to get out of the way. Caravan dogs bolted and barked between the dnu. Cy's team laid their necks low and shot forward into the open just behind Ki's wagon.

Fear, fear, panic. The chase. Cut them out and course them.

Nori kicked her dnu hard. *Ki's team, not Cy's,* she snarled. The hunt-lust was strong. She caught up to the end of Cy's wagon just as another outrider attempted to force the team left, and veered off between the trees. She was barely in time. The team swung back, knocking the outrider aside like a dog and slamming into another wagon instead. Repa's wagon tilted like a half-crazed drunk. "Haw, haw," Repa yelled. Her beasts twisted back, away from the rest of the line. Hunter leapt his dnu forward to grab at the harness and actually got one hand on the trace. Then Repa's transport slammed into the back end of another wagon. Steel felloes crumpled like tin. One of Repa's wheels popped off. The axle cracked. The opposite wheel snapped, and the tirewood split and whipped out like a snake. The back end of the wagon slammed down on the road like a hammer, and Repa flew off the footboard. Hunter was almost trampled as her team plunged left, dragging shattered wood and metal straight into the barrier thorns.

Cy's team leapt over the debris and through the opening like rabbits. "Gee," Cy yelled. *"Gee!"* He hauled with every ounce of strength, but he hit the end of Repa's transport. The wagon smashed over, and the Z-fold walls splayed out like cards. Boxes came loose and smashed through the thin walls, bouncing across the road. Hunter barely had time to dodge off between the trees before he was into the debris. He leapt the beast over the root-balls and into the other lane, cursing under his breath as the motion jarred his shoulder. Then he whipped the mount in a tight circle and forced it back toward the cozar.

Cy's team was now rearing and chittering madly as the outriders tried to calm them. Blood streamed down into the one dnu's eye, spattering the cozar. Ki's team was away, out-and-out racing down the open stretch with Leanna clutching the driver and the seat, and the driver fisting the reins.

Run them down. The hunt!

"Yes," Nori ground out. She was laid low in a wild gallop with two other *chovas*. "Ki's team. Now!" Her violet eyes gleamed. She passed two more outriders as if they stood still, then another pair that jerked away, leaving them to the chase. The hunt-lust was a fire in her blood. Someone shouted to clear her way, but she barely noticed. She just plunged through another knot of riders who had started after Ki's wagon and left them behind like moss.

She didn't know that her lips were wrinkled back, her teeth bared as she raced up on the side of Ki's wild wagon. All she knew was that the prey was ahead, there, to the right, on the footboard by the driver while the wagon careened down the rootroad, swaying with its speed. She beat Wakje there by four heartbeats.

Leanna clung to the jolting wood and gave her a terrified look. Then Nori reached out, caught the girl's forearm, and jerked her across to the saddle. Her hands bruised the girl, but young as she was, Leanna was a child of the Wolven Guard. She went with the motion, wrapped her slim arm around the wolfwalker's waist, and clung like a barney limpet. Nori swung away through the trees.

A moment later, Ki's wagon rod snapped free of its hitch. The driver went off the footboard like a fish on a pole and was dragged, arms-out, a full forty meters before he finally let go. Other cozar sprinted to drag him out of the way before any other teams panicked and crushed him.

No one seemed to notice the tano that dragged itself up on top of Repa's ruined wagon. One of its legs had been caught and pinched in the accordion folds of the ultralight panels, and now it crouched like a lepa, licking its wounded leg. Hunter pulled up beside B'Kosan, and as a knot of men tried to get Repa's dnu to back out of the bushes he asked warily, "Should we help?"

"With your shoulder?" B'Kosan snorted. "They've got it. Besides, too many hands will spook them worse."

B'Kosan raised his arm to wave a signal down the line, and the tano screeched and leapt. It hit B'Kosan's mount like a mudsucker. The man reacted instantly. With one gloved hand, he caught the tano and flung it instinctively off his mount—

Right into the Tamrani. The six-legged beast hit Hunter's chest like a small, ham-sized spider. "What the—" Hunter swiped at the furred body, but it swarmed onto his neck like a rast. "Piss of a—" He started to grab it. Claws pierced flesh near his throat, just above his wounded shoulder. The blood-scent made the tano's eyes gleam. It dug in, instead of fleeing.

"Hunter, freeze," cried Nori. Her voice was a knife through the melee. The Tamrani froze, his body half twisted, as his dnu skittered beneath him.

Beside Nori, Wakje's eyes narrowed. Then he caught the expression on her face. She was the predator now, focused on the tano. He reached out and transferred Leanna neatly to his own saddle. The wolfwalker was away almost before it was done.

She eased her dnu close to Hunter's. "Don't move," she snapped at the Tamrani, then at B'Kosan, whose dnu still skittered nearby. The tano raised its head and bared its fangs like a worlag. Instantly, Nori looked down and away, keeping her eyes hidden. The tano watched the wolfwalker with a hiss, then finally subsided.

Kevinel Runitdown rode up. "Black Wolf, it's right on his—"

"I see it," she cut in tersely. Rishte was growling loud in her mind, and she shoved the wolf back down. "No, don't dismount," she said to Hunter. "Stay in the saddle. Can you turn slowly—*slowly* to the front? Good. Now don't stop riding. It's got your blood-scent. It won't let go, not for a while. Keep it to a walk and ride straight ahead."

He wasn't about to argue. The tano's claws now lightly pierced his neck around his throat and carotid. He managed, "I'm thinking that's good advice—" The tano's claws dug in harder, and he broke off.

"And hush," Nori added sharply. She almost snarled at B'Kosan as the *chovas* shrugged his apology. If someone really was after the Tamrani, not just after her and Payne, they could not have planned this better.

Hunter slanted her a look, but her eyes weren't unfocused. She was thinking like a scout, not a wolf. That, at least, was reassuring.

Kevinel Runitdown eyed the Tamrani and the two small trickles of blood that were now running down his neck. "I'll get Brean," he said and spurred away, unaware that the tano rose and hissed after him.

To Hunter's credit, he rode quietly while the cozar line slowly stopped. Up the road, the Hafell reined in and slowed his dnu so that Hunter's beast caught up. The tano bared its four fangs more clearly, but the Hafell made no sudden moves. After a few tense minutes, Brean was riding side by side with the wolfwalker and the Tamrani.

The Hafell noted the tano's perch and kept his voice calm. "Can you remove it?"

Nori didn't shake her head. "They don't usually respond to humming."

Hunter opened his mouth to ask what *humming* was, and the tano hissed in his ear. One claw snapped out and hooked around his jaw. He closed his mouth abruptly.

"Alright, then, can you kill it?" Brean asked.

She studied the angles. "Probably not before it bites him."

Hunter slanted them another look. The Hafell caught his expression. "Don't worry, Tamrani. If there's a way to do it, we'll save your skin. It's a rich enough hide to warrant it."

Hunter muttered a curse under his breath at all nine moons on a solstice.

Nori glanced at Brean. "What about getting Mian back here? The tano's hers. It knows her voice, her hands. It might be more comfortable with her."

Brean didn't quite give her a look of disbelief. He reminded himself that the Wolfwalker's Daughter had been raised since birth with creatures like the tano. It probably hadn't occurred to her that one didn't usually expose a child to such dangers when they weren't already caged. He said instead, "Mian is already under Trial Silence. Either way, I wouldn't want her near that thing again till it's calmed down. What about simply grabbing it?"

Nori smiled without humor. "Even I am not that fast." She shot Hunter a considering look. "We could let it ride."

The Hafell raised his eyebrows. "Let it ride?"

She nodded. "Look at its legs and its eyes. It's all spiked up right now. Give it half an hour, maybe more, and it will settle down on its own and go to sleep. They always do after they hunt. Then we pluck it off and put it away."

"You want him to ride for half an hour with that thing on his neck?"

"Unless you have a better idea?"

"Black Wolf, I don't," the Hafell said wryly. He looked back along the line, saw that the teams were being calmed and reharnessed. Ki's wagon had been pushed to the side of the road, and the Ell and others now examined it and the wreck of Repa's wagon. One didn't often see such damage. Cozar wagons were remarkably strong for their light weight. With more than eight hundred years to experiment, they had perfected the use of laminated thinwood, coated chancloth, and their formulas for fish glue and proteins. The spring-loaded panels on the sides and tops of each wagon were light as silk, and strong enough to snap back into place even after a hard bash. But even with their design and strength, one of the few things they couldn't withstand was a direct collision or a roll.

Now there was wood and chancloth debris all over the road, not to mention smashed boxes, limp bags, and the personal gear that Repa Ripping White had carried. The vari birds had been recaptured and were being put back in their cages, but they wouldn't lay again for ninans. Mian was lucky the expensive chameleon birds hadn't been trampled. She was luckier still that the Ell was still looking over the wreckage, and had yet to address the girl. From the quick survey the Hafell had made, Repa's wagon would have to be completely rebuilt. Ki's wagon and the other one could be repaired, possibly even at the next circle, but neither job would be easy.

Damaged wagons, tainted lice wash, an attack inside the circle, and now this? Brean shot Nori a sharp look. The wolfwalker had reacted too quickly when the teams panicked, almost as if she had expected it. He looked ahead to Mian. The girl, perched behind one of the outriders, tried not to cry as she looked at the damage, but her small face was pinched and pale. It ought to be. The Tamrani's family wielded power that reached across the nine settled counties. Should he die among the cozar as a result of Mian's pet . . . The Hafell glanced at Black Wolf and then back at Mian. He had thought the wolfwalker's words last ninan had been harsh enough for the girl to take them to heart. This time, it would be Trial judgment, not Black Wolf's, and like a grave, the words of the council were final.

XXVIII

Decisions are easy. Anyone can make decisions.
It's making the decisions stick, that's difficult.
Making them come out right in the end,
Now that's the real challenge.

—Jonha Thalker, in *The Chevres Play,* traditional staging

The claws that pinched into Hunter's neck were hot needles that kept on shifting. His dnu's pace was a dog-slow walk along the halted caravan, but he was starting to sweat at the tension. Drivers and other cozar watched him warily as he passed. All it would take was one man waving his arms, one woman to scream at the tano, one dog to lunge, and the well-grooved fangs would snap down.

He was almost ready for it when it happened. One of the outriders wheeled her dnu unexpectedly. The tano screeched and half rose on his neck. Nori reacted instantly, shouldering the *chovas* dnu aside. Then the Hafell jumped in between them. "Watch out," Brean snapped.

"Sorry," maSera returned quickly. The woman backed her dnu away, but Nori stared after her. MaSera was out of Sidisport and was friends with B'Kosan and Murton. And a woman had been in their wagon.

Brean caught her taut expression, but thought it was for Hunter's safety. "He'll be lucky to make it five more minutes, Black Wolf, let alone half an hour," he said sharply. "I can see more riders coming up from behind, and there are ring-runners ahead on the southbound track."

Nori took a breath. "Then there is one other option."

The Hafell had been watching the Tamrani with sharp eyes. Now he looked back at Nori. She had rarely spoken to him so much before, and he wasn't sure how to judge her. He waited.

Her voice was flat. "I can try to call it off him."

She had his attention now, and Hunter's. Brean frowned. "I thought you said they don't respond well to humming?"

"They don't. I would try to call a prey tone, like a wounded jackbraw or a young pelan, not hum to soothe it. It might be willing to jump to someone else if its hunting instincts were triggered."

Hunter started to speak, but stopped himself in time. The Hafell was already shaking his head. "No. No, Black Wolf, I cannot allow it."

Nori held up her hand to halt him. "I'll wear a double jerkin and a second pair of gloves under full gauntlets. We wrap my neck and upper arms with leather, and someone rides close by with the cage."

"No," Hunter said clearly. The tano's head whipped around to his jaw, and its claws stiffened on his neck.

"Quiet, Tamrani," the cozar snapped. "Black Wolf—" he started.

She cut him off. "Hafell, I acknowledge your braid, and I take this Choice from you."

Brean stopped midword. Hunter stared at Nori. For a moment, her violet eyes looked almost frightened, as if she couldn't believe what she'd said. Then she raised her chin stubbornly and met the Hafell's gaze.

With the tano on his carotid, Hunter could do nothing. He had heard of the Choice, but he'd never heard the actual words spoken. Nori had just taken the duties of the Hafell onto her shoulders for the task of caging the tano. The words had been simple, but the reality was not. A Hafell was, basically, a second Ell. He was responsible for the safety and needs of the entire caravan, not just for the one person who was in trouble at the moment. Among the cozar, a Hafell had the authority of a Lloroi. He could command someone into danger, cut someone out of the train, judge, sentence, banish, even order a death. Any action he took or refused to take was judged with full hindsight, and not tempered with might-have-beens. The only real difference between a Hafell and an Ell was that the Ell's wagon was the head of the train, while the Hafell's wagon was last.

With her words, Nori had just become the Hafell for this task. Brean could still step in as his duties required, to fix the mess she might make of the job, but the task now belonged to Nori. Should Hunter—or any other cozar or rider—be endangered or hurt by her decision or her actions, she could forfeit everything. She would stand Trial anyway, even if it was simply the Hafell judging the way things worked out. The Choice was always judged.

The Hafell looked at her unflinching expression. She was afraid, yes, but she wasn't backing down. And there was . . . conviction in her eyes, he realized. It was not something he'd seen before when she had faced elders in the past. But here, now, she was as certain as her mother. He waited a long moment for her to take back her words, but she said nothing. Finally, he said quietly, "You have a second Choice, maDione. Make sure it is not out of pride."

It was a deliberate use of the name she'd inherited, and she blinked. He was offering her an out. In spite of her words, he would let her back away without risk to herself, without trying to step into the shoes of her legendary mother. No one could truly be like Ember Dione maMarin; Nori and Payne knew that better than most. The Hafell had just reminded her of that in the clearest way he could.

Nori stared at the man without seeing him. Grey and yellow stirred in her mind as she reached inside herself. It might have been the yellow taint that did it, the sense of power behind Aiueven eyes. It might have been Payne's words from before. It might even have been the grey strength of the wolves, but she realized with clarity it was not the tano she feared, but that one of her kind was in danger.

She knew without looking how the tano's ruff bristled against Hunter's thick hair. How the venom sacs pulsed up inside the hollow claws. How the dark blood trickled down and mixed with the sweat on Hunter's weathered neck. She met Brean's gaze steadily. "I see no second Choice."

The older man regarded her for another moment, but although her violet-grey eyes seemed to glint in the sun, they were clear and her voice was calm. Finally he nodded. "The

Choice is yours, as is the judgment." He added softly, "May the speed of the wolves be in your hands." He stated simply, "You have needs."

"Work gloves. Medium, but broad-palmed, with the fingers cut out." Quickly, she tugged on her own gloves and held up one hand so he could judge her size. "Also venge gauntlets or work gauntlets, again with the fingers cut out. A venge jerkin, yours or one size smaller than yours. A leather wrap for my neck. Overwraps for my arms. A smithy apron or venge chaps that will cover my legs but leave me free to ride. And a towel with a deep pile."

He frowned, not understanding. "Would bandages not be better?"

"It's for the tano, not me, to tie onto my front to help its claws tangle as soon as it leaps."

The Hafell nodded and reined away. Nori glanced at Hunter. "And no," she told him evenly, as his green eyes glinted. "You don't have a choice, either." She dropped back at the tano's hissing, and he could only glare as she left.

She used a knife to cut the fingers off her gloves. Then she let herself reach toward the grey. She could feel the taint in her mind. It was watching her, almost stretching toward her as she tried instead to grasp the grey.

The wolf had been moving along the road, paralleling her as she rode. Now his mental voice grew stronger, clearer, and she knew he loped near the barrier bushes, just inside the forest. She closed her eyes and gathered her mind. If this was to work, she would need all the speed she could get. *Rishte, can you open the packsong to me?*

Danger, threat, danger—

Aye, she answered. *I need your reflexes, your instincts. Will you help me?*

She could feel him reaching out to her. There was an underlying excitement in his voice from the racing dnu and wagons. In spite of the damage, in spite of the danger to Hunter, in spite of what she was going to try to do, Nori echoed that animal joy. It was the first seductive hedonism, the one most often fought by wolfwalkers to keep their human selves separate, but she didn't draw back from it.

She caught a glimpse of grey as he came through one of the barrier channels. For a moment, their minds meshed as his golden eyes met hers. *Packmate, trouble.*

His nostrils flared, and she wondered if he could smell the tano through her nose or if he saw it through her eyes.

Sharp venom, burning venom, Rishte identified. *The death-fang from the shadows.*

"Aye," she breathed softly. Hunter's gaze flickered, and she knew he had glimpsed the wolf before Rishte slunk back into the forest. She said softly, "Aye, your chances just improved."

A few minutes later, Payne, Wakje, and another outrider wrapped Nori in as much metal and leather mesh as they could lash on her and still give her movement. The outrider handed the tano's cage over to Payne, and Wakje got out a knife.

Hunter stiffened, but Payne said dryly, "Don't worry, Tamrani. He won't skewer the beast right on your throat—not unless he has to." Behind them, knots of cozar watched from a distance, some with binoculars, as others cleared debris.

Nori ignored them. "Watch its thighs," she told her brother softly. "Its eyes will stay on me, but its thighs will start to flex when it's getting ready to leap." She got a small strip of metal from her pocket and fit it onto a small, U-shaped piece of wood. "It will dig in hard," she added to Hunter. "Don't flinch, or it may not actually leave you. Even to a tano, a palt in the hand is worth two in the bush." She checked her gauntlets one more time. "When it hits me, I'll try to catch it around the neck or arms. It's got carry nerves there, like a kitten."

She closed her eyes for a moment. *Rishte?*

Hereherehere.

I am ready.

She opened her eyes, but kept the link open. She could feel the grey lapping at her mind like a sea. It didn't rush to drown her, but held back with Rishte till she needed its speed in her hands. She let herself get used to the sense of it, then moved slowly toward Hunter until her dnu was almost against his.

She blew experimentally on the wooden caller just once. The

sound was a faint scream of metal and air, and she adjusted it against her lower gums. She was beginning to focus, to reduce all movement and sound to the small point that was Hunter's neck. A spark of yellow flickered beneath the grey, and Rishte paused. The packsong seemed to split in Nori's mind, as if it met a strong current. *No,* she sent sharply. *Stay with me. Me. Mememe . . .*

Nori opened her arms to ready herself for the tano, and then blew across the caller. It was a soft shriek of metal and woman's voice, like a creature being torn apart. Brean shuddered, and Nori blew again.

Facing forward, Hunter couldn't see what she could: that the tano's eyes now gleamed wide open. That they centered now on Nori. Its thighs began to flex so slowly, it took Payne a moment to realize it was happening. Hunter felt the tension like a knife carving away at his flesh. The sound was continuous, like a scraping on his nerves. Then he felt the tano's claws stab deep.

The creature launched itself like a war bolt. Nori's hands flashed. Claws reached toward her chest and neck, and her dnu jerked instinctively. The tano hit her sternum like a shot, and its claws tangled in the towel's pile. It yanked, but even as it tore one limb free and dug into thick leather, she caught its neck like a vise. Her fingers pinched. Its mouth opened soundlessly; the tano's body went limp.

Hunter stayed frozen.

"Have you got it?" Brean snapped.

She shook her head. Her gloves were too thick to detach the tano's claws, and the wooden caller kept her from speaking. She adjusted her grip cautiously.

"Now?" Brean demanded.

"I'e got it," she finally answered around the caller.

Hunter let out his breath. Carefully he raised his hand and rubbed at his bloody neck. "I thought I'd wear that thing to my grave."

"You might have," Payne agreed dryly. He reached over warily and disentangled the beast from towel and jerkin while it hung half paralyzed from Nori's hands. Then he held the cage door open till she popped it in.

Quickly, she started to latch the cover. "Da' it," she muttered. She fumbled with the latch. "Wha' is the 'oblem with this—" she cursed around the wooden caller.

"Hurry up," Payne said sharply. "I don't want this thing loose on me or mine."

"I need a 'iece o' 'ire," she said over her shoulder to Wakje. "Q'ickly."

Wakje snapped open a saddle pack, drew out a small roll of wire, and cut a piece off. He reined up and thrust it into Nori's hand. She tried to wind it around the latch, but gave up after a moment. "We need to get this 'own to ground."

The Hafell swung off his dnu and, with Wakje and Payne, eased the cage to the road while Nori held the door shut. The tano hissed and clutched its perch branches, but didn't try to escape. Carefully Nori threaded the wire through the latch hole, then back out through the side of the cage, till she could twist it into a crude lock.

"Done?" Payne asked sharply.

She sat back on her heels, removed the caller, wiped it off, and tucked it back in her pocket. "Done as best I can. Wait a minute." She ran her hands over the joints of the cage. The Hafell didn't interrupt her until she nodded to Payne to lift the cage away and secure it on Wakje's dnu. When she started to rise, Hunter would have helped her up, but the Hafell reached out instead. He gripped her arm for a long moment. "The Choice was made, the task is done. The Choice returns to me."

"I return the Choice as is right."

Brean nodded.

Nori forced her face to be expressionless, but she couldn't help holding her breath. Brean could give her judgment now, or make her stand before the cozar council. From the hard look in Wakje's eyes, the ex-raider hadn't realized she'd taken the Choice from Brean. Wakje's hand was already on the hilt of his sword as if to attack should it go badly for his niece.

The Hafell ignored the ex-raider. He met Nori's violet gaze and said quietly, "With challenge, you chose to act in my place. With hindsight, you have been judged. No harm has come from your actions; harm has been averted and this man's life was saved. Be at peace, Wolfwalker."

She let her breath out almost audibly.

Brean nodded. "You did well, Black Wolf." He glanced at Wakje, then Payne. "In spite of the fact that I don't believe you knew what you were saying till after the words were out."

She flushed, and Payne knew the man was right. Wakje nodded curtly to the Hafell, then trotted away with the tano. If it had been his choice, he'd have killed the damn thing on the Tamrani's neck, then buried both of the bodies.

Payne watched him go. "That latch was broken," he said softly.

"Aye," Nori agreed. "The metal was torn right out of the wood."

Brean looked from one to the other, then at the blood trails that ran down Hunter's neck. He glanced back toward the caravan that was only now getting underway. This had not been just a mishap. There were three wagons damaged, one destroyed; at least five of the dnu were injured. Ki's driver was lucky not to have broken half his bones, and Nonnie Ninelegs was still unconscious. To have a wagon of exotics wasn't all that unusual, but to have one cared for by a child? He'd taken the chance, since Mian was Nonnie Ninelegs's daughter, and since Black Wolf was among them. It had not been a good decision. His usually mild voice was hard as flint. "Mian is supposed to maintain the cages, not just the beasts within. There will be Trial tonight at fireside."

"Hafell," Nori cut in. "I didn't see anything wrong with the wood. I felt it when I pushed the wire through. It's firm enough, not rotted." He opened his mouth to retort, but she added, "What I did feel were some gouges by the latch, like the kind made by a prying tool."

"What are you getting at?"

She glanced at Hunter, but the Tamrani said nothing. She realized with surprise that he was leaving the decision to inform the Hafell up to her. She looked at Payne, who shrugged almost imperceptibly, then said to Brean, "I think the latch was deliberately loosened. It was only a matter of time before the tano got out. In fact, it probably would have happened last ninan when the weibers broke free and all the animals panicked, but Mian had the tano in its grazing cage at the time."

"That's a serious accusation, Wolfwalker. The only reason to let a tano out is to kill, and there are no grudge hands among us. I know almost every family, even the ones who joined us on the coast. There are two families I've never driven with, but they were in my grandfather's train last year and came with references. They're solid."

Hunter was wiping his neck with a damp cloth, and he paused. "Did you check with your grandfather yourself?"

The Hafell barely glanced at the Tamrani. "Including you and your brother," he went on to Nori, "there are also only eight *keyo* with us. I know almost all of them. None of them would have done this."

"What about Murton and his partner and Hoinse?" Hunter asked sharply.

The Hafell said irritably, "Murton and his partner, and the man from your own caravan, were *chovas,* not cozar and not *keyo.* They're hired-ons. We're not like traders traveling with unknown companions who don't have references, Tamrani. We're not strangers working solely for gold, with our loyalties easily bought. We're family groups. We choose to travel together to share safety and ease trade. We agree to certain guidelines, we live with certain rules. Issues are raised and dealt with at fireside, as they are at your breakfast tables. Among us, they're settled long before they become deadly, or the caravan is split. There have been only two challenges since we set out." He glanced meaningfully at Nori, and she had the grace to look faintly guilty at the reminder of the puffball fight. "Neither of which was serious," he continued. "Conflicts that can't be settled that way are worked out by me or the Ell if it goes beyond the council." He turned back to Nori. "If there's a grudge hand now among us, it's from among the *chovas,* the Test youths, or the Tamrani you brought here."

Hunter was clearly irritated, and Nori murmured, "He's testing you. You've brought him trouble, as have we. He wants to know if you're worth it."

Hunter scowled at her. "I'm beginning to wonder myself."

Brean gathered the reins of his dnu. "At least I can take Mian off Trial Silence."

"Hafell." Payne caught his attention. "If you're willing, there is another option."

Brean glanced from Nori to Payne. The brother and sister had changed on this trip, he realized. Black Wolf had stood up to him twice, and The Brother was looking more serious than he had ever seen. He said slowly, "The Brother has always been welcome to offer his opinion."

Payne's jaw tightened for an instant, but he said, "Keep Mian on Trial Silence. Say nothing about the cage. Let it come out at fireside. Let us bring it up."

The Hafell glanced at the approaching train. "You're talking about a child at Trial, neBentar. There's a burden of compassion, not just truth here."

"Aye."

But Payne didn't turn a hair, and Hunter suddenly realized that there was one thing the songsters never seemed to mention: Payne had been raised by raiders.

The Hafell studied the brother and sister. "There could be Trial for you as well."

Payne nodded. "If Mian wishes it."

Brean said flatly, "You've played too much with girls, neBentar. You know she'll be so grateful at the verdict that she won't blame you for putting her through that. Black Wolf, what do you say?"

He was deferring to her like an elder, and she hesitated. "There is more going on—" She broke off as both Hunter and Payne flashed her warning glances. She shook her head at them both. The Hafell didn't miss it.

His voice was cold. "Black Wolf?"

Nori met his gaze without flinching. "Whoever did this has been among us for some time. There have been more . . . incidents than you know of. We believe we can flush out some of the doers at Trial when they hear what we have to say."

"And for this, you want Mian to suffer."

She glanced at Payne, but said softly, "Aye." She hesitated. "Hafell," she began. "I respe—"

"No, Black Wolf." He cut her off with a sharp gesture. "This Choice is mine. I just want to know why I should make it at all."

She felt her stomach untense with relief. One Choice had been enough for her. She glanced at Payne one more time, but he didn't stop her as she answered, "Weapons have been sabotaged, Hafell. Gear has been ruined in ways that might not be noticed before it was used. I found two ring-runners dead on the trail to Bell Rocks, where raiders were camping out. Last night, well, Condari didn't fall into the shrub line. He was shot, and possibly by Harumen, not raiders. The wolves . . ." She took a breath. "The wolves themselves are uneasy, and I cannot tell you why." Would not, she added silently.

Brean regarded her thoughtfully. "Three questions, Black Wolf. Three answers." Payne took a half step forward, but the Hafell held up his hand to stop the younger man. "If you leave the caravan, does this trouble leave with you?"

Nori hesitated again. She didn't look at Hunter. "This trouble is countywide, Hafell Brean. It will not stop with us."

He leaned across the saddle horn and asked harshly, "Black Wolf, are you bonding?"

It was unexpected, and she stared at him. Rishte growled in her mind. She couldn't seem to move her lips, but her bared teeth and her silence were their own answer.

"If I hold Trial at fireside, you believe that, through the wolves, like your mother, you can feel out the raiders?"

Again, she couldn't answer. Finally, she jerked a nod.

"So be it." He straightened. "Be ready at first flame, Wolfwalker."

He started to rein around, but she stopped him. "Hafell, if you're willing, don't call me that. Not here, not yet."

He studied her, then Payne. She had always been reserved, distant even from the cozar, and he had wondered sometimes if she was even half connected to the humanity she so avoided. Now he saw something in her violet eyes that made him think she was too connected. Emotions churned there like a plunging river. With the wolf, she could no longer hide it. He glanced at

Payne and saw the set of the younger man's jaw, and the way his hand rested on his knife. So. The Brother was still protecting her, though why the title she deserved should make her fear come out . . . He shook his head to himself, but nodded curtly. "Black Wolf," he acknowledged. Then he reined around sharply and cantered back to the wagons.

Hunter murmured down at her, "He must respect you two a great deal to take that."

Payne frowned. "Take what?"

"You telling him what to do so flatly when it goes against the grain."

The younger man scowled. "We didn't tell him what to do. We made a request."

Hunter's voice was dry. "It must be the cozar way, to be that direct when asking. If a *tondi* servant made a request like that, he'd be looking for other work." He rubbed at his neck, looked at the blood on his fingers, then back down at Nori. "I didn't say thank you yet for saving my life."

She shrugged. "I'm a vet and a caller. It was mine to do."

"No, it wasn't. Not when they loosed a tano at us."

"That can't have been aimed at us. No one could predict whom the tano would attack once it got loose. And it's pure luck I was close enough to help."

"You weren't that close at first, and it was more predictable than you think." He nodded at her frown. "As you say, you're an animal healer. According to fireside gossip, you've taken the duty position, even if it's unacknowledged. And you spend a lot of time with that girl, teaching her to care for her pets. All a Haruman would have to do is wait till you're in with the girl, then startle the animals." Payne gave him a sharp look, but he kept his eyes on Nori. "The tano would break out. You'd try to catch it. It would have bitten you like a mudsucker, and there's the end of Black Wolf."

"It might not have bitten me," she said sharply. "And don't call me that."

"The cozar do."

"They've done it all my life. I don't notice it from them."

"But you do from me?" He smiled slowly. "How very interesting." He leaned close and kissed her, quick and hard. He let go almost before she jerked back. He grinned down at her. "Interesting indeed. I look forward to fireside." Then he mounted his dnu and trotted down the road.

Nori scowled darkly after him, but he didn't look back.

Down the road, Wakje gave the Tamrani a hard look as he trotted past, but the Tamrani merely raised an eyebrow and went on by. Wakje looked back at Nori. It was the first time he'd seen her take a kiss. She could have dodged the Tamrani before he grasped her chin. She could have taken Brithanas down completely before the man had actually kissed her. But she'd stood there like a four-legged deer with three of its legs in a rast hole. And that wasn't all. She'd taken a Choice. He'd never heard her do that. She was changing, he realized. Changing to be like her mother. He followed her gaze toward the forest and knew she was reaching for the wolf to steady herself. Soon, she would no longer need him.

Nori couldn't meet Wakje's eyes, or Payne's. Instead, she pretended to listen for Rishte as the wolf loped back from the road. It was an excuse that couldn't last, and she finally turned and took her own reins from a brother who was carefully trying not to grin. She was swinging up into the saddle when he teased in a whisper, "Big, bad Black Wolf. Can't hit a Tamrani when he's right in your face."

"Leave it alone, Payne." But she could feel her face burning. She nudged her dnu into a fast-paced trot, and left Payne chuckling behind her.

XXIX

Lady Sinial looks at the mess of tangled dnu and
wagons. "Who did this?"
Grasp looks guiltily down.
"Was it you?" she demands.
He shakes his head.
"Was it you?" she demands again.
He looks up. "No, Madam. It was my arm, and aye,
My wrist, and even my hand on the blade,
But it was not I who did this."

   —from *Playing with Swords,* traditional staging

The cozar wasted no time on the road. The caravan had already snaked its way to meet them as they rode back. Cy's lamed dnu was tethered behind his wagon, and its thin middle leg was drawn up tightly against its body in a quickcast. Extra mounts were harnessed in place to replace teams that were bruised or damaged. Repa's wagon and goods had been broken down and packed onto other wagons. Repa, Nonnie Ninelegs, and Ed Proving, who'd broken his wrist, had been seen to by the healer.

Ki's wagon had suffered little damage, considering the force with which Cy had hit him. Ki's gear and goods had had to be repacked around the splintered back corner of the wagon, and a broken shaft replaced, but that was all. Ki's driver, bruised and scraped as he was, went on with Leanna beside him.

On the Ell's wagon, where everyone approaching the caravan could see her, young Mian sat silently beside the old Ell. Trial Silence had been invoked, and she would not speak or be spoken to until the cozar held their council. The sick expression on Mian's young face was visible even from where Nori rode. The Hafell reached over, tucked the girl behind him in the saddle, and rode her, crying now, back to her own wagon. He could do that, at least. Even though her parents couldn't speak to her, she could stay inside their wagon.

Nori, Payne, Kettre, and Wakje rode in a tight knot far to one side of the wagons. They spoke little, listening instead to the cozar and *chovas* around them. Sober faces, tense drivers; even the wagon banners seemed to hang flat, as if they were afraid to wave and flutter.

Nori glanced at Rezuku as they passed his wagon. Like the Tamrani and other wealthy merchants, he dressed carefully. Today he'd chosen a somber green cloak with black edging and silver embroidery. He looked serious as he spoke with one of the cozar elders. How terrible about all that damage, all the injuries, and how careless the girl must have been to let such a beastie loose, and moons, but they'd been twice blessed that the Tamrani hadn't died. Why, if he had, just think of it. His family might even hunt each one of the cozar down and destroy their fortunes in revenge. It had happened before, you know . . .

Nori looked away so that he didn't see the anger in her gaze when he glanced at her. There had been a glint in his eye that made her think of a sly tamrin. She wondered how much gold he could make with some of those cozar out of the way of his trade. She also hadn't liked the looks of some of the outriders who had worked the wrecks. Several of them seemed to hinder more than help the repair work. On top of which, there was a weight of rain in the clouds overhead, which seemed to slow the cozar further. By the time they passed Grimwood, both the Ell and the Hafell were up and down the line, urging the teams faster and even snapping at the message master when the old woman's dnu wouldn't hurry.

When Hunter joined Nori, Kettre murmured to the others, and they fell back to leave the two together. Nori scowled after her friend.

Hunter glanced at her frown. "Something wrong? Is it your wolf?"

"Condari," she warned. She looked around quickly at the cozar on the road.

"No one heard me," he reassured in a low voice. "And you

called me Hunter when you thought I was in danger. Is it? Your . . . other?"

She said sourly, "It's the thought of Trial, my well-bruised back, and Kettre abandoning me so obviously to you."

He chuckled. "That last can't be the end of the world."

The end of the world . . . On his neck, the marks of the tano seemed to pulse, and fire seemed to burn in her blood. Memory flashed in the grey. Plague, burning in the womb, plague killing the wolves. Disease striking the Ancients down and leaving them dead as they fell. And Harumen and raiders like rats after the dead. Yellow, slitted eyes flickered, and Nori tried to pull back, but the wolf shivered into the pack. Even at their distance, Nori felt it echo. Close, too close. *Death, alone, alone, fear. Lonely, wolfwalker. Need.*

Hunter glanced at her as she didn't answer. His cool green eyes narrowed. She had stiffened, and her face was tense. There was something in her gaze akin to a deep-seated fear. "Nori-ana?" He frowned. "It's not Kettre who's bothering you. That's your—" He glanced around to make sure no one was near. "—partner."

His words seemed to anchor her, and she shook off the sense of slitted eyes. The sense of men with the plague was closer, as if, since the wagon wreck, such men were now among them. It was crazy. She stared straight ahead until she got control of her mind. It wasn't easy. That flash of fear had been an icy fire. The sense of plague lurked in the packsong, and she would swear it was growing stronger, not weaker as her link with Rishte tightened. It was as if the alien mother-mother in the back of her mind was using the wolves to reach her, while each moment of tension over the Harumen made her more susceptible to fear. She glanced at Hunter and grasped at the yearling for an excuse. "It's Rishte," she said finally. "He's alone, away from the pack, and running through worlag country. I'm just . . . worried."

"He's a wolf. He's got fangs and the speed of a wilding to back them up. Why, by the ruins of the Ponduit Bridge, would you worry?"

She fingered the reins, pulled in spite of herself to the west. "He's barely a year old."

"Old enough to bond."

"Any wolf can bond," she returned sharply.

"I don't see the problem."

She was almost relieved. This she could talk about. "Rishte isn't an adult yet," she explained. "He doesn't have the experience of years in the woods to draw on. This is not . . ." She looked west and felt for that danger sense. Now that she knew what to listen for, she could feel it hovering on the edge of the grey. "This is not the safest place to be," she said finally. "And judging from what's happened in the last three days, I'm not the safest person to be around, either. Yet he's left the pack to follow me. I'm all he has right now."

"You sound almost . . . sad," he observed.

"Aye." Her voice was quiet. "If I stayed near his pack, it wouldn't be an issue. He'd have guides, mentors among the wolves to teach him what he should learn. But as long as I am on the road, he'll be alone for the rest of his life. He'll have no pack, only meetings with Grey Ones in passing."

"What if you formed your own pack?"

Her gaze flicked back to him. "I don't understand."

"You're running with your brother and uncle right now. The wolf can never be part of that because you have too much history among the three of you. What if you formed a new pack, new friends to ride with? He'd be part of those new bonds as they strengthened out of nothing. He would feel as if they were his pack, too."

She had started to frown at his words. Now she scowled. "Moons, Condari. It has nothing to do with who I ride with. I could Journey with no one but the Grey Ones and still not give him a pack. It's the link, not the pack, that matters. That's what separates him from others of his kind, since he's bound to me, not them."

"Then why don't you Journey? You can't say you're not qualified. You're, what, a second? A third in Abis?"

Her face grew expressionless. "That was feeble, Condari. You know I've never Tested."

"Do you want to?"

She wanted to snap, but she forced herself to say simply, "No."

"You're sure? A wolfwalker like you. All these open trails . . ."

She gave him a long look. To have the recognition of rank, to have the elders stop accusing her of wasting her skills. It wasn't the first time she'd wondered what it would be like to be able to stand up to the elders with pride, instead of the stubborn shame of knowing they thought her a coward.

Wolfwalkerwolfwalkerwolfwalker . . .

She pushed the wolf down and turned her face away. She was wearing Hunter's shirt again over her own, and she rubbed the fabric absently. She surprised herself by wanting to answer him truthfully. She liked the strength in him. She liked the way he talked to her, that he teased her like Payne did, instead of treating her like a legend. To have someone other than her brother to confide in, someone who understood? She almost answered, but behind them, Payne called out a greeting to a ring-runner who cantered past. Nori shut her mouth with a snap. The man was a godsdamned Tamrani, practically a councilman by birth, and carrying secrets in that belt of his that might tear her life apart.

Hunter watched curiously as the expressions flickered through her violet eyes. He said softly, "So you do want to Test, and you do want to Journey. I didn't know if you hid your desire or if you were simply unsure about it."

"You're wrong." She forced her words to be firm. "And I'm as sure as the sea hits the shore."

"Ah."

She said sharply, "What does 'ah' mean?"

He shrugged. "Considering what you did for me with the tano, and that you now have your own wolf to work with, I'd think, after living so long in your mother's shadow, that you would jump at the chance to Journey."

"Not hardly."

"By the First House, Black Wolf, you could be anyone, anywhere in the nine counties, if you'd just let yourself take the road."

"I already have duties—" She broke off. Moons, what made her say that?

"Ah, yes, the duties."

"Moonworms, stop ah-ing as if you understand." She started to rein away, then paused and looked back over her shoulder. "One more thing."

"Yes?"

"Touch me—kiss me—again without my permission, and I'll cut your lips from your bones and feed them to the wolf pack."

She spurred her dnu ahead.

The Tamrani rubbed his square jaw and watched her ride off to pace another wagon. "You have no idea," he murmured, "how that challenges a man."

He rubbed the thin stitches on his belt. There had been a particular tone in Nori's voice when she'd spoken of duties, a tone under her anger, and she'd looked at his belt again. She had been anxious, perhaps even afraid, and it had not been his imagination. He didn't think it had to do with the accidents in the train, either. She'd been too calm when they had discussed them, and she hadn't hesitated when facing Brean or dealing with the tano. No, there was something else that worried the wolfwalker, and it was that which worried him. He wanted a scout who was focused on her duty. He couldn't risk his family's lives on someone so caught up in other things that she'd be no use to him. He fingered the belt and watched with a frown as she rode ahead at a canter.

That evening, no one lingered at dinner, and fireside was a jumble of unease. It was crowded, too, and not just from the other three cozar trains who had to share the circle. Almost every cozar from Ell Tai's train was there at Trial, including children and *chovas*. Lookers-on from the village had ridden in, along with locals and messengers. It wasn't often one saw a full cozar trial, and this would be severe. Tai had had to borrow four elders from the other caravans to make up the panel of judges.

A line of elders made up one half of the innermost circle of the stone amphitheater. The judges ringed the other half. Mian's advocate, the old Ell himself, sat in the midst of the elders, with the girl silent beside him. Nori watched Fentris frown at the tight ring of men and women. He was across fireside from

Hunter, ignoring the taller man while trying to check out the cozar. The wolfwalker hid a wry smile. She understood his confusion. If she hadn't known who the elders were herself, Tai and the others would have looked like just more white-haired men and women nodding off at fireside. They wore little to indicate rank. Ell Tai wore just a thin braid of brown, almost invisible on his worn cuff. It was a standard joke that a Hafell was known by the cuff that had no braid. Even the judges wore no robes, only simple stoles with small, heavy metal pins of the oldEarth scales of justice. It was a reminder that they were not above the law themselves, and that the weight of law was a burden, a responsibility, not a power to be used for themselves. They were not gods who passed judgment from the cold distance of legal words, but members in a community who struggled to keep it intact for every one of their folk.

Nori wondered how welcome she would be if they knew she was linked to the enemy of the Ancients, the ones who had passed judgment on all humanity and then had sent the plague. She felt an echo of the dread she'd felt years before when she herself had stood Trial.

It had started with a chance meeting of a scout who had seemed simply friendly. Then the man started turning up, watching Nori at the university, following her to classes. To her relief, he'd disappeared for a while, but then he'd returned, this time trying to get her alone. When he'd tried to touch her, she'd backed away. When he'd attacked, she'd struck back hard. Then he'd turned up dead.

Yellow eyes flickered in the back of her head at her thoughts. There was a sense of satisfaction in the gaze of Nori's mother-mother as Nori remembered the Tumuwen elders, and she tried to stifle a chill. For her, Trial had been an exercise in hiding a truth that could break the counties apart. She remembered every word, every truth she'd swallowed, and her dread as her uncles were questioned.

Yes, Wakje and Weed had noticed the man stalking Nori. No, she had not gone to them for help. Yes, they had warned the man off on their own. The scout had left town, but he had returned.

They had seen his assault, and they'd seen Nori hurt the man badly and nearly destroy herself.

Did the man even get Trial?

Wakje had answered, "He was taken to the trial block, he spoke for himself, he was sentenced by his peers."

Nori had tried not to blanch at that, and the elders had looked at Wakje sharply. "Did you punish him?" they'd asked.

"No," he'd said.

But Nori had not imagined the flicker she'd seen in his flat, blue eyes. She knew that look. She had it herself every couple of years when she faced her mother-mother.

"Did you take him into the forest?" The elders had asked.

"No." Wakje had answered.

"What did you do with him?"

"Nothing." Wakje's voice had been remarkably expressionless.

"Then how did he die?"

"Looked like worlags to me."

The elders, dissatisfied, had turned to the other uncle, Weed, but the answers had been the same. Both uncles had been seen in town the night the stalker disappeared, and Nori had been in a coma. The elders had recessed, then called Trial back. Both Weed and Wakje had been sentenced to guard duty one day a ninan for a month. It was a token punishment that had grated on the ex-raiders even as it had relieved them.

Nori remembered waiting for her own sentence, her stomach a cold knot as the elders finally spoke. Even though she had had nothing to do with the man's actual death, it had been her silence about the stalker that had put her uncles in the position of having to commit violence to keep her from greater harm. The judgment—that she would work four ninends for the poor, tending to their livestock, another token punishment, since she already volunteered for that duty each month—didn't change the sick fear she'd had of waiting for it to be spoken. She would have had nightmares about Trial for years, but there was something worse in her mind.

The link between Nori and her mother-mother had always

been strong, and those yellow eyes had reached into that coma with images even harsher and stronger than usual. After the coma, it took nights of waking with screams on her lips to realize that what she'd been seeing was not solely in her imagination. Nor had it been dreams like the nightmares she'd grown up with.

She had always dreaded sleep. Day or night, she would close her eyes, and in that half-sleep state, when the mind is open to odd connections and to images in the unconscious, she could hear her mother-mother. She could feel the slitted eyes, the icy breath of the sky-chipped mountains, the hatred of humanity that lurked in other birdmen. She saw memories of walls that twisted in on themselves, blasts of light, collapsing heat, and patterns that fractured in coil after coil and disappeared into nothing.

After the coma, there was something else in that nightmare state of sleep. She saw clear, crisp memories from her mother-mother that had nothing to do with the mountains or light or icy winds or patterns. And she could feel a sense of herself in the memory, as if she had tainted her mother-mother's telepathic mind as much as the birdman tainted hers.

For years afterward, she saw her mother-mother each night in nightmare dreams. A white, feathered arrow striking down, tearing the stalker from the callused hands of Wakje and Weed. She looked through slitted, yellow eyes and heard the scout scream in his coarse human way as she locked her claws into his shoulders. Saw him clutch at her smooth, scaled legs. Saw him dig in to hang on as she hovered over the worlag pack like a farmer holding a frantic grasshopper over a flock of hungry chickens. The Aiueven's hands had been like her own, and she'd felt the soft squidiness of human flesh pierced by her finger-long talons. She'd felt the stale coverings of leather and cloth as they slipped and tore in her grip. There had been a futile bite of dull human nails. And then she had released the man, and Nori had watched him fall, fall, tumble and flail in the cold, dark air. And the worlags reaching up with their claws before he hit the ground.

She took a breath and let it out carefully so the cozar wouldn't notice. It had been a terrible risk, for both the Aiueven and for Nori. Since the time of plague, there had been an uneasy truce between humanity and the birdmen, and almost no contact between them. One hint that the birdmen had left their mountains to kill another human, and the counties could rise up in terror of another plague and attack the breeding grounds.

She had always feared the demon inside herself, the taint that erupted with her fear and fury, and which could kill at a single touch. What she dreaded even more was the alien who had defended her daughter-daughter. The taint, the link between the two, could destroy what was left of her world.

Someone jostled her elbow, and she flinched. Then Payne caught her attention with a sharp gesture. She shook off her dread. Someone else had death on their mind. Someone close among the cozar.

She located her uncles, then Kettre and Hunter. The citymen and Sidisport *chovas* were easy to see. Almost all of them wore some sort of rank or House symbols. Guild men wore guild signs, Tamrani had their crests, and the *chovas* pinned the bars of their rank onto their inside collars. Fentris had the most complex knot of all, in silk, of course, not chancloth, and its two-toned iridescence caught the lamplight like luminescent moth wings. She wasn't the only one to notice. The slim Tamrani had just turned to a woman who seemed to be complimenting his fancy war cap. The Tamrani didn't turn a hair as he offered a compliment in return, and the woman preened and fingered the cuff of her cheap blouse where the crest of her trade guild had been unevenly embroidered. He must have asked a question, because the woman launched eagerly into a description of some sort of trade, while on his other side another merchant waited impatiently to interrupt.

The oldest elder finally came forward. People quickly seated themselves, and the crowd quieted as the circle of judges adjusted their stoles.

The old man used a cane to steady himself as he walked, and a girl walked at his elbow with the basket he could no longer carry himself. As the old elder stopped in front of each judge, he reached into the basket, drew out one smooth, red stone, and placed it on the curved table. There would be four stones in front of each judge in the end: black for absolution, green for punishment. White for banishment, red for death.

As the elder set down each smoothly polished, blood-colored stone, he murmured, "May your judgment be careful, made without self-righteousness, without hubris, without hate, without haste."

Each judge nodded slightly at the blessing, and did not touch the stone.

The second oldest followed with another basket, setting down a white stone carefully beside each red one. "May your judgment be tempered," murmured the white-haired woman. "Made without whim or caprice, without assumption, without conspiracy, and without greed for the assets of others."

Another, balding elder followed with green stones. He said quietly to each judge, "May your judgment be balanced, made with humanity in mind, not the letter of the law. May it be made without arrogance, without anger, without a desire for revenge. May it be made with all hands on the scale."

A fourth elder carried the basket of black stones. "May your judgment be made without fear for yourself or others, without vanity, without ambition, and without debt. May it hold steady when all truths come to light."

Now the youngest elder—his hair was still partly grey, not wholly white—came forward. The thin man chalked a black line around the long, curved table in front of the judges. The elder stepped back when he was done and his voice rang in the silence. "This is the finality of the words that will be spoken, the line that all must cross who pass judgment on another, the line where trust may be broken or mended, where faith may be broken or restored, where we will be bound by truth and responsibility, not emotion and the flaws of the self. May this line be a mirror each time you speak, here and before the moons."

The Ell nodded as he finished, and patted Mian's clenched hands. The girl's fingers were white, and she sat like a trapped bird beside him. Nori's jaw tightened. Although she had known several of the judges at her own Trial, they had all seemed like strangers. Stern-faced, flat eyes, watching, weighing, judging her statements and every action she'd taken.

Now Nori glanced at Mian and had to force herself not to re-assure the girl. She looked instead at Payne.

He nodded once, a small motion. Then he glanced at Wakje and caught the older man's attention. The ex-raider nodded in turn. Kettre was with a group of *chovas,* he noted, watching two other outriders. Hunter was in front of a group of elders, and Fentris was now idly scanning the crowd with apparent bore-dom as he listened politely to a pudgy man tell jokes. Payne couldn't see Leanna, but she should be keeping an eye on the outside of the circle, watching to see if anyone left. Payne nod-ded back at his sister.

When Brean called Mian, the girl stood and then looked as if she would throw up. The judges were silent, and the crowd's ex-pression was closed and angry, as if the girl had somehow be-trayed them. A few more minutes, Nori told herself, and then all of them would know.

"Declare yourself," Brean stated flatly.

The girl's voice was reedy and thin. "I am Mian Enna maB-Brekiat," she stumbled. "D-daughter of Nonnie Ninelegs and Cy Windytrack. I am cozar-born and cozar-raised. I accept cozar law, and so stand before the c-council."

"Do you understand why you are here?"

Her voice dropped to a whisper. "My tano got loose. It caused the wrecks, it almost killed Repa and Bere and my mama. And the Tamrani," she added belatedly.

Brean turned to a woman and nodded. The white-haired elder stood and read from a long list: "Repa Ripping White's wagon, almost fully destroyed. One wheel, eight panels salvaged. Dam-age: fifty-six gold. Goods damaged, sixteen gold, eight silvers. *Keyo* Ki's wagon, splintered side and back, and bottom of the wagon damaged: eight gold, three silvers . . ." The list went on in that calm, steady voice, and Mian seemed to shrink with each word. ". . . Eight dnu injured. Two broken legs and numerous gashes and punctures, four gold, nine silvers for treatment and medications. Lease of replacement dnu for teams and for riding, four coppers a day per riding dnu, one tenpiece a day per harness team . . ." The tally grew. Then came the injuries. "Repa Ripping White: sprained wrist, one deep gash, bruises and scrapes. Nonnie Ninelegs: concussion, open gashes, bruising. Kened Catchall, severe bruising on his right arm and a sprained wrist. Gallo Cantaway Soon, kicked by a dnu in the thigh. Bere Quiet, dislocated shoulder, drag-burns on the arms, extensive bruising." And Frecka Wrongway, Ed Proving, Jeri Dancing Mad, four others, and two Yorundan *chovas*. And finally, the Tamrani. The woman's voice grew darker. "Condari Rahnbada neKeatus Brithanas, Tamrani, First Son, First House, Sidisport, Ramaj Eilif, punctures on the shoulders and neck and threat of death by venom." The list finally ended. The woman glanced at Mian with an expressionless face and sat down.

Brean asked, "Do you dispute any of these damages or injuries?"

"No," the girl managed.

She might be over the age of Choice, but she was still before the age of Test, and Brean asked sternly, "Does your family dispute any damages or injuries?"

The girl's father stood up. Cy's mate was sedated in the healer's wagon, unable to move without pain. Now his daughter stood before the council, and he had to let her stand alone. His voice was tight. "No."

Brean had not taken his eyes from Mian. "Do you understand the extent of the damages and injuries?"

The girl's eyes flew to her father's. "Yes," she managed.

"Do you understand the danger the caravan was in? Do you understand the danger to the cozar?"

She whispered, "They could have died."

Brean continued flatly, "What is your statement, Mian?"

The girl answered shakily, "I brought the tano into the train. I did not check the cage often enough, and it rotted and broke open. The tano—*dyen p'ya jen ai.* Its release is my f-fault alone. The damages and injuries are my fault alone." She sucked in a breath. "It's my fault," she burst out. "I almost killed them. My mama's almost dead, and it's all my fault." Her voice broke.

Nori stood abruptly. "May I speak?" Her voice cut across the circle.

Heads turned. No one missed the fact that the Hafell did not rebuke her for interrupting. There was speculation in many faces.

Ell Tai took Mian's hand firmly, and the girl choked in a breath. The old man pressed her back in her seat and murmured something to her.

"Black Wolf," Brean acknowledged.

She said without preamble, "I have examined the cage. It did not break open by accident."

There was dead silence. Then Cy was on his feet. "How dare you. What, by the eighth hell, are you sa—" One of his friends clamped a hand on the man's forearm to keep him quiet. His face twisted, but he broke off. The air tasted of violence.

Payne's dark eyes glittered as he studied the faces around the circle. Hunter's cool green gaze met Payne's for an instant, then slid on past in his own scan. Someone there would not be surprised at what the wolfwalker had discovered. Someone had to be thinking now of how to react or how to hide his face.

Brean didn't look at the girl's father. "Explain," he ordered Nori.

She answered flatly. "I looked closely at the latches to see how the tano had broken out. A prying tool had been used to distress the wood where the latch screws were sunk."

"But that's—" Cy's friend gripped him hard, but an ugly murmur grew up around them. Payne, his gaze on Rezuku, saw nothing in the merchant's face. Like Fentris, the merchant looked bored at being required to sit through another cozar event. But when Payne shifted his gaze to the woman beside Rezuku, for an instant he thought he saw fury on the outrider's face. MaSera, he recognized the *chovas*. That's one, he said to himself.

Brean waited till the noise began to subside, then questioned, "If Mian had checked the cage, would she have noticed this damage?"

"Aye, if she had rattled the door sharply." The girl blanched, and Nori glanced her way. "But I checked the cage myself when she bought it in Sidisport. I checked the cage again two days ago when I was teaching her how to transfer the tano from one cage to the other. There was no damage to the latch screws then. There was also no reason to check the cage for another ninan. Once a ninan during cleaning is considered more than adequate for safety. Many do it only once a month."

Brean gave no indication that he had heard any of this before, and Nori admired his control. Her own control was slipping. She could almost feel the animal within the crowd, the fury of the cozar that their own had been harmed deliberately, and that another one of their own—and a young girl, by the moons—had been singled out for blame. The sense of the beast roused the wolf in her, and she found her gaze held first by B'Kosan's dark, angry eyes, and then by the *chovas* beside him.

The Hafell barely got her attention back. "Two days ago," he prompted. "How closely did you examine the cage?"

She forced herself to look back at Brean. "Closely, Hafell. I wanted to show her how to look for damage from the tano's claws."

"Could not the damage have been made by exactly that, the tano's claws?"

Payne was no longer visible, and Nori knew he'd seen something and had slipped back in the crowd to follow someone or change his line of view. The wolf in her began to sharpen. "No, Hafell," she answered tautly.

"Why not?"

"Chisels leave flat marks with a beveled tip where the chisel point meets the wood. A tano's claws are tapered, curved and round. The marks they leave are also like that. Also—" She looked beyond Brean and met the gaze of the outrider beside the man. Her violet-grey gaze locked on to his and hinted of something violent. "—the marks were beneath the latch, where the screws bit into the wood. The latch had been replaced to hide them."

There was silence for a moment. Brean stood before the

cozar could erupt. "Black Wolf." His voice was sharp. "Do you have any other statement?"

The outrider's eyes bored into hers.

"Black Wolf?"

"No, Hafell." She brought her gaze back to Brean. "What is needed has been done."

Brean resisted the urge to turn and see where she was looking. He'd set two of his best people to watch Payne and Wakje. Then he'd set his own mate to note anyone that Black Wolf took interest in. If anyone had sharper eyes than his mate, he'd never met them yet. He looked around fireside. "Is there anyone else who would speak?"

Payne stepped forward from another part of the crowd. "I, Payne Aranur neBentar, ranked scout; first bar, general science; Ramaj Ariye and Ramaj Randonnen, witnessed the examination of the cage. I offer my corroboration of all that my sister has said."

Hunter also stepped forward. "I, Condari Rahnbada neKeatus Brithanas, First Son, of the First House Wyakit, also witnessed the examination of the cage. I offer my corroboration."

Brean looked at Wakje. The ex-raider's gaze flickered, but he said curtly, "It's as she said."

Brean stifled his irritation. Like others of the Wolven Guard, Wakje consistently refused to identify himself when speaking to the council.

The Hafell let his gaze sweep the crowded circle. He could see the closer faces clearly, but many of those in the back were in shadow from the lanterns. He projected his voice harshly. "Is there any among us who will admit to this action?"

No one moved.

Brean waited. Finally, he looked at the girl. Mian sucked in a breath and forced herself to stand. The Hafell's voice was flat. "Mian maBrekiat, do you accept the judgment of the council and the reparation sentence for those who have been harmed?"

"Yes, Hafell," she whispered.

Brean then looked across the circle to where the injured were present. "Repa Ripping White." He called the woman forward. She limped up to the front. "You are among those injured in person and in goods. You have the right of second verdict, if you so choose."

The woman's face was badly swollen and bruised, and Mian had to force herself to face the wagon driver as the woman met her gaze. Repa's face was tight with anger, and her words slurred as she spoke around the swelling of her lips, but she nodded curtly to the girl as if in apology for what she had thought. "I hold no grudge hand to the girl, but my pain and my anger have influenced my judgment. The wisdom of the elders will be greater than my own. If they are willing, I ask that they speak for me in this."

Brean identified the next man. "Bere Quiet, also known as Bere Verian and Bere Never Bet, you are among those injured in person and in goods. As the driver for *chovas* Ki, you have the right of second verdict, if you so choose, or of separate trial."

Ki's driver stood stiffly. His ribs were bound tightly, making it difficult to bend, and his hands and arms were heavily bandaged, but his face was as expressionless as Repa's had been angry. His voice was so low as to be nearly a growl. "I hold no grudge hand to the girl."

"You will allow the council to speak for you in this matter?"

The man nodded.

Frekka Wrongway, Jeri Dancing Mad, One For Brandy, and each of the others whose cargo, wagons or dnu had been damaged rose when called and relinquished the verdict right. Cy Windytrack started relinquishing his verdict rights against his daughter almost before Brean finished the question, as did the woman who spoke for Mian's injured mother.

Then it was Hunter's turn. An edge of distant formality entered Brean's voice as he called the Tamrani. With his open collar, the blood marks on Hunter's neck stood out harshly. Mian couldn't hide the tremble in her hands when that last name was called. Tamrani were powerful, sometimes even more so than a county's Lloroi, and they had long memories. It was almost moot that this one was a First Son, and that he'd survived the tano's attack. Most Tamrani would consider it unforgivable either way, to have been set upon by some cozar's untamed pet.

Brean said to the Tamrani stiffly, "You are among those injured in person and threatened with death, yet you have no ties to us. You have the right of second verdict, or of separate trial or of transport trial, if you so choose."

Mian made a tiny sound.

Hunter looked at her directly. "I do not require separate trial or transport trial. Your council may speak for me with regard to the girl."

Brean hesitated, but nodded. He'd been fairly sure the Tamrani would not insist on a Sidisport trial, but like most Ariyens, he didn't quite trust them. With regard to the girl alone . . . Brean bit back the question and let it pass.

As Hunter stepped back, the Hafell looked at the eleven judges and finally nodded his permission. It was a large council, and a larger crowd. The damage and injuries had been extensive, and the men and women chosen to judge included almost every one of the train's highest-ranked elders, as well as the four borrowed from the other caravans who shared the circle. Now the first woman in the long line of elders leaned forward and used her middle finger to push the green stone forward. Green for punishment. Mian looked as if she would faint.

The second elder used his middle finger to push his green stone forward across the black line. None of them looked at each other. There was a hesitation before the last elder stretched out his gnarled finger. Then he shifted and pushed the green stone forward as had all the others.

A long, low murmur ran through the crowd. The unanimous line of green was an unusual verdict. It was tradition for there to be one dissent when all other votes had gone one way. That dissent, token as it was, was the responsibility of the elder who had served the longest and whose duty it was to make sure all sides, even those that weren't known, were represented. The single black stone, the traditional dissent, represented the fallibility of man, and the possibility that the issue at hand could be revisited. By voting with the others, the elder was stating that there would be no revisiting of the issue, no matter what happened and what truths came to light in the future.

Mian stared at the line of green and began to breathe too

quickly. Her father started to shove through the crowd. He barely subsided at a sharp look from the old Ell.

Brean stepped back and the center elder stood. The old woman waited a moment, but none of the other elders stood for discussion. The woman relaxed slightly. Especially with a unanimous vote, it was a sign of trust, that her wisdom was enough for them all. She had never confessed to anyone but her mate how nervous she was each time she stood alone. She could make a mistake. She might have missed something in someone's voice, an expression that would make a difference in her perception of truth, something someone else would have seen. And she knew Mian. She knew the girl could not have done something so deliberately careless as they had first thought. But as she looked at the girl and felt compassion uncurl in her chest, she squelched it sternly. It was not her job to soften the blow, but to make sure the blow was fair.

Her voice had grown frail in the last few years, and she gathered it carefully. "Here is the judgment of the council," she stated. "Mian maBrekiat, you are not responsible for loosing the tano. The damages and injuries will not be held to your account. You are released from that burden. Be at peace. However—" The elder paused, and her voice grew more serious. "—you are responsible for bringing the tano among us. When evil arrived, in the form of this deliberate act, it had a weapon in its hands through you." Mian's face was white as linen. The elder said quietly, "This is the first responsibility in the chain, and that burden is yours alone. Are you prepared to render your punishment?"

The girl sucked in her breath three times before she choked out, "Yes, Elder."

"Then we will hear your amends."

Mian looked at her father. Cy's hands clenched, but his daughter had reached the age of Choice last year, and it had been her choice to raise the exotics.

The girl tore her gaze from her father's taut face and forced herself to look back at the elder. "I sh-should have the tano put down. I should not be allowed to take care of the other exotics until I am older. I should tend Repa and Bere and my mama, and the Tamrani and the others," she added belatedly again, "until they are healed. And I should take care of the wounded dnu. Then I should b-be b-banished after that until I'm old enough to be more responsible, so that my animals c-can't harm anyone again." The girl's voice broke at the end.

The elder waited for her to regain her control. "We have heard you, Mian maBrekiat. We believe your punishment is too harsh." An almost visible wave of relief washed through the cozar. The other elders nodded their agreement. "The council renders these amends instead. You will purchase a new cage for the tano and give the old one to the Hafell for study. You will re-structure your wagon to comply with the vestibule rule used by city vets, so that, if one of your animals is released from its cage, it will still be inside a holding area. You will spend an hour a day, at least three days a ninan, for the rest of this caravan sea-son, with Healer Sastry. From him, you will learn to treat wounds made by venomous animals. After the season, you will continue this study with other healers in your family's town for a period not less than two years. You will also spend half a day with Black Wolf—" She glanced at Nori and got a nod. "—learning to call a tano. And might I suggest," she added more gently, "if you intend to continue raising such creatures, you spend additional time with Black Wolf, Vindra Twitch-Whickers, and other callers learning to calm your other beasts."

The elder waited several seconds, but none of the others stood up to add to her judgment. She nodded curtly. "This is the judgment, Mian maBrekiat. Be at peace when it is done."

Mian nodded numbly.

Ell Tai rose and patted the girl's hand. He raised his voice. "The block is cleared, this Trial is done. Lay your comments in the fire."

The crowd milled forward to the firepit, some speaking quietly into the flames as if to apologize to Mian for thinking the worst of her, some spitting the physical expression of their anger into the low blaze, and some saying nothing at all.

Cy Windy Track had barely held himself in check when Ell

Tai closed the Trial. Now he shoved through the crowd and caught his daughter up closely. The girl was crying openly now. She wiped her face with her sleeve as her father took her away, and it made Nori's lips curl back. She didn't realize she was snarling as the Ell gestured, and two men started casting water on the fire. Sparks and smoke blasted up into the night sky, and the crowd murmured loudly. It was cathartic to the cozar, and they watched in satisfaction as the fire hissed and spat.

"Black Wolf?"

She whirled.

Brean stiffened.

"My apologies," she managed. "Hafell. Ell Tai." She acknowledged the older man who leaned on his crutch beside Brean.

Brean said flatly, "You will speak to Mian?"

It was not really a question. "Aye, immediately."

"And then you will speak with me."

Nori gave him a sharp look. His light brown eyes were as angry as hers. She raised her chin. "No, Hafell," she said steadily. She watched his eyes widen. "This is not cozar business."

As she said the words, she knew they were true. As Fentris had pointed out, these mishaps were not aimed at the cozar, but at the county leaders who rode among them, or even at something else. Mian had not been a target of mischief; she had simply been convenient. And Hunter believed that whoever was behind it all was dangerous enough that even the Ariyen council should know. She suspected that both Tamrani were holding back when they said they knew nothing about why the accidents were happening. Both men were too experienced, too decisive in their actions, to be completely uninformed. Yet they were still uncertain enough to form a partnership and back each other up. It made her think that they didn't know enough to identify the full reasons behind the mishaps. Had Nori not seen the damaged cage with her own eyes, she might still have not believed them. She might have been willing to believe it was only raiders who had caused the attacks. That the rest was simply bad luck.

Now she believed, like Hunter, that the Harumen were controlling the violence. What she was afraid to add to the theory was that the Harumen might somehow be linked to the plague sense that had broken out at the same time as the Harumen's actions. Fear flickered along her bones. Only one person in the world could survive the plague on her own. That person wasn't Nori. The best Nori could do was try to keep trouble from the cozar as long as she traveled with them. They weren't a violent people, the cozar. It took a great deal to get them riled, which was one of the reasons they traveled and camped and traded so well together. The problem was that the cozar might have hired guards to protect themselves as usual, but if the Harumen were the hired guards, then the guards might as well be worlags.

Brean stared at her stubborn chin. The old Ell murmured something, but Brean barely glanced at the older man. His voice was tight as he answered the wolfwalker. "This is a cozar caravan, a cozar circle. It was cozar lives at stake. This has been a cozar trial."

Nori kept her voice low. "But it will not be a cozar solution." His face hardened, and she added sharply, "Do not put your watchers or your mate in danger, Hafell. Do not let them interfere."

"How did you know I—" Brean broke off as Ell Tai put his wrinkled hand on the other man's arm.

The Ell's faded eyes were sharp as he studied Nori's face. There was something in her steady violet gaze that belied her calm words. "You are on an uncertain edge, Black Wolf," he said softly. "Be careful you do not slip."

She flicked her gaze meaningfully at the people who swirled around them. "If you're willing, perhaps we should talk more privately."

The old Ell shook his head. "We cannot delay fireside, not after Trial. You have given them a fear that rides with them on the road, and they must let off their tension safely."

She nodded curtly and started to turn away.

"Black Wolf." The Ell stopped her. He searched her face. "Some choices are made silently, but all choices must be judged. It is the cozar way."

"But I, I am not cozar."

"Yet you have ridden with us since you were a babe." The old Ell smiled faintly. "Ramaj Randonnen is not the only claim on your heart. Ride safe, Wolfwalker." He glanced at Brean and nodded for them to move on.

She stared after them. She said softly to their backs, "With the moons."

XXX

Don't corner the wolf

  —Tumuwen saying

Nori met Kettre on the outskirts of the circle. "This way," Kettre said in a low voice. "Payne and Leanna are waiting in the stables. We're meeting at the Broken Mug."

Nori didn't argue. She'd just left Mian, Cy and Nonnie. The look Cy had given her when he realized she'd known for hours about the latch—it had not been pleasant. She'd had to explain about the trial, that it was important they watch for anyone who might have been involved. When he demanded to know whom she had seen, she merely looked at him steadily and said, "Discuss it with Ell Tai." He'd cursed her then.

She'd taken it, but it had burned in her brain, her gut, her hands. It had been all she could do not to reach out and slash back at his face. She'd swallowed it, swallowed the lupine rage and the guilt at putting the girl through Trial. She'd said only, "Better alive and cursing, than burning on the funeral pyre." That had stopped him. He'd let her go then, and she'd stalked quickly away. She'd found her hands clenched like paws.

In the center of the circle, fireside was already tense and noisy. The cozar were speaking too loudly, as if the volume would somehow offer them safety from the unknown saboteur. It had been long minutes before she could force herself through the milling crowd and work her way to the stables.

"Did you see anything?" she asked in a low voice as she led her dnu out beside Kettre's.

"Not during the trial," Kettre answered. "But I did see one of the Sidisport *chovas* meet two others right afterward. They never raised their voices, but I'd swear one of them was cursing. Leanna saw a woman make a beeline for the stables as soon as Trial ended."

"What about Rezuku?"

"He snagged his two outriders and holed up in his wagon. Judging by the cozar reactions, that was probably safest. The cozar aren't too happy right now, and they're talking scared. A smart outsider would make himself scarce for the night."

They swung out on the access road. It was gaily decorated with painted lanterns, but the colored lamps made Nori think of predators' eyes, not lights. She shivered as they trotted past groups of cozar. Some folk walked, some trotted smoothly on dnu-back, but all of them stayed close together. It was as if even the shadows in the barrier bushes stalked them down the road.

Nori glanced at the shrub line and stretched toward the grey. Rishte was out there alone, slipping down the game trails, his ears flicking at every sound as if worlags were everywhere. She could feel his unease, the grind of loneliness in his mind. He howled there for the pack, and the grey answered, but it was a faint grey and a distant call. . . . *alkerwolfwalkerwolfw* . . .

She broke off as Kettre made some comment. She hadn't heard what the other woman said, and it disturbed her. Kettre didn't seem to notice. Instead, the woman pointed at Hunter and Fentris up ahead, and they spurred their dnu to catch up. A moment later, Payne and Leanna cantered up behind them. They could see Wakje waiting by a dark clump of bushes.

"Did you see Rezuku?" Nori asked Payne.

"Aye, but he didn't turn a hair. Looked bored with the whole trial."

"So did Fentris," she said sharply. "And he was doing duty."

Payne gave her a warning glance. "I know you don't want to hear this, Nori-girl, but in spite of the stinger in your bonnet, it wasn't the merchant who caught my eye. It was the *chovas* woman beside him."

She digested that. "A woman," she said slowly. A woman had been in their wagon.

"MaSera, aye," he answered. "She's been with us since Sidisport."

"Ah."

"Exactly."

"You know her?"

"She rode guard for Ell Tai till he broke his ankle. Then she transferred to general guard duty. She sits sometimes with the other Sidisport outriders, but she's mostly kept to herself."

Nori glanced back at Hunter. "What about you? Who did you see?"

He hid a wry smile. She didn't even bother with titles. "I saw two men I wouldn't mind questioning."

"I, too, saw one man," she told them. That man, his eyes had burned into hers long enough that she would know him like a worlag at a tea party. Like humans, worlags weren't indigenous to this world, and their eyes glittered like oldEarth rats—too intelligent for their primitive ways, and too intent on killing to look anything but evil. Nori had seen that same violent intent in the eyes of the man by B'Kosan.

They fell silent as they passed several groups on the road. Wakje had chosen a tavern farther away, hoping it would be less crowded, but it was a futile choice. By the time they arrived, both back rooms were already rented, and almost every table was full. They snagged one of the last two tables in the place and crowded around it. Even then, they had barely a few minutes to enjoy the crush before they were joined by others who shoved their way in, asking about the tano's cage, viewing Hunter's punctures, and declaring their outrage at this latest insult to the caravan. Other than the news that Ki had sent word south with a relay runner, and that he would be heading back at dawn, there was nothing to discuss.

It wasn't long before the tavern began shifting toward the dangerous hour, when belligerents took offense and chairs were turned into kindling. Wakje's dark mood affected them all, and when the ex-raider rose to get his dnu, the others began following quickly.

Hunter stopped Nori as she made to follow Payne. "Stay. Talk with me."

She hesitated, but when Payne looked back, she shrugged at him.

Hunter glanced at Fentris, who was watching silently. "Give us a moment, will you?"

The slender man got to his feet. "I believe I can find something to intrigue me." He nodded to Nori and moved away to order a spiced ale to take outside.

"You're teaching him bad habits," she murmured.

Hunter didn't smile back. "It's your habits that concern me, Black Wolf."

She eyed him warily. "What do you mean?" She didn't need another lecture on duty.

Hunter watched her gaze shutter. "You always seem to be walking away from me just when I think we're getting somewhere."

She shrugged. "There is no somewhere for us to get."

He leaned forward. "You know what I want."

"Aye, but I'm not willing to give it."

"Nori—"

"Don't push, Condari. It won't get you where you think." Not unless he was willing to give her a look at the papers he kept in that belt, something she was sure he'd refuse. Still, even if she satisfied her curiosity, she couldn't ride with him. Land wars were a concern for merchants and farmers, not for wolf-walkers or scouts. She was concerned with bigger problems, with Aiueven and plague.

He studied her for a moment, but the set of her chin told him she was serious. "Why not?"

"I can't answer."

"Can't or won't?"

She smiled faintly, shook her head and made to stand up, but he put out a hand and stopped her. "At least explain why you won't tell me."

She looked at him steadily. "It serves no purpose, Condari."

"Hunter. You called me Hunter before."

"I did," she agreed.

"Then why?"

"It's a duty, Hunter, one I will not speak of again except to say that, as Tamrani, you should understand and respect the seriousness of some obligations."

He tilted his head slightly to study her more closely. "Whatever it is, it scares you."

"That's nothing." She snorted derisively. "I scare myself."

He leaned back in his seat. "All that fear," he mused, "in such a lovely body. I could help, you know."

She bristled in her chair as he knew she would. "I'm not looking for help," she said sharply.

"Why?" he persisted.

"Because I have Payne. My uncles. Kettre. My parents."

He leaned forward slightly. "They're obviously not enough to take away the fear."

"It's not their job to do so."

He said softly, "I could make it my job."

She stared at him. Her hands had tensed, he saw, and her eyes were starting to go grey.

"What are you afraid of, Noriana maDione?"

Plague. Death the way the Ancients died. The taint in her mind. Striking out with the fury hands. Burning out of control. The images tumbled through her mind. She clenched her jaw and breathed in, then out, three times before she thought her voice might be steady again.

"What are you afraid of?" he repeated more softly.

She gazed at him, but he did not think she saw him when she finally whispered, "Myself."

It surprised him. "Why?"

For a moment, she didn't answer. Then she shook it off and said flatly, "Because I can be dangerous."

"Not to me."

"You have no idea," she said dryly.

He reached out and tilted her face up with one finger so he could read her eyes. "I do not fear the Grey One."

She drew back from his hand. "It's not the wolf in me you should fear." She looked at him soberly. "You cannot trust me, Hunter. I cannot trust myself."

He shrugged. "I've seen you in action. I'll take that chance."

"But I won't." She was starting to feel trapped, and her voice had sharpened.

He kept his expression calm. "We spoke the travel oath, Black Wolf. I took your burdens as you took mine. We can share your duties, too, if you're willing."

"I've already given you my answer." She started to rise. "I'll bid you ride safe, Condari Brithanas. It's been an interesting half ninan."

He interrupted. "Do you know what the songsters say about you?" He waited till she sat reluctantly down, forced by her own courtesy. "They say you're reserved. That you keep to yourself and to your family, that you're full of wolfwalker secrets. They say you're another Dione. I've wondered about that, about how much like your mother you really are. I saw her work once, you know." His cool green eyes watched her carefully. He wasn't disappointed.

Her face went carefully expressionless. How could he know? Ovousibas was secret, and he was out of Sidisport. "That is not something we speak of."

He could swear that a note of fear was back in her voice. "But it was so very . . ." He let the words trail off deliberately. "Interesting," he finished.

She glanced quickly around the room and dropped her voice. "Hunter—"

"Can you do what she does?"

"No," she said sharply. The taint could, but she could not. If she tried, it would burn out her mind. "You don't understand."

Yes, there it was, the unreasoning fear. Like a child told she'll drown if she goes into the ocean. A hard note crept into his voice. "I understand enough. You're afraid because people have told you that you can't do this or that. For all that you're a better scout than Payne, you've been overprotected all your life. You haven't earned your fears; you've been taught them, and it's made you distrust every instinct you have except when someone else is in danger."

Startlement flickered in her eyes, and he wondered if he'd

made a mistake. She stared at him. "What are you talking about?"

He stared back. If it wasn't about her mother . . . He tried to buy time to think by brushing a stray hair from her cheek, but this time, she jerked back swiftly. "Don't," she said sharply.

He studied her face. "Moons, Noriana. Were you this skittish before the wolf or just since you started bonding?"

"That's none of your business, Tamrani."

Now, that reaction he knew. He smiled slowly. "Oh, I'd say it is."

"Since when?" she snapped.

"Since we started riding together. You're good for me, Jangharat, even if you're young."

She bristled. "I've known more duty for my age than an elder twice your years."

He kept the satisfaction out of his face. "Maybe you know duty, but you don't know life at all. Frankly," he added deliberately, "I think you're terrified of it."

Her eyes narrowed. It wasn't life that scared her, but the demon in her mind. She'd killed two men intentionally in the last six years, and although they were ghosts she saw in her sleep, the ghost that was worse was the accident, the man she'd almost killed. It was the lack of control of herself that she feared. It was being able to touch the energies of her mother-mother, the power that could erupt through her hands like a dozen knives in a whirlwind. The energies that were linked with the plague. It wasn't meant for humans, and it wasn't meant for wolves. That the Ancients had been able to control it at all was a miracle of the moons. In the end, it had nearly destroyed them.

To the Ancients with their partner wolves, to the Wolfwalker Dione, Ovousibas was a healing force. To Nori, with the Aiueven link within her mind, the energy was stronger, violent and less discriminating, and a wolf-bond might not save her. She feared it like flames in dry grass.

The Tamrani thought she was frightened of life? She was terrified she would destroy it. "You know nothing about me," she snarled.

"Then we're even," he retorted. "Because you sure as the second hell don't know yourself."

He was fast, but she was faster, and it wasn't some light-fingered, ladylike slap that she gave him, but the open-handed blow of a scout, trained and honed by years on the trail, with wolves gathering in her violet-grey eyes and not quite under control. He barely registered that she had moved when he felt the stinging blast, and it took all his will to keep his head from rocking back. He grabbed her hand and slammed it down on the table. Her left hand flew to his, and he covered it with an iron grip and jerked her forward so they were nearly face to face. "Once, with the wolves, because you're still young. But not again," he said softly.

Heads turned toward them, and several men and women seemed suddenly poised. Hunter ignored them.

"Release me," she hissed. She almost vibrated with anger.

"Is that you or the wolf?"

Her lips curled back. "Release me."

He smiled slowly without humor. "Then speak to me as Noriana Ember maDione."

She jerked at her hand, but he was stronger than she thought. She couldn't budge his grip. She felt the snarl crawl into her throat. She didn't want to hurt him, but she would if he didn't let go. He pressed down hard between two of her fingers and watched without guilt as she stilled.

Someone's chair scraped back, and Hunter turned his head and looked at the man coldly. "This is personal," he said softly. "Do not interfere."

The man stood anyway, as did his friend, and Hunter looked back into her eyes. "We'll take this outside, Black Wolf."

"Aye," she snarled. "That we will."

"To talk," he corrected.

Her teeth bared further.

His voice was soft. "We can do this two ways, Jangharat. I can yank you up into my arms, haul you out of here kicking and howling like a wolf in front of all these people, or you can walk out on your own two feet, if you swear, by the moons, to answer one question honestly."

She hesitated.

He started to jerk her up, and she bit out, "I'll answer."

He released her. She sprang back, and he watched out of cool green eyes as she rubbed her hands where he'd pinched the nerves. He could see the conflict in her eyes: run, flee to the pack, or stay and honor her word. She stayed, but it was a struggle. He gestured toward the door, and she stalked in front of him, past the three tall men who eyed him as if they'd like to break more than his nose, past the table of burly *chovas* who watched him darkly, past the barkeep whose meaty hands rested lightly on the bat only half hidden by the bar.

"That's far enough," he halted her in the courtyard. She whirled, stared at him for a moment, then began to pace irritably on the stones. He watched for a moment, then asked quietly, "Do you want me?"

She halted. It wasn't what she expected, and he startled the truth out of her before she thought. "I—I don't know."

He nodded once, more to himself than to her.

She licked her lips. "Do you . . . do you want me?"

"You really are an idiot." He gestured at the ground in front of him. "Come here."

She didn't move. "Why?"

"Jangharat, come here."

She took one reluctant step forward. He raised an eyebrow. She stepped again, a smaller step, more warily. He waited. It was like convincing a wild animal to come close. He waited again, and she stepped forward until she stood within arm's reach, but she was balanced on the balls of her feet as if she would flee at any moment.

"Put your arms around me," he said softly.

"Why?"

"Gods, you're like a child. Just do it, Noriana."

She seemed to fight with herself. Then she reached out and rested her hands lightly on his waist.

"I said around me. Around my neck. Like a hug."

For a moment, he didn't think she would. Then she reached up tentatively and rested her hands on his shoulders.

"Around me," he commanded.

"You're too tall," she said defensively.

"This should help." He grasped her by the waist and lifted her against him. Instinctively, her hands locked on his shoulders to take some of her weight, and she stared down into his cool, green eyes. Then slowly he lowered her along the length of his body until her breasts pressed into his chest, and her thighs rubbed at his waist. Her heart was pounding, and her breath feathered on his lips.

He said softly, "Should I worry about my finger bones going to feed the wolf pack?"

She stared at him out of violet eyes. Mutely she shook her head, one short, slow motion.

"Then kiss me."

"No," she whispered. But she didn't draw back.

"Kiss me, Noriana."

Her eyes greyed.

"No harm," he said softly. "No harm to you."

She stared at him.

He waited.

When she finally touched her lips to his, it was the faintest pressure, there one moment, then gone. He felt the grey in her and something else, as if she was almost sparking.

He said nothing, just watched her. Slowly, she leaned in again. This time her eyes closed, and she took in his scent. She could sense the life on this world, through the Aiueven in her mind. She could sense oldEarth life, through the wolves. This man, she sensed on her own. His energy beat at her pulse. She could breathe him in, and he was smooth to her, a clean musk only faintly clouded by the odors of the tavern. She could feel the heat in his thighs, his chest, his hands. It made Rishte growl in her mind, as if the yearling could feel her reach out toward someone else. She hovered above his lips, then touched hers to his. His hands tightened on her waist. It was enough, and she stiffened. Firmly, without haste, without letting her struggle, he set her down, and she stepped swiftly back.

"What am I to you?" he asked softly.

She looked up at him. "Big," she said dryly.

He chuckled. "Alright, I asked for that. But what could I be to you?"

Kettre's teasing popped into her head, and she said without thinking, "A good source of tesselskin boots."

"If that's what it takes to get you to ride with me, I'd consider it fair trade."

She lost her smile and stepped back again. "I told you once, Hunter, that you were pursuing, but that I wasn't running. Find what you want somewhere else."

"I have what I want right here."

"You have nothing, Hunter. Don't presume more than that."

"You do want me."

"And that should matter . . . why?"

He studied her. "Because wolves mate for life."

Her voice was dry. "I'm not a wolf."

He reached out to touch her cheek, and watched her flinch back. "Close enough," he murmured.

Her lips stretched into a feral expression. "It makes no difference, Tamrani. That mating for life? It's a myth. Wolves mate for years, sometimes a decade or more, but there's too much turnover in the pack for the Grey Ones to mate for life. Most of the animals the oldEarthers thought did that just didn't live long enough in the wild to have their two or three mates during any given study."

"The wolves mated long enough for the myth to form."

"Why does it matter? Are you asking me to ride with you or Promise?" she challenged in turn. "Because we've known each other for barely half a ninan."

He smiled sardonically. Women learned early that they could make a man run by bringing up the Promise. "If I thought it would snare you, perhaps."

"Breaking the Promise isn't lightly done, even for Tamrani."

Anger flickered in his eyes. "Tamrani do not break the Promise."

"Neither do I," she shot back. "Nor any others. I've made oaths, Tamrani. You're not part of them. Find some other wolfwalker. Find some other scout." She stalked away without looking back.

He almost missed the grey shadow that detached itself from the barrier bushes and slunk along beside her. He didn't miss the hand that reached out and brushed the edge of Rishte's ruff. Her eyes would be unfocused, he knew, listening to the wolf. He'd roused her enough that she would be deep in the Grey Ones, her lips curled back and the violence close to her fingers.

Payne straightened from where he had been leaning against the stable. "It's amazing how well you bring out her temper. Rather like poking at a lepa with a stick."

Hunter barely glanced at the younger man. He had prodded the wolfwalker deliberately, just as The Brother accused, and she had reacted just as she had with her uncle. Touch the wolf in her, and she turned feral, defensive, ready to fight. "We seem to rub each other the wrong way," he said mildly.

"Agreed."

Hunter studied Payne. "She's on the edge of the grey, you know. She shouldn't ride alone."

"I don't intend to let her."

The implacability of Payne's tone made Hunter's green gaze sharpen. "Moons, neBentar, you're like twins joined at the intestines. Haven't you ever wanted to be on your own? Don't you want to be known as something other than The Brother?" Payne's violet eyes shuttered, and Hunter knew what The Brother hated most. "She doesn't have to be glued to your side. She could ride with someone else. Someone who would look out for her like you do."

Payne regarded him for a moment, then began to smile, then grin. To Hunter's startlement, The Brother started laughing hard enough to draw looks from the cozar who left the tavern and were walking across to the stables. "Oh, aye, I look after her. And you think she's just waiting for another man to do the same?" He gestured helplessly after his sister. "Tell that . . . to Black Wolf. I want to watch the back blast."

The young man spurred his dnu after his sister, chuckling to himself.

Perplexed, Hunter looked after the two. He would swear by all nine moons that Payne wanted to Journey on his own, to be out from under his cozar name. But the Tamrani had just given

Payne the perfect opportunity to pass the responsibility for his sister on to someone else, and even though it should have been like sweet tea on the tongue, the young man had turned him down without hesitation. He'd laughed when Hunter offered.

There was something not right about either one, Nori or Payne, he realized. It was as if they projected an image that did not fit their persons. They joked and spoke lightly when among the cozar, yet he'd caught them uncharacteristically sober when they thought they were alone. They seemed too informed to be as repelled by the elders as all the rumors stated, yet they refused to kowtow to the council requests for taking on duties. And although Payne had finally scheduled to Test, Nori still refused. He'd heard it again when she was teased urgently by one of her uncles, and Hunter did not think it was out of fear that she refused, but for some other, deeper reason. She was too skilled, too capable, too interested in finding out what he knew. The children of legends. Either they were as shallow and dissolute as the rumors suggested, or—and this he thought more likely— they were subtly and secretly becoming legends themselves.

He stared after the young man, his green eyes cold and distant as he fingered the belt at his waist. They held secrets, those two, perhaps not unlike his own. Whatever they were, they frightened the wolfwalker more than worlags, more than raiders, more than Harumen. By the First House, the woman needed to be on her own. Payne, Wakje, Ki—they were making her afraid of life itself by hovering so close. For someone who professed to be a scout, it was an odd way to take the trail, with so many chaperones.

His jaw firmed. Whatever duties she thought she had, they could be assigned to someone else. He'd make her see that. He'd dare her into it if he had to. There were lives at stake, and someone with her skills could make the difference between tens rather than hundreds, even thousands, lost. Moons willing, he'd have her riding with him by the end of the Test ninan, or she'd find out just how much power a Tamrani family wielded.

XXXI

"Do you really want the wolf to lead?"

—Drendon, in *The Hidden Night*

Nori caught up to Wakje and Leanna and Kettre, and a few blocks later with Payne. After that, Hunter and Fentris joined them. The spiced ale hadn't been as smooth as what the slim Tamrani was used to, and he belched, flushed so badly that they saw it in the dark when they turned and stared at him, and apologized profusely. In the front, Kettre hid a grin.

The pub had been on the back outskirts of town, and they made their way as a group back into streets that were dark and nearly empty. A few people stood on corners or walked down sidewalks as if going home, and one ring-runner clattered out of the stables a moment after they left the pub, but the rider turned south, not west toward the cozar circle.

"Not much traffic this late," Kettre murmured.

"Aye," Nori nodded. "Good night for raiding."

The woman shot her a sour look. "I was thinking that, but I wasn't going to say it, especially not at the dark end of town."

They turned off onto a shortcut to avoid the spillover from another tavern, and then went down one of the more shadowed streets to go around the brawl. Nori glanced back as a pair of riders appeared in the intersection behind them. "Something up?" Kettre asked in a low voice.

She shook her head. But a few moments later, the riders followed them onto another street, and Wakje caught her eye. The ex-raider jerked his head toward an alley. She guided them into it without question, down the narrow length, around the empty crates, and onto another side street. No one came out behind them.

Nori didn't relax. She didn't need Wakje's direction to lead them across the street toward a dark corner. She didn't need Rishte's growl in her head to stay tense. Hunter started to ask a question, but she made a sharp gesture almost absently. The Tamrani fell silent, but his hand crept to the hilt of his sword and loosened the thong. Fentris and Kettre followed suit. All but Fentris were dressed in dark colors, and Nori frowned at the way the light glinted off the Tamrani's buttons. At least Hunter had convinced Fentris to leave off his House ring. The glint from that massive stone could have blinded a dozen raiders.

Nori hesitated before rounding the corner. She could smell the laundry, the yeasts of the night bakeries, and the dry dust of the brick ovens, two blocks down. There was an occasional burst of noise from a nearby tavern, and the distant chock-chock of someone chopping wood. A dog barked far away. She could hear the night women singing as they wrung out clothes and hung them on the lines. She felt hemmed in by the village build-ings.

Rishte called her from the edge of a whittiny field, and Nori tried to answer. *Can you hear them. Are they behind us?*

Worry, he seemed to send back. Wariness, and a confused im-pression of man-things.

She shook her head, unable to understand without the eye contact. Worry—trackers? Man-things—the Harumen behind them? No, man-things were simply the sense of other humans around her, like Wakje and Hunter and the others. She was sure of only one thing: that he wanted her to slide into the shadows and slink away from the town.

Payne moved up beside her, and even under two of the moons, she could see the worry in his face.

No one followed them as they zigzagged through two more blocks. But as they trotted out onto the main road, two riders ap-peared behind them. It could have been anyone, a couple of cozar or late taverners going home. It could have been a pair of ring-runners readying themselves to ride the black road. But Nori glanced at Payne. The Brother nodded silently, and they urged their dnu to a slightly faster trot. No one questioned the pace.

The riding beasts felt the tension and their muscles bunched more as they trotted. Still, nothing happened. The two riders behind them continued to keep their distance until they were halfway back to the circle. Then a third rider joined the pair. Wakje told Leanna sharply to move forward into the middle of the group. Hunter and Fentris automatically flanked the girl, while Wakje pulled back to the rear.

A few minutes later, a fourth rider joined the other three.

Payne's voice was low. "Nori-girl, we're in trouble."

"I see them," she answered softly.

"Should we run for it?"

She shook her head. "No. There's only four behind us."

"Only four?" Kettre asked dryly from behind.

"Aye." Nori glanced back at the other woman. "That means the others are up ahead."

"Can you—?" Payne let the question hang.

She knew what he meant. "He's off to the left, back of the fields. I can sense him, but I can't tell what he's seeing or hearing except that there's man-scent in his nose."

Payne looked at the dark mass of trees, then at the faintly glowing road. They would be dark targets against the light if they stayed where they were. "You know the trails here better than I do."

"Nori?" Hunter cut in impatiently.

She kept her voice low. "There's a track off to the left about eighty meters ahead."

"I know that one," Payne answered. "It cuts between property lines, but Nori, it doesn't go through."

She raised a hand to hold Hunter quiet for a moment as he started to speak again. "The main track doesn't," she agreed. "But there's a footpath in a hundred meters or so that breaks off to the north. It's an old track that heads straight up and over the hills."

"Alright then."

Hunter said sharply, "You're going to take us off-trail?"

She glanced at him, then back at the others. "Get ready," she told them softly. "There are riders behind us and in front. We're not going to meet them. Instead, we're going left at that hanging tree, the one that looks like a gallows. Start staggering the dnu when we reach that dark notch in the barrier bushes. When I give the signal, light out. Hug the saddle, keep your head shielded and low. Your dnu will follow mine."

"Weapons?" Fentris asked.

Payne shook his head. "They'll see them in the moonlight and know they've been made. Better to dodge them than start an all-out fight. Right now, they don't know we know that the rest are up ahead."

"Well, I still don't," Fentris returned dryly. "I can't see a thing."

Payne grinned, a flash of white teeth in the dark. "Trust us, Tamrani," he said.

"Drop back, Payne," Nori told him softly. "Take up the rear with Uncle Wakje."

"Don't ride us into any traps."

She grinned ferally. "Perhaps we'll set a few."

They kept the pace till they reached the notch, then subtly shifted so that the dnu were staggered in line. When Nori saw the break where the trail split away, she made a low, sharp sound to warn them. Then she spurred her dnu into the darkness. The creature, tensed with the increasing pressure from her knees, was just waiting to be released. It jumped like a beanpod and hit the trail at a dead run. Fentris was hard on her heels.

Nori's dnu thundered down the dirt path, its hooves clipping divots and flinging them back. As the first branches snapped down, she threw one arm over her face and lay low around the saddle horn, along the dnu's lean neck. She heard a single shout as the riders following saw them disappear. Then she had ears only for the trail.

Jackbraws and pelan blasted up from their night roosts, and at least one forest cat leapt away. Small creatures skittered into holes. Nori's dnu bunched up to jump a log, and branches overhead scraped her back. They were a quick slap and burn; they didn't even tear her jerkin. Then she was away again, with the others sailing over behind her.

It was Rishte who signaled the break in the trail. He pulled at her from the right. She whistled low, then whipped her dnu over. The riding beast charged down the rough path. She caught a glimpse of wolf; then the shape disappeared into shadow, but she could feel the Grey One ahead.

She kept them at a canter for almost fifteen minutes. By the time they stopped, they were all brush-whipped and stinging. "Shake off," she told them as she pulled up in a clearing. None of them needed more urging. They were off their beasts and brushing off their clothes for ticks and gelbugs like a host of frenzied dancers. Fentris slapped at his hat, then cursed as he put a dent in its smooth top. There was a streak of sap, too, on his cloak. He muttered as he pried the sticky stuff apart where it held the folds together.

"We'll head farther north at dawn," the wolfwalker told them. "We should be able to circle back and meet the caravan the day after tomorrow."

Wakje nodded, as did Payne and Kettre, but Hunter frowned and took her aside. "Nori, we can't stay out here for two days."

"I know," she returned absently as she brushed her dnu down and checked its breathing. "We shouldn't make the cozar worry, but we don't have much choice."

"I was thinking more of our gear," he returned dryly.

That caught her attention. "What do you mean?"

"One night, it'll be a bit cold, but alright. Two nights? We need cooking gear, sleeping bags, water filters, matches, that sort of thing if we're going to stay out here. Rations would be nice, and skinning knives," he added. "Wire for snares. Harness repair tack, extra socks." He gestured at the overcast sky. "Bivvy sacks for rain."

"You don't, um, carry that with you?"

"Are you saying you do?"

"Well, yes."

"Right now?" Now it was Hunter who stared at her in the dark. "You went out for an ale with all that in your saddlebags?"

She asked warily, "Why? What do you carry in yours?"

"A clean shirt, in case someone spills grog on me. Money. A

hoofpick, an extra cinch strap. Riding things. Things that are useful in a tavern or on the road."

She stifled a sigh. "You're irritated."

"You could say that. You're telling me that you could keep going on this trail right now. Payne, too? And your uncle and your cousin?"

She exchanged a glance with her brother, then shrugged her answer.

"Piss on a dik-dik," he muttered.

Payne watched the tall man stalk away toward Fentris, who was dabbing at a stain on his jerkin. "I think Tamrani style will be taking a bath this trip."

She snorted a laugh, then sobered as he added, "It's going to be interesting finding out how many *chovas* left the caravan when we did."

"Aye. They must not have gotten what they wanted at the wagon if there are so many riders out here."

"You didn't leave the second scout book?"

She shook her head. "I've been copying the one to the other."

He lowered his voice. "And Brithanas still has his belt on. You don't still think this is about delaying the council meetings, do you?"

"I don't know." She glanced over her shoulder, then back at her brother. "We have two completely different problems, Payne: the raiders—Harumen," she corrected, "and plague. We're still not sure about the first."

"Or the second," he pointed out.

She caught the carefulness of his voice and knew what he was thinking: to have Harumen fall into his lap was almost a guarantee of a high-level Journey. He was praying that Nori was reading the wolf wrong, that there would be no plague to shut down the county first. But the timing of the two problems bothered her.

"I don't see how it matters right now." He gestured with his chin toward their backtrail. "As Uncle Dangyon would say, first things first."

"Aye," she agreed softly. She went to the edge of the clearing and hunkered down. A few minutes later, Rishte crept forward and gazed into her eyes.

Wolfwalker, Nori-mine.

She smiled. The Grey One stretched his nose and nudged her hand. She closed her eyes and let herself feel him through her mind. There were the dank smells of earth, sweat-scent, hot breath, hot dnu. She opened her eyes again. "Grey One," she whispered, "can you guide us? We want to run the trails tonight, escape the hunters behind us."

He was both eager and reluctant. To have his wolfwalker in the forest, yes, but to have the others with her?

"They are packmates." Her voice was sober. "You must choose them if you want to choose me."

He snarled.

She waited.

His golden eyes gleamed, but she didn't back down, and finally he subsided. *This way,* he told her. He broke the contact and slunk around the edge of the clearing.

She sent him a mental shaft of thanks.

His answer was a growl.

They rode another three kays in the dark up a dozen winding game trails. Their calves and knees were aching by the time she pulled up on a small plateau. She said they'd camp there for the night. No one spoke except to murmur. Even the dnu were quiet, and although Fentris looked sadly at his finely tooled jerkin, he didn't complain when Kettre simply took the garment out of his hands and plopped it down on the damp, grassy ground as his pillow. That the wolf was nearby let almost all of them sleep easier. Only Wakje and Nori were alert on watch for signs of predators.

It rained slightly in the night, and dawn was cold and damp, but the sky was clear with six of the nine moons visible, and the stars bright and distant. There was a clean scent to the air, as if the leaves had been washed and were now turning out to be seen. Nori smiled faintly as she lifted her face to the cold breeze. It was spring, dawn, and time to hunt. Rishte howled his agreement.

Hunter glanced at her, then at the oval patch beside her bed where the grass had been pressed down. The wolf might not be in sight, but he'd definitely been there that night. The grass was dry and musky.

They made cold camp, no fire. Kettre surprised them all with a handful of cold meatrolls, and Nori added a small bag of sour berries picked from an early vine, and a bark plate piled with raw tubers. With Payne's jerky, and Wakje's dried trail mix, it was almost a feast.

Hunter hid a grimace as Nori and the others ate quickly. He'd had to eat this way once before. It had been on a trail, when he'd met a scout who had graciously offered to share, but that had been on a dry summer evening, with a warm fire for roasting the tubers, and with fresh water, sweet berries, and grilled eerin. On a grey spring morning, chilled by a cold night and colder dew, with mud on half his gear, and no fire to warm his hands, he had to force himself to nod for his share.

Fentris took one look at the raw, dried and bitter foods, and blanched. He tried to follow Hunter's suit, but when Nori pulled out a fresh extractor root with the dirt barely scrubbed from its skin and the acrid scent sharp in the cold air, Fentris started shaking his head. "No, no no."

Nori paused in handing him a slice of the root. "What's wrong?" She looked at Payne, puzzled, but her brother shrugged. Kettre caught the horror in the Tamrani's eyes and hid a grin.

Hunter looked at the bare root in her hand and found himself agreeing with Fentris. "Wolfwalker, we appreciate that you saved our necks last night, but perhaps we could make yours a bit easier this morning." He went to his saddlebag while the others watched curiously. He returned with a small velvet pouch, and Fentris breathed, "Thank the moons."

Nori scowled at him.

"No offense, Black Wolf." Hunter smiled faintly. "But I believe this, at least, we could contribute."

She caught the small bag and opened it carefully. Her eyes widened. "Oh."

Payne leaned over. "What is it?"

She tilted it toward him so he could see the fine, pale powder inside. Since the Ancients had intended to land on a different world, not this one, they had not been prepared for this world's ecosystem. Almost all the indigenous plants and animals produced toxins for human bodies. A bite here and there wouldn't kill, but there was a cumulative effect. Five or six meals without first extracting the toxins, and the brain grew sluggish. After that, the body grew slow, joints and muscles began to ache, strength disappeared, convulsions started, the senses went. Eventually there was coma. The Ancients' solution had been a series of root plants based on oldEarth ginseng and horseradish. Raw or cooked, the extractor roots bound to toxins and passed them out of the body so that what was once poison became palatable. Unfortunately, most of the extractor plants that could grow in the wild were bitter as an un-Promised woman.

Nori touched just the tip of her finger to the fine, pale powder. "Hothouse?" she asked. "Gindenda?"

Hunter smiled wryly. "You recognize it."

"I've a friend who specializes in exotics." She touched her fingertip to her tongue and almost sighed in pleasure. Reluctantly she opened her eyes. "But this is too expensive. We can use wild root while we're here."

He shook his head. "There is plenty for a ninan for all of us. And frankly—" He glanced at Fentris. "—I think it's safe to say that we'd just as soon use this."

The other man nodded sharply. Kettre hid another grin as Nori shrugged. It was Tamrani gold, after all.

As they got ready to ride, Leanna hovered near the dnu while Fentris checked the saddles. The slim Tamrani glanced at the girl and hid a wry smile. She reminded him of Jianan, Hunter's sister, a few years ago. Here, now, Leanna was as eager as he was, and it made him feel as if he were a Journey youth himself.

Leanna caught his indulgent smile, flushed, and edged uncomfortably away. Fentris lost his smile. He'd had Jianan's blood on his hands. He prayed he wouldn't see Leanna's. He tugged at the last cinch strap, patted the dnu, and brushed the roan hairs off his sleeve, but he knew his expression was stiff.

Leanna glanced back warily. For all that the Tamrani acted the gentleman, he was supposed to have murdered his brother. She didn't know what to say to him, or to Brithanas, for that matter. Black Wolf seemed to think both could be a threat, and that made Leanna tongue-tied. She couldn't do much physically either. Her father had tried to teach her the basics in the martial art of Cansi, but she didn't have the same determination that Payne or Nori had. That, and her two brothers could block every move she made and laugh at her while they did it. Her father had told her once that it wasn't her fault. Women could be as quick as men, with better balance and timing, but they weren't usually as strong. Unless they'd given over their morals, they weren't usually as ruthless, either. It was because of their differences, he'd said. Men drew boundaries in their minds and cared nothing for what was outside them. They had no trouble striking at anything outside the wall. Women saw decision points, not walls, and changed themselves to suit the choice. Women could be more treacherous, aye, but they couldn't afford to be hit. Their bodies weren't made to survive the kinds of strikes a man could walk away from. Kilo for kilo, it was almost always easier to take them. Leanna looked at Hunter and Fentris, then at Nori, and wondered.

Nori caught her glance and murmured to Payne, "I wish Uncle Ki were with us."

"He and Liam and Mye," Payne agreed. "But that's a wish on the second moon." He watched her study the two trails that led out of the clearing. "We could keep going," Payne suggested. "Head north, cut back toward the road near dawn. We'd end up somewhere near Camber. It's a small place, but it's right off Willow Road. We could get the jump on them that way."

"There are still the message towers," she reminded him. "And there's the cozar to consider."

Hunter came up beside them. "You mean that they'll call another search?"

She shook her head. "We're a large group, well armed, with more than one ranked scout. Especially after last night, they won't call the search. The Ell will assume we've gone after the Harumen we picked out at Trial." She hesitated. "North," she said to Wakje. "And we'll continue north until we get to a good vantage point and can tell who's leading them and how big their group is."

It had been more of a question than a statement, and the ex-raider nodded slowly. "North," he agreed. "And west toward the cliffs. Lots of room there to set up ambushes, weak trails, rock-falls—"

But his words struck a chill in Nori. "No," she said too sharply.

Wakje broke off. The others looked from Nori to her uncle.

Payne raised one eyebrow almost imperceptibly. Nori answered the same way. Rishte had been willing to take them north, as long as they avoided certain places along the line of the cliffs that were cut by a series of flooded creeks and sluggish swamps. Nori had already tried to turn them west into the canyons and take the water routes upstream, north and over to the River Phye. It was a rough route, difficult, and possible only if one knew the places to climb out and around the falls. Once in, one had to go all the way or be washed back down again. It would have lost them a day in getting to Shockton, but it might also have lost them the Harumen. With the clouds holding back a heavy rain, few city hunters would follow their prey into what could become a flash-flood death trap.

But Rishte had growled audibly when she'd tried it. He had picked up her sense of commitment—that once in streams, she would have to lead them all the way up to the end of that set of canyons before they could climb out again. He'd almost blinded her with the sense of death that he'd picked up from other wolves. It wasn't the open streams that he feared, but the upper canyons where they'd end up, where the ancient cliffs were pocked and cracked, and at least two men had died.

Nori had felt a chill at the sense of human death. It had been recent, as if someone had been trapped in the canyons a month ago, died in the rains, and finally been washed out to the south. Plague left little to show itself, especially after the bodies had been in the water. Even if the bodies were recovered by scouts, they would have seen nothing that could not have been caused by spring fever or pogus flu.

"Not the cliffs," she said flatly. "We stay on this side of the cliffs."

Wakje hadn't missed the exchange between brother and sister. He watched the wolfwalker expressionlessly for a moment. Then he nodded curtly.

Hunter and Fentris were left to frown after the three.

They rode for two hours on game tracks, following Nori and Rishte. Then the clouds darkened, and it rained, then poured—a shower that left the trees dripping and the trail slick on the steep parts. Heavy splats sounded each time a cupped leaf gave way beneath its load of water. On one side, then the other, branches shivered loudly and dropped short sprays of water when the pelan and palts took off. The dnu almost steamed with body heat. Nori ran her hand around the brim of her hat to release the last of the rain and scowled down at the trail. The rain made it even easier to see where they had gone, and there was nothing she could do about it. Until they hit a rootroad again, their tracks would be pressed almost permanently into the clay like a map of their intentions. Off-trail or on, they were too large a group. They simply couldn't hide their passage.

When they reached one of the main trails, she pulled them up well back of the path and crept forward with her uncle. Together they studied the dirt track, counted out the prints they saw, and tested the soil for moisture.

"It's early," Nori murmured. "With that rain, it will be at least another hour before any ring-runners come through." She hesitated. "We could leave a cairn."

Wakje didn't nod, but he didn't object when she gathered some fallen bark and worked her way carefully through the brush parallel to the trail. Some ways away, she built a tiny lean-to with the bark, then took a stub of dead branch and slashed a message into it. She used redleaf and winter-dried podberry for dye to emphasize the symbols. Then she suspended the stick in the lean-to. Any ring-runner taking this trail would see the cairn, pick up the stick, and carry it on. A day or so and the message would be up at the towers, heading north with the speed of mirrors. There was no "from" on the message ring, but Nori's parents would understand. She just hoped she got to a message tower before the message did. Her mother might not run with the wolves at this point in her life, but Dione knew all wolfwalkers in this part of the county. Nori could find herself hunted by the Grey Ones, not just men.

"We'll cross here," she told the others when Wakje gestured for them to approach the trail. She pointed to a thick patch of mud. "Fentris, slip there, as if you weren't careful where you put your feet. Leanna—" She snapped the end of a brittle branch. "Leave some hair here, on this joint, as if you got caught and jerked free."

"What was she doing down the trail?" Fentris asked Payne in a low voice as he led his dnu across the path.

"Leaving a message ring," Payne answered.

"Won't that be obvious to the Harumen?" He scudded one foot near a low branch as if he'd tripped over it, then dug his toes in on the other side. Then he carefully scraped the mud off his boots and wiped them down with leaves. Payne said nothing about the latter. It would be even more clear to their followers that the signs were from one of the Tamrani.

Fentris glanced up as he finished. "Why am I making such deep marks?"

Payne led his dnu after the slim man. "The message cairn is out of sight from this crossing. Your marks here will catch their attention and make them more eager to go on rather than look around in case there's something down the trail."

"Smart," the Tamrani murmured, then he frowned back at Hunter. "Why didn't she ask him to scuff his feet?"

"Because he is more experienced out here," Payne answered sardonically. "He wouldn't be so clumsy."

Fentris swallowed his retort.

They rode swiftly for three kays before stopping again. Then up and over a rocky hill and through a tiny valley. Noon came and went, and they paused only to rest the dnu. Afternoon was a winding set of trails. After another hour of that, they were within eyesight of a small clearing with a jumble of boulders, where they drew up again. Rishte had grown tense as the trail approached the rocks, and Nori didn't question him, but simply motioned the others back.

With Payne behind her, Nori went forward just to the edge of the trees. The trail went directly across the clearing, but there were almost no tracks on it, no deer, no eerin, not even rabbit or stickbeast or downdrey. Nori's nostrils flared as she checked the scents. Then she began carefully lifting the leaves nearby that lay in clumps on the ground. She found what she was looking for almost immediately.

Payne nodded as she showed him the tiny dung piles protected under the leaves. Then she glanced meaningfully toward the boulders. He raised both eyebrows. She wasn't seriously suggesting . . . But she shrugged and grinned slyly.

Judging by the size of the dung piles, that boulder pile was a fairly large woodrast colony. The wild rodents didn't usually attack humans, but the six-legged beasties would swarm like tiny worlags when disturbed in their denning ground. They were fast, too, and they'd chase anything that ran—dnu, deer, or eerin.

Nori began flicking the nearest piles back into the brush. Payne did the same on his side of the trail, and both of them carefully reset the leaves so that they no longer looked like clumps. They froze when there was a burst of chittering to Nori's left, but Nori closed her eyes and started humming, and the chittering subsided. They eased their way back to the others.

When they got back, Payne kept his voice low. "How do you propose we go around?"

She smiled slowly. "I don't. If you knew that I, Black Wolf, was leading this party, and you saw our tracks go straight across on the trail through that clearing, what would you think?"

He cocked his head at her. "I'd think there was no threat there." He started to say something else, then stopped. Slowly he began to grin.

She nodded and explained to the others. "If your Harumen are woodswise, they'll check the edge of the clearing for signs of a colony. When they don't find the dung piles, they'll assume the den is abandoned. If they're in too much of a hurry to catch up, they won't wait till the woodrast start popping up again. Instead, they'll go right through on our tracks. The beasties will hunker down till your Harumen are within a meter of the den. Then they'll panic and attack." She looked back at the boulders. "I figure there's perhaps three hundred rast in that mound, and that's if they haven't dug deep. It should give your Harumen quite a fright. At the least, it will slow them down whenever they get near a rock pile."

The tall man looked past her. The clearing wasn't large, but the area around the boulders had been nibbled down to the ground. With the soft earth, the lack of hoofprints on the trail was clearly visible. "You said we wouldn't go around. So how do we get our tracks on that trail?"

She just stood there and smiled at the two Tamrani. "Do you trust me?" she asked softly.

The two citymen were alike enough that both their gazes narrowed. "It depends," said Hunter slowly.

"I'll take you through, one at a time."

Fentris looked past her. "Take us through where? There?" The boulder pile squatted in the forest like a pile of lava bombs. Even he could see the movement now—two small bodies that popped up, then dropped back out of sight. A glimpse of eyes that he knew would be red as thin blood as they watched their party. City rasts were as bad as oldEarth rats. They could swarm a man and tear him apart before he could run twenty meters. He startled as something shifted nearby.

"Don't worry." Nori looked back over her shoulder, then reassured, "Just stay quiet and calm. Leanna first."

The girl nudged her dnu forward without hesitation.

Fentris shifted uneasily. "Black Wolf—"

"Hush," she told him. "It's critical that you be quiet."

Hunter grinned sardonically at the other man. Fentris set his hat more firmly on his head and muttered a silent curse.

When Rishte growled in her head, she sent, *You, too*. Then she took Leanna's reins and ducked her head in a silent question: Ready?

The girl nodded back.

The wolfwalker closed her eyes for a moment, centered herself, and began humming. It was a soothing sound, more like a purr than a tone, and the dnu responded easily. Its head drooped, and its breathing slowed. She smiled faintly as she heard and felt the change. When she opened her eyes again, her gaze was distant, as if she looked past the rocks, not at them. She started to lead the dnu forward.

Carefully she picked her way across. She never quite looked at the rocks. She simply followed the trail, stepping lightly and avoiding the small rocks that littered the ground. A few minutes later, she released Leanna's dnu in the woods on the other side, and the girl walked it ahead.

She walked back as easily as she'd gone across. When it was Hunter's turn, he simply nodded to the wolfwalker and handed over the reins. He couldn't stop the hard pulse in his neck—he swore he could still feel the prick of the tano's claws as they neared the den—but he sat calmly on the dnu and rested his hand on its neck to reassure it.

Twenty minutes later, all seven were across, and moving quietly down the trail. Then they trotted, then cantered to put distance between them and the rock pile. A few hours later, when they slipped across a ridge, Nori started smiling.

"What is it?" Hunter asked.

"I'm thinking that your Harumen should be crossing the denning ground about now." Her smile turned into a grin. "I'm thinking, I wish I was watching."

He studied her for a moment. "You've a mean streak in you, Black Wolf."

"All in a day's work," she returned blithely.

Evening finally found them at another main trail, where a stream curled in toward the path. Nori led her dnu quickly down to the stream and let it drink at the edge. It pulled toward the shallows, but she clicked her tongue and drew it back. Dnu didn't like deep water, but they liked to bathe and roll in anything knee- or waist-deep. She had no desire to canter a soggy beast.

Hunter's dnu nudged hers aside, and she shifted to make room. He kept his voice low. "We need to stop, get trail rations, gear."

She patted his dnu and scratched its haunch as it arched under her hand. "There's a place. Six more kays by trail, then another three by a backroad."

Hunter searched his memory for the names of the village nearby. "Maupin?"

She nodded. It was an end-road village between the harvest homes and Willow Road. "There's a storekeeper there who won't mind selling to us at night." Her own dnu almost pulled out of her hands, and she murmured a quiet command.

Hunter didn't notice. "They'll expect to see us head there."

Aye, the Harumen would probably keep a few riders on Nori's trail, and send the rest out to the farm tracks to see if Nori's group made a run for Willow Road. She glanced at her uncle. "What if we get in and out fast, and avoid the roads completely? Take the trails till we get farther north?"

Wakje hid a wary twinge that she'd asked. She still didn't see inside him, still seemed to accept him and he cleared his throat before answering. "They'd have to stay on your heels. They can send word out to Willow Road and Deepening Road to watch for you, but they won't know which way you'll go, or where you'll break for the road." He tried not to glance toward the wolf. "You'd be forcing them to play your game, not theirs."

Hunter frowned, but Payne smiled grimly. Playing with Nori in the wilderness was like boys sharpening claws with a worlag. It was always her game, not theirs.

Fentris felt the warmth of his dnu. "We'll need to trade our dnu for new mounts."

Nori shook her head at the other man. "It'll be evening. There won't be anything in town."

"How do you know?"

"It's coming on to the Test ninan. Anything we come on at night will already be used up by the spring planting or be the dregs of what's left from the town's Test youths."

"It's nine kays," Payne murmured.

"Aye." She looked at the sky, judging what she could see of the moons that skimmed the rims of the clouds. "But we've ridden easy for the last three or four. We'll go swiftly from here. Give the dnu a good breather in Maupin. The cliff meadows start a few kays past the outer farm boundaries. We'll spend the night there and get a good vantage from there at dawn."

Hunter touched her arm as Wakje and Payne took their dnu to

the trail. He felt her tension like bone and lowered his voice. "You don't think we lost them at the rast den."

"No." She stared out at the forest. "They know we're out here. They know we're heading for Shockton, and that there aren't many bows and bolts between them and your paper belt." She had the satisfaction of seeing his green eyes shutter. "All they have to do is watch the roads and trails and listen to the towers."

Hunter studied her carefully. "Will they catch up?"

"Not if I can help it."

"You've taken us this far on the game tracks."

She shook her head. "Game trails wind around, dead-end and disappear, and this is worlag country. We'll have to watch the land every minute, scout the paths, backtrack around the lairs and poolah traps. It's slow, and we can't hide our trail, not with so many of us on it. At some point, we have to get back to the roads." She rubbed absently at a fresh scratch on her hand. "We're eight days out of Shockton by caravan. That's four days hard riding on the roads, but five or six days by trail, and that's if nothing bad happens. We'll stay ahead of them, but we'll lose time overall. It's a blessing we've been so lucky."

He shrugged, winced at his shoulder, and said dryly, "Define 'lucky.' "

"Lucky enough," she amended.

He studied her in the dark. There was a faint glint of moonlight off her hair, and her violet eyes gleamed. She was uncomfortable with him so close. Perversely, it made him shift closer, crowding her against her dnu.

"Condari—"

"Con," he corrected. "Or Hunter." He stepped back abruptly. "Lead on then." He mounted and trotted back to the trail with Kettre.

Nori stared after him. Then she shook herself. She said nothing as she took point again on the trail, but she cast more than one look over her shoulder.

XXXII

Red snake, death snake, diamond head;
Use dried curcuma or you're dead.
Greenback, dogtooth, checker snake;
Tincture broote and dried mandrake.
Redeye viper and hooded asp;
Use weiber venom and tano trasp.
Harmless snake is venomous;
There is no cure if bit by this.

—from *Cures,* by Sevin maRegna, Randonnen healer

The town was dark as the forest, set off only by the low lamp-lights that marked the stables and inns. The stores were just black windows on dark walls, and their porches like steps leading up to shadowed maws. Nori led them at a trot halfway down main street, turned off near the public bathhouses, and then zigzagged through the silent streets. As they approached the outskirts, businesses began being backed by the owners' homes. Dogs roused at their passing, but like a wolf Nori snarled at each oldEarth breed, and the dogs slunk back in the shadows.

Finally, the wolfwalker reined in. She sat for a moment, listening. Rishte was in her ears, and the yearling deafened her with sounds that were too close for being far away.

Payne shifted impatiently. "Well?"

She didn't answer. Her nostrils flared, and she breathed lightly in and out. The others were silent. "Fresh meatrolls," she said finally. "Pork and bollusk. Carrot casserole. And pie."

Payne perked up. "Pie?"

She nodded. "Early peaches, but there's a hint of something else."

"Probably gingered extractor root. I'll take the kitchen. You take the store."

"Keep it under four silvers," she warned.

392

He made a face.

Fentris cleared his throat. "You're going to break into their kitchen, not just their store?"

Nori studied the store's porch. "Solvini's one of the top ten cooks in this area. She supplies two of the larger towns when she has time outside of her own café. Just think of it as an early sale for her." She dismounted and handed her reins to Kettre.

"Moonworms," Fentris muttered. Hunter hid a smile.

Kettre led their dnu to the hitching post and waited while Nori and Payne climbed the steps to the porch. They both eyed the black rafters. "It's this one or that one," he murmured, pointing with his chin.

She frowned. "That one, I think."

Hunter followed their gaze but saw only shadow. "What are you looking for?"

"An old night spider nest. Stand back a bit," she said softly. Payne cupped his hands and hoisted her up, and she caught the rafter while she balanced on his callused palms. She took the hilt of her knife and tapped slowly, then more rapidly on the beam as she leaned toward the eave. She began humming deep in her throat. For a moment, Hunter saw nothing. Then the shadows seemed to writhe. Insects, spiders fled the rapping of the knife and the resonance of her voice. Like angry stingers, they scuttled and jumped from the corner. Quickly, Nori reached into the blackness. "Got it," she said breathlessly.

Payne dropped her back to the porch and ducked as she scrubbed her hands over her hair. He flicked something dark off her shoulders and jerked as she accidentally brushed another bug right at him. "Moonworms, Nori-girl. Watch it."

"Sorry." She twisted to look at herself. "Are they off? No, there's something on my back."

Fentris's eyes widened, and Hunter stiffened, but Payne didn't even blink. "Night spider," he acknowledged. "Small one. Can you get it? It's moving down toward your waist."

"I think so."

She started to reach around, but Hunter grabbed Payne's arm. "Stand still," he snapped at Nori. "I'll do it—"

She didn't look up. She simply wiped her hand across her lower back and brushed the insect off.

Hunter said, "Dammit, woman, are you insane? You could have been bitten and dead as a six-day corpse."

She grinned faintly. "Anything's possible. Am I clean?" she asked Payne.

"Turn around again." She did so, and he nodded. "Clean, I think."

"Good. That always makes me feel itchy, as if I missed something."

Fentris swallowed. "You've done this before?"

She brushed her hands over her hair one more time. "Ogoli has been leaving a key there for me for years. It's a good place to hide it." She tugged her tunic back in place. "No one's going to reach into a spider's nest willingly."

Fentris's voice was dry. "I'd say that was truth enough."

She grinned over her shoulder as she unlocked the door. "Shall we?"

Hunter gave Fentris a satisifed look and followed her inside. The fop muttered and went in after them.

She fumbled for the lamp, lit it, and turned it up to an easy glow.

It was Hunter who said, "Isn't that going to attract attention?"

"We're not stealing," she returned. "I don't want to wake him, but Ogoli won't worry as much if he sees the lights on." She reached over the counter and got out the tally pad. "The dried meats are over there," she directed Hunter. "And the dried fruits are in the canisters on the second shelf." She glanced at Fentris. "Trail socks—"

"I see them."

Quickly, they assembled and tallied their goods, while Nori searched the shelved canisters and boxes. Hunter glanced at her as he wrapped his bundles. A moment later, he caught her sniffing the contents of a glass jar. "What are you looking for?"

She stepped back and shoved the jar back in place. "Nothing," she said shortly. But he could have sworn she had flushed as she turned away to the jerky packs.

They had most of the goods together when she tensed. Her

head shot up, her gaze going toward the back door. "Quiet," she snapped the whisper. In the near-silence, the command was sharp as a shot.

Hunter slid the pack of arrows onto the counter and started to draw his sword when Nori relaxed. "It's okay," she said. A moment later, when the latch on the back door began to ease up, she said in a normal voice, "It's alright, Ogoli. It's just me."

" 'It's me?' " Hunter whispered dryly.

She went back to pulling out glass jars. "Only someone you know is going to assume you know them by saying 'it's me.' It's strangers who use names, since they know you don't know who they are."

"I'm terrified to think that that almost made sense."

Kettre choked back a laugh, and Fentris shook his head, but even though the slim Tamrani trusted the wolfwalker, he didn't slide his own sword back in its sheath.

The latch turned and the door opened, but no one stepped through. "Sorry to wake you, Ogoli," Nori said. "We were trying to be quiet."

Now the mountain of a man appeared. If Hunter had been the type to fear size alone, he'd have been stepping back quickly. On the other hand, the storekeeper held his bow as if it would turn and bite him. The massive man glanced at Nori, then at the others before lowering the weapon. "You were quiet enough," he agreed casually. "But I put in a thread alarm last year after thieves hit me twice. I take it you're in a hurry. Finding everything alright?"

From anyone else it might have been sarcastic, but Hunter caught none of that in the man's tone. "Almost," Nori answered. "Where are you hiding the salt packs?"

"Under the counter, by the uncuts. It's alright, Josu," he said in a low voice over his shoulder. "It's Jangharat."

The boy stepped around his father and grinned. "I told him it was you."

"Good ears, smart man," she approved, and earned a wider grin from the boy. He didn't rush to hug her this time, and she smiled wryly. "Too manly for a hug?" He glanced at the Tamrani, and she followed his gaze. "They're just cityfolk," she told him. She glanced back at Ogoli. "Can't see in the dark," she explained, "or we would have left the lights off."

Hunter snorted.

She offered Josu her arm, and he grasped it, eager to return the adult greeting. He'd been five when she'd found him on search after he'd been kidnapped; he was twelve now. Too young to draw a man's bow, but old enough—he slanted a look at his father—to be greeted like a man by Black Wolf.

Nori started to step around the counter, but the storekeep did it for her, pulling out three white salt tabs and setting them on the counter. "Five, please," she corrected, and he added two more. She tossed one each to Fentris and Hunter. It was almost amusing the way the two men ignored each other as they took their bundles out to the dnu for packing.

Ogoli studied her tallies upside down, then took the pad from her when she started to add the salt. She glanced up from under her lashes, and her violet eyes gleamed as she stuffed her own dried foods in her saddlebag. She lowered her voice carefully. "You don't, by any chance, still keep a few balls of modichoc in the store?"

The storekeep didn't look up from his tally, but he smiled slyly. "I might. I'm surprised you can't smell them."

She glanced back, but the Tamrani were outside. "Ogoli, you sneak," she whispered. "Where are they?"

"I thought, with the Test ninan and all, there might be unexpected visitors in the valley, so I took the liberty of hiding the modichoc from thieves with sharp noses. Just in case," he added with a wider smile.

"I'm hurt."

"That'll be the day." He moved to the tea shelf and opened a canister, drew out a wrapped package, opened that and the package inside, and the package inside that. "This what you're looking for?"

She grinned. "I had to throw mine out a few days ago. I've been dying for a bite." She reached out, but he drew it back before she could grasp it.

"Now, Wolfwalker. You owe us a dinner. Solvini's made up a special dish just for you."

She glanced meaningfully at the boy and sobered. "On the way back, perhaps."

The storekeep followed her gaze. He gathered the last three bundles. "Josu, take these out to the cityfolk." He waited a beat till the boy hurried out, then said soberly, "Riding at night, sneaking gear? You're in trouble."

"We're being followed," she admitted.

He stood straighter, seemed to puff out his already massive chest. "I'll take care of it. I'll tell them I haven't see you. Or I'll tell them I heard you were near Tochoars."

"Ogoli—"

"Better yet—" He shook his thick finger at her to hush her. "—I'll tell them you stole from me. Broke in and took what you wanted, then fled west or south when I nearly caught you."

She put her hand on his thick arm. "Ogoli, I thank you for the offer, but you're a terrible liar, and they'd know it. They already know we've got to head east, fast, to hit the main road. I hate to leave you with danger on your doorstep but—"

"Jangharat," he interrupted. "Whatever you need."

She nodded. "If you really want to help . . . ?"

"You insult me," he chided her.

"Then get a few friends, armed, to join you here tonight. Stay up with the lights on low, as if we snuck in and you're trying to inventory what we took. The men tracking us will come here, I know it, and you don't want to meet them alone. If you have to, tell them what they want to know. It won't matter," she said quickly over his instant denial. "We have a good lead on them already, perhaps even hours. Don't fight them, Ogoli. They're the nasty sort. They kill carefully, but easily."

"Raiders." Ogoli cursed quietly.

"Worse, I think. They're out of the city." She jerked a nod at Hunter as he stepped back inside. "Harumen, he calls them."

Ogoli's face blanched at her steady tone. He'd heard the term before. It wasn't said lightly. He forced his voice to be stern. "I can send a message to your parents, warn them that you're in trouble."

"No." There had been that ring-runner who rode out unpaid with that message from the *chovas*. And the other messages going missing. She gave him a lopsided smile. "The Harumen will be watching the message towers and ring-runners. If they see you sending a runner out to the tower line, they'll know that we're more to you than some late-night irritants." She paused in her swift packing and put her hand on his arm. "Ogoli, friend, you have mate, a son, a sister and your sister's children to watch out for. You have a home that can burn. You have livestock, a store and a livelihood. Don't get caught up in this. We're ahead of them, safe for now. Trust me. We'll be alright."

" 'Trust the wolfwalker, follow the wolves,' " he murmured.

"Aye." Nori started to dig in her belt pouches for coins, but Hunter drew out a handful of thin gold and silver pieces. The wolfwalker glanced at the coins, then at the tally and quickly counted out what they needed.

The heavy man raised his eyebrows at the Tamrani. "Even charging cityfolk, that's too much."

She teased, "A storekeep who argues about overpayment?"

His meaty hand pushed four of the silvers back across the counter. "You know, if you'd come in the daytime, we'd have bargained, you'd have argued, we'd have settled, and you'd have paid less."

"Yes, but." She grinned slyly. "If we'd come in the daytime, Payne wouldn't have been able to steal the ginger-peach pie that was still cooling in your kitchen."

"The pie? Payne? Why that—"

She leaned forward and gave him a quick kiss on his stubbled chin.

He tried not to look pleased. "What else has that damn tamrin taken?"

"If I know Payne, he's gotten into your leftovers."

"I should have alarmed the kitchen."

She pushed the silvers back. "Tell Solvini we loved the meatrolls and appreciated the fresh cheese."

"Nose like a hound dog," the storekeep muttered.

She hefted her saddlebag to her shoulder and didn't bother to complain when Hunter plucked it from her hands and slung it over his own. She punched Josu lightly in his chest, then looked meaningfully at the boy's father. "Send for your friends now,

Ogoli. Don't wait. You want to be protected when they get here."

"I hear you, Wolfwalker." He watched her from the door. "Ride safe."

"With the moons," she answered over her shoulder.

Hunter slapped her saddlebags over the horn and stepped back as she lashed them down. He murmured, "See why I want you with me? You're a handy woman to have around."

"Handy?" She tightened the buckles, then tugged on the tabs to check them.

"How many scouts know a storekeeper who leaves the key to his store for you, doesn't moan about getting up in the middle of the night to find you raiding his home, doesn't argue over the payment you figure you owe him, and then sneaks you modi-choc candies?"

"I didn't think you saw the candies," she muttered.

"With the size of that package, you must have one heck of a sweet tooth."

She let the sense of the wolf in so that her lips curled back. "*Teeth* is the operative word."

He bit back a laugh. "I'm curious, Wolfwalker. Just how many contacts like that do you have, in how many obscure towns, and in how many of the first nine counties?"

"Are you asking for a reason, or just trying to irritate me?"

"Will you blush again if I irritate you enough?"

"Moonwormed Tamrani," she said, not quite under her breath. She ducked under the dnu's neck to take the reins from Kettre.

"He saw the candies?" Kettre whispered slyly. "You're slipping."

"Just hush and give me the reins." She mounted as Payne trotted up. "Hurry up," she told him shortly.

"For pie, we can wait sixty seconds." He thrust one of his bundles at Kettre. "Find room for this. And don't squish it," he added quickly.

A moment later, they cantered away down the road.

Inside the store, Ogoli watched them go, then turned to his son. "You feel like a man tonight?"

The boy puffed up his chest as his father had done. "Aye."

"Then run fast, to Libri's house, and wake him. Tell him to bring his sword. When you've done that, go wake Ursgor and tell him the same."

"Rhyk'ka?"

Ogoli hesitated. "Him too, if he's not too drunk."

The boy started to dash from the store, but his father caught his shoulder and spun him back around. "You see anyone riding in town, anyone at all, and you go into the bushes and hide." Josu's eyes widened at the fear that flickered in his father's gaze. "You hide, and you don't make a sound," the man added sternly. "You don't breathe, you don't move, you don't come out for any reason, not until they're gone. No matter what you hear, no matter what you see, come home only if the roads are clear and none of the dogs are barking."

"They didn't bark at Jangharat."

"They never do," he answered.

XXXIII

Petty men steal all but strife;
Thieves take from the money wheel;
Killers take each family's life;
What then do your friends steal?

—Sixth Riddle of the Ages

At first, the trail was well used and wide enough that the branches didn't whip them as they rode. Nori had them stop and stand silently more than once while she listened to the night. Then she led them on again.

Rishte was closer now, out of sight, but near enough for her to feel the grey. He fed her impressions of dew-dank earth, night-chilled leaves, the musk of day creatures sleeping, and the rustle of creatures that warily watched them pass. He was getting used to the sounds of the dnu, and he ventured close enough that twice Nori caught a glimpse of movement off within the trees.

It was well past midnight when she finally led them off the trail and into a stand of pintrees. Decades of needles dropped on the ground made it spongy, and they set out their bedrolls and sleeping bags.

At dawn, they were up again. At midmorning, they watered their dnu at a steep stream that rushed down the hill they had just urged their dnu to climb. While the others rested, Nori rolled her neck and shoulders to ease her tiredness before changing her riding boots for running moccasins.

"Where are you going?" Hunter looked at her suspiciously.

"Up there." She gestured with her chin at a ridge. "We need to know how far they are behind us."

"Not far enough." Kettre dropped to the ground, staggered a bit, and grimaced. "Are you taking Payne?"

Nori shook her head. "He and Uncle Wakje are the only other scouts among us. He'll have to stay here with you."

Hunter nodded. "Then I'll go up with you."

"I don't think so," she returned flatly, and hid a smile at his look of surprise. "You're next best on the trail. If something happens to Uncle Wakje or Payne, you'll be needed here. I'll take Fentris or Kettre."

He tried not to be pleased at the offhand compliment.

"I'll go," Fentris offered.

Kettre barely glanced at the other Tamrani. "I'll go. Best to keep the cityfolk together."

"Toss for it," Nori said flatly. She turned to Hunter. "Do you have a coin?"

Kettre murmured, "Does a poolah pee in the woods?"

Fentris coughed, and Payne hid a grin. "He is a Tamrani," he told her.

Nori rolled her eyes, but took the silver from Hunter and then glanced the silent question at Fentris.

"Heads," he affirmed. The coin flicked up, glinted white in the sun, and fell heads-down on the dirt. "Well piss on a brick and bake it," he said in turn.

Kettre kept her voice bland. "At least he's learning something from us."

The slender man smiled sardonically and turned to loosen the cinch on his saddle, but Nori stopped him. "You can't rest here." She glanced at Wakje. "Move on down the trail, maybe half a kay." The ex-raider nodded, and she closed her eyes to think over the land. She'd wandered here for ninans one summer. Her mother had taken her out with the wolves to teach her about the river. She could still recall the trails, the smell of the dark, wet canyon as they approached it in the morning. The steep cliffs, black water racing and boiling into white froth below . . . She opened her eyes. "The ground will start getting rocky within a kay. The closer you get to the gullies that lead down to the river cliffs, the rockier it will get. You'll have to cut across some of the ledges. Kettre and I will meet you near the top of the gullies when we cut back down from the ridge."

Hunter frowned. "This is rough country to bushwhack."

Kettre tugged on her running boots. "We only have to bush-whack if Nori can't find the trail."

He glanced at Nori. "And can you find the trail?"

She shrugged. "I've been here before, back in '34, I think. It was the year the Phye flooded at the ten meter level. Dankton was completely under."

" 'Thirty-four?" Fentris raised one elegant eyebrow. "What were you, twelve?"

She frowned, counting back. "Aye, about that."

He couldn't hide his disbelief. "You remember trails from when you were twelve?"

Payne snorted. "She remembers every blade of grass, every print and every pebble on every trail she's ever run. Don't ever bet on her sense of place or direction. You'll lose more than your shirt." Nori scowled at her brother, and Payne added to Fentris as he took the reins of her dnu, "I bet you remember every copper you spent at the same age."

The Tamrani exchanged a glance. He had a point.

"I know I'm showing my city ignorance again," Fentris said dryly, "but if we need to rest the dnu, why can't we do that here? It's shaded; there's water and grass. Plenty of space for the dnu."

Payne merely nodded to Nori. She sighed. "Do you hear that tree sprit?"

The slim man cocked his head. "No."

"Or that pair of stingers?"

"What stingers?"

She gave him a lopsided smile. "You wouldn't hear the Haru-men, either. Not till they were upon you. Water deafens your ears, but bounces sound so that others farther away can hear you." She turned to Kettre. "Ready?" The other woman had changed her boots also, but made to remount until Nori shook her head. "Belt packs, on foot," she told her friend. "This side of the ridge is too much of a scramble for dnu."

"By the second hell, Nori. If I'd known that, I would have lost the toss."

She slung her own belt pack on. "If your pride wouldn't stop you, you could still give in to the Tamrani."

"I'll think about it, when laceflowers grow in the seventh hell."

The wolfwalker grinned.

It took the two women half an hour to jog-walk to the base of the ridge. They didn't speak. Kettre had learned scout signals from Nori when they were young enough to have thought of it as a game. It was one of the reasons she'd been invited to ride on the city venges when they hunted raiders outside the outskirts. Kettre snorted to herself. In the city, Kettre was considered a sharp-eyed scout. Compared to Payne, she was barely adequate. Next to Nori, she might as well be blind and deaf and half crippled on one side.

Nori caught her wry expression and grinned. Between the wolf and the hand signals, their silent conversation, went something like this:

This way. Clear. Clear. Hold. Watch: tick nest.

Got it.

Clear. Clear. Clear. Hold. Wait. No, it's okay. Stickbeast.

I see it. Good eye.

Nori raised an eyebrow.

Kettre grinned back.

This way. Clear. Watch this bush. Clear. Clear. Red lily.

Pretty.

Aye, it is. Good thing you're not hungry or there'd be none left after we passed.

Kettre made a face, and it was Nori who grinned this time.

This way. Clear, Clear. Loose rock. Clear.

There was a sudden edge in the faint sense of grey. Midstep, Nori flung up her palm and froze. Instantly Kettre stilled.

Hundreds of meters away, Rishte was only a slightly sharper voice in the din of the distant packsong. Still, his wariness was like a needle to Nori, and she signaled the other woman. Wait. Wait. *What is it?* she sent back to the wolf. The mental words were unheard, but the impression of the question, the alertness went through.

Blood-scent. Death-scent.

That she understood. Wait, she told Kettre. Listen. Watch for predators.

Blood-scent, kill-scent . . . Rishte circled, tested the wind. *Movement. Hunger. Defend. Above, moving.*

Nori closed her eyes. It took almost a minute for her to separate Rishte's thoughts into things she could understand. Movement? On the ground? What was above? Something overhead, something flying. She peered up through the canopy but she'd never be able to see if there were lepa in the sky. *What is it?* she sent again.

Sharp. Movement, movement.

Death-scent, sharp—that was the smell of old guts, of stomach acid and bile and half-digested grass rotting in the air. The gut-scent wasn't fresh. If it had been, Rishte would have been more interested, more eager to get near it to help with the last of the kill. This was old enough, hours perhaps, that it made the wolf think of fighting for his share of the carcass, fighting to eat, not taking a creature down.

The movement, the skitterings, she didn't understand, till her brain kicked back into gear. She stiffened. Rast? Near a den, the ratlike creatures would leap forward, tear out a bite from carcass or intruder and dodge back. What if it was bihwadi? The dirty-seeming, doglike creatures would attack a badgerbear if there were enough of them to pull it down. Rishte was small enough and lone enough to be an easy target.

She could almost feel the sense of movement around him. Skitterings: rast. But the feeling that some of the threat was overhead? Something above the yearling? She felt a chill. Not bihwadi, she realized. Jays.

OldEarth jays were blue and handsome, crested birds, even if they were vicious to smaller creatures. The Ancients had found similar birds here and named them jays, but where oldEarth jays were small with short beaks, those here were large with wickedly hooked beaks that could tear into any beast. They would flock over a carcass like oldEarth crows. *Rishte,* she called urgently. *Get away.*

The sense of hunger made her stomach twist.

Rast. Bihwadi. Jays, she warned. *Without the pack, you're not predator, but prey.*

The grey wolf felt only the sense of restraint. He growled angrily back. *Human. Small nose.*

Nori's eyes flew open in shock at the insult. *You worm-eared mutt,* she breathed. *Stay back from the carcass,* she said sharply, almost harshly into the grey. *You have no one to protect you. Stay. Back.* She didn't know she snarled the words. *Back.*

Slowly, carefully, Kettre drew an arrow and began to nock her bow. Some part of Nori's brain noticed, but she was too focused on the wolf. Her presence was growing stronger in his mind, and he was still young enough to submit to a strong pack leader, but he was also eager, male and hungry.

She clenched her fists. Her violet eyes were unfocused now, and her lips began to curl back. *Rishte,* she breathed. She called it into the grey until it echoed like balls in a rubber room. The grey din seethed and swirled. She could feel the pull between them like a faint tug of war. She centered herself and Called sharply. *Rishte.*

The sense of resistance faded suddenly, as if he had pulled back to answer her voice. He growled angrily, but she could feel him obeying. She unclenched her fists, but kept her mental voice firm until she was sure he was returning.

"Grey Rishte?" Kettre asked as Nori lost the tension.

"Aye. He's . . . willful, stubborn."

"They say like calls to like."

She gave the other woman a look. "I never ran around by myself all unguarded and unarmed."

"Of course not," Kettre soothed. "That run on Ironjaw Trail was just an accident."

"It was."

"So was the time you took off to collect the hotflowers to pay Davoni back for that prank with the dye-laced tea. And the time you ran off with Grey Hishn and ended up dragging the old wolf back in a travois you made out of your poncho when her arthritis acted up. Oh, and there was the time you wanted to see why the night-beating birds were hooting. That was definitely not on purpose—"

"You're one to talk," the wolfwalker retorted. She grasped

one of the boulders and hauled herself up. "You were the one who started almost every bit of trouble we ever got in."

Kettre watched her move smoothly up the steep slope. "You needed trouble," the woman told Nori's back. "You were too reserved as a child."

Nori grinned down. "And you were far too wild." She fit a fist into a wide crack in the rock and levered herself up. She studied the slope for a moment. "You can come on up. It's a scramble, but it's no real climb."

Kettre eyed the rocks and muttered, "Define 'real.' " But she jumped, got a hold on the top of the boulder, and followed the wolf-walker up.

Like the cliffs close to the River Phye, the west side of the ridge was riddled with ancient caves. They might have been den for lepa once, but they had eroded and fallen in until they were only pockets and shallow depressions. Now they gave the steep path the semblance of a set of giant, eroded stairs. There were signs of wolves, forest cats, eerin, bihwadi, even wild goats along the rocks. Rishte followed a goat trail back until he hung his head over the cliff up above and panted curiously at them down below. Nori couldn't help smiling.

Rock mice and cliff birds had nested among the old rocks so long that the debris had built up like tumors in the rocks. Kettre slipped and stepped on one, and the puff of dust and spore that burst up had her coughing for minutes. Nori climbed back down to see what had happened, and she examined the old nest carefully. At first glance, there seemed to be a faint vein of turquoise behind it, but when she pulled the back of the mat away, the color was nothing but an old stain. She breathed shallowly to avoid the dust from the old nest. "That's odd," she murmured. She ran her finger inside the depression that Kettre's boot had left. "There's swamp fungi in here."

Kettre choked, coughed, and yanked her water bota from her belt. "It's years old, Nori. Why wouldn't there be mold?"

"Because this is a swamp fungus. It only grows this thick where it's been wet for years, like in a stagnant pond or seep. Look at this stuff. It's even stained the stones." She rubbed her finger and thumb lightly together under her nose, but couldn't smell anything but rain-damp detritus. She left the crushed nest finally, and led Kettre on.

Nori had just climbed to the edge of a depression when she halted so abruptly that she actually rocked back on her heels and almost toppled over backward. She cocked her head, her nostrils flaring. "There's something . . ." She turned her head from side to side, trying to catch a better scent. She'd smelled this before. Or rather, she hadn't smelled it. The wolves—

"Get back," she said sharply. "Go left. Left." She scrambled back and found her heart pounding with sudden fear as Kettre clambered left over the rotten rock. She wiped her mouth and nose as she rejoined the other woman.

"What is it?" Kettre studied her pale face.

She shook her head. She couldn't answer. But the death-scent, the sense of old death had been there in that depression. It wasn't strong, not like the seep that night with the worlags, or the other place Rishte refused to go, but it was definitely here in the packsong. Moonworms, was this what her mother sensed all the time? Memories of death, of kills and fevers and plagues? She had to learn to pull back from that.

Rishte urged her away, and she listened carefully, but kept her mind clear. Now she could hear the echo, or rather, the reso-nance of other wolves behind him, the ones who had passed along that plague sense, and who now strengthened the year-ling's growl. She had been around enough wolves to know it was another pack, close enough that the wariness of the other Grey Ones rode on top of Rishte's faint impressions. That, and their sense of hunger was strong. Nori rubbed her ankle ab-sently, then scratched her ear and studied the next stretch of stone before she realized she had once again sunk toward the grey. She drew back again abruptly. But when she started up again, she angled farther left to avoid the places where Rishte's growl was harsh.

It was a scramble, then a climb, then a scramble. By the time they reached the top, they were dusty, dirty, and their faces were streaked with drying mud where they had rubbed at a nose or chin. Nori's ankle throbbed where she'd banged it again on the rocks. Kettre shook out her arms and grinned at the wolfwalker.

"Now, that's the Nori I know. Dirty, dusty, and looking as if she'd go again in a flash."

She looked down the cliff. "Go again? You're crazy." Then she grinned back at the other woman. "Perhaps," she admitted. She closed her eyes and reached out to the wolf. He was above them now, but a hundred meters away. With no threat to sharpen his nose, she had only impressions of the scents of different bushes, the occasional sharp odor of woodrat or vole, and the smell of day-old dung as it dried in the mild spring air. She raised her hand to her nose. She could smell damp dirt as if it was in her own nails. She smiled faintly, and gestured for Kettre to follow.

It was steep enough that they used the trees to pull themselves up. They left small scars in the detritus where their feet dug in, but they didn't worry about the marks. With the brush as dense as winter wool, it was unlikely anyone would see their trail unless they bushwhacked down the same route.

As she clambered up over yet another a boulder, Nori almost stepped onto the ridge path before she realized she'd hit the trail. She barely managed to thrust forward and jump the trail awkwardly to avoid leaving a print. It wasn't a graceful move. She landed on a lumpy root, teetered for a second, waved her arms like a scarecrow, and finally landed on the other side where her footprints wouldn't show. Immediately she pressed herself against the bole of a silverheart tree.

In the distance, Rishte snapped to attention.

Be silent. Be still, she returned unconsciously.

Kettre had gone still and flat when she'd jumped so abruptly. The other woman now lay against the ridge, waiting for Nori's signal. For several moments, neither moved. Finally, Nori eased up so she could peer around and over the roots. The trail had been almost hidden by the fresh spring grasses, but the boot print on what she could see was fresh. She could also see the marks of a deer's split hooves flattened beneath the print, and the deer must have gone up right around dawn. Their tracks had disturbed the dewfall. But where the deer prints were slightly fuzzy at the edges, the pressure ridges of the hiker's prints had barely begun to crumble.

Nori listened, then gave a low bird call to Kettre. The other woman poked her head up, saw Nori, and nodded. Neither woman heard anything other than the small sounds of creatures getting used to their presence again. The wolfwalker signaled for Kettre to come forward, pointed out the tracks on the trail, and waited while the other woman stepped over carefully. Then they squatted to study the tracks.

"Is it from a scout?" Kettre breathed in her ear.

"Aye. We're too far out for a solo hiker, especially in worlag country."

"There are deer and eerin hunters."

"Not in spring." She pointed. "Besides, this is no hunter. The animal prints point both ways on that trail."

Kettre waited, then prompted. "So what does that mean?"

Nori glanced at her. The trees were dense enough that the lower branches had died back. Columns of streaked brown trunks rose out of the clumps of brambles and redstick, and new growth covered the ground in billows of soft, pale greens and spotted leaves that offered shelter to woodrast and hare. It was a denning haven for deer and eerin, but those creatures would graze much lower. She gestured at the trail. "A hunter would have seen that this is a well-traveled path both up and down the ridge. He'd have set up near the lower grazing areas, not up here. He wouldn't want to pack the meat all the way back down. No," she said softly. "This man would be no hunter. They've got themselves a tracker."

"One who would come up here?" Kettre pursed her lips.

"Aye, if he knows this country well enough to be comfortable by himself on the ridge. He'd be local, not Harumen," she added. "Probably someone they picked up in Maupin." She studied the ridge. "Some lookout trails are easy to find, but this one can be a bit tricky. You have to know how to get over the rocks to the trailhead, and a cityman wouldn't likely find it."

Kettre hesitated. "Could he have seen us coming up?"

It was a question whose answer Nori dreaded. "If he was still climbing up or down to the lookout point, I'd say probably not. But if he was already on the ledge when we were at the base, then yes. There are places where the trees are thin, and we disturbed enough birds that he'd have noticed that for sure."

Kettre couldn't help asking, "What are the odds he was up on the ledge?"

"If they're close behind us? Fairly good."

Kettre didn't have to ask who *they* were.

Rishte snarled, and she nodded mentally at the wolf. "Come on." She stepped over the path and waded through the ferns. Kettre followed carefully, and they lay down in a shallow dip caused by a long-ago fallen log.

They had been settled only a few minutes when Rishte snarled more eagerly in Nori's mind. She glanced back, then cursed under her breath. "Don't move," she breathed in Kettre's ear. Nori shifted so that she had one arm and one leg over Kettre. "Put your arm over your mouth and nose," Nori ordered in a whisper. "Breathe shallow and into your elbow."

Kettre closed her eyes as Nori tucked her face beside Kettre's and started to hum. The tone was deep and slow, so soft that a man a meter away wouldn't be able to hear it. It wasn't a man she was humming for, but the four deer that were picking their way through the ferns. Spook them, and any watcher would know that something was right there by the trail. Keep the deer calm, and she had a near-perfect blind.

One doe froze. Only her tail twitched, right, left, flicking sharply. The creature took a tentative step forward, her ears flicking now. The buck remained on guard, and the doe slowly lowered her head to nibble at the soft grainy weeds. After a moment, the buck raised his head and tugged at the new leaves on a vine that wound up and overhead.

Kettre tried not to breathe. For all that Nori was trim, she still weighed almost seventy kilos, and that didn't count her belt pack or weapons. Right now, Nori's buckle was digging into Kettre's stomach, and there was a sharp branch under her thigh.

The four deer picked their way through the brush single-file, their nostrils flaring as they approached. The buck paused, and Nori could see his antlers clearly. They were well branched and curved in, unlike the eerin, whose short, spiraled, two-pointed horns were curved out toward the front of their foreheads.

Rishte snarled eagerly. The sense of prey was clear, and the hunger of the wolf pack nearby made Nori's stomach tighten.

No-prey, Nori returned sharply. *No-harm, no-thought.*

She kept her head down and hummed in her throat. The deer moved closer. One doe nibbled at the new growth, then raised her head and stared at Nori. Nori breathed calmly. She could almost feel the doe's wary curiosity, her tentative testing of Nori's scent. Of all the creatures the Ancients had brought to this world, deer were some of the few that could survive on their own. They were four-legged, not six-legged like the eerin that moved like quick centipedes. They had delicate heads and huge black-rimmed eyes, not the hammer heads of the dnu. One of the does limped, and another had the flat, black hump of a parasite knot, but the others looked healthy. They were moving normally, listening. If there was a tracker on the ridge, he was either watching like Nori and Kettre, or he wasn't close enough to spook them.

Nori kept the hum in her throat. The deer moved closer, sharp hooves cutting into the humus. One of the does stepped around a tree near Nori's legs until she was nibbling near Nori's arm. The deer shifted a few steps away, then raised her tail. Nori caught the sharp scent an instant before the pellets started to fall. She caught her breath and cursed silently. She could only pray her braid was out of the way of the steaming heap. But she could hold her breath only so long. Then she half coughed, forced herself to be still, took in some wary air. The odor was heavy and sharp. She started to gag, clenched her fists, and forced herself to keep humming.

Beneath her, Kettre seemed to be choking.

Nori flicked a finger against the woman's thigh, but the woman's body started to tremble, then shake. Then Nori's hum grew ragged as she, too, started to giggle silently. Kettre only shook harder. Nori finally had to pinch the woman to stop her from laughing so hard.

The doe simply walked away.

Nori felt Rishte snarl and hissed a warning. Both women went still.

A few minutes later, a man came down the trail. He didn't see them. His gaze was on the deer as the small group wended its way up through the trees and over the forested rise.

Kettre lay utterly still until they heard some small pebbles down the trail falling away to knock on the rocks below. She started to move, but Nori tapped her thigh. Stay. Not clear, she told the other woman.

From below, Rishte was watching the man. Nori could feel the sense of movement in the lupine gaze. He must have suspected something; he had stopped on the trail. He waited. They waited. A long ten minutes passed. Finally, he seemed satisfied and moved on. This time, Rishte watched him go.

Nori raised her head and listened to the forest. "Stay quiet," she breathed to Kettre. "He's moving on down, but let's be safe about it." She levered herself up—away from the fresh dung.

The other woman sat up. "For a moment there," Kettre whispered back. "Poised as she was, I thought that doe was thinking about acting as a career."

"What do you mean?"

Kettre started grinning. "To doo or not to doo, that is the question."

Nori tried to hold it back, but she couldn't help it. She giggled.

"Well, then," Kettre whispered, "doo we go on?"

"Stop it," Nori whispered back. "No one likes a punster. And yes, we go on. We have to see where they are. After all, this isn't just a job, it's a dooty."

Kettre stuffed her fist in her mouth to keep from laughing out loud. Her shoulder shook even after Nori reached over and pushed her down into the leaves.

Nori looked up to see the wolf watching in disgust from the brush to the side. He panted at her silently, and she just shook her head.

With Rishte to watch before them, they went on with more speed than care. It took them half an hour to climb the rest of the way, and Nori's thighs and calves were aching by the time they reached the lookout.

She took her belt pack off, lay down and wormed out to the dusty edge. "Just in case," she told Kettre over her shoulder. The other woman sighed and followed suit. A moment later, they were side by side on the rocky ledge, looking out over the forest.

It was a decent lookout. The ridge was steep enough that only a few trees managed to cling to the slope. Most of them topped out below the ledge. Far below, the dark canopy swept up the ridge like a wave that crested in a slide area just below their perch. There were no breaks in the trees and only a few thin spots to indicate clearings or small meadows. The only hint of Oracle Creek was a faint dipped-out line through the green. Birds darted up, arced out, and plunged back into the purple-green canopy of spring growth, while wind sent cat's paws through soft leaves. Just below the lookout, two blue-winged palts dove at a flock of red-shafted, shivering finches. The small birds weren't unarmed. Twice, they turned and attacked the palts before diving back into the trees. Nori listened to their harsh cries with half an ear, her other mental ear catching the sense of Rishte nosing in the brush behind them. She wormed out a bit further until Kettre hissed, "Not so far."

She thumped on the rock with her fist. "I know this ridge. It's solid."

"A lot of comfort that will be when you fall."

Nori snorted. "I'm as likely to fall here as in love."

Kettre cast her a speculative glance. "And how are things going with Condari?"

Nori stared out at the forest. "Things are fine with the Tamrani."

"*The Tamrani,* is it?"

"It is," she said firmly.

"Dangling dogs, Nori, you haven't been interested in a man for years. Maybe it's time to think about trying it again."

Nori shrugged. As she'd grown, even those boys she'd known for years wanted the legend more than the girl. Aside from Kettre and a few others, her friends had been as bad as the raiders, the betrayals worse than beatings. Payne said she was still picking the knives out of her back. She didn't disagree. So she simply shrugged. "You only have to club me two or three times before I learn my lesson. Besides, it's not men in general. It's elders, councilmen, guildmen, and Bilocctans."

"And citymen, traders, and Tamrani," the other woman added.

"Just on general principle," Nori agreed with a grin.

Kettre made a disgusted sound. "You can't go through life distrusting everyone."

"Why not? I don't even trust myself."

In spite of herself, Kettre laughed. "You're a strange one, Jangharat."

"As are you, Kettre 'Nother Knife." Nori pointed abruptly. "There. Eight o'clock. Follow the line of the creek, to the right-angled bend, then look east two or three hundred meters."

Kettre followed her gaze. "Oh, crap on a stickbeast and scrape him clean."

"Aye. We'll have to hurry."

"Look at all those birds flying up. That's not a small party. That's twice the size of the one that chased us out of town."

"They must have found some friends."

"I'd like a few more friends myself."

"The woodrast den must have made them wary." Nori wormed her way back. "We'll have to find a few more ways to slow them down. Perhaps a snap-back or two on the trail, with a puffbag from a clove bush, just waiting to break on their heads."

Kettre smiled slowly. "Hunter's right. You're nasty, Nori-girl. But then, you learned from the best."

"That I did." Nori gave her a grin. "You ready for a fast skid down?"

"I thought you'd never ask."

XXXIV

Dik-dik hunt the forest mice;
Rast can hunt the dik-dik;
Forest cat hunt forest rast;
Worlags hunt the wounded cats;
Bihwadi suck the worlag dry;
Who will hunt bihwadi?

—from *Who Hunts Whom?* by Capira Rhodaback Thyme

They regained their group only an hour ahead of the trackers. When Nori told Wakje what they'd seen, he snapped at the others, "Mount up."

Fentris stopped Payne. "How could they catch up so far so fast?"

He barely glanced at the slim Tamrani. "We stopped in Maupin, we didn't start today till an hour after dawn, and they can follow a trail like ours at a run." He swung into the saddle. "And we're scouting the trails for them."

This time, Wakje didn't even hesitate to motion Nori into the lead. The ex-raider fell in at the rear, then dropped back far enough to be able to see the entire line ahead of him.

The trail was open, then shuttered and tangled with spring growth. They twisted through massive trees as big around as small houses. They took a steep game trail to shave off some switchbacks, then worked their way carefully over two small hills to avoid skylining themselves. Wakje set two snap-backs on their trail to slow their pursuers. They didn't bother to try hiding their tracks. They couldn't, not with so many dnu. Better to find a place to stand and fight, he told them, or simply outride the trackers. Nori agreed. They rode swiftly, but she kept her mind open to the grey so that the sense of the wolf could guide her. It was like having an invisible compass inside her. She

knew which way to go. The only problem was that she sometimes struck off-trail to reach the wolf instead of following the
paths.

She could hear other wolves behind the yearling. It was the
pack of hungry ones she had sensed up on the lookout ridge.
She couldn't tell if they were drawn to Rishte or to her, but they
seemed to add to her tension. She kept looking ahead as if she
would see them. It only made her more nervous.

They crossed a swollen stream and spent ten minutes trampling the mud into a sinkhole. Wakje was pleased. By the time
they left, the sinkhole was deep and its surface smooth. If they
were lucky, it would mire the first rider who tried to cross it.

When a clump of pinmites flurried over Kettre and Hunter's
heads, Nori told them to ride ahead. While Kettre and Hunter
combed the mites out of their hair, she located the nest, gathered it carefully, and set it just above the trail, on the back side
of a tiny fork on an overhanging branch. When the Harumen
passed and disturbed the bough, the entire nest would burst.

At noon, Nori guessed they were a few hours ahead of the
Harumen. While the others made cold camp, she went into the
brush to find some clove bushes. It was early in the year, so not
many of them were ripe, but several had that translucent look
that spoke of spice. She broke three off. Hunter watched as she
carried them back to a steep part on the trail and set them
against a flattish rock, then bent a soft, new-growth twig back in
front of them. That was held back by a thin upright between that
twig and a low sweeping branch that hung over the trail. The
first dnu past would brush the branch aside, the twig would slip,
and the clove balls fall and burst.

She caught Hunter's grin and smiled without humor. "As long
as it's not raining when the balls burst, it will make their eyes
water for hours."

They rested the dnu for an hour, and Nori ate hungrily—too
hungrily. She coaxed Rishte close enough to take some jerky,
but her stomach stayed cramped after she'd eaten, and it wasn't
until she met the yearling's eyes that she realized it was the
sense of the other pack in the hills. The Grey Ones were hunting, tracking some eerin, but the grazers had moved swiftly, dis-

turbed by so many riders. The wolves were turning south, back toward smaller prey.

Two hours later, on the outside edge of a steep trail, Nori found the trail washed out and the earth crumbling into a rocky stream below. They had to backtrack quickly and work their way farther east. They lost what time they had gained. Payne confirmed this when he caught a glimpse of movement one hill back.

Hunter led his dnu up beside Wakje's as they quickly watered their mounts at a small pond. He glanced back at Leanna and murmured to Wakje, "They've got to be close by now."

"They'd have seen where we backtracked," the ex-raider agreed.

On his other side, Fentris tucked a tear in his sleeve up under the edge of his jerkin. If they didn't get to a wider trail, he'd be dressed in rags soon. He glanced at The Brother's clothes. He should have worn heavier leather. "Why doesn't the wolfwalker muddy the trail?" he asked Wakje. "Make it look as if we've gone in different directions?"

The older man raised one cold eyebrow. "All our tracks are different. We'd have to split up for real to make that work, and that means one group takes the brunt of the Harumen."

"But the Harumen would split up also."

"No." He took up his reins. "They'd follow the group that has what they want."

Fentris glanced at Hunter and said softly, "The question is, which of us do they want?"

Hunter's hand itched to touch his paper belt. "We could switch dnu."

Wakje snorted. "First time you peed, their tracker would know."

Fentris looked startled. "Excuse me?"

Payne hid a grin. "Women don't stand," he explained as he led his dnu past.

They rode another hour at a hard pace. Nori looked wistfully at two clumps of bluebells and their ripening seeds. She mock-whimpered as she caught a glimpse of a thick patch of ali herbs between the trees, and then passed up a patch of roostertail.

Payne grinned at her back. He could almost hear her cursing their pace.

By the time Nori pulled up for the next resting spot, Fentris had been branch-whipped a dozen times until his cheek was cut twice and his arms marked by welts. His fancy shirt was in ribbons, and he was now wearing one of Payne's jerkins. His hands, which might have been callused for swordfighting, weren't used to such long hours grasping rough branches and being stung with sap. He sported four blisters the size of Wakje's thumbnails.

Hunter had fared little better. His jaw was scraped where a rough branch had whipped back, and his calf had a bruise the size of his fist. He pulled a twig out of his war cap, yanked a fern from his stirrup, and muttered a city curse.

"Nori?" Payne asked softly as she studied the trail fork.

"We're too far west," she answered worriedly. "We need to stay away from the cliffs." As if there were any land in Ariye that didn't have ridges and canyons, draws and folds of mountainous hills. She glanced at the trees. They were shifting into stands of heavy evergreens, the kind that dug their roots deep into rocky ground and clung where lighter trees washed away. It wasn't a good sign.

"There's Loblolly Trail," he suggested. "The lower loop leads back toward one of the main trails to Willow Road."

"We're already fourteen or fifteen kays from the road, and Loblolly doesn't curve away from the gullies until after it goes down through three canyon swamps. It would slow us down like snails in dry sand. If it rains, we'll be trapped in there for days. Even the ring-runners avoid it in spring. And—" She lowered her voice. "—Rishte refuses to go there."

Plague. She didn't have to say it now. "Is he close enough to find us a better way?"

"No. He's uneasy, though, and it's getting worse."

"The Harumen?"

"Perhaps." With the Harumen close behind them, and Nori growing more anxious about their direction, she didn't blame the wolf for dwelling on the hunters. She stretched toward the yearling. When he snarled at the fork, she looked back on the trail, then turned left.

Two kays later, she realized she must have misinterpreted his sending. The wolf had pulled in, closer to the group, until Nori glimpsed him almost continuously. His voice was a constant stream of almost-impressions, like a set of extra senses in the back of her head that were never quite clear. Smells, movements that weren't there when she looked. Yellow-black shadows that distorted what she saw. Itches she couldn't scratch. She found herself shifting awkwardly in the saddle, as if she wanted to run, not ride, and move at a faster pace. She had to shake herself to set aside the growls that filled her mind with the tension of being hunted. When a pair of bluewings exploded out of the brush in front of her, she jumped and almost unseated herself.

"Dammit," she cursed. She pulled up and soothed her dnu.

Danger, the wolf seemed to growl at her.

I already know that, she muttered under her breath. It's on our heels like clay. She tried to focus her thoughts. "How close?"

He sent back an impression of intensity, hunger, of hunting.

"Harumen." She looked over her shoulder. The muggy spring sun was shafting down between the heavy, puffy clouds, and now shot low through the trees. It was getting on toward evening, and her riding beast stamped its feet impatiently. It could smell water up ahead. "Easy, easy," she murmured. Her nostrils flared as she took in the smells. She frowned. The predators would be stirring soon for their evening meals, and if she wasn't careful, she could find her party caught between two sets of fangs.

Behind her, Fentris asked softly, "Wolfwalker?"

She held up her hand to silence him. Still, she heard nothing behind them.

"Let's pick up the pace," she ordered flatly.

In her mind, Rishte growled, and she sent him a mental thanks. He snarled more loudly as she shifted into a smooth trot. She tried to soothe him, but he seemed to bare his mental teeth. He wanted her to leave the group, but she wasn't obeying. Instead, she headed for the stream at a canter.

The rushing stream muted the sounds of the dnu. The scent of water and the mud of the streambank masked other, more subtle odors. With weak light filtering through the breeze, the leaves were in constant motion, making the land deceptive even to one who was used to the forest's motion. Nori looked back one more time.

And the first clawed beast flowed out like a red-brown net from the depths of a massive root-ball. Her dnu half reared, but paws caught it on the shoulder, and the riding beast screamed. The forest seemed to erupt. Nori yanked her dnu up, but its foreleg snapped, and it shrieked, then screamed again as the first badgerbear ripped its thigh.

Run. Dodge! Danger—

A second badgerbear tore out of the brush. Payne yelled, and Fentris's dnu bucked and corkscrewed back from the second beast. The badgerbear went for its belly, slashing into flesh.

Blood. Hot acid. Strike, bite—

Nori jerked her leg up as black claws slashed through the cinch strap. The saddle started to slip. She grabbed her bow, tried for her quiver, and kicked off desperately, but there was no purchase on the loose leather. For an instant, she was face-to-face with a small badgerbear. She jabbed instinctively with the bow. The beast's teeth snapped on air. Then she kicked free and landed hard on her shoulder under the hooves. The youngling staggered as the dnu kicked it. It jerked back and swiped at the bony leg, and Nori scrambled away.

Payne's dnu tried to bolt. Hunter's mount spooked and slammed into a tree, tangling in the roots. It bucked and shrieked as he fought it. Fentris's dnu twisted, spun, kicked out, and sprayed blood across the crumpled brush. Leanna screamed at Wakje to shoot, shoot, but the ex-raider held his fire. There were two adult badgerbears, not just the cub; his war bolts wouldn't kill them, just enrage them to greater violence. They'd take the dnu before the humans if Nori could get away.

Hunter was down, shoving quickly away through the brush, holding his bow up over his head. Fentris was still in the saddle. The slim man slashed at the badgerbear, but it was like trying to hold water and hack it. The beast wasn't there when he cut. Another paw raked his dnu. The creature bolted. Fentris clung for an instant, saw the rock pile ahead, and hauled hard on the reins.

He barely missed Nori. She scrambled to her feet, felt the hot sense of beast, and jerked as a war bolt slashed past. She whipped around. An adult was almost on her. But the badgerbear stuttered as Hunter's second bolt caught it in the back.

"Nori, run," he shouted. The beast twisted and clawed at its back. The bolt snapped off, and the creature lunged forward. The wolfwalker plunged off-trail. She dodged around a deadfall, took two steps, and slammed into a log masked by the ferns. She vaulted it blindly and landed half on ground, half in the soft hole on the other side. For a moment, the badgerbear hung over the log, snarling down at her face. Then it whirled and screamed its hunting cry as a third bolt ripped its neck.

Wakje aimed again. He was on one knee, coldly clear: Draw, nock, wait, wait, *there*, when it turned toward Nori. Draw, nock, wait—He shifted, then released, caught the adult in the side. The beast finally whirled and charged back.

Fentris's bloody dnu actually leaped toward the wounded badgerbear as the man forced it away from the rocks. The adult opened the dnu's second belly as it charged. Thin legs wavered. Fentris felt his mount start to go down. He kicked frantically out of the saddle. Black claws cut leather where his leg had been, and he landed hard in the tangled deadfall, gasped in shock. Then he was ripping at the branches, crushing, snapping them like twigs as he tried to get away from the beasts. The badgerbear didn't notice. It had swarmed on his dnu like a blanket and tore at its flesh and neck. Nori grabbed the Tamrani by the arm and hauled him out of the brush.

"Nori," Payne yelled urgently. His dnu was stuck like a dog on a spit, a branch jammed through its cinch. One of the badgerbears had seen him and now changed direction abruptly. *Nori*—

Nori saw the beast turn toward her brother. She didn't stop to think. She let go of Fentris, only vaguely registering the fact that he fell as if she'd thrown him, and ran back to the thick, fallen log. She vaulted on top of it and threw out her arms. "Ayuh-chuh-chuh," she roared. "Ayuh-chuh-chuh."

All three badgerbears whipped around. She screamed her challenge again, and the adults rose and thundered their challenge back, the young one's voice a thin cry beneath them. They began to flow toward Nori. Payne spurred his dnu viciously. The branch snapped off, and he leapt the creature away. "Nori, run—" he yelled over his shoulder.

Go, Go! she screamed back. She didn't know it was in her head. *"Ayuh-chuh-chuh,"* she roared again as the badgerbear rippled around the dnu.

Kettre turned and slapped her bow down on Leanna's mount. The dnu spooked down the trail. Wakje leapt toward Payne as he passed. The older man landed on a boulder, launched himself, and grabbed the young man's arm. Payne slung his uncle up behind him, and they both dug their heels in. The dnu raced away like fire.

Nori roared her challenge one more time, got a glimpse of Hunter off to the left and Payne disappearing into the trees. She jumped off the log and fled. Fentris was still standing, half bent where she'd left him, and she caught his arm in a vise. "Are you alright?" she demanded.

He staggered up. "Good enough. Go!"

She dragged him after her. Behind, the red-brown beasts paused as she left the kill to them. One turned and gave a last swipe at Fentris's shuddering dnu. It opened up like a coin purse, and the badgerbear dug into pink guts. The cub rushed in, was slammed aside by a large paw. It swarmed toward the other beast and was thrown back by its father. It shrieked its small fury back. The adults kicked at it irritably, and the small beast grunted, caught another scent, and flowed away toward the deadfall.

Moons, moons, Nori cursed under her breath as she ran. What had she done? There were only four true predators in the forest—worlags, poolah, bihwadi, and badgerbears—and she knew them all, how to see them on the hunt, how to hear them approach, how to feel almost all of them. She'd never before been so stupid as to walk into a trap. Oh, aye, Rishte had warned her, but she'd been so sure she could interpret the grey, so sure she could keep them ahead of the Harumen and bring them all to safety. She'd always wondered how other scouts got caught like this. Now she knew. She'd been so worried about the Harumen, and so enamored with the bond, that she'd forgotten to use her own eyes. Now they were split up, on foot, and on the run. With the Haruman tracker so close behind, she'd just given them up like gold to a hungry beggar.

She used her bow like a machete, smashing through the brambles. Twiggy branches snapped, crushed leaves released their odors. Stalks of blackthorn and greendup clawed at their ankles. There was a game trail somewhere ahead, and Nori thrust almost blindly toward the grey. Her ears were full of the sounds of eating. Fentris faltered, and she snarled, "Hurry."

"Keep going," he snapped back. "I'm alright."

Wolfwalker, the hunter—

I know, she hurled at the wolf. Gods, she was an idiot. Hunters: not Harumen, but badgerbears. She risked a glance over her shoulder, tripped on a root and barely caught her balance. This time, she didn't mistake the grey. There was something red-brown behind them. She yanked free of a bramble and started to run.

Fentris stumbled behind her. "What is it?" he asked urgently.

"There's one in the brush behind us."

"Badgerbear?"

"Don't stop." She jumped a tiny seep and threw up her bow and an arm to ward off the brush that grew thickly on the other side. A cloud of gnats released. She batted at them and plunged through the waist-high bushes. Payne and the others were away down the trail; Hunter was somewhere nearby. If she and Fentris could get to a ridge, they could meet up with Hunter and combine their weapons. Then they could travel together to get back to Payne, make sure he was alright.

Fentris cursed under his breath, jumped the seep, and went to his knee on the other side as he slipped on her muddy prints. He got awkwardly to his feet only to find Nori grabbing his arm again and yanking him up.

"Hurry," she snarled. "It's closing."

They ducked under brush and then shoved through twiggy branches that stuck out from the trees like atrophied limbs. They left white scars where they stripped off tender bark. Birds burst up and away, and something large fled through the undergrowth. Small stands of ferns hid the woodrast that Rishte smelled. She thought she saw a clear line through the trees, one that might be a wider trail, and she sped up, but Rishte howled in her head. The danger sense was sharp as a talon. *I know,* she sent back. *We need rocks, a cliff, something to climb.*

He seemed to understand. He shifted and pulled farther right. She changed direction abruptly.

Fentris was caught off-guard. "What is it?" he managed.

"Watch out. Stay clear of the redstick. We've got a chance now." She called mentally, *Find Hunterhunterhunter. Bring him to me at the cliff.* She glanced back. Fentris stumbled again. "Be careful," she snarled.

He caught her sleeve. "Black Wolf, I've been bleeding."

She whirled. Her gaze dropped to his leg. Blood was staining his fingers, and it marked the grass by his leg.

"Damn you," she breathed. "You said you were okay."

He stiffened. "I can still run."

On top of her ignorance and arrogance, Tamrani pride would kill them all. "Dammit, it's not about running." Her violet eyes flashed with fury. "It's about leaving a fresh blood trail." Her gaze jerked past him to the crushed growth. She could barely see the stains, but to a badgerbear they would be glowing. She could have bound the wound. She could have carried him to break the blood trail. "Gods." She looked around desperately. She had three knives and a bow, but no hunting bolts. Fentris had his sword, but no bow or bolts. Against Harumen who might want them alive, it was a pitiful arsenal. Against badger-bears, with their ferocious speed and claws as long as her finger, it was almost suicide.

They'd been so lucky. They'd been breaking trail, really, for the Harumen ever since they took to the forest. They'd had to move carefully to avoid spring poolah and worlags. They'd had to stop for supplies, find crossings for runoff streams, backtrack that washed-out trail on the ridge. Even with all that, they'd managed to stay ahead. One mistake—her mistake—and they were scattered like bloody chaff. The Harumen could now run them down like well-culled, three-legged eerin. Her stomach clenched. Even if it was Nori or Hunter the Harumen wanted, they wouldn't leave Payne alive.

Rishte growled. With the other wolves strengthening his voice, she could almost see the trail through his eyes. *I know,* she hurled back. Hunter was somewhere behind to the right. He'd seen her go off her dnu; he knew she had no arrows, but there was no way he would get there in time.

"This way," she snapped at Fentris. "Hurry."

He glanced over his shoulder. "Black Wolf—"

"Hurry up!" She started to run. "We've got to get to a clear spot."

Twigs snapped audibly behind them, and her heart stuttered. *Wolfwalker,* Rishte howled.

We're coming, she cried to the wolf. She burst out into a tiny clearing where the brush was mostly grass and only thigh-deep. "Here," she said quickly. She ran to the other edge of the clearing, turned, and scanned it at a glance. It was six or eight meters across, bordered by scarred trunks whose lower branches had been broken off long ago. Claw marks had left dark streaks in the bark where the sap had become a breeding ground for black fungi. The grass was all wispy and new. The only dried stalks she could see lay on the ground, scattered like a loose bed beneath the light growth. "Oh, moons," she breathed. It was a bedding place for badgerbears. They would know it from the year before.

Rishte slunk beside her and stared at Fentris, then at the brush. *Blood, fresh blood. The hunter breathes. Too close, too close, wolfwalker.*

"We have to face it here," she returned.

"Black Wolf?" Fentris clutched his leg and tried to catch his breath.

She snarled, shook her head, and re-formed the words at him. "Get ready."

"For what?" He broke off and stared past her, and she knew Rishte was there.

"To kill it." She ran back to him, stooped and squeezed his leg at the wound site.

He almost hit her. "Shit on a stickbeast—"

"Shut up," she snarled, shoving his hands away. She smeared the blood around on the grass, then along a sloppy path toward the other side of the clearing. "How good are you with that sword?"

"Good enough," he snapped. He straightened up.

"This isn't pride, Tamrani," she shot back. "This is life and death, and we might have one minute to decide." And it was her own damn fault. Her hands itched to snatch the blade. She forced herself to ask, "Do I get the sword or do you?"

"No offense, Wolfwalker, but I'm much better than you."

Rishte snarled. Nori agreed with the wolf. "How much better?" she demanded.

Brush cracked back on the trail, and Fentris spoke quickly. "In swordsmanship, I'm fifth rank, Dangu style, third rank Abis, third rank Cansi. I've trained six years with Master Edon, three years with—"

She cut him off and pointed at his leg. "And with that?"

He said flatly, "I'm still very, very good."

"I pray, by the moons, that you're right. Have you killed?"

"Men, yes. Badgerbears, no."

"Then aim for its heart or its spine." She jammed her bow up in the branches and drew her long knife. "The best we can hope is to bleed it out before it tears us apart, or paralyze it before it can call its parents. Move over there and stay behind me." She pointed with the long blade and kept her eyes on the brush. "And try not to bleed when you move. It will follow the blood trail, not you." She unsnapped the guard for her hunting knife and drew the sharp, curved blade as he stepped past her carefully. "Stand still in place. Don't move, don't breathe. Watch and wait. When I turn it away from you, strike."

"Black Wolf—"

"Be quiet. For gods' sake, be quiet." She stared at the edge of the wavering grass. Her voice was a whisper. "It's here."

XXXV

Make your bargain with the moons,
Run the silver trail;
Make your bargain with the wolves,
Run the black, blood trail.

—Randonnen saying

The badgerbear was a mottled shifting of red and brown. A subtle movement that nudged aside the broken ferns and flowed, rather than stalked up the slope. It reached the edge of the clearing, licked the bloody grass, and raised its flattened head like a snake. The smooth drums that covered its ear bones were pulsing with eagerness. The age marks on its head were small and piggish, barely red enough to see, but they seemed to widen as the beast's fur flared and shifted. The maw was beginning to open, and the camouflaged eyes above its teeth flicked toward the wolfwalker.

It could hear her breathing.

She sucked air in slowly and fingered her knife.

It raised up another handspan. She could see the fur shift and ripple along its length. The maw was half ringed with teeth, thinner than a poolah's mouth, but with longer fangs. The creature's paws spread, and the claws slid out. They were black and smooth, unnicked by time and hunting. The detail stuck in her mind.

Danger, danger, run. The wolf's voice was a blinding snarl.

She found her voice and began the hum. The badgerbear froze. Its eardrums pulsed as it located her, and it flowed forward another meter.

Rishte's bristle stiffened like wood. He edged back. Nori sent him a shaft of approval, and he clawed at the inside of her mind. *Danger, death. Run, wolfwalker. Quickly.*

She shook her head, not realizing that the motion was physical until the badgerbear keyed in to it. She saw the blur of the beast, and screamed as she threw up her arms. "Aiyu-chuh-chuh."

The beast froze midair and landed short, four meters before her. Then it lunged up on its hind legs. The teeth in its maw seemed to grow in length as its lips retracted slowly.

Nori's vision blurred. She screamed again, *"Aiyu-chuh-chuh—"*

The youngling seemed to compress. Then it leapt like flight.

She jumped left, ducked her head, and struck instinctively with both blades. Rishte felt her sudden fear. He leapt, fangs bared. He closed on fur and yanked his head, ripping deep into badgerbear muscle. The badgerbear roared. Fentris lunged. Nori felt the claws start to rip at her shoulders. She stabbed in with both hands. The left blade sank deep. She slashed back with the other and jerked the deep blade down. The beast turned on her, and she stumbled back. Its maw was open and claws slashed as she cut, slashed, stabbed. Claws, claws caught on the laces of her jerkin and yanked her up and sideways as she started to fall. Black claws tore through leather. She felt the bite of the bear, and then it engulfed her. Teeth pressed into her stomach. She hit the ground, her face smothered in fur. It trapped her arm, her legs. She stabbed blindly with the hunting knife, wild beneath its weight. She bit at the fur. It was grey, a grey beast with white-black eyes. Black ears, black age marks, black blood—

There were insects, mosquitoes, things in her ears. She kicked out as her legs were freed. Her mind was snarling and snapping, and she howled as she got a breath. Then she heaved the beast off and lunged after it like a wolf, stabbing into its body. Right, left, off-rhythm, stabbing, cutting deep, ripping down and hot blood and she slashed through gums and teeth caught on her wrist and skin tore and blood, hot blood.

"Noriana—" Fentris's fingers dug into her shoulders like spikes. Slender as he was, he yanked her up by her shoulder and belt and threw her bodily away from the carcass. Her long knife caught the edge of his sleeve and cut it, and he cursed as she hit the ground and rolled back to her feet so smoothly he might have helped her do it.

He stepped in front of her, between her and the beast. "Stop, stop it," he yelled. "It's dead."

She didn't register the words. Instead, she went past him as if he wasn't even there. One moment, she was in front of him, her nose wrinkled and her lips curled back until her teeth were fully bared. Then he felt the light touch of her hand and hip as she lunged, and she simply shifted past him. Her violet-grey eyes weren't quite human, and the sound that came from her lips as she dropped to the carcass was the snarling of a wolf. She stabbed the badgerbear again, again, her blades going in unopposed. She was breathing far too quickly.

Fentris whirled, but when he stepped toward her, she turned her head and snarled at him so viciously that he stumbled to a stop. Beside her, Rishte yanked at the flesh, opening part of the gut. The wolf barely glanced at him before turning back to the carcass. Nori sucked in a breath, gagged, turned her head, and spit out fur. Her fist clenched on the handle of the long knife.

Fentris swallowed and touched his sleeve where she'd cut him. The thin line was barely bleeding, but he knew it could have been worse. "Black Wolf?" He cleared his throat. "Noriana, it's over. It's dead."

But Rishte sang in her head. *Fresh, dead. Hot meat, fresh. The hunt, the hunt!* He tore at the gut where Nori's knife had pierced flesh and released the scent of the internal organs. It was a hot, blood-and-bile-laced sensation, and Nori sucked air and spit again. She shivered. There were other wolves nearby. They were coming, drawn by her unconscious projection into the packsong. The weight of them behind Rishte filled her mind with a sea of grey snarls that crawled on the inside of her skull. She could hear them, could almost see them. Her vision was all wrong.

She blinked, shook her head, and realized her hands were so clenched on her knives that her knuckles had gone white. "Gods," she managed.

"MaDione?" the Tamrani said more sharply.

She shook her head again, trying to make sense of his words.

She could still feel the tips of the claws that had pierced her back, but the badgerbear was young, and it had made only small punctures, blunted by her jerkin. The blood was sticky across her back, but there wasn't much of it, for all that the taste of it was in her mouth. She got to her feet shakily. It was Rishte's tongue she tasted, and she tried to shut him out. He paused and snarled at her, and she had to close her eyes. *Back off, back off,* she growled back. *I can't have you in me now.*

Hunger, hungry, he growled.

Deliberately, she formed the words, but they came out more like snarls. Eat, then. Fill your belly. There's time for that, at least.

He turned back to the dead beast eagerly. When he dragged a strand of something ugly out of one of the punctures, Nori turned away. She was shaking, and her vision wasn't yet right. She needed to . . . needed to tear at the badgerbear, taste it again.

Fentris moved around to the other side of the beast. His sword had been wrenched out of his hand when he'd cut deeply into the spine, and the bones had locked around the steel. He muttered a curse and worked it free, then wiped it carefully on the grass. He gave Nori a wary look as he slid it back in its scabbard. "Black Wolf," he started. Then, harder, "Black Wolf, shouldn't we go?"

Nori shook her head in answer, but it was a shaggy motion. She closed her eyes and scrunched up her face, then rolled her neck and shoulders until she felt her own muscles, not those of the wolf. "No," she managed. She opened her eyes and looked at the wary Tamrani. "If the adults had heard this, they'd have been here by now. They'll be occupied for hours with the dnu. We'll wait for Hunter."

"He's here?" Fentris looked around quickly.

She nodded shakily down the slope. "He's coming up now."

Carefully, she set her hunting blade in the grass. Then she wiped her longknife on a handful of leaves, but the blood was already drying. She had to spit and work the leaves over the blade before she could put it away. Then she took her hunting knife, nudged the wolf aside, and started to skin the beast.

Fentris stared at her. "What are you doing?"

She jammed two fingers into one of the slits she'd made and slid the blade between them. "I want the fur." She cut the pelt back in a long line toward the abdomen. She left the inner membrane as intact as she could, and had to snarl at Rishte when he tried to tear through it again. *Not yet,* she snapped.

"Hmm, Wolfwalker, I know this is your wilderness and all, but it seems to me that there might be better times to take a fur."

"It's not for me," she returned sharply. "It's for the Harumen." Her hands were bloody, and she had to grip the knife sharply to cut down the insides of the legs. *Just a minute,* she snarled at the wolf. She cut away a large, bloody chunk of haunch, and the Grey One almost took off her fingers when he yanked it from her grip. By the time she'd freed the fur of both rear legs, Hunter was at the edge of the clearing.

He took one look at Nori's bloody arms, another long look at the carcass. "What the hell happened here?"

"My fault," Fentris said flatly. "I left blood on the trail."

Hunter's expression closed, and his cold green eyes seemed to pierce the other man. Nori glanced at him. "And mine," she told him. "I didn't notice he'd been injured." She went back to work on the carcass and explained tersely before he could ask, "I'm taking the pelt. We can use it against the Harumen. We need every advantage now." If they hadn't run into that trap, she'd have tried to hunt something like this down herself, once the Harumen got closer.

Hunter reached for his hunting knife, but its leather hanger was torn and the blade was gone. Fentris silently handed him his own knife, and Hunter tried not to snort at the patterned steel and inlaid handle. The blade was still master-sharpened and unscratched, and Fentris almost winced as Hunter stropped it twice on his trousers to wipe off any oil. But when he started to squat beside the wolfwalker, she snarled at him and refused to shift over. Carefully, he eased back. He kept his voice calm. "Use the pelt how?" he asked instead.

She reached in through the abdomen to cut out the tissue around the glands inside the anal cavity, and Fentris looked quickly away. "Tied to a bent-back on a thread-release." Her voice was still too much of a growl, and she steadied it. She didn't touch the glands with her knife. Instead, she took a leaf from the pile nearby, and used one to pinch each gland shut, so she could pull it gently out and set it carefully on the ground. She had to force herself to add, "It will spook their dnu. It might even put some of them afoot like us."

She rolled the pelt up against the spine of the beast, then grabbed its knees and heaved it onto its other side. The head stayed where it was, the neck twisted limply. The ribs sagged where they had supported the guts. All three tongues tangled in the sunken circle of fangs, and the slashed gums drained blood and saliva onto crushed grass. There was something obscene about it. Fentris swallowed again but, with some sort of horri- fied fascination, couldn't look away.

The wolfwalker had worked the pelt up to the shoulders when both she and Rishte stiffened. Hunter whipped to his feet, and Fentris slid out his sword. "Stay still," Nori snapped at both.

She crouched over the carcass and stared into the brush. She could hear it now in her own ears, the quieting of birds just over there, the stopping of the insects that then started up again as the somethings, the creatures, passed. A moment later, the first wolf slunk into view. Rishte growled. Then the pack leader slipped into the clearing, to the left, forcing Nori to turn. He bristled at her as the other wolves moved in then and made a half circle around the carcass. Two of them licked their teeth.

Slowly, Nori straightened. She could almost hear the quick- ened heartbeats in Fentris's and Hunter's chests. Her own was pounding like hooves on a hard, stone road. Her lips curled back as she fingered the knife.

The pack leader growled. *Back away. Ours now. Back away.*

She didn't have to meet the wild wolf's eyes to hear his in- tent. Rishte started forward and she snapped, *Back.* He froze, startled. She glared at the pack leader. *My kill. Mine first. You wait.*

Golden eyes gleamed as they took in the humans. *Weak pack.* He bared his fangs. *Hungry. Our kill.*

Nori's lips curled into a feral smile. *My kill. Mine first, and I am well armed. Do not challenge me.*

Human. Hungryhungry pack. We take the beast now.

"No." All eight wolves flinched at the spoken word. Rishte growled low, and automatically Nori hushed him. *Twenty minutes for me to finish, and Rishte gets first meat. Then the beast is yours.*

Ours then. Our meat, our pack.

Aye.

The male wolf licked white fangs and considered that. Nori noted the broken tooth in front, the scar that split one ear where he had fought another wolf in the past. She could feel the strength in his voice from the years he had led. He had seen humans before, but had always avoided them. Now she stared him down.

Wolfwalker, he acknowledged.

"Aye," she said softly. She didn't turn her head, but she ordered the two Tamrani, "Stay where you are, make no threatening moves. I'll be done here in a few minutes." She waited till the pack leader sat. A minute later, the other wolves did also, and the wolfwalker turned back to the carcass. Rishte didn't lower his head. She snarled at him, and he finally dropped his head and began tearing at the haunch. Around them, the other wolves watched. They looked as patient as poolah, but Nori could feel the edge in them. They were poised, ready to leap forward when the pack leader gave the signal. They would fight for the meat if she let them. She looked up every few seconds to meet the male's gaze and let him feel the taint in her mind. It made the wolf more wary.

She worked the pelt off over the skull. Then she rolled it up, blood-side out, to keep the mites from jumping from fur to her. Finally, she stood and looked at Fentris. "Let me have your shirt?"

Quickly, he shrugged out of his jerkin and stripped off his shirt. He was putting his jerkin on again when he realized what she intended. "Wait, what are you—"

Hunter snorted a laugh. She had tied the sleeves around the bundle, turning his shirt into a makeshift bag. The blood had already stained the fine cloth. Nori merely slung it onto her shoulder, then looked at Rishte. He had torn and glulped about half the meat from the haunch, and she waited patiently till he finished. Then she called him softly in her mind.

He looked up at her. *Wolfwalker.* There was a new note in his voice, and he didn't argue when she gestured for him to leave with the Tamrani. Instead, he trotted past the two men, then through the other wolf pack, bristling only slightly.

Nori looked into the gaze of the pack leader one more time. The Grey One snarled in response, then stalked forward and, ignoring her, began tearing at the carcass. The other wolves shied away as she walked through them after the Tamrani, but they lunged eagerly forward as she cleared away from the badger-bear. She glanced back only once. They were growling over the guts and limbs, eating as fast as they could.

XXXVI

Knife in hand
Wolf in mind

—Randonnen saying

Payne had seen Nori throw herself into the trees, dragging Fentris with her. He had no time for more. When his dnu panicked, he could only hunch low on the neck and pray he could stay in the saddle. Wakje clung behind him, the man's face tucked into Payne's back to protect his eyes as the forest clawed at their limbs. Trunks of bent trees, low boughs slammed their shoulders, calves and knees. One stirrup caught on a branch that whipped back with the dnu, then shattered across Payne's ankle hard enough to bruise it through his boot. Then the dnu hit a stand of greendup and, with the double weight of two men, floundered like a deer in a mud hole. "Easy," Payne commanded sharply. He had already begun pulling back on the reins, but the dnu was mindless. It felt the pressure on its face and started to rear.

Wakje went off and landed hard, barely missed by the hooves. Payne pressed his knees in and pulled firmly down on the dnu's neck. Its sides were heaving and its eyes were wild, but after a minute it came to a halt. "Easy, easy," he murmured. He didn't dismount. Greendup was hard enough to wade through on a dnu. On foot it was worse than brambles.

Carefully, he eased the riding beast back until one of its hooves tangled. Then he dismounted carefully, kept his hands on its trembling body to soothe it, and peeled the vines from its leg. He stood for a moment listening. He couldn't hear Kettre, but she had to be nearby with Leanna. He tried not to curse as

436

he caught sight of Wakje wading toward him. Nori—gods only knew where she was. The two Tamrani were with her, that was something, but it would take time for her to circle to meet them, time the Harumen wouldn't have to take.

Something crackled in the brush to the left, and both men stiffened. Then an alder bird cried out softly. Payne let his breath out in relief. Wakje waited till the cry came again, then returned it three times. A few minutes later, they led the dnu free of the rest of the greendup stand.

At first, they didn't see Kettre. Then she and Leanna stood. Wakje nodded his approval. The two women had crouched and forced their dnu down to the ground to stay out of sight till they knew him. He gave them a quick once-over as they met up. Kettre was solid, her weapons ready, but he could see the fear in Leanna's eyes. "Alright?" he asked sharply. The girl stiffened. She threw her loose braid back over her shoulder and nodded tersely. "Fine."

Kettre exchanged a wry look with Payne. Pride had always been one of the best and simplest goads. She kept her voice low. "What about Nori?"

Payne sobered. "We cut left. She went off to the right. She could be anywhere." He squinted ahead, but the brush was thick even outside the greendup stand, and he couldn't see clearly more than thirty or forty meters in any one direction. "High ground is that way," he pointed. "She'll expect to meet there."

Wakje nodded. He looked back along their trail. They had crushed brush in long swaths where their dnu had smashed through the forest. The tangled mass was the obvious work of a panicked creature—no eerin or deer would go into such a patch unless driven by a predator. They needed to regain the trail, get to a point where they could see far enough behind them.

Payne's gaze sharpened. Three birds flew abruptly up in the distance.

"I see it," Wakje said flatly. The Harumen had found them.

Kettre murmured, "We're short a dnu for running."

The ex-raider didn't answer. He simply took the reins to Leanna's dnu and motioned the girl up behind Kettre. The woman hesitated, but didn't argue. Weight was everything, and the ex-raider weighed as much as she and Leanna together.

They forced their way quickly through the thick growth. Twigs snapped, ferns broke, waxy leaves split and bled. Animals fled from their path, and a pair of jackbraws called the warning raucously as they trampled too near a nest.

It was Payne who first saw the party behind them. He'd been scanning the forest constantly, looking for signs of Nori when he caught a glimpse of movement too high up for a predator. It was a hat, and he took a second to verify it. Then he whistled low and sharp.

Wakje looked back and caught the jerk of Payne's head. They had regained the trail barely four minutes before, and after doing the tick dance to shake off the forest mites had spurred their dnu to a quick trot. Now the ex-raider pulled up and studied the forest. The skyline had the thinness of a sharp drop-off, and Payne felt a chill. High ground, yes, but Nori had told him to avoid the deep ravines. "We're only a kay from the canyons."

"No choice," Wakje snapped back. They'd have cover among the rocks and first choice of high ground. When the wolfwalker found them, she and the Tamrani could flank the Harumen or come up behind them and put the group in a crossfire.

"What about Nori—" Kettre snapped.

"She'll find us," Payne threw back. "Run for it." Then he leaned low over his dnu and kicked it into a canter.

Behind them, they heard the first horn.

*

Nori halted abruptly on the trail.

Fentris almost ran up on her. "What is it?" he demanded.

"Horns. The Harumen have seen them." They were close enough to Payne not to worry about being subtle. She looked to where Rishte had loped ahead. "Hurry," she told them. "They're near the ravines."

"Is that a problem?" Hunter asked sharply.

"No," she said shortly. Gods, Payne, don't climb down.

But the fear was back in her eyes, and Hunter started to ask, "Black Wolf?"

She shook her head. "It's nothing. Let's go." She broke into a run.

He steadied his bow and quiver. Fentris's sword was useless at a distance, and Hunter himself had only seven bolts left. What Nori expected them to do against moons only knew how many Harumen . . . He swore under his breath. But he had seen the tightness in Nori's face, and as Fentris stumbled in front of him, he matched Nori's pace without question.

*

Payne's dnu pounded over the trail. Small, slick rises slowed him down, and new growth tangled the trail. He guided the beast around massive boulders and ducked broken branches that hung head-high, while behind them, the Harumen came into view. He risked a glance back, caught the blank intensity in Kettre's expression and the top of Leanna's head as the girl tucked in behind the woman. Wakje leaned so low on the saddle he was almost off his dnu.

Payne jumped his own beast over a deep puddle, skidded on the other side, and spurred the dnu back to a gallop. They were close to the ravines; he could see sky through the trees. For a moment the brush thickened. In the rear, Wakje saw the same thing. He whistled, low and sharp. Payne, keyed up like an overtight bow, obeyed blindly. He grabbed his weapons and dove off his dnu. When he hit, he rolled instantly under the ferns and wormed away on his belly and elbows. Leanna kicked free of Kettre, hit the ground after him and bounced, then scrambled into a root-ball.

Kettre gasped as she felt the girl kick free. She started to shout for her to hang on. Then she understood. She looked back, but her dnu had plunged on after Payne's, and the thick brush was already behind her. She'd been too slow. The Harumen could see her.

"Faster!" she yelled, as if at Payne. "They're almost on us." She didn't look back again.

*

Nori ripped through brush to get to the trail. Ahead, Rishte howled the hunt, and her senses seemed to sharpen. She could smell the broken leaves; she could clog her lungs with the odors of mud, but she tried to hold herself away. She had to see clearly to run.

Fentris struggled behind her, and she left it to Hunter to help him. She was focused ahead, on the horns, on her brother, on the thudding that seemed to beat in her ears with the pounding of hooves of dnu. She registered movement, the shift of creatures away, a bursting in the brush as an eerin startled and bounded away. The late-afternoon breeze was rising to a wind, and the day's warmth had leached away until the shadows were chill with sweat and fear. Payne, turn away, get away from the cliff. Moons help her to reach him in time.

*

Payne watched Kettre gallop past and cursed, cursed under his breath. He slid his bow into position and huddled so that he could leap to a crouch when the Harumen passed. He could hear the pounding now, the Harumen approaching. Five of them slammed past on the trail; they looked neither right nor left. Seconds later, the other six whipped by. Immediately he started squirming after them, staying low in the brush.

Ten meters, twenty. Wakje was working forward to the side. Leanna was somewhere behind him. None of them risked standing; the Harumen would have people watching for exactly that. Gods, careful was so slow. How long had it been? Ten minutes already? The Harumen were at the rim, moons alone knew what they were doing, but they weren't moving on.

There were few shadows to help Payne hide as he worked his way forward. The fragments of sky that he could see were half grey and half blue with that thick mugginess of spring, and he couldn't see the moons. He made enough noise that the forest remained silent to watch. He squinted past the dark perion shrubs, then around a massive root-ball. He froze at a glimpse of movement, but it was just a fern collapsing; the Harumen were not yet starting back. Kettre must have misled them enough. But his bones chilled as he heard her cry out. Then he heard her scream—

He scrambled to his feet and sprinted toward the rim, staying behind heavy trees. Wakje thrust up after him and high-jumped brush to catch him. Payne tripped, fell but didn't lose his bow, and leapt back to his feet. He could hear men talking now, arguing. He could hear dnu being trotted away.

The forest thinned but the tree trunks thickened where they got more light, making it easier to work his way forward. Brush scraggled out on the ravine rim. He caught sight of half a clouded sky, pieces of an open trail, and ragged coats of lichen, and then the Harumen. They had Kettre. He could see the blood on her temple and torn cloak. He brought up his bow as three men turned. Wakje's bolt was an instant behind him. Both arrows sank into the same heavy man, the one holding Kettre. Both Payne and Wakje dropped to their knees and shot again as the first man sagged, and the others brought up their weapons.

Payne dodged instinctively, and the first war bolt phuttered through the leaves he'd been sprinting past. He leapt, dove, rolled into a clear spot, and came up on one knee. He fired as he caught his breath. He missed. One dark-haired Harumen woman dodged into cover; the blond man went down with Wakje's bolt in his throat. The blond thrashed and tore at the bolt, but it was sunk all the way through his neck. The Haruman started choking. Three arms reached out and dragged the man behind the rocks. One arm jerked back as Payne's arrow caught it.

He cursed under his breath. Nine Harumen, and only two dead, and Kettre already down. Leanna wasn't armed except with a knife, and he had a half-empty quiver left of hunting bolts, not war bolts. Only Wakje was still armed for fighting. Payne studied the layout quickly. There were packs on the ground, and a fallen knife. The Harumen must have decided to stop and question Kettre rather than chase the riderless dnu. There were no dnu of their own, either. That would have been the sounds Payne heard. Someone had taken the dnu away from the rim to tether or corral them. There would be too much temptation for Wakje to spook them off the cliff and leave the raiders on foot. This far out in the wilderness in a hungry Ariyen spring, the Harumen would take no chances.

If they had to be caught against the cliff, they had chosen an excellent spot. The rim trail was well packed and curved along the ravine, and a few older trees leaned out like lookouts, clinging with shallow root-balls and ready to fall in the next storm. The boulders that tumbled down from the hills behind left a protected trail along the edge of the cliff all the way back to the forest. There was a seep for water, places to shelter from rain, even shade for the sun if it came out. It was perfect cover, and the Harumen were taking full advantage. It was no less than he expected. Not from men who didn't waste movement, shout commands like uncertain raiders, or expose themselves carelessly. In fact, nothing moved now except the chill breeze that cut the rim. They were waiting for Payne's group to break first.

Payne shifted carefully until he could see Kettre. The woman was half crumpled near the edge of the brush. The end of a war bolt poked out of her side, and her hand moved restlessly in the soft earth. Two fingers, then one. Then she grew still. He rose up a hair on his knee to see better—and dropped flat as a war bolt flew out of nowhere to rip through his sleeve. He hit on his belly, caught his breath, then began worming toward the rim. Behind him, he heard rustling and knew it was Leanna.

A low whistle came from his left, but Leanna ignored her uncle. The girl had seen Kettre and was trying to reach her. Payne cursed under his breath, but Wakje whistled again more sharply for Leanna to stay back. Finally, she grew still, but only for a moment. Then she began creeping forward again.

"Dammit," Payne breathed. Moonwormed girl thought she could play the hero. He caught a glimpse of a Haruman moving between trees and fired. This time he was lucky. The bolt caught the man on his calf, and the leg jerked back behind cover. As he shot, another man burst out of the trees and sprinted to the right. He missed that one, but Wakje clipped someone to the left. Dammit, he cursed under his breath. If the Harumen got away from the cliff, they could surround Payne and the others and take their time with the killing. And where the hell was Nori? He gave a low birdcall to Wakje. He waited till he heard the single soft trill in response. Then he started worming toward a log.

Leanna had other ideas. She could see Kettre, she could see the blood. If she just eased farther right, she should be able to creep up, perhaps even drag Kettre back into the forest. The girl's heart beat fast, and her hands shook, but she elbowed up to a fallen tree, slid over its rotting husk in the shelter of a large bush, and began wriggling through a patch of grassy vines. She didn't see how they pulled overhead, bending the branches down.

Far to the left, Wakje loosed another bolt, and a man cried out but cut himself off. The movement south ceased abruptly. Wakje shouted, "Got a bit of a standoff, looks like." Two war bolts sped in his direction, but he was already moving. They split leaves and earth, not flesh.

Someone shouted back, "I'd say we have the advantage. Your *chovas* is in our sights."

Wakje didn't answer, but a moment later he sent a shaft into the rocks and heard another man curse.

Leanna eased forward from behind a bush. Carefully she lifted the lowest branches. She could see the upper half of Kettre's body. The woman lay still. Blood seeped from her temple, soaking her hair, then dripping into the grass. The girl elbowed a handspan forward, then another—

And froze at a tiny rustling. Slowly, slowly she looked to the right. The war bolt with its wicked steel head was aimed right at her. The man holding the bowstring taut was expressionless and flat-eyed, just like the eyes of her father. It was Gretzell, one of the Sidisport *chovas,* and he gestured with the arrow. Eyes wide, she shook her head. He loosed the bolt. From bare meters away, it tore the earth between her outstretched hands. Leaves burst into her face; the shaft slid beneath her arm. She sucked in breath to scream but the man's flat eyes seemed to burn into hers, and he already had another bolt at the string. He gestured again with the arrow. This time, she obeyed.

*

Nori sprinted toward the ravine. She scrambled over boulders, banged her ankle again, then her calf as she slipped on slick rock. She muttered, then heard Fentris curse behind her. Hunter jumped the boulder entirely and landed hard on the ground.

"You'll break an ankle," she snarled over her shoulder.

"Not before you break our necks with this pace," he hurled back.

She spit out an oath. The wolf was far ahead, sliding through the brush as if he didn't notice the vines, the roots, the branches that whipped her face. He could feel her urgency, and even with his belly full it fed his eagerness. The hunt, the forest, his wolfwalker—he had everything he wanted. He snarled at her in his head to keep up. She snapped back, and he bared his teeth in a fearful joy.

He could smell the humans now. The breeze blew up over the edge of the cliff, and there was blood in the air, blood and dnu. The beasts were tethered nearby.

Behind her, Fentris stumbled again, and Hunter hauled him up by the arm until the other man shook him off. "Dammit," he cursed. "Let go."

"Be quiet," she snapped over her shoulder. "Quiet." She tore down their pace a fraction, then halted and dropped to her knees as the trees thinned abruptly. She'd caught a glimpse of dnu in a clearing, so the Harumen had to be close. Her chest was heaving, and she was breathing too fast. She drew back from the sense of the grey. Rishte howled, but she snarled back in her head, and the yearling crept back toward her.

She unslung the bloody pelt as Hunter drew down beside her. His jerkin showed blood at his shoulder, as if he'd torn his older wound. Fentris leaned against a tree trunk, his weight on one leg. She glanced at the slim man, watched him stiffen up, and nodded curtly at his determination. Then she unrolled the fur, rolled the soiled shirt into a ball, and stuffed the bloody garment under some leaves. "They're coming this way," she said harshly.

"All of them? Moonworms." Hunter started to nock his bow.

"No, two. Just two." Rishte smelled them. There was clove oil on one of them, on the man, but it wasn't Payne. She would have known. With the man was a female, one from Nori's pack. That meant Leanna or Kettre was hostage. She could try a straight-on attack to break the girl free, but it was the risky approach. And if it failed, the girl would still be a hostage. The Harumen would want something in exchange. Her scout book? Aye, they'd want that, but they'd want something more, too. Her gaze flicked to Hunter's belt. She shook out the badgerbear pelt. "Give me your laces."

Holding his bow in one hand, he yanked the laces from his jerkin with the other. "What are you going to do?"

"What I have to. Go that way," she motioned sharply along the cliff. "Don't let them get past you or get to their dnu."

He nodded and took off. Fentris shoved himself away from the tree and tried to follow suit. He took five steps before he could force himself back to a run. Then he found the mindless pace he'd learned so young and blanked his thoughts to the pain.

Wolfwalker, Rishte sang.

Her nose wrinkled at his eagerness. He could smell the rancid pelt in her hands, and his teeth bared, as if he would tear it away. "Back off," she snapped. "I need this." But her nose wrinkled like his. Gnats crawled on the edges of the skin, and more landed every moment. Gelbugs had wormed their way inside the bundle as she'd run, and they were already feasting on the patches of flesh left by the crudeness of her skinning. She snarled deep in her throat but forced herself to lay it out. Then she wrapped the pelt around herself and began to tie it on.

XXXVII

You can choose
The knife or the bow,
The sword or the stone,
But still you'll have to kill.

   —from *The Chevres Play,* traditional version

The trail petered out where the cliff had washed away, and the heavyset Haruman ran right out onto the overhang before he realized it had ended. He felt the ground tremble and staggered back onto more solid ground, dragging Leanna with him. He'd never liked the wilderness, and with one of the Wolven Guard in the woods, he expected a shaft in the back every second. Get the girl, get the dnu, hold the hostage clearly, and flank the Ariyens if he could. Had he been on the road, he'd already be done by now.

"Moonwormed trail bait," the Haruman cursed. "Where are the godsdamned dnu?" He could have sworn he'd led them straight this way to make camp and had tied them there by the grass. Maybe around those boulders. He ran toward them, hauling Leanna at his side. The cliff was tempting. The little bitch would break like a teacup when she hit the rocks below, but he might need her if—

The arrow that was meant for his back slashed past and broke on rock instead. He jerked his bow up and loosed his own bolt as he whirled. Leanna hit the ground hard, then cried out as the Haruman ground his boot down on her knee, trapping her in place. The man's bolt flew hard toward Hunter.

The Tamrani jerked back—right into the arrow's path. It tore through his outer thigh, and for a moment the shock froze him in place. Gretzell drew again and fired at Fentris, and Hunter staggered against a tree. The fletching stuck out of his leg on one side, and the arrowhead had punched through the other. Instinctively, he went for the shaft, felt the wash of blindness begin, and grabbed for a new arrow instead. His shoulder was soaking his shirt now, but when he nocked his bow, his grip was iron-steady.

Fentris dropped and crawled up behind a tree to the right. The Haruman threw down his bow, yanked the girl up in front of him, and put his knife to her throat. "Hold, Tamrani."

Hunter's voice was harsh. "Let go of the girl."

Instead, the man tightened his grip. The knife pricked pale skin, and blood began to trickle. Leanna clutched his arm. The Haruman didn't even notice her nails digging into his skin. He edged toward the trees.

Hunter's heart was still pounding from the run, but Nori was nowhere in sight. Moons, had the wolfwalker run for her brother instead? "Release the girl," Hunter snapped at Gretzell. "And we'll let you go from here."

"No way in hell," the man snarled back. He looked back and forth like a trapped dog. "Godsdammit. Where the hell are the dnu?"

Fentris had worked his way to the edge of the trees and now stood with his sword in hand. "You're lost, you idiot." As he would have been. He had no idea if Wakje's group was right or left on the cliffs.

The Haruman took one look at Shae and laughed without humor. "Fat lot of good that sword will do against this. Stand down, Tamrani, or I dump the girl off the cliff like so much garbage."

Hunter's arrow didn't waver. "She's the only guarantee you have."

"True enough." The other man shifted his grip again, and the trickle became a finger-width wash. Leanna stared at Fentris with wide eyes. Her chest rose and fell like a bird's, rapid and shallow. Gretzell watched Hunter like a hawk. "I can scar her good and deep." He bit out the words. "And you're far from the nearest clinic. Easy to get gelbugs or hairworms this far outside of town. Although the wolfwalker has a way with healing. You could chance it."

"Nori's a vet, not a healer."

"The mother, you fool." Gretzell stared at Hunter. "By the moons, you're taken with the daughter."

"Enough to consider her cousin my own," he agreed. His arm was beginning to burn.

"Then you'll want to keep her whole."

His lips thinned. "You can't back all the way to find your dnu. And you'd better make sure that I'm dead first before you harm the girl."

The Haruman shifted his grip on Leanna, then stiffened as something moved in the brush. "Stay back," he started to snarl. Then he caught a glimpse of the red-brown fur. "My gods—"

"Ayuh-chuh-chuh—" The badgerbear screamed its hunting cry as it burst up out of the shrubs. Fentris cursed, and Hunter's head whipped around. He had a single glimpse of the wounded beast flowing across the rocks. Another beast? Gods, and all of them were bleeding.

On the rim, Gretzell's breath froze in his lungs. Then he thrust Leanna in the badgerbear's path and threw himself back and away. Hunter jerked his aim to fire at the beast as Gretzell stumbled, fell, and scrambled back. The creature plunged toward Leanna like a starved wolf—

And leapt over her.

Hunter's war bolt flashed between Leanna and the beast. Leanna screamed and went fetal as it passed over her. Gretzell shrieked in turn as it whirled at him, bloodied claws, bloodied fangs. The Haruman flailed with his knife, and Hunter felt his leg start to fold as he grabbed another arrow. It was nocked and releasing when he finally saw it. "My gods—" He barely deflected his own shot. Moccasin feet stuck out of the badgerbear's calves. Black Wolf's feet. But Fentris was still lunging forward with his sword, and Hunter yelled, "Shae, get back."

Fentris staggered to a halt. The wolfwalker hit Gretzell head-down, midchest, and drove him toward the cliff.

"Nori—" Hunter shouted. Leanna crawled toward the brush, like an animal, and Fentris went for the girl. Hunter leapt for Nori. He took two steps, hit a soft spot, felt his leg crumple, and sprawled across the root-mass. The arrow shaft pressed against a root, and blackness washed his eyes and ears. He forced himself up and staggered blindly toward the ravine.

Nori and Gretzell were locked on the edge of the cliff.

Tear, slash—

The wolfwalker slammed the Haruman, raked at his face with her claws while her other hand slashed with the knife. He didn't see her inside the skin; his eyes were blind with terror. He stabbed, stabbed into the flaccid skin and screamed into the fur. They slammed into the boulders and she lost her knife. The metal spanged on the stones. Hunter saw the exact instant Gretzell realized it was no badgerbear. The man's lips pulled back in a rictus of a smile. He slashed for Nori's throat.

Wolfwalker—

The wolf lunged from the trees as Nori went down. Gretzell's blade passed across, then back, as he whipped his head toward the new threat. The wolfwalker seemed to fall back limply. Hunter threw his knife like a bolt. His heart stopped as she went down.

And then Gretzell flew off the cliff like a doll. She kicked him up and out as she fell, and as the ridge crumbled, there was no place for him to land. Hunter's blade flew right over her arms and sank into the Haruman's gut. The heavyset man couldn't even cry out as he felt the air beneath him. He made no sound as he plunged over the edge. He made no sound as he fell.

Rishte sank his teeth into the bagderbear pelt and pulled at Nori as she clung to the crumbling edge. She scrambled back with him, but watched till the Haruman cracked on the stones below.

Hunter staggered to her side and hauled her up. "By the moons, are you alright? Are you hurt?"

Rishte snapped at him, but he ignored the yearling. Then Nori got her feet under her and felt the head of the pelt slip back over her face. She was shaking, and the bloodied fur lay on her like a collapsed beast. She pulled at the laces but they were slick with blood, and she couldn't undo the knots. She began struggling against the skin like a demon. "Gods, gods." Her fingers fumbled at the thongs, then yanked at them. "Get it off me," she said tightly. "Get it off." Instinct, not intelligence jerked at the loops, and they tightened like nooses. Rishte tore at the pelt, but it was loose, and he only spun the wolfwalker around. Hunter barely caught her to hold her upright. He caught a glimpse of her eyes, and they were flickering with horror. Her voice was rising. "Get it off me. Now. Oh, gods, get it off."

He grabbed her and dragged her away from the edge. She half screamed at him as she twisted in the skin. "Stop it," he snapped. He dropped to his knees and tried to pin her, but he almost fainted when she bashed his leg. Then Fentris and Leanna were beside him.

"Dammit, hold still," Hunter cursed. He grabbed one of her claw-hands and trapped it against her body, but there were gelbugs on the inside of the fur, and their flat, wormy bodies writhed in the clots, wriggled by her skin. He saw the scream rising in her throat and slapped her with enough force to stun her for a full second, long enough for him to get the blade under one thong and cut it. She felt it loosen and ripped her arm free, hitting Leanna in the cheek. The girl just ducked her head and held on to Nori's leg with her small, tight grip. Then he had a second loop cut, and a third.

She shuddered out of the fur as he slashed, and she kicked it away from her body where Rishte tore at it for her. Now the jerkin clung to her like a dress, loose and bloody. "Gods, gods." Her voice was still tight and rising, and Fentris grabbed the jerkin and yanked it off over her head as Hunter cut it away.

She scraped at the writhing gelbugs to get them off her clothes, her skin, her fingers. She could feel the nausea rising, but it wasn't from the taint in her mind, nor from killing Gretzell. This was the sick flash of memory. She shoved Hunter away and crawled toward the trees. "No," she cried out, when he tried to support her. "Don't touch me." Blood. The smell of blood, thick and sweet, cloying, fat and fleshy. She jerked free again and bent, rocking as she tried to hold in the bile. "Rishte," she cried out.

The yearling leapt to her. He licked at the blood on her hands, her face. It was a steadying sense, that rough tongue licking and cleaning, as if the world stopped sucking away. The black void in her sight began to fade, and she could hear past the roaring in her ears. Hunter was murmuring to Leanna, rolling up the pelt, moons only knew why. It would be a long day in the second hell before she'd touch that thing again.

"Rishte," she whimpered.

Here, here. The pack is here. Wolfwalkerwolfwalker. The prey is down. The danger is gone. The prey is dead.

"No," she managed. "The hunt is still up." Payne was still somewhere along the cliff, facing the rest of the Harumen. He couldn't feel them the way she could, couldn't tell how close they were. He'd never had that sense of life. He had no taint in his mind. She shuddered in a breath and tried to control her shaking. Blood had already dried under and around her nails and in her knuckle lines. It was sticky between her fingers, and even Rishte's tongue couldn't clean it off. She wiped her hands in the moss, then rubbed them with dirt and scraped them off with crushed leaves. She scrubbed her face with grass. Rishte sniffed her carefully for gelbugs and nipped the one he found on her braid. She couldn't hide her shudder.

"Nori?" Hunter asked quietly.

She looked up, away from him, and forced out the words. "Leanna, are you alright?"

Fentris was dabbing at the girl's throat, and she answered quickly, "It's shallow. I'm okay, but Kettre's down. They shot her in the side when she passed us. They had her for a while, Black Wolf." There had been the slightest hesitation in Leanna's voice as she named her cousin. She had seen the wolfwalker's eyes when the badgerbear—when Black Wolf in the badgerbear pelt—leapt toward her. She couldn't quite bring herself to name her cousin more closely. "She's bleeding, Black Wolf. Badly. And they have her as a hostage. That way, along the cliff."

Nori thrust herself to her feet. She was still shuddering. She tried not to look at her bloody hands as she tried to calm herself. "What about Payne?" she demanded.

Leanna answered almost before she finished. "He's okay. He and Wakje are keeping them pinned down."

Two men against eight or nine? Hunter started to speak, but Nori turned to the wolf. *My brother, our pack, can you find them?*

He snarled and backed away. *The blood-place. The death-place.*

Nori stared at him. Blood-scent and plague sense mixed in his mind. She demanded, *Here? Along these cliffs?*

His golden eyes seemed to snap.

She started to reach out, but he slid back. Plague, the curse of the Ancients. Lower, below, near water. She tried to think, but his dread pounded at her like a drum. She felt the hum begin in her throat. *Trust me,* she tried to send. *I will not take us there.*

He snarled, and she closed her eyes, reaching through their minds. *Trust me, trust me. Just take me to my brother.*

He leapt away into the woods.

Bile churned in her stomach. She took a deep breath and tried to calm herself. She needed her mind, not just her hands. "Stay with her," she ordered Fentris curtly.

But Leanna shook her head. "I'm alright by myself. Take him with you."

"Not a chance."

Fentris saw Nori glance at the pelt and understood. There were still badgerbears in the area, and other threats less visible, and Leanna had joined the rest of them in bleeding enough for a predator to scent. He said flatly, "If we're not on your heels, we'll be soon enough behind you."

She glanced at Hunter.

"If it's short, I can make it," he answered obliquely.

"Give me your shirt and belt."

He yanked off the shirt. "You're making a habit of taking men's clothes off."

She dragged it on and tried to ignore the stickiness where the blood on her skin wasn't dry. "The belt," she said curtly, keeping her eyes down as she gathered up the shirt.

He hesitated.

"Hurry up." She forced herself to meet his eyes. "I don't have time to explain." She took it from him almost before he had finished slipping it off. She wrapped it around her waist, cinched it up, and tugged the oversized shirt into place. Then she put her hands on the arrow shaft still in his leg. "Ready?"

"For that? Moonworms, give me a minute."

"It's in the fleshy part," she told him. "It looks like it missed the major vessels and nerves. It will bleed, but that's a good thing." And it would make him weaker, not stronger. He wouldn't be able to stop her. She tightened her grip.

He glared at her. "Bleeding is good? You're kidding."

"No, actually I'm not. The better the bleeding, the cleaner the wound." It was truth, but not the whole truth.

"Black Wolf, your bedside manner really needs work." He took a breath. "Alright. Go."

She snapped it fast and cleanly, but for all that, he almost bit through his own teeth. By the time he could see again, she had wadded half his shirt into pads and was binding them onto his leg. "Ready?"

He cursed under his breath. "I wish you'd stop asking me that. You always follow up with something that could kill a dnu."

"Come on, then." She sprinted toward the standoff. She didn't look back, and he was grateful. As he forced himself onto the path, the blood pulsed out of his leg into the hasty bandage, and it jarred with nearly blinding pain at every step he took.

Ahead, Nori ran near silently, ignoring the gnats that flocked to her sticky skin. After the race, the struggle, the image of Gretzell falling, the forest was eerily silent. Whatever had happened was over. Payne, she cried under her breath.

She shoved through brush and cut into the forest instead of following the cliff path. She could hear Hunter limping more irregularly, then falling behind, but she didn't dare stop.

Ahead, Rishte answered, but he snarled as he sent it. The sense of death was stronger.

Old death, burning death, not the death from blood. She understood too well. *Trust me,* she snarled in return.

She halted when she caught Payne's scent in the yearling's nostrils. She gave a low birdcall, and waited. A second later, the response came from up ahead. She pulled the wolf back, then dropped and wormed her way forward. He growled in her mind, caught in the sense of the hunt and the fear that she walked into danger. She had to snap at him to keep him in place. *Your fur is no protection,* she snarled. He subsided angrily.

Hunter staggered up, and the wolf sent a shaft of hurt into her mind that she accepted man, not wolf. She shook her head and sent the image of the bow and bolts. "His fangs reach further," she told him sharply. Rishte slunk back to watch.

She looked back at Hunter's face. It was grey beneath the tan, and she wondered that he was still standing. Then he pushed himself down behind a tree and worked his way forward behind her. When she eased through the ferns to her brother, Payne glanced back and stiffened at what he saw. Nori shook her head. It's not mine, she signaled, but she could see he didn't believe her. She shook her head more sharply, but he caught her scent and nearly gagged. "By the gods, Nori—"

"Badgerbear pelt," she whispered. "Fresh. To get the drop on the one with Leanna."

Payne swallowed. She looked monstrous, Medusa-like with blood-streaked skin and clotted hair. There were bits of flesh glued onto her clothes. The gnats tried to land on her hands where her nails were grimed with red and the dirt she had crawled through. He flicked a gelbug off her shoulder and didn't tell her. She had a horror of the things.

He nodded forward. "There are seven left in the rocks. Wora, maSera, B'Kosan, and four others. We've got them pinned, but they've got Kettre."

She nodded. She could just see Kettre. The woman lay half on her side, a blood swath on the ground where they had dragged her into reach. Nori's stomach clenched at Kettre's stillness, but she could still feel the other woman. She prayed it wasn't delusion. Then Kettre's fingers moved, and she knew she was still alive. "Uncle Wakje?" she whispered.

He pointed with one finger. "Thirty meters, last I saw."

She nodded slightly. Keep moving, don't settle in, fire from many positions, don't let them pin you down. It was classic raider tactics.

Payne said almost under his breath, "We can get in on them from the right if you're up for it."

"No bow. No sword," she whispered back. "Hunter's down to four arrows. He's wounded, Payne. He'll get his shot off if he has to, but he's like to pass out any minute."

"Dammit. And he's got a seventy-pounder." Which meant Nori could draw the Tamrani's bow if she had to, but she couldn't shoot it as well as her own. "What about Fentris?"

"He's weak; he's lost a lot of blood." They both looked back as the slim Tamrani and Leanna limped through the woods behind them. She pointed with her chin toward the rocks. "They want safe passage?"

"Aye. And something else."

One of them called, "Time's almost up, neBentar. Hand them over or watch us start the carving. She can take a lot of pain before she dies."

Nori's jaw tightened. She took a breath, then let it out, controlling the grey rage inside her. "They want Condari's papers."

Payne nodded. "And your scout book. Can you get them?"

"Already did." She unknotted Hunter's belt.

Beside her, the Tamrani's hand shot out as he realized what she intended. "No," he said sharply. "My sister nearly died to get those letters and maps. That's two years of research, of information. It could stop a citywide war."

"Did your sister survive?"

"Yes, but—"

"Kettre won't."

His fingers dug into her wrist. "Black Wolf, Jangharat, I can't let you do this. That's evidence, and I need it for the council."

Payne shifted, but Nori didn't take her eyes from the man. "Do you know what's in those letters?"

"Of course, but that's not enough."

"It is enough for me." She rotated her hand, and his own wrist nearly snapped before he jerked it back. Then she kicked him just above his leg wound. He blacked out like a stroke.

Payne cursed, but Nori was already worming forward. By the time Hunter could see again, Payne was layering broad leaves under the pad on the wound, and Nori was near the ravine.

Nori didn't let herself look back. She squirmed over roots like a snake and scraped past a spiny brush. Her lips pulled back at the stronger sense of plague death. It was close, below, at the base of the cliff, somewhere down near the streams.

She crouched on the roots and caught her breath. There were

two things she still had to do. She gathered her scout book and Hunter's belt, then dug a small branch out of the soil and got out her skinniest blade. A few moments later, she stood up by the silverheart tree. "I have what you want," she called flatly.

"Step forward," Wora called back. "Away from the trees."

She obeyed. Gnats flitted around her head and arms over the dried blood. There were twigs in her hair, and her teeth were bared.

"Shit on a worlag." The curse was startled out of the Haruman. She looked like she'd bathed in blood. He studied her for a moment, then stood, his own war bolt nocked and pointed at Nori. "Let's see them," he ordered harshly.

She unrolled the belt, opened the hidden pouches inside, and pulled out the nearly transparent papers.

"Open them." Obediently, she unfolded the papers. She turned them so he could see them, but he snarled, "Read one."

Hunter cursed her audibly from the forest, but she ignored him. " 'The east–west trade route is falling off. Four caravans that usually trade across Ariye have rescheduled along the Sidisport route and back up on the Randonnen border for the fall. The following properties have changed hands on the Eilian route and appear to be fallow, but there are rumors that builders have been scheduled for future work: Lot Five Sixty-one in Sakas Borough, Lot Five Sixty-four—"

He cut her off. "That's enough. Seal them back in the belt and toss it here."

"Damn you, Black Wolf," Hunter snapped. "I'll kill you myself."

Behind Wora, B'Kosan heard the Tamrani and smiled without humor. His hand tightened on his own bow. The sharp, narrow arrowheads he carried would tear through a war cap or jerkin like hers like thick paper. He couldn't help imagining Hunter's or The Brother's expression if he skewered Black Wolf's head. Wora snorted as one of the men behind him murmured, "That would save us a lot of trouble."

Nori watched Wora like a wolf as she tasted the air around them. The cliff was cracked and stained with old water trails, and she smelled swamp fungus faintly up from below. Wora found himself shifting uncomfortably at her steady gaze. It angered him, and he straightened. "The papers, Black Wolf."

She folded them, tucked them back in the belt and sealed it, then flung it toward the rocks. B'Kosan caught it one-handed like a snake, rerolled the leather, and stuffed it in a belt pouch. "Now the scout book," Wora commanded.

Nori hesitated.

"The scout book, Black Wolf, or this woman dies now, and from what I hear you can't afford to lose one of the few friends you have."

She reached into her own belt pouch and pulled out the slim book. He could see the hole in the stained cover.

"Toss it to B'Kosan." The other man caught it, grinned at her with a leer, and tucked it into the pouch with the belt. "Now back away," Wora commanded.

"No." She remained standing, and her violet eyes burned in her bloody face. She could smell the clove bush on the Harumen, the blood, the sweat-scent. She could see the kill-thought in their eyes.

For a moment, there was silence. Then Wora said very softly, "Back away, Black Wolf."

She shook her head slowly, and the silence of her answer was more menacing than the nocked arrows he knew were aimed at him from behind her. Wora glanced at the forest as if it were filling with wolves, but there was no movement among the trees. He couldn't see the ex-raider or The Brother or the two Tamrani with them, and his eyes narrowed. He dropped his aim to point at Kettre's back. "Get back. Now."

Her voice was harsh. "We will not allow you back into the forest to attack us from behind or to track us back to the towns."

"Don't be stupid, Black Wolf. Your friend's life is under the bow."

"Her life will be in as much jeopardy if we let you go here, up top."

Up top? Her words made him pause. "You have another option."

She didn't nod. She could hear Rishte behind her, not in her ears, but in her skull, and even within his fear of death, the yearling wanted blood. She didn't blame him. It was her need the wolf was picking up, not his own. She pushed him back hard. He must not learn that from her.

She looked at the Harumen. "Your dnu are scattered. You'll spend hours rounding up enough of them to ride out, if you can get them all in the first place. The carcasses we left half an hour back on the trail will be calling predators here from kays around. They'll be eager for any kind of flesh, and your wounded will be like candy."

His eyes narrowed. "What do you propose?"

"You take the papers, the scout book, and go down the cliff." She felt her stomach twist.

Slitted eyes sharpened in the back of her head. *(Death/danger.) Warn them,* whispered her mother-mother.

She ignored the icy voice. "We will stay here with Kettre."

He was silent for a moment. "We'd need a rope."

"We have one." The slitted eyes blinked, and Nori swallowed visibly. Her lips curled back, and she cursed the taint till it faded under the grey.

"Your rope?" Wora snorted at her offer, and he started to raise the weapon.

"It's alright." Nori's smile held no humor. "It's new. It's not the one from the wagon."

The Haruman's expression went carefully blank. So she'd known. That explained a few things. The question was, how much did she know for sure, how much had she guessed, and what did she suspect? His fingers itched to get into her scout book. "What would keep you from shooting us on rappel?"

"Kettre," she bit out. "She's under your knife till the last man goes down."

"Not good enough. The last man down would be dead meat."

The cold yellow eyes grew sharper *(Old/gone) death, blood-debt, and burning . . .*

She met Wora's gaze with difficulty. Her stomach had tightened, and her fists were clenched. She had to force the words into her voice. "By the time he is ready to descend, you'll have clear shots from below if we approach the edge of the cliff. Besides, it would do us little good to kill one man here and leave the rest alive. We couldn't follow you down, or you'd shoot us as we descended." She felt his wavering. She made her voice quiet, firm, oddly soothing. "I swear to you as a wolfwalker, I swear to you on the souls of the wolves, I swear to you as—" She hesitated almost imperceptibly. "—the Daughter of Dione that we will let you go unharmed if you give Kettre to us alive, as she is now, and take the cliff route away."

"We keep the letters and the book."

"Aye."

He glanced at Kettre.

"Alive," Nori snarled softly. "As she is right now."

He stared at her. "Get the rope," he said finally, harshly.

The greasy twist of nausea tightened. She stayed where she was, waiting while Leanna crawled to Wakje and retrieved the rope slung over the ex-raider's shoulders. Then she waited while Payne brought it forward. Her brother half rose carefully behind the tree and handed it out, then dropped and wormed his way back to another shooting point. She threw the rope out by the rocks.

Warily, one of the men eased out to get it. It wasn't a Haruman, but their hired tracker, and Nori's eyes narrowed at him. She knew him. She'd seen him before in Maupin. He was an older man without family, one who spent most of his time in the woods. He'd take almost any duty. So that was how they'd known more closely where she'd taken her group. "Broziah," she said flatly.

"Black Wolf," he acknowledged. He handed the rope back to the others.

Wora had dropped his bow point, but he'd kept the arrow nocked. Nori knew that, like Wakje, he could draw and fire in a second. She ignored him and looked only at the tracker. "You don't belong with them."

Broziah rubbed a grizzled chin. "I took their silver. I'll want the rest they promised."

She felt the snarl in her voice and steadied it. "How much was the offer?"

His eyes glinted. "Two silvers to go on the job, three coppers a day, plus gear costs—two silvers, three coppers—up front. A five-silver bonus if I managed to corner you."

She raised one slim eyebrow. "Steep."

His grey eyes were shrewd. "Black Wolf and two Tamrani?"

Slowly, she nodded. "About six silvers then, still owed."

"Aye, that's what I figure."

"Stay here, and I'll pay it to you."

Wora stiffened, but Broziah cocked his head at her words. B'Kosan's eyes narrowed.

Nori kept her violet gaze on the tracker. "Stay, and I'll pay your fee."

Broziah didn't look at the Harumen. "You'd have to do better than that. They'd want a break-duty fee, too."

"Ten silvers."

"Black Wolf bidding against the Haruman?" The tracker smiled faintly. "Now that's worth a bit to the songsters."

Her jaw tightened to a white line under the grime. "Go with them then. You'll get what you bargained for." Her gaze swept the Harumen. She took a step forward, menacing as a wolf. "Go," she said softly, "but take this knowlege with you." The blood on her face had smeared into a gruesome camouflage, and when her lips curled back, her teeth were too white against it. "I know you now. Your voices, the way you move. I know your scents." Her voice was chill, and even B'Kosan shivered as it caressed him in the growing shadows.

Hunt. Rishte's satisfaction was savage in her mind. *Sniff him out. Man-sweat, man-scent. The easy trail at night.*

Her hands clenched like paws. "I give you free rein to run today, but follow me again, any of you, any Haruman; bring harm to me or mine, and I'll tear your ligaments from your joints and use them to tie on my gauntlets." She took another step forward, and Payne breathed a sharp warning. She could feel the hot pulse of the wolf in her hands, her neck, her chest. She could feel the bile rise in her throat. "Meet me on a trail, a road, a street in town, and I'll rend your tendons from your flesh and make baskets of your bones." Not one of the Harumen moved. "I know you now," she snarled. She flexed her fingers as if they ended in claws. "A glimpse, a scent, and I'll hunt you down like rast in the rotten timbers."

The words hung on the edge of the cliff like their thin, threadbare safety.

"Wolfwalker," Broziah breathed.

Her lips wrinkled back.

B'Kosan swallowed. Nori had been a target to him, someone to pursue and taunt, to keep on edge. Now she had turned, and her eyes weren't those of the frightened rabbit or wary deer, but the wolf seeking challenge. He had to force himself to look away and go back to knotting the rope.

Wora kept his nocked arrow pointed at Nori, but his hands had tightened. Wolfwalker. There were legends about them. And Black Wolf had violet eyes.

Broziah watched Nori thoughtfully. She trembled, but it wasn't with fear, he realized. Even though the wolf was in her eyes, it wasn't the hunting rage that filled her. He rubbed at his aching hip and then stepped forward, toward the scout.

B'Kosan looked up and spat to the side. "Cross us and go with her, and we'll hunt you down like a hare."

The tracker shrugged and said over his shoulder. "She's paying you a break-duty fee. Doesn't really matter to me, but I've never been good on rappel." He walked to the side and sat down on a rock to watch.

Nori dug into her last belt pouch, counted out the thin silver coins, and tossed the four to Wora.

The Haruman didn't move. He murmured something, and one of his men reached out and picked the coins from the dirt. Behind them, B'Kosan and maSera began lowering the man with the bleeding calf. Forty long minutes later, after the others had gone down, B'Kosan lowered himself down. Even with a leather pad, the rope began to chafe on the edge of the cliff, but it held as B'Kosan rappelled down. Then only Wora was left. By this time, it was almost dusk. The Haruman looked at the wolfwalker. Then he slid his bolt back into his quiver and slung his bow on his shoulder, without taking his eyes off Nori. Quickly he gripped the rope.

She stopped him with a sharp gesture. "You could have taken

my scout book," she said. "You could have taken the belt from the Tamrani almost anytime. Why harass the cozar and Elder Connaught? Why go after any of the others?"

She had the sense that he was surprised by her question, but the light was failing, and he was between her and the west horizon. She couldn't read his eyes. Then he smiled, and she knew.

She'd been right, but not right enough. It hadn't been about the cozar, or Nori and Payne, or the scout book or Tamrani papers. Those were barely the opening moves, the ones played out by secondary actors in short scenes on the sides. And Wora wasn't the only one chipping away at Ariye. He couldn't be. He was too sure of himself, almost smug in his certainty that she would never touch him. He was a man taunting the badger-bear because, behind him, out of sight of the beast, were a dozen ready archers. She felt the edge of the wolf curl her lip and fought for control. There had to be more Harumen in Ariye, in other caravans, among other cozar wagons. More heading for Shockton and council.

"There are more of you moving up through the county."

She didn't realize she'd spoken out loud till Wora's eyes shuttered. He didn't answer, and she recognized the ease of his own self-control. Wakje had tried to teach her that—to shutter her eyes, give nothing away. Wora had done this long enough that he wasn't even tempted.

"Why?" she asked again. Behind her, Payne and Hunter stared at the Haruman.

Wora shook his head slightly and smiled without humor as she tried to get him to answer.

"Is it to get to the elders?" she demanded.

He gripped the rope and prepared to step off the cliff.

She took a step forward. "Is it the council?" She could swear his knuckles tightened for an instant. Her parents, her uncle Gamon, even a cousin was on the council. "How many are dead?" she snarled.

He glanced at her. "Not enough. Not yet." His smile grew broader. "You can't guard your back every moment, maDione. We know you, too, Wolfwalker."

Rishte bristled in her mind. She let her lips curl in a feral smile of her own. She said softly, "Woraconau."

He stiffened almost imperceptibly as she used his full name. Then he turned and stepped off the cliff.

Nori stared after him for a moment. Then she dove for Kettre. She turned the woman gently, closing her eyes in relief when Kettre's eyes opened blearily. "Nori-girl?"

"Aye, it's me."

"Hurts like hell."

"Aye, it would."

"You're always . . . so agreeable."

Nori choked out a laugh. Then Payne was beside her with the bandages from his belt pack, and a handful of broad leaves. "You'll be alright," Nori told her friend. "You've got a finger-long gash up here, but even on knock-headed humans, I'm a darned good hand with a needle."

Kettre managed weakly, "No, Payne, don't let her. She'll put cross-stitch in my head."

The Brother shook his head and continued packing on the leaves. Wakje stood, and Nori could see the blood on his wrist where a bolt had cut too close. When Hunter and Fentris began limping over to join them, Payne grinned without humor. "If they'd seen us as we are right now, they would have fought, not fled."

Nori didn't disagree.

He glanced at her expression, back at the Tamrani, then lowered his voice. "Which scout book did you give them?"

Her hand went to her waist. She was trying not to throw up, and she pressed her hand hard against her stomach. She managed, "The one they expected, not mine."

"But the hole in the cover?"

"Pierced with my knife, poked through with a branch, in case they'd seen the real book in camp. We were watched too many times."

He nodded his approval. "And Condari's papers?"

Hunter's shirt billowed on her without the belt, and she discreetly tucked the few papers she had stolen more securely into her pants. She glanced over at the Tamrani. "I took two from the packet, but I don't know how valuable they'll be without the others."

"He said he knew what was in them."

"I meant for us," she returned soberly. She broke off as the Tamrani approached. She glanced at the rim and her stomach roiled. Death, old death, and fresh death soon. She swallowed against the bile.

Hunter sat down heavily on a boulder. He was pressing a pad against his shoulder with one hand, and another against his leg. His face was still grey, and he didn't even object when Wakje began bandaging him up. He grunted when the ex-raider pulled the knot tight across his leg, then tamped it twice to check it.

Nori let her brother and uncle finish up. She could still feel the wolf in her hands, and she moved to the edge of the ravine to look down into the blackening shadows.

Gingerly Hunter limped over to join her. His voice was expressionless. "We'll have to go down after them."

She kept her eyes on the ravine. "It would be you, alone, wounded and weak, against seven armed Harumen who have trained for decades to kill."

"I need those papers, maDione."

Her stomach twisted at the formal name. She wasn't sure it was all nausea, and she clenched her fists. "You said you knew what was in them."

"Yes, I know. But that was evidence."

"For Ariye or Sidisport?"

His jaw tightened. "You have no idea what those papers are worth." His green eyes were cold. "You took them from me deliberately. You traded them for your friend. The least you can do is help get them back, you and your godsdamned wolf."

From the tree line, Rishte bristled.

"I have other duties," Nori said softly. "And you cannot reach them now."

"Cannot reach them?" His eyes narrowed sharply. "What do you mean?"

The smell of his blood was making her stomach whirl, and she had to make her voice hard to use it. "You, Fentris, and Kettre can hardly stand, let alone ride. Wakje is wounded, Payne and I are bashed up like a wagon wreck. Leanna, well, she's had a fright that will last for a while, and she should never have been in this anyway. We've got barely a dozen arrows between us." She swallowed stiffly against the nausea. "Your Harumen have only one badly wounded man who won't last out the night, and so will hardly slow them down. The rest of them are ready for revenge, not just killing. On top of which, they're heading into worlag hunting grounds. It's suicide to go after them."

"So you won't help me?"

She smiled without humor. "Trust me. In this, I am helping you more than you know."

He gestured with his chin toward the woods. "Like you did back there?"

When she kicked him near his wound. Her voice was low. "Kettre was dying."

His expression hardened. "Do you have any idea how many could die in Sidisport, in your own county, because of those letters?"

"I would do it again."

He stared at her. His voice was soft. "You owe me, Wolf-walker."

"And you owed me the truth, Tamrani," she shot back. "You knew there were Harumen in Ariye long before we were attacked, yet you never passed word to the county. You—and Fentris, too—knew the Harumen would try to affect the council, yet you never warned the elders. Instead, you let the cozar—and Payne, and Leanna—bear the brunt of your secrecy." Her stomach roiled, and she pressed both fists against it.

His voice was quiet. "You saw that Haruman when you questioned him. This is bigger than the cozar, maDione. Bigger than your brother or your cousin, even you. If Ariye ever was wary of Sidisport, they should be doubly wary now."

She could barely see him now, and she glared at his blurred image. "Why?"

"Because Sidisport is a worlag, biting what it can reach. Right now, it's reaching into Ariye. I needed those letters, Black Wolf. I needed that proof for your councils."

She just shook her head. She had proof enough in her scout

book, proof in the code she'd taken from the raiders, proof in the two letters she'd stolen. Ariye didn't need the Tamrani to tell them when threats were on its borders. Not when the Daughter of Dione stood up in council to speak to the Ariyen elders.

Hunter eyed her silently, then turned and stalked away. He was angry, but it was more with himself. He had known innately she would do whatever she had to for her family, for her friends. If it had been her brother under the knife, she probably would have sacrificed Hunter himself to keep Payne alive. He should have guessed she would use him, as he had been trying to use her. It made him pause at the edge of the trees and look back. She was standing tautly, her fists clenched, staring down at the shadows. He almost turned to go back, but the Harumen's tracker moved over to look down over the rim beside her.

Broziah had moved quietly, and his voice was as mild. "You were lucky."

She swallowed her nausea. "Aye."

"They won't get far tonight."

"They'll camp at the base of the cliff, then try to make their way south tomorrow."

"You're not worried that they'll circle around and come back up to hunt you?"

Her voice was low. "There are swamps at the lower ends of the canyons, and it will rain tonight and tomorrow. The swamps will fill, and they'll be trapped. It will take at least two days to get through those waters, maybe more if it rains hard enough on the ridges." She swallowed hard. "Once they make it past the swamps, it will still take one more day to reach the lower trail. Another day to get to a town. By then it will be too late."

Broziah didn't understand what she meant. "They still know where you are heading. They can send word ahead to Shockton."

"No. Not them." She rubbed her wrists as if she could soothe the fire that seemed to burn in her own veins. Her mind was beginning to whirl like her stomach. There was death below, but she hadn't even considered any other way. Trial block or trial bolt, that's what Randonnens said, and Nori, she was Randonnen. She forced her voice to be steady. "They won't make it out of the forest."

He gave her a sharp look. "You swore you would let them go."

She stared out at the deepening twilight. "It's not me that will be the death of them. But it's me who sent them there."

The tracker eyed her warily. "What is down there, Wolfwalker? Worlags, bihwadi?"

"Death," she said harshly. "Fire and death. They are already wading through it."

She forced herself back from the cliff. Rishte was growling in her head, clawing at the slitted eyes. Yellow snapped back at the grey. Her stomach turned. She clenched her fists harder as if that small pain could cut through them both, and the flesh split beneath her nails. Blood began to trickle. She could smell the trees, she could feel the boulders that stubbed her feet, but her human eyes were blind. Nausea rose and choked her. She couldn't see the edge of the cliff anymore. She didn't know her spine stiffened as the slitted gaze cut into her skull. She had never fought back against the creature that claimed her with mother debt, but this time she screamed in her mind. *Damn you,* she cried out silently. *They were not harming us at that moment. Would it have made us any less their kill?*

(Old/new) debt, death-debt and fire . . .

She stumbled and went to her knees, and began vomiting into the moss. A moment later, a strong arm slipped around her body and held her as she retched. Rishte snarled at the Tamrani, but Hunter ignored the wolf. Instead, his other hand pulled her bloody hair back from her face and tucked it behind her ear. He was murmuring something, but she could hear only the tone of his voice. Later, when Payne asked what he'd said, she could only shake her head. All she knew was that Rishte had accepted him. It was the only explanation for the sense of his voice in her head.

Epilogue

"You've already started your Journey, girl.
You just don't know it yet."

  —Shendren, in *Tracking the Moons,* by Vergi Vendo

Nori hovered over the village healer like a hungry boy over dinner. "Watch that spot there." She pointed to the stitches on Kettre's scalp. "It was the deeper part of the gash."

The healer hid a sigh. "If you'd step back just a bit, Black Wolf, out of the light?"

"Of course." She did so, by moving to the healer's other shoulder. It was late, and they were lucky the tiny village had a healer to wake. She moved the lantern to bring the light closer.

"How does it look?" Kettre asked the healer. "Will I have to part my hair on the side from now on?"

"Hmm." The grey-haired woman dabbed at the hair that had become clotted into the wound. "It will scar, but lightly. You did a good job," she said absently to Nori. "Not but what I'd expect from the Daughter of Dione."

Nori shrugged and pointed. "There was a lot of dirt in there. You might want to irrigate that before putting the dressing back on."

The healer said mildly, "Aye, I thought the same." The woman reached for the syringe. Nori already had it and handed it across. Kettre almost swatted Nori's hand away when the wolfwalker pointed again. "There, and there."

The healer bit back an acid comment. Black Wolf had her first bar in healing, and so was essentially an intern, someone to be tolerated and taught as well as possible. The healer understood Nori's worry for her friend, but if the girl didn't step back or go tend some farmer's dnu . . .

Nori couldn't seem to stop herself. "Don't forget the other edge."

The healer held her breath for a moment, then let it out before saying, "It's clean, Black Wolf. There's no sign of infection." She started to reach for a cloth to dab away the fluids.

"Here." Nori handed her a double pad. She was ready with the dressing almost before the healer was done. "She's hard on her head. You'll want to pack it well."

Kettre rolled her eyes, and the healer said sharply, "Black Wolf—" The woman broke off. When she spoke again, she said firmly. "MaDione?"

"Aye, what do you need?" Nori looked quickly down at the tray of instruments and dressings. She thought she'd anticipated every move. Perhaps the cotton strips for binding the pad?

"I need for you to wait outside. Now."

Nori looked up. "Outside? But—" Her gaze flew to Kettre's face. The other woman raised one brown, sculpted eyebrow at her, and she stared. "Kettre?"

The woman didn't bother to hide her satisfaction. "*Keyo* 'bye, Black Wolf."

"Outside," the healer repeated firmly. "Now." She took up her tweezers again. "I believe the door is that way, Black Wolf."

Kettre's brown eyes danced. Deliberately, she ignored Nori. "So how does it look?" she asked the healer.

"It's healing well," said the woman. "You might have a headache for a few more days, but that's normal. Now let me see your ribs."

Nori hesitated at the door with her hand on the knob, but the healer looked up and jerked a nod sternly outside. As the door was closing behind her, she heard Kettre say, "One more thing about that gash: just tell me if it's cross-stitch."

Outside, leftover rain dripped from the old woman's gutters, and the sound was like an interminably slow drum. They had been two days in the forest before they reached the village. Nori had spent both nights stalking six of the Harumen's riding beasts, as well as two of their own. She was dragging with exhaustion by the second dawn, but she had come back with eight dnu on a long-line lead, a bag of washed tubers, a small pack of sour early berries, and a handful of limp, dead woodmice to scramble with eight fragile eggs from a pair of palts that had nested too high on the cliff. The rest of the dnu would filter back to the villages or become badgerbear meat.

They'd been more than lucky, Nori acknowledged. Neither Tamrani had been in good shape by the time the rains hit hard. Kettre had been wan as bleached-out silk, but the shallow claw marks in Nori's own back had scabbed cleanly, as had Leanna's neck from the Haruman's knife. Wakje's arm was barely gashed, and Payne had only a bruised hip.

She looked across the road. Fentris was limping out of the general store where he'd bribed the storekeep to break into the latest shipment of clothes for a fanciful elder. The garments might be a bit old in their style, but at least they weren't made of chancloth.

Nori paced irritably, tried to sit, and stood again almost immediately. She was waiting only for word of Ki. With a bit more luck of the moons, Payne would come back with news of the ex-raider and his sons within the hour.

Rishte growled softly from the tree line, and she closed her eyes. His voice was clearer, easier to hear. The fear and tension, the kills by the cliffs—everything had combined to sharpen them for each other. There was a . . . brilliance to it, she decided. Like water under a harsh sun. It should be hard and grating, but instead she slid into it and simply felt the grey.

Rider closing in on the town.

That would be Payne. She opened her eyes to watch the end of the street. With five of the moons climbing over the steep roofs, there was light enough to see every paving stone, and plenty of light to identify her brother at a distance when he cantered onto the street.

"I've sent the messages for Ki," he told her as he reined in.

"What word on the archers he tracked?"

"They dropped out of sight like three stones in the sea." Payne shook his head. "Either they know a hidey-hole he doesn't, or someone was covering for them and covering well."

She nodded. Wora had all but confirmed for her that there were more in the county.

Payne glanced at the clinic. The doors were conspicuously shut, and Kettre was not in sight. "The healer kicked you out?" he guessed. She scowled, and he hid a grin. "Serves you right for kibitzing."

"I wasn't kibitzing." She made a face. "I was . . . helping."

"You helped yourself right out the door." He looked across at the Tamrani. "I've arranged for a wagon in the morning. Are they finished packing?"

"Soon enough. If Fentris doesn't stop buying fairly quickly, Uncle Wakje will just wait till the Tamrani turns his back, then toss his pack in the waste pit."

Payne chuckled. "Once they're on the wagons, they won't have to worry about it. They can eat like spoiled elders, ride like kings, and sit on their bums all the way to the road as safe as a cozar at fireside." He grinned as she snorted. "So, Wolfwalker, are you ready to ride?"

"Aye." And Rishte was more than ready to run. "We're still going on tonight?"

"You think I want to stay? We're a five-day ride out of Shockton, and we have three short days to get there." He wheeled his dnu.

"Then I guess I'll say my ride-safes."

"Be quick, Nori-girl. I'll wait on the road."

She nodded. She wasn't looking forward to this. The papers she'd stolen from Hunter's belt burned in her mind. He had tried to speak to her several times as she led them out of the forest to the village, but their argument on the edge of the cliff stood between them like a worlag.

Hunter saw Payne trot away and raised his hand to catch her attention as he limped aross the street. He frowned as he watched her expression close up when he stepped up on the sidewalk. He hadn't realized how free she had been with her laughter when they were out in the forest. Now she was as stiff and reserved as the day they had met.

For a moment, the two looked at each other. Then Hunter

said, "I've been meaning to ask, make baskets from their bones?"

She shrugged, uncomfortable. "I thought it had a nice sound to it."

"Remind me not to get on your bad side."

She looked toward the forest. "All my sides are bad."

"Not from what I've seen." He studied her closed expression. "You know we'll still have to get eight or nine venge riders and go after the Harumen."

"My mother will take care of that."

"Dione?" She couldn't be serious. He'd seen Nori's face when she'd pressed the Haruman on the cliff. She'd been intent, digging at whatever the man knew, at any signal she could read. That wasn't the act of a woman who could just walk away from trouble. He stared at her. "After all that's happened, all we've learned, you're still handing this off to your mother?"

If it's about plague, yes, she thought silently. There was no other who could survive it. And if there was a way to get those papers back from the bodies of the Harumen and out of the mouth of plague, Dione would find that way. Only after that would the rest be up to Nori. She said finally, simply, "There's no need to hurry to find the Harumen. They never left the forest."

"How do you know that?" he said sharply. "Through the wolves?"

Her lip curled. For a moment, he caught something other than the grey in her violet eyes. The wolf snarled through her throat, and his skin seemed to crawl. Then she blinked, and became just a woman again standing in front of him, turning away for her dnu. He caught her arm. "I need those papers, Black Wolf. I need them for the council. I can get a venge together in a day and head back into the forest."

"No," she said sharply. "No," she said more calmly. "You can't." He hadn't called her anything but Black Wolf or ma-Dione since she had kicked him in his wound, and she bit back another apology. She said finally, "It would be suicide."

"Why?" he demanded.

She shook her head.

"It's suicide, so you send your mother in? And then rush off to Payne's Test?" He caught the guilt in her gaze. "You—" His voice broke off. "You aren't dropping this at all," he realized. "You are going to speak to the council. You're going to tell them about the attacks, the Harumen, the threat to Ariye."

She looked away, unable to meet his gaze.

His green eyes narrowed. "Even the Wolfwalker's Daughter would need some sort of proof to back up a story like this." He caught a flicker in her gaze, and it fell into place for him. "Damn you, not all my papers were lost. You held some back." He felt the fury build and nodded at the fresh flash of guilt. "You stole some reports, then traded the rest for Kettre."

Silently she nodded.

"How many?" he demanded. "How many did you hold back?"

"Two."

"Which ones?" His voice was too harsh, and he didn't try to soften it.

Her own reply was stiff. "One report and a letter from your sister. There wasn't time to be picky." He glared at her, and she shrugged and started to turn away.

His hand shot out and he gripped her arm hard. "I want them."

She didn't meet his eyes. Instead, she stared after Payne. "They're in your pack," she said softly.

"But you read them." He didn't need her nod. "And you understood what they implied."

Silently, she nodded.

"So you know of the threat to the counties, that the trade routes look to be ready to shift, and that something must happen to cause it. Something big and something deadly. The Houses are already on the edge of war. They'll erupt over something like this. The violence will spill out into Ariye if it isn't already here."

Again, she nodded.

His voice was flat. "You now have a duty, Wolfwalker."

She looked up at him, and he wasn't surprised to see his own anger mirrored in her violet eyes. Her voice was soft. "House

Wars, Sidisport, Harumen, and trade. Those are your duty, not mine, Tamrani. I already have a duty, and it reaches farther than any Haruman or House can strike."

"So you will stand before the council."

"Aye." Her voice was quiet. "It's time." He started to grip her arm, but she stepped back. She was still wary around him, even though she could still feel his hands on her waist, the heat and strength when he'd lifted or held her, the timbre of his voice. She looked away. She had to remind herself that they weren't friends. They were barely allies, and he was from Sidisport himself, from one of the greater Houses. He would be approaching the council for his own ends, not to help Ariye.

This time, Nori would be there. She'd have to be. She would not let Hunter—or Fentris, she acknowledged—hide their secrets from the elders when they could harm Ariye. She didn't worry that she might not be believed against two First Sons of the Tamrani. She had worked for her parents for years, taking in information from their contacts and reporting to the Lloroi. Her word had been proven again and again. And she was the Daughter of Dione. Even the elders who didn't know her would listen when she spoke. After that, when the councils broke up for the day, and the doors closed for the inner circle, she would speak again, about plague. Payne might get a solo Journey after all, she thought. With Grey Hishn gone these past two years, Dione would need a partner wolf to heal herself with Ovousibas after exposing herself to plague. She might take Nori and Rishte with her to use their lupine link.

Hunter frowned as she said nothing else. He prodded, "It's time you take up duty, but you still won't ride with me."

She smiled without humor and shook her head. She yearned for Rishte, she pulled the wolf as much as the wolf pulled her, but this Tamrani pulled her, too. This close, he was in her senses until she wanted to touch his skin, feel his hands, taste his breath. She forced herself not to move toward him. With plague and the wolf and the taint in her mind, she couldn't afford another link that could tear her loyalties. Instead, she slipped off the boardwalk and walked toward her dnu.

He stared after her. "I can't believe you're just walking away."

For a moment, she rested her forehead on the warm neck of her riding beast. Her voice was low, and she breathed into its fur, "I cannot believe you'd let me." She didn't think he would hear her, and she started to mount.

But Hunter dropped onto the street, took two quick steps, and plucked her from the saddle. He spun her around to face him. She didn't fight the movement, nor would she look at him, but when he tilted her chin up, he could see both hunger and fear in her eyes. "What if I said I would not let you go?"

She looked down at his long, tanned fingers. They were scratched from the ride and one bore a long, shallow cut. And they were barely holding her. She could brush him off. She could slip past, even simply step away from him, and she knew that this time he wouldn't try to stop her.

"What if I don't let you go?" he repeated more quietly.

She almost reached up to touch his arm. From the edge of the village, Rishte growled. She dropped her hand, but met his gaze and smiled so faintly he wasn't sure he saw it. Her voice was soft. "Then I'd say you'll see me in Shockton."

This time, she did slip free.

She mounted and turned her dnu after Payne. Shockton. Council. Duty. In the dark, she could see it with clarity, and it wasn't just the grey in her eyes that sharpened her sight. She was stronger inside, as if standing up to the taint on the cliff had given her a foundation from which to launch herself or challenge it again. Or challenge anyone, she realized. She would no longer wait till she turned twenty-three to stand before the council. She stared at her hands, then up at the moons. She almost laughed at the sense of freedom the simple decision gave her. It was dark and muddy and still damp from the downpour, and yet she felt as if everything was light. Every sense was alert, like the words of the Fourteenth Martyr: The moonlight glistens like ice on the leaves, and I am blinded by its brilliance. Every image she saw was so crisp with its edge of rain that it seemed indelibly etched on her mind. She could still smell Hunter's hands on her skin, taste wet leaves on the air, hear her dnu's soft breath in the wind. It was as though paths that had been fogged up before were now clear. As if, when duty rose and her goal became clear, it would no longer be dreaded, but welcome.

Wolfwalkerwolfwalkerwolfwalke—

She answered with a growl. She glanced back at Hunter, and he raised his hand once. She was almost to the edge of the trees when he called, "Jangharat."

She twisted to look back.

"You could have kept the shirt," he called.

In the moonlight, he saw her teeth flash. "What makes you think I didn't?" She shrugged out of her jerkin and stuffed it into a saddlebag. It took him a moment to realize she was wearing an oversized blouse, or rather, a blousy shirt of blue-brown silk. His shirt, in fact.

Slowly, he grinned. "I'll take that back someday."

He thought she laughed, like a moonmaid in the night. Then she turned her dnu in a tight circle as a salute, and spurred the beast after the wolf.

Author's Note

Wolves, wolf-dog hybrids, and exotic and wild cats might seem like romantic pets. The sleekness of the musculature, the mystique and excitement of keeping a wild animal as a companion . . . For many owners, wild and exotic animals symbolize freedom and wilderness. For other owners, wild animals from wolves to bobcats to snakes provide a status symbol—something that makes the owner interesting. Many owners claim they are helping keep an animal species from becoming extinct, that they care adequately for their pets' needs, and that they love wild creatures.

However, most predator and wild or exotic animals need to range over wide areas. They need to be socialized with their own species. They need to know how to survive, hunt, breed, and raise their young in their own habitat. And each species' needs are different. A solitary wolf, without the companionship of other wolves with whom it forms sophisticated relationships, can become neurotic and unpredictable. A cougar, however, stakes out its own territory and, unless it is mating or is a female raising its young, lives and hunts as a solitary predator. Both wolves and cougars can range fifty to four hundred square miles over the course of a year. Keeping a wolf or cougar as a pet is like raising a child in a closet.

Wild animals are not easily domesticated. Even when raised from birth by humans, these animals are dramatically different from domestic animals. Wild animals are dangerous and unpredictable, even though they might appear calm or trained, or seem too cute to grow dangerous with age. Wolves and exotic cats make charming, playful pups and kittens, but the adult creatures are still predators. For example, lion kittens are cute, ticklish animals that like to be handled (all kittens are). They mouth things with tiny, kitten teeth. But adult cats become solitary, highly territorial, and possessive predators. Some will rebel against authority, including that of the handlers they have known since birth. They can show unexpected aggression. Virtually all wild and exotic cats, including ocelots, margay, serval, cougar, and bobcat, can turn vicious as they age.

Monkeys and other nonhuman primates also develop frustrating behavior as they age. Monkeys keep themselves clean and give each other much-needed day-to-day social interaction and reassurance by grooming each other. A monkey kept by itself can become filthy and depressed, and can begin mutilating itself—pulling out its hair, and so on. When a monkey grows up, it climbs on everything, vocalizes loudly, bites, scratches, exhibits sexual behavior toward you and your guests, and, like a wolf, marks everything in its territory with urine. It is almost impossible to housebreak or control a monkey.

Many people think they can train wolves in the same manner that they train dogs. They cannot. Even if well cared for, wolves do not act as dogs do. Wolves howl. They chew through almost anything, including tables, couches, walls, and fences. They excavate ten-foot pits in your backyard. They mark everything with urine and cannot be house-trained. (Domestic canid breeds that still have a bit of wolf in them can also have these traits.) Punishing a wolf for tearing up your recliner or urinating on the living room wall is punishing the animal for instinctive and natural behavior.

Wolf-dog hybrids have different needs than both wolves and dogs, although they are closer in behavior and needs to wolves than dogs. These hybrids are often misunderstood, missocialized, and mistreated until they become vicious or unpredictable fear-biters. Dissatisfied or frustrated owners cannot simply give their hybrids to new owners; it is almost impossible for a wolf-dog to transfer its attachment to another person. When abandoned or released into the wild by owners, hybrids may also help dilute wolf and coyote strains, creating more hybrids caught between the two disparate worlds of domestic dogs and wild canids. For wolf-dog hybrids, the signs of neurosis and aggression that arise from being isolated, mistreated, or misunderstood most often result in the wolf-dogs being euthanized.

Zoos cannot usually accept exotic or wild animals that have been kept as pets. In general, pet animals are not socialized and do not breed well or coexist with other members of their own species. Because such pets do not learn the social skills to reproduce, they are unable to contribute to the preservation of their species. They seem to be miserable in the company of their own kind, yet have become too dangerous to remain with their human owners. Especially with wolves and wolf-dog hybrids, the claim that many owners make about their pets being one-person animals usually means that those animals have been dangerously unsocialized.

Zoo workers may wish they could rescue every mistreated animal from every inappropriate owner, but the zoos simply do not have the resources to take in pets. Zoos and wildlife rehabilitation centers receive hundreds of requests each year to accept animals that can no longer be handled or afforded by owners. State agencies confiscate hundreds more that are abandoned, mistreated, or malnourished.

The dietary requirements of exotic or wild animals are very different from domesticated pets. For example, exotic and wild cats require almost twice as much protein as canids and cannot convert carotene to vitamin A—an essential nutrient in a felid's diet. A single adult cougar requires two to three pounds of prepared meat each day, plus vitamins and bones. A cougar improperly fed on a diet of chicken or turkey parts or red muscle meat can develop rickets and blindness.

The veterinary bills for exotic and wild animals are outrageously high—if an owner can find a vet who knows enough about exotic animals to treat the pet. And it is difficult to take out additional insurance in order to keep such an animal as a pet. Standard homeowner's policies do not cover damages or injuries caused by wild or exotic animals. Some insurance companies will drop clients who keep wild animals as pets.

The reason wild and exotic animals damage property or cause injuries is not that they are inherently vicious. What humans call property damage is to the animal natural territorial behavior, play, den-making, or childrearing behavior. Traumatic injuries (including amputations and death) to humans most often occur because the animal is protecting its food, territory, or young; because it does not know its own strength compared to humans; or because it is being mistreated. A high proportion of wild- and exotic-animal attacks are directed at human children.

Although traumatic injuries are common, humans are also at risk from the diseases and organisms that undomesticated or exotic animals can carry. Rabies is just one threat in the list of more than 150 infectious diseases and conditions that can be transmitted between animals and humans. These diseases and conditions include intestinal parasites, *Psittacosis* (a species of *Chlamydia*), cat-scratch fever, measles, and tuberculosis. Hepatitis A (infectious hepatitis), which humans can catch through contact with minute particles in the air (aerosol transmission) or with blood (bites, scratches, and so on), has been found in its subclinical state in more than 90 percent of wild chimps, and chimps are infectious for up to sixty days at a time. *Herpesvirus simiae,* which has a 70 percent or greater mortality rate in humans, can be contracted from macaques. Pen breeding only increases an animal's risk of disease.

Taking an exotic or wild animal from its natural habitat does not help keep the species from becoming extinct. All wolf species and all feline species (except for the domestic cat) are either threatened, endangered, or protected by national or international legislation. All nonhuman primates are in danger of extinction, and federal law prohibits the importation of nonhuman primates to be kept as pets. In some states, such as Arizona, it is illegal to own almost any kind of wild animal. The U.S. Fish and Wildlife Service advises that you conserve and protect endangered species. Do not buy wild or exotic animals as pets.

If you would like to become involved with endangered species or other wildlife, consider supporting a wolf, exotic cat, whale, or other wild animal in its own habitat or in a reputable zoo. You can contact your local reputable zoo, conservation organization, or state department of fish and wildlife for information about supporting exotic or wild animals. National and local conservation groups can also give you an opportunity to help sponsor an acre of rain forest, wetlands, temperate forest, or other parcel of land.

There are many legitimate organizations that will use your money to establish preserves in which endangered species can live in their natural habitat. The internationally recognized Nature Conservancy is such an organization. For information about programs sponsored by The Nature Conservancy, please write to:

The Nature Conservancy
1815 North Lynn Street
Arlington, Virginia 22209

Special thanks to Janice Hixson, Jill Mellen, Ph.D., Mitch Finnegan, DVM, Metro Washington Park Zoo; Karen Fishler, The Nature Conservancy; Harley Shaw, General Wildlife Services; Mary-Beth Nichols, DVM; Brooks Fahy, Cascade Wildlife Rescue; and the many others who provided information, sources, and references for this project.